Impulsively, Anna came up onto the tips of her toes and reached out toward him.

Before she lost her nerve, she pressed a light kiss to his cheek.

He turned his head and pressed his lips against her own. Shocked at herself for the quick warmth that stole over her body, she would have drawn back at once had not his arms come around her waist, preventing her escape.

However, he did not draw her in more closely toward him. Her body fell of its own accord against him, without her having consciously willed it.

Was this supposed to be his punishment of her? she wondered. For the kiss did more than simply stimulate her. It inspired her. And she found herself wanting more—of him, of the kiss ...

Other **AVON ROMANCES**

ELUSIVE PASSION *by Kathryn Smith*
HIGHLAND ROGUES: THE FRASER BRIDE
by Lois Greiman
HIS BETROTHED *by Gayle Callen*
THE MACKENZIES: ZACH *by Ana Leigh*
THE RENEGADES: RAFE *by Genell Dellin*
ROGUE'S HONOR *by Brenda Hiatt*
THE WARRIOR'S DAMSEL *by Denise Hampton*

Coming Soon

A MATTER OF SCANDAL: WITH THIS RING
by Suzanne Enoch
AN UNLIKELY LADY *by Rachelle Morgan*

And Don't Miss These
ROMANTIC TREASURES
from Avon Books

THE BAD MAN'S BRIDE: MARRYING MISS BRIGHT
by Susan Kay Law
THE MARRIAGE LESSON *by Victoria Alexander*
ONCE TEMPTED *by Elizabeth Boyle*

KAREN KAY

WAR CLOUD'S PASSION

AVON BOOKS
An Imprint of HarperCollins*Publishers*

AVON BOOKS
An Imprint of HarperCollins*Publishers*
10 East 53rd Street
New York, New York 10022-5299

Copyright © 2001 by Karen Kay Elstner-Bailey
Map and poster by Trina C. Elstner
ISBN: 0-380-80342-9
www.avonromance.com

First Avon Books paperback printing: July 2001

Avon Trademark Reg. U.S. Pat. Off. and in Other Countries, Marca Registrada, Hecho en U.S.A.
HarperCollins ® is a trademark of HarperCollins Publishers Inc.

Printed in the U.S.A.

10 9 8 7 6 5 4 3 2 1

Acknowledgments

For some outstanding people
at the Blackfeet Nation
HELP Learning Center.

In particular:

Toni Running Fisher
Patricia Running Crane Deveraux
Harold Dusty Bull
Kinder Hunt
Maria Ferrara
Jeff Butler
Dave Bolger
and last but not least, my husband,
Paul Bailey.

You are making a difference.

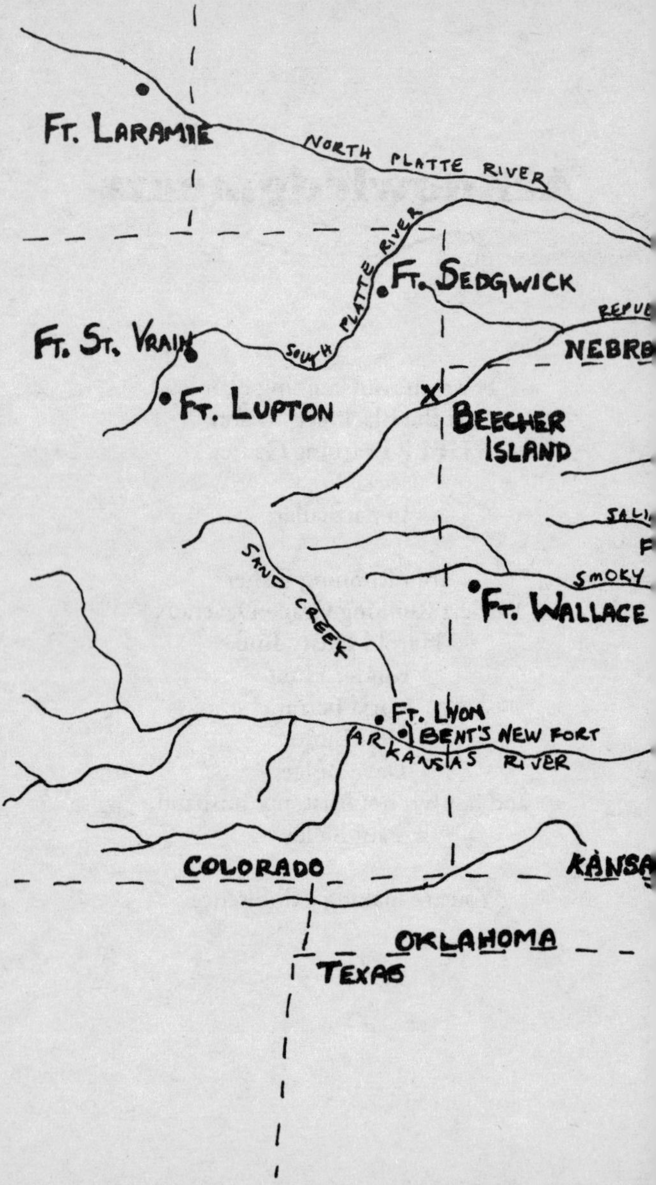
FT. LARAMIE
NORTH PLATTE RIVER
SOUTH PLATTE RIVER
FT. SEDGWICK
FT. ST. VRAIN
FT. LUPTON
NEBR
BEECHER ISLAND
SAND CREEK
SMOKY
FT. WALLACE
FT. LYON
BENT'S NEW FORT
ARKANSAS RIVER
COLORADO
KANSA
OKLAHOMA
TEXAS

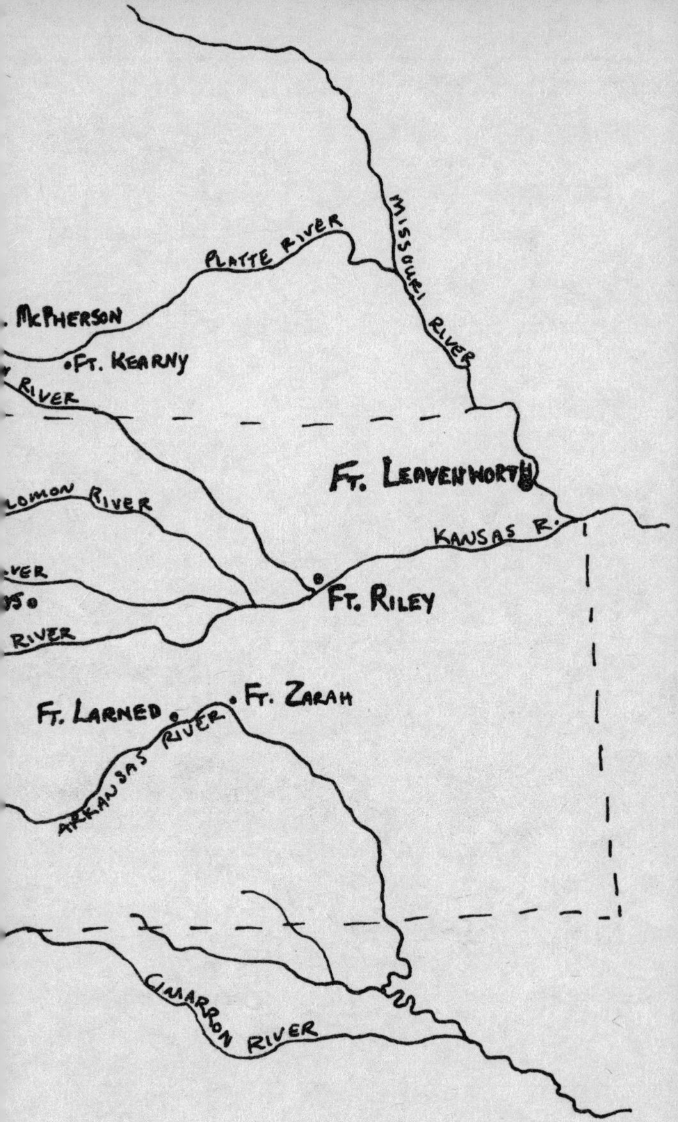

PLATTE RIVER
MISSOURI RIVER
McPHERSON
FT. KEARNY
RIVER
FT. LEAVENWORTH
LOMON RIVER
KANSAS R.
VER
FT. RILEY
RIVER
FT. ZARAH
FT. LARNED
ARKANSAS RIVER
CIMARRON RIVER

NEEDED

HOMES for ORPHANS

A PARTY OF ORPHANS WILL BE ARRIVING AT: HAYS, KS., ON SATURDAY, MAY 16TH, 1869

The children, ranging in age from 5–15, are coming to us in care of the Society of Orphans in New York City. It is hoped that these children will be able to find a new life in our community. Good Christian homes are needed. Applications can be made to the church committee. Prospective parents will be asked to treat these children well, as though members of the family. Parents must promise to attend to the child's schooling, as well as his spiritual nature and must agree to send the child to Sabbath school every week. Additionally, parents must agree to properly clothe each child until he or she reaches the age of 17. The following good citizens of our town have agreed to act in the capacity of agents for the children.

A.K. SIMMON; E.M. NORFOLK; H.G. WILLIAMS; P.C. WILSON

Come and view the children.
Dispersion of the children will begin at:

THE OLD CHURCH, SATURDAY, MAY 16TH AT 2:00 P.M.

A.T. BILSWORTH; C.B. PAGNEY AND A. WILEY.
AGENTS FOR THE SOCIETY OF ORPHANS. NEW YORK CITY, NY.

REV. W.P. MATTHEWS

Prologue:
The Legend of
Sky Falcon

It has been said that Sky Falcon was a good, if misguided merchant. His was a strong, passionate nature; his face, as well as his body, pleasing to the eye. Some even say he was beautiful.

The tale always begins with a flute. Some say the instrument was enchanted; some maintain otherwise. All that is known with certainty is that whenever Sky Falcon played his melodies, women threw themselves at him. And Sky Falcon, not being the sort of man to deny himself, soon lay claim to quite a reputation.

Now, being a merchant, Sky Falcon spent most of his time roaming the West from village to village, exercising his trade and indulging his sensual nature.

But such could not last forever. As it does to most young men, there came a time when Sky Falcon's aimless ways had to bow to the winds of change.

It so happened that on this particular day, such a transformation took place during Sky Falcon's first meeting with the beautiful and vibrant Spirit Woman—she who was from the Cocopa tribe in the Southwest. It is said that Sky Falcon lost his heart to this maiden.

However, there were problems.

"How do you intend to win her when there is not a man in the village who does not desire her?" asked He Who Limps, his name signifying a family name rather than a characteristic of the kinship.

The two friends were slowly approaching the village where Spirit Woman lived. They led a convoy of several dogs, each one pulling a travois stacked high with merchant's goods: wampum, shells, cloth and string, among other items.

Villagers, alerted to their approach, had come out to watch them, some to greet the two merchants. But Sky Falcon barely noticed the townspeople.

He smiled at his friend instead and held up his wooden flute, the object boasting a multitude of feathers as well as charms, all attached to the instrument and hanging from it like a cascade of silk. Said Sky Falcon, "Ah, it is good that you ask me about this, my friend, for I will tell you gladly how I intend to do so. I visited a medicine man in that last village who gave me a new song, one that is sure to win her, I am certain."

He Who Limps scowled. "I fear you will need more than a song, my friend. While your flute may charm the young maiden and the discontent wife, to try to win a wife in this way . . ." He Who Limps tittered. "I do not need to tell you that when a young lady wishes to marry, she follows not her heart, but the dictates of her father.

And I do not believe that this maiden's father will approve of you."

"Why not?" Sky Falcon asked, still smiling.

"You forget your reputation, my friend. Her father will not want a son-in-law who has charmed every young maiden in the country."

"I think you exaggerate my talents," observed Sky Falcon.

He Who Limps merely shrugged and continued, "Her father will not care if you can play a song. I think he would more want you to be a steadfast and an honest man. He will look to you to be a good provider and a good hunter, for there will come a time when he will depend on you for his own sustenance.

"But most of all," continued He Who Limps, "I think he would want you to be constant, so that you do not make his daughter weep with jealousy."

Sky Falcon acknowledged his friend with a self-satisfied smile. He said, "That may be, my friend, that may be. Yet, I think I will win her nonetheless."

He Who Limps shrugged, saying only, "We will see."

However, He Who Limps' warning proved to be true. For, as he had pointed out, while the vibrant Spirit Woman might have loved Sky Falcon on sight and might have married him posthaste, such was not to be. Her father, a formidable medicine man, heartily disapproved.

Yet, as a man might learn to his own detriment, Spirit Woman's father could not forever control the heart of his daughter.

* * *

Spirit Woman sat beside her friend as they worked over a skin. Because the Cocopa women wore only short skirts with wide sashes, their feminine charms from the waist up were amply laid out to view. And close to hand, admiring that view, sat Sky Falcon, playing his flute.

"His eyes never leave you," observed First Antelope.

Spirit Woman did not lift an eyelash to take notice of the man, even though she was well aware of every move that Sky Falcon made. She responded, "Think you that he courts me?"

"Think I? Who else is he playing to? Certainly not to me."

Spirit Woman shrugged.

"Have a care, my friend," First Antelope continued, "for your young suitor has a reputation that precedes him, and I fear he may stir your father's resentment. It is well known that since your mother died, your father guards you too well, protecting you as a man might a favorite wife, rather than a daughter."

Spirit Woman nodded. Even though she loved her father, she was not unaware of his shortcomings. It was one of the reasons so few suitors came to call on her: most young men were afraid of her father. All knew that if her father's disposition were mixed with one of his magical incantations . . .

But Spirit Woman held no such fear. She had long ago learned that a sweet smile calmed her father's savage instinct. And so Spirit Woman grinned at her friend, when perhaps it might have been wiser to covet discretion.

Spirit Woman said, "It could not hurt me to talk to the one they call Sky Falcon."

First Antelope sucked in her breath. "It could do much harm. Do not do it."

But the heart knows little fear and Spirit Woman was already enchanted with her young suitor. And in little time the couple had fallen in love.

Now, as has been said by generations of wise men, there are many different kinds of love. There is the love between a parent and a child; the love of a man for his comrades; the love of one's people for their culture. There is even the love one feels for all things living. But sometimes there is a devotion between a man and a woman so potent that it is remembered within the hearts of the people for all time.

Such was the adoration between Spirit Woman and Sky Falcon. And though her father disapproved, Spirit Woman had already determined that she would marry her sweetheart.

And so it came to pass that they eloped, fleeing the Cocopa village and hurrying on toward the North, toward Sky Falcon's people and safety. For Spirit Woman feared for her husband.

Happily they reached the camp of her husband's people, and it was here that they began their lives together. And oh, how well they loved.

For many years they lived in contentment. But never did they dare to return to the Cocopa people, for Spirit Woman's father had threatened to kill Sky Falcon if ever the two men were to meet.

Now, it happened in the spring.

Dark Star, a lovely young woman who had been captured from a warring tribe, had come to live with the people. With her she had brought a curious pet, a mountain lion.

In little time, Dark Star outgrew her slavery and went on to win the attention of the tribe's young men. In truth, she could have picked a husband from several of her acquaintances. But Dark Star had eyes for only one man: Sky Falcon.

However, her desires were met with firm resistance, for Sky Flacon's heart belonged to another.

Now, while it is true that Sky Falcon could have married Dark Star, since the old ways permitted a man more than one wife, Sky Falcon refused to do this. His was no fickle heart. Once pledged, Sky Falcon's devotion remained faithful.

And perhaps it was this that held appeal to Dark Star. But whatever her reasons, she had determined to have what was not hers to take.

It is said that Dark Star flirted openly with Sky Falcon. And although the custom of Indian life forbade an unmarried woman to speak to a man alone, Dark Star ignored these rules, and invited Sky Falcon to her lodge.

"Come and feel this deerskin that I have made for your wife. You will like it and it will make a good dress."

Instinct clamored within Sky Falcon, the desire to run away intense. But alas, he could see little harm in answering Dark Star's appeal. He said, "My wife has many pretty skins with which to make beautiful clothes. I thank you for your consideration, but we do not require them." He turned to go.

"But this is a special skin," Dark Star insisted and she caught his arm.

Sky Falcon shrugged off the woman's touch and spun away from her, every impulse within him crying out in alarm.

Dark Star, however, remained determined and she pushed the skin farther toward him, coaxing, "Here, feel the texture of this pelt. It is special."

"I think not."

Dark Star's smile, however, cajoled. "Come," she said, "do you think it will hurt you? Surely not. And it is so pretty."

Perhaps Sky Falcon only wished to put a quick end to the conversation. Mayhap he might have thought the skin winsome. But too late, he chose to do the wrong thing. He touched the skin, a very unwise thing to do.

For this was no ordinary deerskin. This hide had been worked over with herbs, with wizardry and witchcraft until the pelt itself had taken on power. Such was its potency that he who touched it—save only the one who had worked over it—would fall at once under a spell.

And so, with no more than a simple touch, it came to pass that Sky Falcon fell under Dark Star's command.

Seeing this, Dark Star purred, "You want the skin."

Sky Falcon, being not now himself, nodded.

"And you will take it home to your wife, will you not?"

Again Sky Falcon found he could only agree.

Dark Star grinned, though the gesture played at odds with the evil illuminated within her eyes. "And you will instruct your wife to make a dress from the skin," she commanded, "a dress for me, my wedding dress."

With the magic of the fleece touching his skin, Sky Falcon agreed. For such was the power and evil of this charm that it forced Sky Falcon to step back from his own consciousness, to fall asleep as his own self and to come under the whim of Dark Star.

"Follow me," said Dark Star, and taking hold of Sky Falcon's hand, she propelled him to her lodge. The large mountain cat, her pet, sat outside the lodge's entryway, as though to guard it. But Sky Falcon little saw it, not even to fear it.

Dark Star commanded, "Put the skin on the ground and lay yourself down upon it."

Having no choice, Sky Falcon did as she instructed.

"Now disrobe," commanded Dark Star.

This he did and when done, Dark Star said, "We shall make love and afterwards, as is tradition, we will be married."

However, this one night of passion was never to be. For no sooner had Dark Star disrobed when Spirit Woman stumbled into the dwelling. Perhaps, some say, it was Dark Star's intention that Spirit Woman discover them. Others, more kind, maintain that it was the huge cat that brought Spirit Woman to that lodge.

And as any woman might upon seeing her husband with another, Spirit Woman screamed.

It is said by the wise ones that only love, true and pure, can cast off an evil spell. Such was Sky Falcon's adoration for his wife that when he heard that scream, the hex lost its power and Sky Falcon returned to consciousness, as his own self.

Miserably, however, as he stared around him, it took no genius to surmise what had happened.

But it was too late.

* * *

No sooner had the scream split through the air than Dark Star's pet, the mountain lion, charged into the dwelling and attacked Sky Falcon. Though Sky Falcon struggled as best he could beneath the huge beast, with no weapon, the fight could only go one way.

"Stop it!" screamed Spirit Woman.

In desperation Spirit Woman turned to Dark Star. She implored, "Make your pet stop."

Dark Star wickedly grinned before saying, "I can only do that one way."

"Then do it. And do it quickly," sobbed Spirit Woman.

But Dark Star did not act at once, her stare at the other woman heinous. Said she, "I fear it will involve you."

"Me?" queried Spirit Woman. "How is this so?"

"A life for a life," clucked Dark Star. "If I save your husband, you will lose your own life."

Spirit Woman straightened her spine. "What sort of magic is this?" she asked the other woman.

"Does it matter?" cackled Dark Star. "Your life for his. I can save your husband in no other way."

Spirit Woman barely hesitated. With head held high, for the love she felt for her husband was true, she commanded, "Then do it."

And so it was that, to the accompaniment of howling winds and ghostly wailings, Dark Star's dwelling fluttered, the wind, the gales and satanic sorcery bringing about so much turbulence, that amidst the flying dust and dirt, no eye could easily discern what had come to pass.

The cat disappeared, taking on its human form; Spirit Woman, too, vanished, leaving no trace that she had once lived. And Sky Falcon, no longer battling the cat, jumped up and hurried toward the place where his wife had stood.

But he found nothing there, not even a lock of her hair or an article of her clothing.

"You killed her," came a deep, male voice, a voice Sky Falcon recognized. It was Lost In Timber, Spirit Woman's father, for it was his spirit that had inhabited the cat.

"I did not kill her," Sky Falcon denied. "That one did it with magic." He pointed a finger at Dark Star.

"Not completely," said the old man. "You were inconstant. Had yours been a strong heart, you would not now be in this lodge, causing my daughter pain. Yours is a frivolous heart."

Sky Falcon uttered nothing, not even in his own defense.

"And you." The old man turned to Dark Star. "You were told not to kill her. You were only to entice him."

Dark Star barely flinched. "Your daughter wished me to save him," came the venomous response. "I did as she asked."

"You did not kill her because of him," screamed the old man, the sound of his voice causing even the heavens to quake in response. "You and I both know it. You did it because you were jealous; jealous of her beauty, jealous because she had him."

Dark Star tried to say something, perhaps a lie, but Lost In Timber would hear nothing more. He vowed, "I will curse you both."

Dark Star tried to run away, but the old man held her back, saying, "You will go from here, never to be seen again. And to seal your fate, your body will turn into that which mirrors your soul."

No sooner had the words been spoken than Dark Star screamed, her form turning into an ugly, old hag, for Dark Star's beauty had been no more than skin-deep.

"And you." Lost In Timber turned to Sky Falcon. "You took from me the one thing that I loved. You stole my daughter's heart away from me and made her hate me."

"No, old man," said Sky Falcon, who stood, oddly calm, before his father-in-law. "If her love for you died, and if she did hate you, it was something you did yourself, for you treated your daughter, not as a daughter, but as one might think to guard a cherished wife."

"I did not so guard," denied Lost In Timber.

But Sky Falcon remained silent, for the truth that Sky Falcon spoke could not be turned aside.

Now, Sky Falcon might have been many things, but he was not without bravery and he little flinched beneath the old man's regard.

Seeing this, Lost In Timber became enraged. "From this day forward, all things yours—your family and all your kin—will be unlucky in love. In this way will your seed upon this earth be wiped away. And it will not matter the handsomeness of your face, nor the bravery of your war record, because from this day forward until forever, none of yours will find contentment in love."

Perhaps Sky Falcon could not fathom the repercussions of such a spell; mayhap he little cared, for he had lost that thing most precious to him, his wife. And so it was that Sky Falcon showed his father-in-law little fear.

But the old man, seeing that calm, became venomous and further incanted, "Think you that you will be united with my daughter in spirit? If so, think anew, for not even in death will you be joined with her. Always will you search for her, never will you find her." And then, in finality, the old man uttered, "So be it."

With these words, Lost In Timber disappeared from the face of the earth, never to return, for, as the wise men have often counseled, an evil deed always recoils upon the one who dares to use it.

It is said that Sky Falcon died a very old man; a man who never again knew the companionship of she who had stolen his heart. Not even in spirit. Ah, yes, do not be misled; the curse held firmly in place.

After Sky Falcon's death, so the legend goes, his spirit wandered aimlessly over the western plains of America, looking for his lost love, searching the heavens for her, but never to be reunited with her. Accordingly, he came to be seen often upon the prairie, always at night, sometimes in the company of other spirits of his clan, but always did he search for one amongst his own lineage who could at last break the spell. But never did he probe with any fortuity until . . .

Chapter 1

Abilene, Kansas
Late May 1869

"**G**uess th' soldiers whipped them redskins so hard this time, they'll think twice afore bothering us again," came the husky, masculine voice in the seat directly behind her.

Having no wish to eavesdrop on the conversation, Anna Wiley gazed steadily out the dirty window of the #17, or the *Choctaw,* the name given to the Kansas Pacific train. In a single glance she took in the station's platform and the few untidy tents set out on a flat stretch of Kansas prairie, and she wondered, was this all there was to Abilene's train depot?

Anna's spirits took a plunge at the thought. She had hoped for more . . . so much more.

Taking a deep breath and inhaling the hot, stale air in her crowded car, Anna set her gaze toward the outside of their caravan. There, beside the train tracks, in a line seeming to stretch off into infinity, stood the telegraph poles carrying the singing wires of modern communica-

13

tions. Farther away rose a building or perhaps two, which appeared to be all that there was to the "sprawling metropolis" of Abilene.

Brushing a fly that buzzed around her face, Anna allowed herself a brief smile, remembering the words of Mr. Bilsworth, the New York agent for the Society of Orphans, the man whom she had, of necessity, left behind in Kansas City.

"You and Miss Pagney go on west. They're expectin' you in Hays. Got a telegram from the orphanage in New York saying that they had contacted the church there. Word has it that this town has got plenty of folks there needin' a helping hand with the chores. They'll make the children part of the family." Mr. Bilsworth swallowed with difficulty. *"You'll be able to place the rest of the children there . . . in Hays. I'm certain of it if only you can . . ."*

The old gentleman collapsed back against his pillow, unable to say the rest of the words. Anna held her breath, barely daring to breathe for fear of disturbing him. She observed the sickly, white pallor of his skin and listened to his breathing. That he gasped for air as he spoke did not bode well for his role in the rest of her mission, she feared.

Although Anna was by no means a doctor, she had seen enough sickness in her young life to recognize the symptoms of cholera when confronted with them. No, Mr. Bilsworth would not be making the rest of the journey westward.

Were she and Miss Pagney capable of continuing the journey without him? Two women alone upon the open stretches of the Kansas prairie? Could they place the rest of their charges, these twelve remaining orphaned children, in good homes?

Well, they would have to, Anna resolved. As it was, she could only hope that the children were not infected with the disease that had so suddenly stricken Mr. Bilsworth.

Patting the elderly gentleman's hand, Anna placed his arm back at his side. She cleared her throat, trying to put a note of cheerfulness into her tone as she uttered, her voice barely raised over a whisper, "Don't you worry, Mr. Bilsworth. Miss Pagney and I will go on. We won't let you or the orphanage down. The two of us are capable, I am certain, of seeing to it that the rest of the children find good, Christian homes. I give you my word that I will not rest until it is so. You just concentrate on getting well, and after Miss Pagney and I finish our task, we'll return and reunite with you here. Then we can all return to New York together."

Upon her declaration, Mr. Bilsworth reached out, clutching at her hand. For a moment, his eyes took on the look of a wild beast as he implored, "Ensure that they are good homes, Miss Wiley. Be certain to obtain a written . . ." he gasped, having difficulty drawing in breath. His hand on hers suddenly took on a death grip, so tightly did he clench at her. "Important to have a written contract," he croaked. "Remember that."

Anna swallowed with difficulty before she uttered, "I understand."

Mr. Bilsworth fell back, his grip lessening. He muttered, "Do I have your promise? Will you vow to me that you will find these children good homes? Christian homes?"

"Yes, Mr. Bilsworth." Anna nodded. "I promise."

That was all he had been waiting for, it appeared, for with her words, Mr. Bilsworth relaxed his vigil, giving her a silent nod in acknowledgment before the doctor rushed in to usher her quickly out of the room.

That had been almost a month ago. Mr. Bilsworth had died a few days later, leaving her and Miss Pagney in charge. The two of them, along with the children, had waited the necessary few weeks in Kansas City to determine if the disease had infected any of the rest of their party.

Luckily, neither she, Miss Pagney, nor any of the children had come down with the illness. But the wait had given her the opportunity to learn sign language, the universal language of the plains. One never knew. It might come in handy.

"But Pa, Ma says that them Injuns is on the warpath again," came the younger voice from behind her. "Ma says she heard tell that them Sioux has joined up with them Cheyenne Dog Soldiers. Said that together they's gonna fight it out with us."

Anna's thoughts came rushing back into the present. Was it true? Were the Cheyenne Indians, along with a smattering of Sioux, on the warpath?

When she had booked passage on this train, nobody had told her anything about an Indian uprising. Nobody had warned her.

Why hadn't she had the good sense to read a newspaper before she had ventured out farther along the Kansas frontier?

Would it have made a difference? a small voice inside

her challenged. Anna glanced nervously toward her small charges, letting her gaze fall tenderly upon each child.

She breathed in heavily. It would have made no difference whatsoever, she acknowledged to herself. Placing these homeless waifs with adoptive parents who would raise and love them as their own was her responsibility.

Responsibility? It was more than that. She and Miss Pagney would scour the countryside for churches, for families, for anyone who would support their project, and in doing so, would always put the happiness of these children, their welfare and their eventual adoption, above their own needs. And why?

Anna had never really thought about it, yet, if she were to be truthful, she would admit that these children had become more than a simple obligation. They had become her life, the very reason for her existence. This project and others she had undertaken these past few years ignited her with purpose; and certainly no Indians, or even a threat of an all-out war, would come between her and the fulfillment of that duty.

Deep inside her a voice added that she would never permit anything to come between her and the role, perhaps for a moment only, of being a mother.

Anna closed her eyes as the truth of that thought found its mark. She might never find any other form of motherhood. At least not in this, her earthly existence, since Anna was painfully aware of her lack of appeal to the opposite sex.

At five foot ten, she towered over most of the gentlemen of her acquaintance, and this, as well as her willowy figure, did little to instill undying inspiration, she had found. Of course, there was also her mousy brown hair and her too pale skin, which only seemed to add to her homeliness.

She drew in an unsteady breath, deciding to turn her thoughts to other things, unaware that there was one trait about herself that she had missed, one that highly recommended her had she but known it: her eyes, green and lustrous. They shone with a kindness of spirit that could not be bought, sold, or bargained. And perhaps this alone was their beauty.

Anna settled back and gazed out upon the Kansas frontier as the train came to a stop. Her glance took in the few tents that had been scattered close to the railroad tracks, and she knew a moment of despair.

"Is Ma waiting for us at Hays, Pa?"

"I expect so, son, I expect so."

Anna let out a deep sigh of relief while she tried to drown out the rest of the conversation between the father and son. If a woman lingered there in Hays, then that town surely had to be better than these few tents in Abilene. *Please, dear Father,* she prayed, *let it be better than Abilene . . . for the children.*

And, on this more optimistic note, Anna tried to settle her mind.

There was a sort of beauty to the plains, she acknowledged as her gaze scanned the prairie. At least there were no mountains here, Anna thought with a shudder. She particularly disliked high places and hated to think how she would have managed had she been required to cross a mountain or two in order to find homes for these children.

But that would be unnecessary, she decided as she glanced out at the stretches of flat land. The panorama from her window reminded her of an ocean of green, for no landmark could be seen to distinguish one area from the next. It made her wonder how, if she were to become lost from the train, she would ever find her way.

The chances of that happening were very slim, she reminded herself. Shaking her head, she brought her gaze closer to the train tracks where, up ahead, there stood passengers, waiting to board the Kansas Pacific Railroad. From her limited vantage point, she could see perhaps thirty people standing upon Abilene's depot, the railroad station being little more than a simple platform.

None of those people looked refreshed, Anna quickly observed. But then, why should they? The train was already close to ten hours late.

Still, Anna reckoned, those passengers would wait rather than risk trekking alone over the prairie. After all, better to travel by this more modern mode of transportation than to depend on the prairie schooners, the only other means of transport across this land.

Slowly the train swayed to a stop, which caused a stir amongst the passengers waiting outside.

Where would they be fitting all those people? Anna wondered. The train was full, with adults and children already sitting or reclining in the aisles.

Anna heard a high-pitched sigh and brought her glance back to the confines of her own car. A small child sat in Anna's lap, the child's head wobbling this way and that with the jostling motion of the train. Tenderly, with gentle hands, Anna reached out to bring the child's head in closer to her bosom.

The scent of the waif's filthy hair drifted up to her, causing Anna to reach a firm decision: as soon as their group reached Hays, she would ensure that all the children had a good wash. And it wouldn't matter the objections of Miss Pagney. Miss Pagney had already complained too heartily at Topeka—the last station—that the meager finances of the Society would not include a bath for each of these children.

But really, Anna reasoned, how else were they to present these youngsters at their very best?

Anna rested her gaze on these six of her twelve orphaned charges who, without a fuss and with nary a complaint, sat clustered around her, their trust in her a real and tangible quality. All at once, a feeling of helplessness, all mixed up with hope, along with a healthy dose of fear, shot through Anna.

Ah, yes, she reaffirmed, she would do all she could to ensure the best homes would be given to these children. Thus, the necessity of baths.

"But Ma said in her letter that them Injuns might still attack us," came the young voice directly in back of Anna.

"Ah, there's nothing ta fear, young 'un," a deeper voice explained. "Didn't General Sherman roust them Injuns outta their wasps' nests like the varmints they are? Survival of the fittest, son, survival of the fittest. Them Injuns is beat." The deep, male voice laughed, though there was little humor in the sound. "Didn't all them Cheyenne chiefs, just last New Year's Eve, surrender at Fort Cobb? Why, them Injuns is no better'n animals and they run from anythin' resemblin' a good fight. Naw, they's got the fear of the good Lord in 'em now. Calm yourself, son, them soldiers has things well in hand."

"But Ma said that some of 'em didn't surrender, Pa. Didn't she call 'em Dog Soldiers? And ain't they still mad 'bout Sand Creek? I heard Ma sayin' that they's out ta kill anything with white skin."

Anna heard the masculine expletive from behind her and felt her face flush in reaction.

"Sand Creek!" came the deep-voiced hiss. "What does yer ma know about Sand Creek? Why, them Injuns was taught a lesson at the Sand Creek battle, I reckon. Got exactly what they deserved, and they would not be on the warpath on account of that. Why, Sand Creek was a victory for them cavalry soldiers, as great as any from the War atween the States."

Victory? Anna nearly choked. She really should not be listening, she acknowledged. Yet, she could not seem to help herself—at least, not without plugging her ears.

But to call Sand Creek a victory? Even she, an easterner, knew that Sand Creek had been no more than a massacre.

With interest, Anna had read about the incident in the eastern papers, and she had been appalled, as were most easterners, over the savage tactic employed by the United States Cavalry.

How could one call the slaughter of peaceful Indians, who had been promised sanctuary by the military, a victory?

For despite orders to the contrary, Colonel John M. Chivington had enlisted the aid of volunteer troops and had forced a seven-hundred-man march in the dead of winter. Then, one cold and blustery morning in 1864, he had reached a camp of peaceful Cheyenne Indians who had always been friendly towards the whites and who had been flying the United States flag within their grounds.

Under Chivington's orders, the volunteers and soldiers

had hit that camp hard, and at a time when the Indians had least expected it, especially since their chief had been invited to move in close to the fort—for the Indian's own "safety."

The paper had gone on to say that not only had the cavalry been intent upon killing the fighting men in that camp, the soldiers had gone on to slaughter, with glee, well over a hundred women and infants, scalping and mutilating their bodies with such savagery, any sane person would have been left wondering exactly who it was in the West that were the savages.

"But Ma says them Cheyenne ain't never forgot," came the young voice again, followed by a snort from his elder.

"Them Injuns is licked, I tell ya. Iffen it weren't safe ta travel on this train into Hays, the train would not be runnin'. Now, don't let's talk about it anymore, son."

Should she believe the unknown man who sat behind her?

"Look, Pa, thar's an Injun!"

Anna glanced quickly out the window, calming herself when all she espied was a child—an Indian child—probably not much older than those children who were currently in her own charge.

But her calm was quickly replaced with indignation. Why, the boy carried upon him, chains: shackles around his arms, holding both his hands together, and links—large and heavy ones—about his neck.

Chains? Lord help them, the lad was a mere boy.

Worse, the Indian lad was accompanied by three men who, as she watched, knocked the boy this way and that, stretching his chains to the limit, causing the youth's arms practically to be pulled from their sockets. Blood ran down the boy's neck and wrists.

All the while the big men laughed. Laughed!

Anna could barely restrain herself. A child was a child, after all, Indian or not.

Oddly, despite the discomfort that the child must be experiencing, no emotion—none whatsoever—could be seen upon the young man's countenance.

Anna came to her feet, settling the youngster she was holding onto her left hip.

"Hold my seat for me, sweetheart," she whispered to the oldest of her charges, Collin, who sat in the stiff, hard seat next to her. "I'll be right back."

Jostling her way through the rest of the passengers, Anna came at last to the door of their car. No sooner had she reached out to open that door when those same three men flung the door wide, pulling the Indian youth through it.

Quickly Anna jumped back, barely avoiding being squashed against the train's walls. Regaining her footing, however, she planted herself directly in front of the men.

"Excuse us, ma'am."

Anna raised her chin in the air. "You are not excused."

The man to whom she had spoken appeared momentarily taken aback.

Anna, however, barely paused, going on to demand, "Unhand that child."

"What child?"

"That . . . that youth you have in chains." With her free hand she pointed toward the boy.

The fellow in front of her—a very large man—laughed

at her before he went on to explain, "This here young 'un ain't no youth, ma'am. This here's the brother of War Cloud. Why, that Injun's become more outlaw than Injun in these here parts."

"War Cloud?"

"That's right, ma'am."

"I don't understand," she said. "What has any of that to do with this boy?"

The big oaf of a man scratched his beard-stubbled chin, as though he were contemplating his words, before he went on to say, "Well, now, ma'am, the way we's fig-urin' it, iffen ya want ta catch a mean old bear like War Cloud, ya gotta sweeten the trap. That's what this here young varmint is fer."

Anna gulped. "Are you telling me that this young man has done nothing? That you are simply holding him here—in chains—only to catch his brother?"

The man, however, appeared oblivious to her tone of voice and he went on to elaborate, as though she were in full agreement with him, "I knew ya weren't no dumb 'un, ma'am."

Anna stiffened her spine, clutching the child she held on her hip as though the small lad were her only lifeline to sanity. She scolded in her very best schoolmarm voice, "Are you aware that what you are doing to this boy is highly illegal?"

The big man appeared somewhat taken aback. "Illegal, ma'am?" he asked as though he hadn't heard correctly. "I don't rightly think so. And this 'un here ain't no boy. This here's an Injun."

"I disagree," Anna uttered. "The child that you hold is a human being, Indian or not."

"Not out here in Kansas, he ain't. Nits make lice." The man gave Anna an inspecting look. "Youse must be one of them silly easterners, ain't ya, ma'am? Not a very pretty one either."

At the insult, Anna lifted her chin.

"Now, look here, ma'am," the man in front of her offered, "we don't want no trouble. We's only holdin' the boy as hostage until we's—"

"As hostage!" Anna interrupted. "A youth who has done nothing more than be a living relative of another man! And in restraints? Look at the poor boy's wrists, and his neck."

"Yeah, jest look at 'em," the man chuckled inanely.

But Anna would not be kept silent and she reproached them even further, "If you are merely holding the youth as hostage, then I demand that you at least let him out of those chains."

"You, ma'am? Demand?"

Again Anna was met with that senseless laughter, but this time from all three of the men.

"Why, ma'am," another of the men, farther away from her, chimed, "it ain't like we's hurtin' the boy or nothin'." At the same time, that man tugged on the lad's fetters, causing a fresh rivulet of blood to run down the child's wrists.

Anna snorted. "Why, shame on you, gentlemen," she chided. "Didn't your mothers teach you any better than to lie? Just you look there at the boy's wrists and his neck! And from my window I saw the way you were manhandling this child. Now, tell me, has this lad himself—not his brother—done anything to merit such harsh treatment?"

All three of the men chortled with laughter—not a pleasant sound. One of them replied, "He's Injun, ain't he?" as if that explained it all.

Anna stamped her foot. "I will not tolerate this kind of treatment. Not of a child." She stood her ground when the three men flashed her irritated looks. "And not within my sight," she added.

All three men guffawed, one of them pushing her aside, none too gently, as though to get by her. Another of them mimicked her accent as he, too, made to move around her. "Then, ma'am, might I recommend that you not watch."

To another round of coarse laughter, the three men pushed on past her.

Anna glanced down at the poor Indian boy when he filed by her. She smiled at him. But it did no good. The boy didn't even look at her.

Anna, however, was not through with these men and she threatened, "I will tell the conductor about your maltreatment of this child, if you do not cease this barbaric approach at once."

The last of the men, the biggest one, turned back toward her. "You easterners, with your highfalutin ways and your big words, seem ta all think alike. Now, I's tellin' ya, ma'am, you go right on and tell the conductor." A foolish grin followed his words before the man added, tipping his hat to her, "You jest do that."

And with nothing more to be said or done, at least for the moment, the three men pushed their way into the next car.

Chapter 2

⟨᠙⟩

The train sped over the plains of midwestern Kansas at a whopping speed of about twenty miles per hour.

The child on Anna's lap slept while the boy in the seat adjoining hers fidgeted, his head hanging down. Oh, dear, something was wrong.

Anna leaned down to whisper into the lad's ears, "Is something the matter, Collin?"

The youngster shook his head.

Anna sighed. She knew what it was, of course. She was, however, reluctant to speak of it.

Collin had been badly abused by his father prior to being brought into the orphanage. It was possible that seeing the young lad, bound in irons, had stirred some bitter and painful memories for her young charge. Anna asked, "Is it because of that Indian boy that we saw with those men?"

Again came that shake of Collin's head, although he added, "If those men are treatin' a boy like that only 'cause he's Indian, what are they going to do to me? Some people hate the Irish as much as they do the Indians. And some people just seem to hate."

27

Anna patted the boy's hand. He had a point. But she said, "Not to worry, Collin. Not to worry. I think the prejudice out here extends only to Indians." *Or at least I hope so,* she added to herself. "Besides," she went on to say, "I'll personally ensure that the family that adopts you will not ill use you. Don't worry, now. It's all part of the contract they will be making with the Society." She patted Collin's hand once more. "I'll make sure of it, all right?"

Collin nodded, although he did not look her in the eye, and after a while, Anna turned her gaze once again to the passing scenery.

The land of opportunity. Wasn't that what the West symbolized? She sighed. Such beautiful plains, yet such a rugged country. What had the man behind her said? Survival of the fittest? Was the concept true? Was it only the fittest that deserved survival?

If that were true, then by the same reasoning these children did not deserve to live, and Anna knew she could never agree to that. Every human being deserved a chance at freedom, and these children, most of whom had never known a mother or a father, much less the warmth of love, were going to have that chance.

Yes, one would have to be strong to exist here, but that did not mean that one could not love his fellows, be they children . . . or Indian . . .

Anna's eyes felt heavy and she realized with a start that she was tired. But why shouldn't she be? She'd had very little sleep these past few days, her worries about the children keeping her awake until the wee hours of the morning.

But she could not sleep, she told herself. She must remain awake; after all, she must register a protest about that Indian boy's ill treatment. Perhaps she should try to find the conductor, but she realized she could not leave her charges.

That gave her only one thing to do. She would have to wait until the conductor passed by her seat, looking for tickets.

Which meant she could not afford a nap, she reminded herself, even while her eyes closed.

Boom!

Anna's eyelids flew open. What was that noise? Worse, had she been sleeping? Had she missed the conductor?

Quickly, Anna glanced around her. What had awakened her?

Another explosion came from behind her; Anna recognized it as the blast of gunfire. As anxiety pumped through her body, she clutched her seat and threw her arms around Collin. What was going on?

Suddenly, the back door of their car burst open. At once, the clanking din of the train permeated their car, followed by a scream.

Anna glanced behind her.

Drama unfolded as the young Indian lad, dragging his irons behind him, pushed the door of their car shut and rushed down the aisle.

Another loud blast sounded from the adjoining car and Anna realized the bullies were shooting at the young Indian.

Within the space of seconds, the boy scrambled over the passengers lying in the car's aisle, pressing on impossibly over them, yet heading steadily toward her. Briefly, for a moment only, she caught the lad's wild glance. But in that moment, she also found the calm within her to smile at him.

The gesture, however, remained unreturned, perhaps not even seen.

Anna stood up all at once, changing places with Collin so that she was in the seat closest to the aisle. It was almost as if Collin had read her thoughts.

Without even a moment's hesitation, Anna gestured toward the Indian as he pushed closer toward her.

"Over here," she urged, wondering if the boy understood English.

He ignored her.

But Anna was accustomed to dealing with children. Reaching out, she grabbed hold of the lad's arm and pulled him toward her.

"Bend down," she ordered, "and hurry."

The youth at last glanced at her, giving her a puzzled look.

Just then the door handle to their own car jostled, another gun fired, and the door to their car fell open.

"Hurry," she urged the young man. "There is little time." And without awaiting his agreement, Anna pulled the boy to her, forcing him to bend down. Without another thought as to what she was doing, she swept her full skirts over him, hiding him completely. Just as quickly she sat back down.

As she had predicted, the three bullies soon followed, scampering over the people lying in the aisle and rushing past her without giving her a second glance.

They pushed open the front door of the car, once more

allowing the noise of the train to filter into their compartment.

All three men, weapons drawn, exited. All three men returned within a matter of minutes.

"The varmint has ta be here, lessen he jumped off the train," one of the men offered, scratching his head with his gun as he spoke. "Ya don't suppose he's gone and jumped, do ya?"

"Naw, we woulda seen him. The varmint's here somewhere. Them irons woulda kept him from jumpin'."

"Pardon, ma'am," one of the roughhousers addressed Anna, using his gun to lift his hat. "Did ya see that Injun varmint, the one you's complainin' about, come through here?"

Anna didn't even lift up her eyelids. Oh, dear, she thought. She had forgotten about the youngster sitting directly behind her—and his father. Neither of them had seemed too sympathetic to the Indian cause. Would they betray her?

"Ma'am?"

At last Anna raised her gaze, addressing the bully who leaned over her. She even smiled.

"Has ya seen that Injun varmint?"

"An Indian?" she repeated. "Or a varmint?"

"They's one an' the same thing, ma'am."

"I've not seen any Injun varmint," Anna said, acknowledging to herself that she did not lie. The young lad was certainly not a "varmint."

The man glanced down at her lap, as though he knew she hid something. But short of forcing her to stand and disrobe, what could he do?

Anna turned her head away from the man.

"Wasn't ya sittin' in the far seat last time I seen ya?"

Slowly Anna turned her scrutiny back to the man. She smiled sweetly and said, "Was I?"

The man looked stumped.

Anna came to his rescue. "For a time I was sitting there, yes." She pointed to the youngster beside her. "But Collin and I switched seats so that he could look out the window."

The man bid Collin to look at him, as though for endorsement.

But Collin merely shrugged and gazed away. And, thank the Lord, not a single word came from behind her.

Anna suggested, "I think, sir, that if you are looking for a 'varmint,' you should look elsewhere. There is no such thing here."

The man seemed reluctant to believe her—and with good cause, Anna acknowledged to herself. Still, in a matter of a few minutes, the man moved on.

One tense moment followed upon another as the three men forced people to stand while they checked under their seats. Anna stood; she even moved aside, ensuring that the Indian youth remained well hidden.

And at last the men left.

Still, Anna waited; not moving, not speaking, fearing to so much as utter a sound. Finally, after almost a half hour, Anna leaned toward Collin, inquiring, "Would you be so kind as to take out a piece of the bread in that basket that we brought with us?"

Collin did so.

"Thank you," Anna acknowledged, tearing off a part of it and handing it beneath her skirts to the Indian lad. She whispered, "He looked hungry."

Collin, a young man of ten, nodded.

At length Anna observed, "Why do you think the two people sitting behind us did not betray us?"

Collin grinned. "Have you looked?"

Anna had not. She did so now. Why, the man and his boy were sound asleep.

She asked, "Have they been that way for long?"

Collin nodded. "Not even the gunfire awoke them."

"Then they must have been exhausted. Far be it for us to awaken them."

She smiled at Collin as the train crawled onward, "roaring" over the countryside at an unheard-of rate of speed—not more than twenty miles per hour.

He might as well have called her ugly.

Anna gulped. It was one thing to admit the fact to herself, another to hear a person speak the words aloud. Ever since the bullies had passed by her, that one man's words kept rolling round and round her mind.

Not a very pretty one at that.

Anna inhaled deeply and tried to console herself with the fact that the man was the same one who thought nothing of fettering a mere boy. The man was a ruffian at best, as well as a fool, she told herself. If she knew what was good for her, she would try to turn her attention to something else. But it was no use.

At length, she felt the stirrings of the boy, who still hid beneath the cover of her skirts. The child must have fallen asleep, she supposed, and was only now awakening.

Oh dear, she thought, the lad must be famished. Reaching across Collin to the basket of food, she grabbed another piece of bread, sneaking it to the boy.

There was a bigger problem, however, than mere hunger. One she had only begun to realize. How was she going to smuggle the lad off the train? Could she keep him hidden when she walked?

Anna was considering several different solutions to the problem when she became aware that the train was slowing almost to a crawl. Glancing outside, she found herself unable to discern a reason for it. No civilization loomed up ahead yet. She leaned forward, trying to look outward, toward the engine.

Well, no wonder. Here were buffalo, the first she had seen on this trip. There were thousands of them literally blackening the surrounding countryside as well as blocking the train tracks.

Even at their snail's pace, it did not take long before the entire train coasted into the thick of the shaggy animals. Within moments, Anna could see the huge beasts from her window.

Shouts of glee sounded from within her car, and soon gunshots rang out over the prairie. One buffalo fell, followed by another and another, all within a matter of a few minutes.

"Dang!" Another of what could only be called "sportsmen" jumped up and rushed from their car.

Anna had heard of this sort of thing, had read of the large herds of buffalo being butchered by these hunters, had read reports of the animals' bones and hides being collected by the railroad and sold back east. At this rate, Anna speculated as she watched one animal after another fall, there would be few buffalo left for future generations.

The train soon came to a complete halt amidst the roaring of gunfire. Anna stole a glance at the children, noting that they appeared uneasy, but she smiled back at them in reassurance.

"They're only hunting buffalo," she whispered to her darlings. "We'll be on our way shortly."

Suddenly a cry rang out over the gunfire. Here was yet another and another.

Anna became immediately alert, for these were not the sounds of animals. These were human cries.

Quickly scanning the area around them, she gasped. A man outside her window lay inert on the ground.

Swish, an arrow flew past her window, followed instantly by the painful cry of a man.

Before her eyes, a man clutched his chest where an arrow had sunk into it; the man fell forward.

Indians!

As if to confirm her deduction, a war whoop reverberated close by her. Another followed, and another and another until there were so many of them, the air fairly rang with the high-pitched cries. Added to this cacophony came the retorts and blasts from guns. But as that particular sound became too few and far between, someone yelled out, "Cheyennes!"

Were they losing?

Suddenly fear washed over Anna; her stomach dropped and she barely had time to consider what she should do. She, herself, carried no weapon of any kind.

"Children, come here, all of you. Now!" Anna jumped to her feet.

Struggling out of their seats, all six youngsters flew toward her.

"What is it, Miss Wiley?" one of the boys asked.

Anna didn't know what to answer. How could she tell them the truth without causing panic? A panic that might cause one of them to scream, which could bring them all to the Indians' attention. Yet how could she not tell them? Especially when the Indians were right outside her window.

As a result of her indecision, she said nothing, and she moved around the children, her object being to place the young ones into her aisle seat behind her and hide them. Meanwhile, she positioned herself in front of them. Hurrying as quickly as she could, she picked up one child after the other, stationing them behind her.

"Miss Wiley, are we going to die?" one of the boys asked.

She paused in order to gather her thoughts, if that were possible. At last she answered, "Of course not," and had barely uttered the words when a group of four Indians broke in through the door to their compartment.

Anna's scream came as a completely involuntary reaction.

Larger than life, with hideous red, black and white slashes of paint across their faces and on their bodies, the Indians wielded guns and knives as though they had been born to handle them. They also wasted no time in using them.

The toll of death, along with the swish of knives, the roar of guns and the wild, war whoops resounded off the walls of their small compartment until Anna's head reeled.

She watched as one after another of the white men fell beneath the Indians' guns and knives. Her heart beat so quickly, she thought it might stop. Desperately she tried to gather the children together in an attempt to shield them from sight.

But it was useless.

A precious few of her children still stood in the aisle, even as the Indians steadily advanced toward them. Anna flung herself forward, in front of her children. She hadn't considered that her action might uncover the boy; in reality, she had forgotten about him. However, it was this action, and perhaps this action alone, that saved her.

At once, a very tall Indian—the one who kept lingering to search under each inert body, the one who kept plodding onward in front of the others—stopped absolutely still as he caught sight of her and the boy next to her. This Indian had not been killing the passengers as had the others; rather he had trod steadily forward, frantically searching under each seat.

Quickly he made his way toward them, and reaching out, flung Anna aside.

At least he hadn't killed her.

"Ne-naestse!" He made a hand motion to his side, obviously telling the boy to come to him.

The boy went.

The tall Indian then raised his weapon and took aim at her. Anna closed her eyes. Dear Lord, she thought, what was going to happen to the children?

As she prepared herself for the worst, it was the last thought she had.

Chapter 3

❝**H**ova'ahane!❞
The shot never came. Anna opened her eyes. The young Indian boy stood between her and that gun.

Anna gulped. Had her earlier act of kindness saved her life?

It appeared to be so, for the young Indian would not leave her side. His action gave the tall one no choice but to kill the boy or let her live.

He chose the latter and turned to leave, at the same time motioning her and the children outside.

Anna moved at once, hustling the children with her, all of them struggling toward the open door of their car. They stumbled over bodies in their path, partly because of her own hurry to get out of the car, partly because Indians behind them kept shoving both her and the children forward.

Someone commanded, *"Ta-naestse!"* Anna had no idea what that word meant, although she thought he might be urging them to hurry.

Behind her came the ear-shattering clamor of more gunfire, followed by so many screams, Anna couldn't bear to think about it. Silently, she thanked the Lord for her own and the children's rescue, and as she did so, she spared a moment to say a prayer for those not so fortunate as she.

In little time she alighted from the train, coming to stand on the firm, yet grassy Kansas plains. The acrid smell of war hit her at once, as did the burning sensation of the sun. But she tried to keep her wits about her, even as the hot, humid breeze pushed its way into her face. That the wind tore the bonnet from her hair, until the hat had no choice but to hang from her neck, she ignored.

She felt light-headed, as though she might swoon, but Anna solemnly refused to give way to the feeling. The children depended on her.

All around her lay death and destruction: the buffalo; some white men, the conductor and engineer amongst them; a few Indians . . . very few Indians. Yet it wasn't over.

Farther away, toward the front of the train, the Indians were shooting at the men and a few of the women who remained alive. And there, amongst those precious few, stood Miss Pagney along with the other six of her orphan charges.

A shot fired. Miss Pagney fell.

"No!" Anna screamed out the word, repeating it over and over as she ran down the distance between herself and the other children. "No! No! No!"

Perhaps it was fate that kept her alive. Perhaps the Indians were merely startled by her behavior. Whatever the reason, Anna reached the children without further incident.

Quickly, she knelt down toward Miss Pagney's body,

running her hands along the woman's throat where there should have been a pulse. There was none.

Gulping back a cry, Anna stood, casting a poisonous glance out toward her friend's murderer. But her effort was wasted. The one responsible for the deed paid her no attention.

A few of the Indians crept closer. As she watched them, nausea threatened to overwhelm Anna, but she resolutely held on to her dignity. She'd be darned if she would give these Indians the thrill of watching her break down.

Biting back the fear that rose up in her throat, Anna herded the children into a circle, placing the youngsters behind her. Breathing deeply, she mustered every ounce of courage she possessed, that she might confront these Indians with some show of composure. She expected no less than the worst.

But again, the worst never happened.

Looking around, Anna at once understood the reason why: the young Indian lad had followed her, had again placed himself between her and the line of fire.

"Ne-ve'-neheseve!" one of the other Indians commanded of the lad.

"Hova'ahane!" came the answer from the youngster. *"Epehevahe!"*

Anna might never know what was said, but of the result she could be left in no doubt.

She remained alive, while those few remaining white men who stood around her soon met their Maker.

In little time she and the children were the only white people still standing, still breathing. They must have made an odd sight, too, Anna determined, for all twelve of the children were positioned behind her. And the only thing that intervened between her and the guns of these Indians was the youth whom she had rescued.

Though another might have whined given the same circumstances, strangely, the horror of the Indian attack had not created that effect on Anna. Yes, it was a terrible thing; yes, it might haunt her in nightmares for years to come, but all she could think of at the moment was to survive, to stay alive. She must live, if only for the children's sake.

She drew in a breath and coughed. If the stench in the air were the smell of fear, Anna knew she would never mistake it for anything else again. That odor and the sight of the bodies lying around her turned her stomach, but Anna swallowed back the bitter taste in her throat.

Later, she thought, later she would allow herself the luxury of breaking down—if there were a later.

The tall Indian strode toward them. *Dear God Almighty,* thought Anna, gazing at the man, *this Indian is huge.*

Even at her height, the man towered over her, and she wondered at it. Somehow she had been led to believe that Indians were squat and homely. Yet, she could not deny what her eyes beheld. Neither gangly nor heavyset, this man had to be well over six feet tall. In truth, none of these Indians appeared to be less than six feet in height. As for homely, even through the man's war paint, she could see that this warrior was anything but plain, the breadth of the man's chest alone causing her to gasp.

"Ne-naestse!" He addressed the boy, motioning to him.

The boy made his own gestures, obviously a negative response.

Again, the man ordered, *"Ne-naestse!"* followed by a firmer hand motion. All to no effect. The boy remained where he was.

Although Anna thought this might serve to enrage the man all the more—and it would have been difficult to tell if it had, for the paint hid the man's expression—the tall one did not raise his voice. Perhaps it was only by some base instinct that Anna knew the Indian was angry.

Without uttering another word, the tall Indian collected a pickaxe from one of the inert bodies lying in the field and, treading forward, took aim.

Wham! Anna flinched as the clamor of metal upon metal hurt her ears, but she remained otherwise unharmed. She watched, however, as the irons holding the boy's wrists came open and fell to the ground.

The tall Indian's scowl next fell to the chains around the boy's neck.

He wouldn't try to . . . Why, he could hurt the boy doing that.

"Wait!" Anna shouted and, sparing little thought to her actions, she ran toward the body of one of the bullies, one of the men who had previously ill treated the boy.

Holding her breath, for the stench of death was sickening, she fumbled in the man's pockets. Anna could barely believe that she was doing what she was. Still . . .

Ah, there they were. Keys.

"Wait!" she ordered again, and rising to her full height, she ran back toward the boy, shouting, "Keys." She jangled them in front of the tall brave's face.

Amazingly enough, the Indian appeared indulgent, and Anna thought she might have witnessed a glimmer of humor, there in the man's hard-set gaze. Although, she

decided as she took better note of the look of hatred shining in his eyes, perhaps not.

Because she was in such a hurry, she fumbled with the
keys and almost dropped them. And to make matters
worse, her hands shook so unsteadily, she could barely
see what she was doing.

The tall Indian trod right up to her side, however, and
growling out, *"Enanotse,"* wrenched the keys from her
hand. With little difficulty, he opened the lock around the
boy's neck. But if the tall Indian had thought the release
of the boy would change the youth's attitude, he was
badly mistaken. If anything, the youngster whirled in
closer to Anna.

"Ne-naestse!" Stepping back, the tall one spoke and
motioned to the lad, the elder's gesture obviously asking
the youngster to come forward. *"Naena'ovo'hame."*
Anna recognized the sign for horses and watched as the
warrior jerked his head to the left.

The boy looked around the barren prairie briefly before
uttering, *"Tosa'a?"* This word was accompanied by a
hand motion indicating "where?"

"Ho'hamose," said the tall brave, pointing toward a
distant hill. *"Ta-naestse!"* Again Anna was able to follow
the conversation in bits and pieces from their gestures,
and she knew that the tall one wanted the boy to leave her.

The youngster made no move. He asked, *"Ne-ta'-ose-
htseohtse . . . e-na'hoho-o'o vo'estanehe?"*

No! Anna could not understand the words, but she had
recognized the sign for kill and for people, along with the
sign for question. The youngster was asking his elder if
he was going to kill them.

Anna drew in her breath and held it, anxiety making

her head spin. Minute by minute passed as she awaited the elder's reply.

At length the tall brave let out a hiss. *"Na-saa-e'hes-tana momoo'o . . ."* he said, and Anna lost track of the conversation, for his signs were too quick for her to follow. Of one thing she was certain, however: the tall Indian had not answered the lad's question.

"Ne-ta'-ose-ese-htseohtse e-na'hoho-o'o-he?" the boy asked, again using the sign for "kill."

The tall Indian shrugged. *"Ne-tsehe-skestovestse naa tsehe-hestovestse, ne-tsehe-axaa'ehemestovestse naa . . . Hooxe'eo'he'e . . ."* The man talked on and on and Anna held her breath, trying to discern the tall one's gestures. But the only thing she could determine with accuracy was that the man spoke of the Battle at the Washita River. And, if she were reading the signs correctly, it appeared that he wanted to take her and the children's lives in exchange for those of his own relatives.

It made her wonder if this man had lost someone dear to him at that battle. He must have . . .

The boy interrupted her thoughts as he cried *"Hova'-ahane!"* The gesture for "no" followed and, if Anna had not been aware of it before, she surely understood now that this boy alone stood between her and death's door. Could the child hold out against this fierce warrior?

To her surprise, the tall brave looked taken aback, even if it were only for a moment. He said, *"Na-to'se-ene-ne-heseeo'otse-he?"* leaving Anna to identify only one sign, the one for "stop."

After a brief pause, the tall brave gave a quick nod toward her and asked, *"Ehaahe?"* She observed the sign for "brave."

The lad acknowledged the man with a nod of his own and positioned himself firmly in front of her, his feet apart, as if he might grow roots.

The light of battle glared from the tall one's eyes, yet he appeared to hold in his anger, even as he demanded, *"Nehe'se, noheto! E-noohta. Ase-sta'xestse!"*

Anna observed several different signs being used with these words, one demanding the boy leave at once.

"Hova'ahane!" Again, the gesture for "no."

"Notaxe-ve'ho'e seve-e'neha nenoveto. Ekase'xove."

Anna tried her best to concentrate on the gestures. The tall one had said something about white men, but she could not tell what it was.

But the youngster did not so much as flinch. He said, *"Na-he-vesenehenotse. E-saa-ne'ame-saa-atse,"* and Anna saw a single gesture for "friend," then one of denial. Ah, she came to realize, the youngster would not leave without her.

That was when it happened: the tall Indian scrutinized *her*, from the top of her head down to the very hem of her dress. And under that intense regard, Anna felt certain that this time her knees would give out beneath her. Perhaps, she thought, it was only sheer willpower that held her erect.

"Eaaa." The tall Indian became silent—too silent. Then, making a quick, distasteful face toward her, he ordered, *"E-he-have'hatsestse!"* and turning, he sauntered away.

He was leaving! He was going to let them live!

Relief made her swoon and Anna reached out to hold on to her hero, the boy in front of her.

In response, the youngster took one of her hands and,

turning around to her, said, *"Ne-hve'ohtsemestse."* He let go of her hand to make the sign for "Come with me."

Anna wanted to obey. But she could not. Not right now. She was too confused and, truth be told, she could barely stand on her feet. She had to take a moment, albeit a short one, to gather her thoughts, perhaps her strength as well.

Glancing up at the sun and then around her, she wondered how long the tall brave would permit her party to live. That he had wanted to kill them was without doubt. That it had only been the actions of the boy that had saved them was also unquestionable.

She did not want to leave with these Indians, because if she stayed here, she might eventually be found. If she went with the Indians . . .

Did she have a choice? Would the Indians permit her to stay?

She would have to try to reason with the Indians and try to persuade them to let her stay.

But, she considered conversely, what if she were granted that request? How long would she have to wait before help arrived? Days? A week? Would she and the children be able to survive here, alone? And she without a weapon, without any way to protect herself and the children from the wolves?

She would have to find a weapon, she decided; it was the only way. But it seemed impossible. With the Indians already confiscating the white man's guns and rifles, there would soon be nothing here with which to defend herself.

Or was there? There, on the ground, close to the left side of her, lay a revolver that the Indians had somehow missed.

Glancing quickly around her, Anna shuffled her feet toward it, finally coming to stand over the gun until her skirts completely hid the weapon. Then quickly, she bent down and scooped up the pistol, depositing it in the pocket of her dress.

Of course, using it would be another trial.

She sighed. Perhaps she should be concerning herself more with how to give these dead and in particular, Miss Pagney, a Christian burial. It would be a hard task; maybe with the help of the children, she could do it. But then what?

"Aren't we going to stay here, Miss Wiley?"

As Anna scooted back to where she had left the children, she glanced down solemnly at a boy who was no more than eight. She answered, "I don't know, David. We don't rightly know when someone might come along to check on us. Besides, I'm not certain we have a choice in the matter."

"Don't you? Somehow I got the impression that the tall one didn't want us."

Anna stared at the figure of the man walking briskly away from them. She not only had the impression, she knew he had wanted to kill them. She would not divulge that information to the children, however.

Soon, the tall brave returned with two of his comrades, the three of them prodding both herself and the children along behind them.

But Anna was not to be so easily coerced. If the elder Indian had not shot her yet, perhaps he did not mean to. And she had to try to do something to save them.

Gathering both her shawl, as well as the armor of her courage about her, Anna raced up to where the tall brave

led their procession. Drawing level with him, she said as
though she had every right, "The children and I will stay
here." She followed her words with sign language, once
again thanking the good Lord that she'd had the vision
and the interest to learn the language when she and the
children had been stranded in Kansas City.

The man didn't even glance at her; he just kept
walking.

She tried again. "The children and I will stay here."
Once more, she used the proper signs.

"If you do that, I will have to kill you." He didn't say a
word and his signs were so quick that Anna could barely
follow them. As it was, it took her too long to analyze his
gestures.

She also had the task of running to keep up with him.

"What did you say?" she asked in sign language and
then queried, "Could you sign a little slower?"

He growled, and at the sound, Anna jumped.

Still, he signed again, a little slower. "If you stay here,
I will have to kill you."

"Why?" she queried.

"Because it is the way of things. We might take people
captive, but do not misunderstand; we leave no one alive
behind us. If you choose to stay, that is fine with me, and
I will get it over with now." He had not looked at her as he
signed his meaning; he did not look at her now. Nor had
he slowed his pace to accommodate her.

"Oh," Anna said, almost to herself and she dropped her
gait to a fast walk. She was not one to give up so easily,
however, and so she hurried forward. "Why?" she
queried again. "The children and I will only slow you
down. Why not leave us? You don't have to kill us."

"It is the way of warfare, and if I had my way, you and your children would not be accompanying us," he said by way of hand motions. "My brother demands that you live, so we must take you. Were I to have my way, you and all things yours would now be lying with the others on the prairie."

"Oh," she uttered again, this time dropping back completely. She tried to remind herself that this was war and that his remarks were not meant to be personal. Still, she could not help it; her life was a very personal thing.

Soon, they had crossed over the top of a hill, and Anna became aware that there were horses waiting for them.

She watched as the tall brave gave orders to the others, watched as the rest of their party mounted and left, leaving her and the children to the mercy of this one Indian.

Luckily, the young boy whom the man had called brother remained with them, somewhat easing Anna's nerves.

In signs she asked the lad, "What is happening?"

He answered her in the same manner. "We will split up into different groups now. It is the best way to lose those warrior-whites who will seek to follow us."

She asked, "But wouldn't it be better to stay together, united? The more of you there are, the less likely you are to be hurt."

The youngster gave her a considering glance. "Why should you care about what happens to us? You are white."

Anna shrugged. "It is only that I do not understand."

He nodded and answered, "To lose an enemy, it is necessary to be able to disappear. One cannot do that easily in a large group, but splitting up into smaller and smaller units, one can at last lead the trail into nothing. In this way we will lose the warrior-whites."

Anna still could not grasp the sense of it and so she asked, "But if you do that, what is to keep them from coming after our party instead? With the children, we will not be able to move very quickly."

"*E-tse-ena'estse-hapo'e-eestse-ve, hova'ehe eohke-saapo' nohtsestahenovo.*" With these words, the boy appeared exasperated. Patiently, however, the boy signed, "My brother will lead us and I will cover our trail. Do not worry. We will lose them."

Again she shrugged. "I do not worry."

Bringing his closed hands in front of him, with his thumbs outstretched, and moving them to the right and then to the left, the youth gave her the sign that their talk was finished. Yet within only a matter of minutes, he asked her, "Why did you come to my rescue, back there on the fire wagon?"

Anna allowed herself a slight smile. Ah, he meant the train. She signed, "You are too young to be treated in such a manner."

"I am not too young!" came the instant signs. "I am a warrior, as brave as any other. I would gladly die for my brother and for my people."

Again Anna smiled. She signed, "Perhaps you misunderstand. I do not believe that anyone of any age should be handled in such a manner. And you are right. You are a warrior, true."

"Humph!" the boy uttered, and left her to go to the rear where Anna could see the youth working to conceal their trail.

Anna did not know why it was so important to her to

appease this young lad. Hadn't this group killed every other white person on the train? Weren't she and the children even now the unwilling captives of this boy's relative, the tall brave?

Yet this boy had saved their lives and he had not been a part of the mass killings, she reminded herself.

At least, she thought, she and the children were alive. They had a chance. It was enough—at least for the time being.

Chapter 4

❦❦❦

"**D**amn!" War Cloud muttered, as he trod along the path he had set, using—and quite aptly, too—the English curse word. Had his own descriptive language carried a few of its own choice words, he might have used them also—and gladly—so sour was his mood. As it was, he had to content himself with English.

"*Na'neha,* my brother, what does this word, 'damn,' mean?" Lame Bird's tongue slid over the blasphemy as he hurried along beside his elder.

War Cloud growled, but answered nonetheless, "It is a bad word and means to speak about the white man's God in a critical way."

"You would do that?" asked the youngster. "You would speak of this God in a harmful manner?"

"He is not the same god as the Cheyenne Creator," justified War Cloud. "What do I care about how I speak of Him?"

The younger brother shrugged, but said nothing, though he did slow his gait.

Meanwhile, War Cloud turned his mind to the problem at hand: a party of whites—he was leading a party of whites to safety—and he, a Cheyenne Dog Soldier . . . who should be killing these people, not helping them. Had this same incident happened only yesterday, and without the interference of his brother, these whites would be lying dead along with the others. Such was his right as well as his duty to the spirits of his family.

A life for a life. It was the justice of Indian law. And as the Great Spirit must surely know, War Cloud still had many more lives to take before he could fully atone for the injustices done to him and his kin.

"Damn!" War Cloud muttered once more.

"Do you use that word because of the white woman?" asked the boy who had once more hurried to War Cloud's side.

War Cloud did not answer. Of course his ill mood had everything to do with the white woman and these children, he thought. But he would not tell his younger brother this. To do so would be a disgrace. For such a confession would be a form of criticism, an insult to the youngster's judgment. It might also serve to cloud the young man's decision making in the future.

No, Lame Bird had made a resolution. War Cloud would try to honor it. Still . . .

"She is a brave woman," said the boy.

War Cloud grunted.

It was a true statement, but War Cloud would not easily admit it, not even to himself. All he could think of at present—all he could consider—was how he had come to this.

Lame Bird lapsed into silence and War Cloud chided himself. He should show more approval for his brother's decision.

At length, War Cloud admitted, "She is indeed a brave woman. And perhaps that is what worries me."

"What do you mean?"

"You know what I would do if we were to meet another Indian party. You know what would happen if they wanted the white woman's and her children's scalps . . ."

"I would fight them," said the boy.

"I would not," War Cloud uttered. "Why should I? What have those white people done for me?"

"She, and she alone, defended me from some men who wanted to kill me," said the youngster. "When they came after me, she hid me from them."

War Cloud cursed beneath his breath.

Lame Bird asserted, "You say you would not defend her and yet you sent the rest of our party on toward Tall Bull's camp. You must have been thinking of shielding her then."

War Cloud did not answer.

And the lad went on, "If this is so, it is good, for this shows that, despite your need to avenge yourself, you would honor me."

Again, War Cloud remained silent.

Lame Bird continued, "We should avoid all Indian parties, as well as the whites, at least until you have decided what to do with these people. Do you have a plan yet?"

A low growl was the boy's only answer.

But if the lad noticed, he cheerfully ignored it. Instead he fell back into silence while War Cloud checked his surroundings.

He had no choice, War Cloud decided. He had to go north. Even now the warrior-whites swarmed over the Kansas frontier, making it difficult for any well-trained warrior to travel safely or to make camp in this country, let alone to attempt it in the company of a band of white children. A band of white children, he might add, who were most likely inexperienced in the ways of the prairie.

After a time, Lame Bird scooted up closer to War Cloud's side and asked, "Do you think Ten Bulls and the others will return and try to do harm to the woman and children?"

War Cloud shrugged, saying, *"Hova'ahane,* I do not think so."

"And if they do . . . ?"

War Cloud squinted his eyes and looked away from the boy. He said, "You know that I cannot take up arms against my own people. Especially when most of our people have lost a son or a daughter, or some other relative to the treasonous guns of the white man. Let us hope that we do not meet anyone upon the trail so that our loyalties are tested."

"But—"

"Did the white man stay his hand when the Cheyenne came to him in peace? Did the white man show mercy? Twice the warrior-whites invited our people to pitch our camps close to him, and each time the white man spoke only of peace. Yet, our people who trusted, our people who believed him, have been slaughtered under the guns of the white man's 'peace talks.' "

"But she is not the same as those."

"She is *white.* She is an enemy. I will not endeavor to help her overly much."

"But—"

"Is it not bad enough to lose a loved one in an honest battle? But to have one taken from you when we were promised only peace . . . You must know that after Sand Creek and the Washita, even those wise men who had been for reconciliation with the whites have begun to reconsider. Those massacres would not have occurred had our chiefs not been trying to make those peace talks."

Lame Bird remained silent. After a pause, he said, "Still, I would let her go before I would let you kill her."

"She would die if you released her. Do you think she would know how to find food? How to find the white man's villages?"

"Then I would stay with her."

"*Eaaa!*"

"*Na'neha*, my brother," said Lame Bird, "I, too, do not wish to have to test my loyalty against my own people. Could we not avoid them and all other parties?"

"We could," said War Cloud, "we can, if I decide that is the best thing we can do."

Again, Lame Bird became silent, while War Cloud kept his own counsel and deliberately increased his pace.

With the weight of the train fight behind him, he had to put distance between himself and that battle. He also had to think.

What he had told the boy was true. At the start of the trouble, only a few Cheyennes had been for war. Armistice should have been an easy thing to obtain, for the peace chiefs had exerted their influence over the people. Only the Dog Soldiers had spoken the war-talk, but no one had really listened.

It had been a hard thing to realize, for within the memories of the people there was no incident by which to compare this thing. Lies had been told to the people in order to get them within fighting distance. Peace had been promised them, yet under the cover of darkness, the Cheyennes had been murdered, killing almost all—leaving no exceptions, not even sparing the women and children. Never could anyone remember such treachery.

It seemed so pointless, too. Had peace been kept, had the white man honored his word, the Dog Soldiers would have been disgraced, the Cheyenne people would have deserted the Dog Soldier camps, and as the peace chiefs had planned, harmony would have come to this country.

War Cloud snorted. He recalled a time when he had been for peace, when he had been amongst Black Kettle's friendly band. But that had been long ago, before Sand Creek, before the Washita.

Now, barely a day went by that did not see War Cloud either considering revenge or exacting it.

He called Lame Bird once more to his side, saying, "I have decided what we will do with these people."

Lame Bird remained silent.

"We will take them to the North, into the Lakota camp of Spotted Tail. I am told that these people live in relative harmony with the whites and that their Indian agent is a man sympathetic to our cause."

"That is a good plan."

War Cloud nodded. "But do not be mistaken. If our people discover us with these whites, I will not keep my friends from avenging themselves upon these white people. It is their right."

Lame Bird nodded.

"You will scout," said War Cloud and then, as if the thought had only occurred to him, he asked, "Do you think that all these children are her own?"

Lame Bird hesitated, then asked, "Does it matter?"

Did it? Of course not. Still, War Cloud could not account for the discontentment that swept over him.

"You go now to these white people and tell them to give me no trouble. You direct them to be quiet and you instruct them that if they do not do as I ask, I will kill them all."

Lame Bird nodded. "I will ensure they will obey you."

"Humph!"

And would they? Would they comply with his wishes? War Cloud decided he did not care. So great was his frustration, he knew he would not hesitate to follow through on his threat if the opportunity presented itself.

But so far, it had not. No, at present the most he could do to vent his rage was to utter another well-chosen "Damn!"

Lame Bird flinched, but War Cloud took no note of it. Instead he set his course to the north and west, toward the south fork of the Republican and Smoky Hill area.

Turning to Lame Bird, War Cloud ordered, "Go and tell those whites what I have said. Then you must leave to determine whether it is safe to journey to the North. We will meet again in three days."

Lame Bird nodded and, turning, trod off in the direction of the woman and her children.

Chapter 5

Dusk had fallen all around them. The children sat huddled close together. Every now and again one of the younger boys would speak, but only so very softly. They were too afraid, most of them, to do anything else. At least not since the young Indian boy had warned them about making any noise.

He had also cautioned them that they were to obey the tall Indian, if they wanted to live.

Anna did not think she would have any trouble doing that. The man, as well as her duty to these children, scared her into being silent.

It was daunting to think that she, and she alone, would have to carry on the mission to place these children, if that were even still possible. She could only hope that it was.

That these thoughts made her wonder what the tall brave had planned for them, caused her yet another worry. Did she dare try to discover his intentions? Would he kill her if she broached the subject?

Somehow Anna doubted it. That his younger relative, his brother, had come to their aid had made the tall brave reconsider his actions, and perhaps that still gave her protection. She had to remember that the tall brave had not yet killed them, and she did not think he meant to do it at all—. She hoped.

Anna tried to remember again the accounts she had read of white people in Indian captivity. She seemed to recall noting somewhere that if an Indian didn't kill his victim, he might intend to rape her. Is this what the tall brave had planned for her?

It seemed plausible, but again, she could not envision the tall Indian committing such a deed. Might he, however, arrange to give her to someone else in his camp who would think nothing of committing that act?

And the children. What would he do to the children? With something akin to horror, Anna realized that she was going to have to discover this man's intentions. Not only that, if those plans did not bode well for herself and her orphans, she was going to have to convince him to change his mind.

And so it was that, upon this note, Anna decided to seek out this savage warrior. She took in a deep gulp of air and, leaving the children with the oldest of them, ventured out of their camp, toward their captor.

As she sauntered toward him, she observed that darkness had begun to creep over the grassy Kansas landscape, bringing with it the evening song of crickets. She stopped to listen for a moment, their familiar chant soothing to her spirit.

Swallowing nervously, she padded up to the tall brave. Since he had stationed himself atop their small hill, she hadn't far to go.

"Excuse me," she began, trying to capture his attention. The man turned a sharp eye on her and in reaction she caught her breath. Goodness, she thought. The extent of this man's masculine beauty had escaped her notice. How had this happened?

Her head spun slightly with the observation. She hadn't expected that. Not really. From the horrid accounts she had read of the Indians, she had expected to find them little more than savages, more animal than human. Certainly she had not thought to discover a man amongst them who more resembled a Grecian sculpture than a brute.

But perhaps the fault was not hers. The man had only recently washed the paint from his face, and maybe it was the war paint that had lulled her into the belief that she had been accompanying a mere savage. However, she needed to rethink her attitude, for with the brilliance of keen intelligence gleaming from his eyes, it took no great effort on her part to observe that this man was no barbarian.

It was strange, because for a moment she wished that the good Lord had given her body more of an eye-pleasing appearance. Yet even as she thought the idea, she knew this wasn't quite right. She was happy with herself, had long ago put away her dreams of knights in shining armor and of romance.

Besides, with only the children to keep the two of them company here on the prairie, she knew she should be thanking the Lord for her limitations, not wishing for more. Still, as she gazed steadily at this man, inspecting him much as he had done to her earlier, she spared a moment to do nothing more than admire him. Surely there was nothing wrong with that, was there?

With a firm set to his jaw, full lips and a slightly

aquiline nose, he presented quite a picture of untamed and rugged masculinity. His eyes were dark, almost black, and his brows were heavy, set in a face that was perhaps only a few shades darker than her own. She knew she shouldn't stare; it was a most improper thing to do, yet so stunned was she by him that she seemed little able to do more than that. Even now, as she gaped at him, a few strands of his hair fluttered forward in the wind, and with the last streaks of the sunset behind him, it created a natural-looking halo effect.

Anna felt like pinching herself, for there was a dream-like quality to this.

But, she cautioned herself, as she finally grasped back control, she digressed. Remembering the children and her mission, she set her observations of this man aside and stiffened her resolve. Once more she voiced, "Excuse me."

However, she was dismayed when the tall brave did not look up at her or acknowledge her in any way. It was also daunting to her since she had been admiring him and had sat herself down in front of him where he would *have no choice* but to see her.

Taking a deep breath, she tried again, this time adding sign language to her words. "Hello," she began. "I would like to thank you for sparing our lives."

But she was unprepared for his brisk response. Grunting in a most unusual guttural manner, he arose and, turning away from her, strode out onto the prairie . . . without a single word or a by-your-leave.

Well!

Her first reaction was to feel that she had done something terribly wrong; her second was that of pure anger.

How dare he! She had heard that Indians had all kinds of odd manners and unusual rituals. Well, she decided, this one could certainly use some lessons in courtesy.

She followed him like a clucking hen, came right up to him and, not sparing a single word, scolded, "How very impolite of you!"

He looked at her, and none too cordially, either. However, his quick examination of her was enough to add even more fuel to her smoldering fire. Using signs to push her meaning home, she continued, "What kind of Indian are you that you do not even listen to the words of a woman? That you turn your back on me?"

He stared at her without a single emotion crossing his face.

"Well," she scolded, letting her hands drop as she spoke without the use of signs. "I think you could use a few manners, and I would like to take a moment to tell you, sir, that you may be handsome of face, but physical looks by themselves mean nothing. After all, handsome is as handsome does and—"

"Humph!" he cut her off, but Anna, far from being irritated at his behavior, took heart. At least she had him talking. The man also had an unusual gleam in his eye, she noted.

She chose to ignore it, however. "I feel compelled"— she voiced and signed the words at the same time—"to ask you, M . . ." She stopped. What was his name? So far she had contented herself with calling him the tall brave or the elder, but he must surely have some name.

Oh, dear, she fretted briefly, she was forgetting her manners. She cringed. She had been taught all her life that no matter one's circumstance, one could always be polite. She cleared her throat and began again, "I am sorry, but I have not introduced myself."

"Humph!"

"My name is . . ." Here she stopped signing. There was no way to signal her name in the language of the plains, since her name, as far as she knew, had little meaning, or if it did have significance, she did not know it. So she contented herself with simply saying, while pointing to herself, "Anna. Anna Wiley."

"Humph!"

"And you are . . . ?" She asked and signed the question at the same time.

"Humph!"

"Don't you know how to say anything but 'humph'?"

"Humph!"

"Well, we're not going to get very far if you won't co-operate."

To this he gave her a curt nod and turned his back on her.

Anna, however, was not to be denied. She scooted around, once more, to the front of him so he would have no choice but to see her gestures.

She signed, again, as though he hadn't snubbed her, "What is your name?"

Using his right hand only, he signed, "A warrior of any merit does not speak his own name."

Well, what do you know? she asked herself. She had elicited a response. She took strength from that.

"All right," she said aloud, not signing the meaning of the words, if they even had a sign equivalent. She began, "I have to address you as something. How about if I call you 'sir' for now?" She followed this last with more signs.

He shrugged.

"Fine," she said, continuing her gestures. "Now, sir, may I ask you what you have planned for myself and the children?"

No response.

She continued, "Do you plan to sell us to other Indians perhaps?"

Again, no response.

"Why are you acting like this? I have done nothing to you."

He turned his back on her.

"Oh! Don't you do that!"

"Humph," he said again and, as she came around to the front of him, he crossed his arms over his chest. He did not look at her either. His eyes, she noted, were ever on the far horizon.

"Now, look here, ah, sir," she began in her best schoolteacher voice. "Just because God gave you a heaping portion of good looks is no reason for you to ignore those around you. I'll have you know that . . ."

Good Lord. That remark was met with a smile, and as she gazed into his eyes, witnessing again that gleam of intelligence, she suddenly realized her mistake. She said, actually stuttered, "You . . . you . . . ah . . . speak English, don't you?"

His grin widened and she groaned.

"You could have told me."

"What? And spoil your attitude toward me?" he asked in perfect English.

"Oh, dear, I . . . I didn't mean . . ." She felt like melting into the ground. "I didn't mean that you were . . . I mean when I said that you were handsome, what I meant was that . . ." What had she meant? "It's only that," she continued, "I hadn't expected to find an Indian so . . . tall, or so . . . well . . ." Her voice trailed away, while his grin grew ever wider.

Goodness, she seemed to be getting herself in deeper and deeper. She felt her face grow warm as color rushed to her cheeks and partly as a matter of defense, partly for something to do, she took in a gulp of fresh air. At length, she asked, "How did you learn English?"

He jerked his chin forward and to the left. "The white man has long been in our camps, pretending to make peace."

"Pretending?"

He gave her a long look.

"Excuse me," she said. "I interrupted you. Please, do continue."

"Humph." He remained silent.

"Please?"

He let out his breath in a hiss before he said, "One time, long ago, when the people believed the white man meant us no harm, I scouted for the warrior-whites."

He stopped so suddenly, she felt as though she had been left in midair. She encouraged, "Yes?"

"That was when I learned English."

"I see."

"Do you?" The antagonism was back in his voice.

She asked, "Did something bad happen there?"

He groaned, letting his intonation trail out in a hiss. He

said, "You are a white woman and have no right to question me. Now leave."

Her shoulders dropped and she hung her head. Conversation with this man was more than a little difficult. It was next to impossible. But she would not give up. She could not. She had to remember the children, had to remind herself that there was a purpose to her talk. Hence she asked, "What have I done that makes you speak to me as though I am not worthy of your consideration?"

"You are white."

"I cannot help that," she countered. She paused a moment and then asked, "Is that the only reason?"

"It is reason enough."

"Well, I'm glad that you have that all settled, then. It makes it all very black and white, doesn't it?"

He raised an eyebrow, obviously not immune to her sarcasm.

She nodded. "All Indians—good. All whites—bad. Is that it? Now do you feel better?"

He glanced away from her. "White woman talks too much."

She countered, "Red man speaks too little. What happened that you stopped scouting for the army?"

"Humph!"

She asked, "Was it Sand Creek? Were you there?"

He turned away from her, his glance constantly scanning the prairie. Still, he said nothing.

"It was Sand Creek, wasn't it?"

He shrugged and said, "I was at Sand Creek. I was also at the Washita. Most of my kin, what little I have, were killed at both these places."

Anna caught her breath. "I'm so sorry."

He went on, "After I have seen the white man's treachery, I regret I ever had anything to do with these warrior-whites and I am ashamed that I once scouted for them."

This last was said with so much loathing, Anna decided to make no comment on it, none whatsoever. Instead, she comforted, "I am sorry for the actions of my people against yours, for I know that they have committed wrongs to yours. And I am particularly sorry about your kin. But at least you had kin, if only for a little while."

This last had him looking at her strangely, but she made no comment, and after a lengthy pause, she found him asking her, "Do you not have any relatives?"

"None," she replied honestly.

"Not a mother?"

She shook her head.

"A father?"

"None."

Perhaps it was more a sort of sixth sense than anything, but Anna felt a spark of life flare up between them. She pressed on, "Please know that I did not have a part in those fights, nor did these children who are with me, and I do not approve of everything that my people have done to yours. In truth, there are many of my people, mostly in the East, far away from here, who disapprove of the actions of the military in this part of the country."

"Humph!"

"I truly feel remorse," she said, and meant it.

Anna again experienced the discomfort of having this man look her up and down as though she were some item of trade. Unfortunately for her, she knew she came up lacking. Still, she pushed back her shoulders and raised her chin, saying, "Do you believe me?"

A quick nod was her only answer.

"You do?"

He snorted. "Did I not just tell you that I did?"

She smiled. "Well, yes, I believe that you did. It is only that I thought you might fight me on that one, too."

He stared away from her. "You helped my brother. I believe that your heart may be good, despite who you are."

She took immediate offense. "What do you mean by that remark? There is nothing wrong with who I am."

Heaven be praised, her remark elicited another smile from the man, albeit a tiny one. Still . . .

He said, repeating himself, "You are white. It is enough."

She paused a fraction of a beat before she responded, "I am sorry, so very, very sorry."

He raised one of those heavy eyebrows of his, an obvious query.

"To have so much hatred for the whites cannot be doing your soul much good, I am afraid," she explained. "Hating all whites is just as bad as the whites despising all Indians."

He shrugged. "Perhaps it is the way of war."

She pressed on, "Perhaps war is not the answer to what is going on here."

"There is no other way to deal with the whites. Even our wise, old peace chiefs are beginning to see this . . . those who have not come recently under the white man's knife."

Anna looked away. She knew there had been many,

many injustices, one side against the other. She did not wish to continue that war, however, on her own home front.

She offered, "It appears that we might be in one another's company for a while, sir. I think it would be good if we were to make a personal treaty between the two of us, don't you?"

This remark must have taken him by surprise, yet, if it had, she would not have known it by his features. He said, "I make no treaties with white people."

"I promise that I will keep my end of the bargain. You can trust me."

"Humph! I have heard those words from the whites before."

"But I am not the same as those other white men."

Again that scrutinizing look fell upon her person. He said, "*Hova'ahane,* no, I can see that."

She pushed on, urging, "I will not demand your signature on a piece of paper. Just a promise between you and me that if you will take me and the children to the nearest white settlement, I will ensure that you and your brother are well cared for and will be given everything that you ask for, if possible."

"*Saaa,* we will visit no white settlements. I will not accompany you and the children anywhere but where I say. No treaty."

She did not even blink. "I see," she said. "Would you do it if I offered you money or gold?"

He snorted. "No treaty."

She drew her brows together; she had to think quickly. There must be something she could offer him. After barely a moment's pause she asked, "Is there anything that I have that you want, for which we might strike a bargain—for the sake of the children?"

This time the tall brave didn't even look at her as he emphasized, "There is nothing." A jerk of his hand and the sneer on his face emphasized his words.

Anna's throat constricted until she thought she might choke. In truth, she could not remember a time she had felt more helpless. And to make matters worse, this man had, without a moment's thought, impressed upon her the idea that she had nothing of worth to proffer him.

Had she failed the children? Was there something wrong with her own person that she could not save them?

It made no sense that she should feel as she did, but logic did not always rule a woman's heart. She felt . . . hurt.

However, as though he were aware that his words had set off a bad reaction within her, he tendered, "Do not take offense. There is no white person alive who could give me anything that I need." He looked her up and down. "There is nothing wrong with you."

Dear Lord, what was the matter with her? There were tears, actual tears gathering at the back of her eyes and it was all she could do to state, without her voice wavering, "I think that you lie, sir. I think there is a great deal wrong with me."

That she should become so emotional with this man was almost more than she could stand. Perhaps the rigors of the day were finally catching up with her and that was all there was to it. Perhaps.

Yet, she could not stop the wetness in her eyes, nor the tear that spilled over her cheek. But she refused to wipe the tear away. Maybe this tall brave would not notice.

His dark eyes did not miss a thing, however, and she consciously had to keep herself standing erect as he reached out to smooth the tear from her face. He said, "Know that I do not like any white people, but if I were to experience any affinity for one, you might be the first, I think."

She snorted.

And he went on, "I do not lie, white woman. I have rarely, if ever, known a woman to be so brave as you. It is a remarkable quality, and one that should be sung about in your camp for many years. All should know of it. I lived with the white man and so I know that these people are not taught the ways of bravery. And yet, when the time was ready, you acted better than many warriors I have known. Yours is the soul of a warrior, *Nahkohe-tseske*."

She could do little more than stand before him, her shoulders gently shaking with each indrawn breath. Worse, under his compliment, her body reacted to his gentle graze as though she found this man to be . . . perfect.

She shook her head, hoping that the simple action might clear her thoughts and induce her to remember that this man was no more than her captor. But it was no use. His soft words, his tender touch, had already become entrenched within some secret recess, and privately, something within her wanted to reach out to him. She asked, "What did you just call me?"

"Nahkohe-tseske?" He lowered his hand.

She nodded.

And he translated, "It means Little Bear."

"Little Bear? I'm sorry, you must have misunderstood me. My name is Anna."

"I did not misunderstand. You have a better name now. A good Indian name. One that you earned and one that shows your courage."

"I do?"

"*Haahe,* you do. Your courage is like the mother bear when her cubs are threatened. Although the female bear is usually a docile creature, she will become a formidable enemy when danger imperils her children."

Anna gasped. *My God,* she thought as a sudden truth hit her . . . hard. *The rumors about these people are all wrong.*

So very, very wrong. Despite his fierce demeanor, kindness fairly emanated from this man, kindness and a compassion for life, for her; she, this man's enemy.

Anna drew in another shaky breath. She had to take care in this situation. She had been the recipient of so little admiration in her lifetime, she barely knew how to react to it. She commented, "I think that you flatter me, sir."

He did not alter his scrutiny of her one bit. "Do you mean that you think I speak with a tongue that is forked?"

"Aren't you?" she asked. "I'm hardly the kind of person to inspire songs."

"Perhaps the right time has never come for others to lay bare your inner qualities, or perhaps the whites are stupid."

"Sir," her voice reprimanded, "must I remind you that when you speak derogatorily of the whites, you speak this way of me, also? Besides, I know my limits, and I know that I am hardly the kind of person to inspire a song in another."

"And yet," he insisted, "my young brother is quite taken with you."

"But that's only because I—"

He held up his hand. "It matters not the reason. He was willing to risk his life for yours. And he barely knows you." The man smiled at her, and Anna had to admit, the result was most attractive. He said, "I think that perhaps you underestimate yourself."

She shook her head. "I think not. But tell me, sir," she said, preparing to change the subject to a less emotional one. "Do you have plans for us?"

"I do."

"And will you tell me what your strategy is?"

"Perhaps," he agreed, "but I must first ask you a question."

"And that is . . . ?"

"Are all these children yours?"

Chapter 6

◦◦⌒◯◯⌒◦◦

She laughed and War Cloud discovered that he could barely look away from her. Although she was not the best-looking woman, there was something about her . . . about her smile . . . a charisma he could little explain. It filled him with the desire to tease her until she would have no option but to grin.

She was speaking, however, and he gave her his full attention, listening to her while she said, "No, the children are not mine at all." She followed this with another chuckle, and War Cloud found himself enchanted.

However, the spell was soon broken; she became more serious and explained, "They are all of them orphans from back east, a place called New York. It has been my duty and my pleasure to escort these children into this country, where there are many people in need of a helping hand. It has been supposed that these western families will not be hard put to feed any extra mouths, since most of the settlers are farmers or cattlemen. It would take little to include the children in their lives. It has also been surmised that because so many of the settlers are in need of a hand to help with the chores, they will gladly take the children in as their own, making the youngsters a part of their family."

War Cloud nodded. "I know many families who would welcome them. There are many of my people who have lost children in the wars. They would not only take them in and treat them as a part of the family, the children would *be* the family."

"No," she said immediately.

War Cloud stared at her for the turn of a second. "What do you mean, no?" he asked.

He observed her closely, witnessed her confusion, saw her grappling with the situation. He could sense that she did not wish to offend him, yet . . .

War Cloud spun around, presenting his back to her. So, he thought, despite the white woman's talk, she was as prejudiced as were these frontier whites.

However, if he had meant to dismiss her—and he had—he soon found it was not to be so easily done. She scooted around him until she stood face-to-face with him, whereupon she said, "You misunderstand."

"I do not think so."

"I know what you are thinking, and it is not completely true. It is not that your people are not good enough for the children," she persisted, "it is only that I have given my word of honor to place these orphans in Christian homes. The society that sponsors these children has made me pledge that I will do this."

He shrugged, refusing to look at her.

"Don't you see?" she asked. "I cannot leave them to grow up without the Christian faith."

"Humph," he uttered, grasping her predicament perfectly. However, in light of all the injustice done to his people, he could not give her quarter. And so he said no more.

But she would not let it rest, and she continued to explain, "I must take them to white settlements and see if I can find them good homes. The society also demands that I receive a written contract from the children's new parents—similar to your treaties—so that we can keep in touch with the children from time to time and ensure that they are being well treated. This is also something I could not do with your people."

"Humph."

"Do you understand?"

He refused to answer, presenting her again with his back. But he was not prepared for her soft touch on his shoulder.

"Please try to understand, sir," she said, and War Cloud realized that, all bias aside, he did not understand what was taking place between himself and this woman. Not at all. Why should her touch make his senses leap? And why did it cause him to want to take her in his arms?

He supposed it was because he had been so long without a woman. Yet, if that were the reason—and he could see no other cause for his reaction—it was something he would have to suppress. It would be a very long time indeed before he would have the opportunity to indulge himself in that fantasy.

He breathed in deeply and uttered, "I do see your problem, but I think you might not be able to keep your promise to your society. There are many of my own people who need children to replace those lost in war. Besides, it is not the custom of the Cheyennes to bring captives back to the same people they stole them from.

As it has always been, women and children are often the spoils of war, and according to the laws of my people, you are mine to do with as I see fit."

"I beg your pardon!" she uttered vigorously, and War Cloud wondered what he had said that should have her reacting so fiercely. He gave her his full attention; he was not long in waiting.

She proclaimed, "I believe the children and I are people, not property."

Ah, so that was it. He uttered, "You are captives and I will speak no more of it to you." With this said, and because he was certain he was done with it, he turned to tread away from her.

But he had reckoned without taking her nature into consideration. She followed him, dogging his every footfall, complaining, "I do not agree."

She had more to say, too, and in due time, War Cloud found he had no choice but to stop and acknowledge her.

Looking down upon her, he said, "You are like the dog that will not stop his pestering until his master gives him a piece of meat."

"I am no dog, sir," was her quick response, "and you are no master."

Though her words had been harshly said, he found himself grinning down at her, for he could not help admiring her. This female was certainly spirited . . . and entertaining. He agreed easily enough with her and said, *"Hova'ahane,* you are right. You are no dog. But you and the children are still my captives and you will do as I say."

"No."

"You have no more say in it. It is as it is."

That he had irritated her was without doubt, for she

immediately countered him, saying, "Could we expand upon that assumption, sir? It is as it is? I believe it is as you are making it, not as *I* would make it."

He decided not to answer her, realizing that mere words would do little to win him this fight. But he had to smile. He could not remember the last time he had more enjoyed such sparring.

"Do not laugh at me, sir."

"I am not," he said, this time more seriously. "It is only that I find you . . . unusual."

"Is that an insult?"

He caught her eye and with deliberate intention, held it. That this woman did not hold herself in high esteem seemed somehow a crime. And although he cautioned himself not to do it, he found he could not control the impulse to comfort her. Of their own accord, his fingers came up to smooth back a lock of her hair. While a part of him registered the silky feel of those few brown tresses, he said, "Do not take offense, for I do not insult you. Know that I speak the truth when I say that I find you . . . engaging." He held her glance for a moment more and then, lowering his hand, made to move around her.

But he was going nowhere. As he took a step to leave, she reached out and seized hold of his arm, causing War Cloud to stop what he was doing, to turn and stare at that hand. Nor did he think he would have been able to move from this spot with any speed, even if a posse of warrior-whites were suddenly to rush their camp.

There it was again. War Cloud drew in his breath and held it. Why did this woman's touch flood his system with excitement?

He stared at that hand as it lay upon him, while at the

same time an ultrafine awareness answered his own question. Silently and inwardly he groaned.

In the meantime she asked, "Engaging?"

He wondered if she knew the inherent danger from his ardent nature and decided that she did not. He would not inform her of that risk, either. There was no need.

He was Cheyenne.

Passion was not a new feeling for him, and it would present no threat to her. For not only could he control his own basic responses, he would nurture those feelings and let them simmer beneath the surface. *Haahe,* yes, rather than give in to its fervor, he would use his eagerness, much like a store of energy. And as the wise men often counseled, the next time he chose to fight, that energy would be there to give him strength.

Eaaaa, it was either that or seek out the attentions of an agreeable widow in the next friendly camp.

He sighed and asked, "Is it so unusual that I might find you attractive?"

Her gaze met his, held his, veered away, finally coming back to recapture his. They were pale, he thought; her irises, that is. War Cloud tried to remember when he had last seen eyes the color of wild prairie grass, but finally decided that he had not ever beheld it. That was not all. He could not help but notice that her body held an answering response to his, mirrored there, in the gentle depths of her gaze. Immediately and without question, every male instinct within him responded to her.

But he held himself back. It was not a sexual hunger he witnessed within her eyes. With the simple logic of a rational being, he realized that the intensity he witnessed in her was rather her own ardor for life. It was not for him.

Yet his body was not so discriminating, and again awareness of her femininity surged through him, causing his blood to surge.

She said, "Sir, I think that you flatter me."

Innocence, he thought. She stood before him completely unaware of her own worth; she fairly radiated virtuousness and purity. War Cloud allowed himself the luxury of staring at her for the beat of several moments, captivated, for there was so much beauty in her guilelessness, so very much, indeed. At last he remarked, "I think, *Nahkohe-tseske,* that you do not prize yourself as highly as you might."

"Sir, really, I . . . I . . ." As though she, too, became suddenly aware of the allurement between them, she let go of his arm. "I . . . I think that we leave the point, sir. Let us return to it."

"I have no more to say on it. It is done."

"I beg to differ," she persisted. "I cannot sanction these children going anywhere but where they were originally intended. Sir, please, I beseech you to help me."

War Cloud's heart went out to this woman and he took a moment to say a silent prayer of thanks for his Cheyenne training which allowed him to keep his emotions hidden. For he could not relent. He must not. And so he said, "Be content in the knowledge that you are still alive."

She hesitated, but only for a moment, before she reiterated, "I cannot do that, sir."

He crossed his arms over his chest and glared down at her, his countenance full of menace. He said, "You will *have* to."

"But, sir, please, you don't understand. I have pledged

my word to find homes for these children as I have told you."

"Then you were unwise. You should have realized that something might come between you and the realization of your accomplishment. You were traveling into a country that was and is at war."

"But, sir," she persisted, "we were told that the war was over. That it was safe to travel."

"Then you were misinformed."

"Yes," she acknowledged at last. "We were misinformed. But it was either that or turn around and take the children back to New York."

He did not understand the abrupt sadness that colored her words, and he scrutinized her features, that he might know her thoughts more exactly. When, after a moment, he still did not understand, he asked, "What do you mean?"

His question seemed to bring on an even greater gloominess within her, and he could not help likening the shift he witnessed to that of a storm cloud passing over a brilliant sky. She did not speak for some moments, nor did she look at him, but in due time, she began, "We left New York with eighty children, sir. We placed most of them in homes as we made our way farther and farther west. These children who remain with me are the ones that were not chosen."

He still did not understand and he raised an eyebrow in query.

She said again, "They were not chosen."

"Not chosen? You are telling me that these children were rejected by the whites?"

"Not exactly rejected," she defended. "They were simply not picked."

"It is the same thing, I think."

"Almost," she conceded. "We—myself and my other two companions—had no choice but to go farther west, in the hopes of finding more homes."

"Two companions?" he asked. "I see no one else."

The color drained from her cheeks as she said, "Our agent, Mr. Bilsworth, died while we were in Kansas City." Here she turned her face away from him before continuing, "And the only other adult who was accompanying the children was . . . killed today at the train fight . . ."

Her voice trailed away as though she might have expected him to apologize.

War Cloud, however, remained steadfastly silent, and after a time, she added, "I could not, then, in good conscience, take the children back to New York and see them left once more on the streets."

"On the streets?" he queried. "What is this?"

She took a deep breath. "Have you no orphans in your camps?"

"Haahe, we have orphans, but they are not looked upon as a problem. Each child is also the son or daughter of the entire tribe. The children are never without aid or assistance or food, for all of our young belong to the tribe and are the responsibility of all. Besides, usually a family will adopt them."

She stared at him in silence for so long, he began to wonder if he had said something she did not understand. At length she admitted, "Then your system of handling orphans, sir, is much better than ours."

He gave her another inquisitive look.

"Our children are not the children of the village. It is hard to find anyone willing to take them in, and most of our orphans are forced to fend for themselves—usually without homes or shelters. There are some places called orphanages which take in the children, but they are so overcrowded that many of the youngsters find themselves cast out and alone."

This War Cloud could hardly assimilate. Was the white man so greedy that he could not share his wealth with his own children? It somehow affirmed, at least to his own mind, that the white man was not quite human. What kind of creature could not hear the silent cries of his own kind?

But War Cloud wisely kept his opinion to himself.

She continued, "I had and I still have no choice but to find good, Christian homes for these children."

So sad was her expression that again War Cloud found himself holding back his urge to give this woman solace. What was it about her that made him desire to reach out to her, to hold her until her cares ceased to exist?

Perhaps, he thought, he had better find a friendly village—one with willing widows—sooner than he had expected.

He muttered something beneath his voice, then softening it, he said, "If you and the children live through this journey, it is possible that they might find good homes."

"If?" she asked. "Sir, surely you are not still considering . . . our demise?"

He did not answer. Instead, he presented her with his back. The woman was too potent, and he a little too weak to her charm.

However, she scooted around him to confront him once more, face to face. "Sir?"

He paused. He needed to think. That he actually considered her predicament, that he contemplated taking her to the white settlements, despite the danger to himself and to his brother, was testimony to the power of her persuasion.

Another admirable quality about her, he thought. War Cloud began to add them up.

However, it was not within his power to give her all that she wanted. It was enough that he was sparing their lives and taking them to a place that could better handle their welfare. He said, "Know that I cannot give you all that you need."

"But you will spare our lives?"

He looked away from her. "Perhaps."

"Perhaps?" she repeated. "Sir, I do not think you are as uncivilized as you might like me to believe."

He turned her a deaf ear.

She, however, appeared immune. "And I think, sir, that if you intended to kill us, you would have done it already."

He made no comment.

And after a moment, she said, "I believe that you could at least share with me what you mean to do with us. You must have some plan."

"A warrior does not talk over his ideas with a woman . . . and in particular with a white woman."

"Oh?" she asked. "More prejudice? You believe there is something wrong with my sex now as well as my race?"

War Cloud let out a low growl. The woman did not

know what she was doing. He needed no reminder of her sex; he was already all too aware of it.

Helpless to curb himself, he scrutinized the contours of her face, her lips, her shoulders, his glance skimming down even lower.

She was a delicate thing, tall but slender. And the more animated her emotions, the prettier she became. It made him want to tease her, or perhaps to anger her, if only to witness the rush of color to her cheeks.

His gaze met hers, and in that look, he found himself . . . spellbound.

She was the first one to speak. "Sir," she said, her voice imploring. "I would do most anything to save these children. Please, isn't there something . . . ?"

He shook his head. "Know that I cannot take these children where you might like. Besides, I do not wish to get myself or my brother hanged. At least not yet."

"Hanged? For what?"

War Cloud could not quite meet her eyes, for the incident was still too fresh in his heart, the injustice of it too hard. It was his turn to gaze away, off in the distance. His attention rested, without seeing, upon the point where the land met the horizon, where, since darkness had fallen upon the land, only the stars in the heavens differentiated the earth from the sky.

Several more moments of silence passed until at last she prompted, "What happened?"

Still he did not answer, although after a time, he began, "It is a sad story. Are you certain you want to hear it?"

"I do," she said without pause.

He sighed and began, "All right. Four years ago, two Oglala Lakota, Two Face and Black Foot, tried to surrender to the whites. Two Face was married to my cousin and I knew him well. He was a good chief, a good man. But in surrendering, there were some problems. Not always could the white men distinguish between peaceful Indians and hostiles.

"But these two chiefs were determined to surrender. They decided the best way to do it was to ransom two white people, a Mrs. Eubanks and her child. These two whites had been captured by another band of Lakota and were being held at a camp that was some distance away.

"This the two chiefs did; they made the journey to this other camp and ransomed these two white people—at great expense—and took the two captives to Fort Laramie. In repayment for this act of kindness, the officers at that fort, Colonel Thomas Moonlight and Colonel Baumer, hanged those Indians."

Anna gasped. "No, that must be wrong. It cannot be."

War Cloud jerked his chin to the left. "I do not lie."

"Please, no. If this had happened, I would have heard of it."

"Would you? I am not certain the white people tell the stories of this war with a straight tongue. What I have said to you is so."

"But please, you must know that I would never let anything like that happen to you. I would testify in your behalf."

"I do not know what this 'testify' is, but I like to think that this Mrs. Eubanks might have tried to explain, too. If she did, she was not listened to. No, I think I will do as I think is best."

She gulped. "Which is . . . ?"

"I do not reveal my intentions to a white woman."

"Are we onto that again? Please, sir, I implore you, please take us to a white settlement. I promise that I will do anything that you say."

He leered at her. "Anything?"

She nodded. "Within reason."

He sent her what he hoped was a wicked glance, his gaze skipping over her physical assets. He asked, "What is meant by this 'reason'?"

She shrugged. "I don't know. I could not climb the highest mountain for you, I suppose."

"But you might do other . . . feminine things . . . for me?"

She had turned her face away from him and he was uncertain she understood his implication, for she said, "I suppose that I could."

He groaned, his sexual reflexes immediately screaming at him. But he did not see an answering gleam of erotic awareness in her physical demeanor—something, anything, more than words that would indicate she was willing to act the part of a kept woman. And so he battled with himself over the desire to take this woman in his arms.

"I assume that I might be able to cook for you and mend your clothing and that sort of thing," she continued, "but I must warn you that I have no experience at working over an open fire—or how to mend clothing without the use of thread for that matter."

"Humph!" he muttered and turned his back on her, hoping she would go away and not witness the telltale evidence of his arousal.

But she would not leave him alone and she persisted,

"Please, sir, as you can see, I am more than willing to act the servant for you, if only you would—"

"These are not the feminine acts that I would require, if I were to even . . . consider your request."

"Are they not? Then, sir, I do not know what you mean."

He reached out and caught a lock of her hair in his fingers, twirling it this way and that.

Still, he witnessed that she did not understand such an insinuation, and she looked at him with barely controlled impatience.

At last, he said, "I mean that an Indian man can sometimes take on more than one woman to act in the capacity of a wife."

She let out a harsh breath, still unaware. She queried, "Can he?"

"He can," he confirmed, "although most Cheyenne men content themselves with only one such woman."

"Is that so?" she asked, although it appeared she really did not care to hear the answer. She added, "Why only one wife when a man could have so many more to *serve* him?"

War Cloud did not miss the sarcastic emphasis on the word, "serve." He said, "Because my people have found that women do not always get on very well with one another when a man keeps more than one. And a Cheyenne man likes to have peace in his home."

She crossed her arms over her chest, causing him to release that lock of her hair. She said, "That seems fair," but her conduct said she grew tired of this game.

"Does it?" he asked. "And could you be this kind of

woman? Could you pleasure a man who has had many wives?"

"I could not," came her ready reply. "My faith would not permit this."

"And yet," he said, "that is the capacity that would have meaning to me."

"What?"

"I mean that *if* you definitely wished me to do this thing for you, you would act, perhaps, in the most feminine role of a woman and assume the pleasurable duties of a wife."

"A wife?" she asked, her arms falling to her sides, her eyes wide and her mouth open.

"At least those specific kinds of duties that please," he said, and into the silence that followed this declaration, War Cloud paced swiftly away.

Chapter 7

Anna found herself suddenly without the means to express herself. Truly, it felt as if the air had been knocked from her lungs and she found herself staring— and possibly quite stupidly, too—at the man's retreating back.

A wife? Had this man just asked her to marry him? She, who had assumed she would never enter into the holy state of matrimony?

Though she conjectured that the man had remarked upon this course in an attempt to throw her off her task, this was not exactly the result she had contemplated when she had chosen to take her stand against him. But it wasn't bad.

Was this possibly a way to save the children? Was there, after all, an asset she had by which she could barter with this man?

Well, good. The knowledge filled her with a sense of accomplishment. She hadn't failed exactly; she just hadn't completely succeeded.

However, the thrill of winning dimmed as she realized that she would never be able to do what he required.

To marry a man of another religion? Of another race? A race at war with her own? A people that might hate her on sight?

Puzzled, she turned in the opposite direction from the man and took a few steps away. Why was she stirring herself up over this? It had been a simple statement, a casual remark, one he had made as an attempt to get rid of her, in all likelihood.

Yet, though it defied logic, she could not stem the flow of memories that his mere suggestion had brought to life. As though her mind had a will of its own, it began to roll back recollections of unhappy years and, like a walking picture that would not be stilled, she could not help but remember . . .

"Yer jest like yer father," her mother complained for the umpteenth time to her eight-year-old daughter. "Ne'er-do-well. At least you dinna inherit his handsome mug, and more's the blessing."

Stumbling to keep up, Anna held on tightly to her mother's hand, fearing the worst. Only this morning, her mother had dressed Anna in her Sunday best. Even though Anna's coat was two sizes too small and her feet were pinched into last year's shoes, Anna had been happy to have her mother's attention.

But her gladness soon gave way to fear.

"Yer pa's gone off and left us, Anna, and Lord forgive me, but I canna keep you wit' me. Where I'm goin' you canna go. What I'm goin' ta do, you canna be a part of. Do you understand me, lassy?"

Anna nodded without thought, while her mother con-

tinued, "Leastways as I see it, I'm doin' you a favor. I'll be marrying no one else, no mistake, and if yer smart, you'll think twice afore takin' up wit' a man, yerself. I kin only hope you'll be outgrowin' yer awkward years. But don't be rushin' it, lassy, don't be rushin' it."

Her mother sized Anna up and down with a discerning eye. "Although you may na have to worry about that anyway. Too tall, you are, with no redeeming features in yer face. Best you keep it that way, Anna. Don't go and make the mistake I did, my girl, do you hear me? Don't you paint an' dress yourself up ta look pretty. Wouldna do you any good, right enough. Have never met a man yet that dinna think all women were the work of the devil, anyway, to tell God's truth. Now, dunna cry."

Her mother had left Anna at the local Catholic orphanage, and Anna had never seen the woman again.

Anna had, of course, overheard the nuns' whisperings. But it hadn't been until she was older and on her own that she had grasped the significance of the phrase, "Her mama has taken to the calling."

Anna had never blamed her mother for what she had done; the woman had been left little choice. In a way, it had been the best thing for Anna.

As it was, although Anna had never received the love and attention that kindly parents might have indulged, she did not consider herself lacking. The orphanage had seen to her education, for which Anna had been grateful. That she had gone on to become their best student was a blessing, for it had been this education that had allowed her to make herself into an invaluable part of the orphan movement.

No, Anna reminded herself, she did not blame her mother. She thanked her. Anna was exactly the kind of woman she wanted to be . . . although sometimes . . . only occasionally, if she were really honest with herself, Anna would admit that she found herself yearning for the love and comfort of a family. For perhaps a husband of her own whom she could love; one who would also love her in return.

But Anna was also realistic enough to know that these things were not for her. They were mere myths as far as she was concerned; fairy tales invented to do nothing more than put children to sleep at night. Although . . . today for a moment, perhaps a brief little bit of time only, she had felt . . . feminine . . .

Anna immediately squared her shoulders and let out her breath. She had to stop this line of pondering and think.

There was only one thing she understood with any degree of certainty: she would have to cause this tall brave to change his mind. That was all there was to it. She was going to have to convince him to take her and the children to a white settlement without the marriage contract he seemed to require. But how to do it?

She frowned. There had to be a way. She lifted her head and raised her face toward the twinkling stars; there must be a way.

Off in the distance, the sky rumbled and Anna watched as storm clouds raced silently across the moon, blocking out its light. The result was, of course, darkness. But what was so strange about it was how quickly it had happened. Did storms come on that rapidly out here?

Her eyes scanned the heavens. Stars to the north, dark clouds to the south. She looked away from the sight, took another step or two, but after a few moments, found herself glancing back up above.

What was it about the heavens out here that made the sky appear so much more vast than anywhere else? It was not as if Anna had never before witnessed a beautiful, starlit sky, nor a magnificent sunset. It was only that the horizon here seemed so much more immense than she would have ever imagined it would be. For a moment, she let herself dream: the dream of being alone on this prairie, perhaps at the mercy of this very same Indian man; a man who would find a beauty in her that others might have missed. A man, she reminded herself, who had mentioned marriage and her in the same breath . . . this tall brave . . .

She pulled her thoughts up short. Alone? At his mercy? What was she thinking? She gave herself a derisive snort and turning, trod back to the children.

"Miss Wiley?" a young voice ventured.

Anna glanced down to find young David at her side. She immediately drew him to her and hugged him.

"What is it, David?"

"Is the Indian going to kill us?"

Anna found herself smiling. "No, he's not. Come now and I'll tell you all about the talk I had with him. Everything is going to be fine."

"Is it really?"

She leaned down and kissed the top of the boy's head. "It is. I promise you." And to herself she added, she would make it so.

"He has said that, given the right circumstances, he might help us find homes," Anna said, knowing it was a long stretch of the truth, but unwilling to tell the children the bald facts. Besides, so long as she lived, she would do everything in her power to change this tall brave's attitude. Perhaps her willing sacrifice might suffice, if there were no other way.

Anna sat on the ground, next to the children; their shelter being the rocks against their backs, and the ground, their beds. She gazed lovingly at each child, finding a great deal about every one of them to admire. No one had whined and no one had screamed or yelled; there had been little talk at all among them. Actually, most of the children were so tired, they had gone to sleep at once, still in a sitting position.

"It's very kind of the tall Indian to help us find homes," said Patty, the only girl who still remained with their party. That Anna's heart went out to the youngster, she could not deny, for Anna was certain that the only reason Patty had not been picked out of this group was because she was plain of face. Also, the girl was petite and because of this, Anna feared that these midwestern farmers looked upon Patty as a liability, rather than an asset.

Anna said, "Yes, it is very kind of him to help us. I think he has a good heart." She situated one of the sleeping children against another child as she spoke, hoping to place each one in a position so that when the children awoke, no one would have stiff muscles. She turned back to those who still remained awake and said, "But remember that we must do as he asks us. Kansas is at war with these Indian tribes, and we do not want to stumble into the middle of another fight. One was enough," she added beneath her breath.

"Yes, Miss Wiley," a few of the children said, some-what in unison. Anna smiled.

"It's quite pretty here, isn't it?" commented seven-year-old Patty.

"Yes, it is very pretty," Anna agreed, then added, "This land is not at all as I thought it would be."

Wide brown eyes stared back at her, then timidly the young girl asked, "What did you think it would be like, Miss Wiley?"

"I'm not sure," Anna said, as she brushed her fingers through Patty's hair. "It's only that the land goes on with-out seeming to end; there is so much space here, so much room. And tonight it was so quiet, I felt as though I could hear myself think."

"Did you really?" asked Patty, distracted. "Look, Miss Wiley, do you see? Over there?"

Anna looked in the direction Patty pointed. There was nothing there, nothing but land and sky.

Patty continued, "Do you see it? That's how to draw the sky. It's not a line at the top of a page, is it, Miss Wiley?"

Anna glanced at Patty as though she had never before seen the girl. What an adult comment, as well as the ob-servation of an artist.

"See," Patty went on to illustrate. "The sky meets the land there and there and there." She pointed. "Now I can draw it."

Anna grinned and hugged the girl. "And so you shall, my love, so you shall."

Several of the boys were already asleep. Anna watched them for a few moments before deciding that she had better take this opportunity to seek out this tall brave once more. The winds had picked up some force, their gusts causing her to shiver, inciting Anna's fear for the children's health.

She arose and plodded toward the man, finding him some distance away from their camp, next to the horses. Unaware that she might have presented a most charming picture, Anna did not think to tie back the long tresses of her hair, which had long ago come loose from her tight chignon. Instead, she let the wind stir the locks against her face.

The wind also caught at her dress, whisking her skirts to and fro, now and again catching the breeze perfectly, the gale outlining her body against the frail cloth. But, still of the mind that her body presented little to stir the imagination of a member of the male gender, she did not consider such a thing.

She raised a hand to her bonnet, to keep it on, not noticing until she did so that the hat had come loose and was hanging around her neck by its ties. After several attempts at sticking the article back on her head only to have the wind chase it away again, she finally gave up and glanced heavenward.

That was when it happened. Truly, it occurred so quickly, and without her willing it, that her reaction took her by surprise. Her spirits lifted, as though in complement with the storm, and she felt . . . free and . . . content, if only for a moment.

It made her want to spread out her arms like wings, perhaps to catch the next gust of wind. Captive or not, at war or not, storm or not, she was abruptly aware of the beauty that surrounded her, and Anna felt like twirling round and round. She did not do it, however. Hers was not an uninhibited heart.

Unaware of the picture she displayed, she glanced up innocently to find Mister Tall Brave watching her. And with that look, although the wind might have continued to whip its worst at her, the world stood still, if only for a moment.

What was it about this man? she wondered. What was it that made her want to reach out toward him, yet crawl away from him at the same time?

Surely, it was a strange sensation, given their circumstances, and yet Anna could not look away. What was happening?

Anna did turn away, however, as though in defense . . . against what?

"You felt it."

The soft masculine words came from directly behind her. But she did not turn around.

"Felt what, sir?" Anna said.

"The beauty of this place has stirred your spirits, has it not?"

"I . . . I do not know what you are talking about."

She heard the harsh snort in his voice and forced herself to keep from turning around, from confronting him with perhaps the validity of her feelings.

He said, "You are just like all white people, I think. You cannot speak the truth even when it is obvious to you."

Anna could not say a word. Instead, she found herself looking straight to the horizon, and unconsciously, she moaned. He was right and she did not know why she could not just admit it.

Perhaps the experience was too new. Perhaps she did

not trust him with so vulnerable an emotion when she did not even understand it herself. Perhaps it was none of these things.

All she knew was that something about this land was taking hold of her. And Anna could not decide if it was for good or for bad.

When she did not speak right away, this tall brave uttered another grumble and she heard his footsteps moving away.

"Sir?" Quickly she spun around. "Sir, I think that you do me a disservice."

He did not pivot to confront her.

"Sir, a moment please."

He stopped, although his posture said that he was anything but amenable.

She began, "You say that I am like all the others of my race. Yet, for a few moments tonight, I think I began to understand what is going on here. You are right, I did feel . . . something stirring in my soul. I do not know why I could not say it a few moments ago, except that perhaps my feelings were too new, too personal, and you, sir, are a stranger."

He looked over his shoulder for a moment, muttered a gruff, "Humph," and glanced away.

She continued, "I think I understand now why the Indians fight so hard to keep this land and their way of life."

He did not utter a word and she took a few cautious steps forward.

"Please correct me if I am wrong, but for a moment here tonight, sir, I think I discovered how the land and the beauty of this place could creep into the soul and the **heart of a culture.**"

Impetuously she padded up to him, and had to stand on her tiptoes to murmur into his ear, "Sir, am I not right to believe, then, that your people love this land and want to keep it the same as it has always been?"

She watched as his muscles grew tense.

She touched his shoulder. "Sir." She was whispering now. "I, too, have tonight witnessed the beauty of this place. And I think that, although I am a newcomer, I speak the truth. The land, nature, the wind and the soil are a part of your people's makeup, a part of their soul, while these same things are perhaps nothing more than assets to be used, sold or bartered by the newcomers."

She could feel his muscles grow stiff beneath her touch, and it was almost more than she could do to keep herself from massaging all that brawn.

He, however, did not speak, did not react, did nothing at all, and she sighed, returning to stand full-footed upon the ground. She drew back her hand, turned away.

"*Nahkohe-tseske.*" He spun around, made a grab at her arm under her elbow and drew her back. As though the wind were in conspiracy with her desire, its blasts whipped up behind Anna, whisking her forward, propelling her into his arms.

Both of them grew quiet. Neither of them moved, Anna fearing even to breathe.

His head came down toward her. Did he mean to kiss her?

Excitement struck her unexpectedly, overwhelming her with a frenzy of hunger so intense, she could barely breathe. And with a shudder she realized that she *wanted* that kiss; she *wanted* that embrace and she felt herself grow weak.

Did he desire her, too? No, it couldn't be possible that he might feel the same for her, yet . . .

Gently, his forehead met hers while his hands came up to caress her cheeks as though she were more precious than porcelain china. She closed her eyes. She dared not think; she dared not even stir. She moaned instead, not being able to suppress it. She had never felt more under a person's spell than she did at this moment.

Yet, to her surprise, she came alive, becoming aware of little things that she had, perhaps, never noticed before. The air smelled crisper, the earth beneath her feet felt more solid, the softness of the night held more warmth. Fleetingly, she could sense the blood pounding through her body, could perceive the rhythm of life flowing within her, and without conscious thought, she experienced a sensation of herself as a spirit growing larger, as though a mere body could not hold that which she was.

Oddly, the universe in which she lived seemed a more vibrant and real universe at this moment than at any time she could remember. And she became fleetingly aware of the life all around her, even to the grasses, which grew so high and green, as they sprang up in the wind, to touch and tickle her ankles.

Truly, she felt above herself, witnessing the sky as though its vastness were mere child's play; the peal of thunder, the wonder of lightning as no more than a toy. And all the while beauty, peace and harmony settled into her soul.

Another flash of lightning, followed by a crisp clap of thunder dispelled the illusion, had her remembering where she was. As she glanced up into this tall brave's eyes, she consciously brought back to mind exactly who she was; who he was and where they were.

She cleared her throat, muttered a low, "Sir," and stepped out of his embrace.

She gazed away from him, from the spot in his arms where she had been, and said, "What sort of game do you play with me, sir?"

He did not answer, which gave her little choice but to continue, "I know that I am not an attractive woman and yet you have offered marriage to me." She stiffened her spine. "Sir, tell me true. Is it your intention to use me?"

When he did not answer, she glanced at him. But all she could witness upon his face was a curious look, one of eyebrows raised in question.

She drew in a deep breath. "All right," she said. "I suppose I must be forthright and speak what I mean quite bluntly. Sir, do you intend to have your way with me?"

Still he did not answer.

She shot a glimpse at him and raised her voice. "To abuse me?" She waved her arms. He crossed his own over his chest, still suspiciously silent.

She shut her eyes and plunged. "To have sex with me, sir? That is what I am saying." She peeped an eye open to steal a look at him and muttered quietly, "To pretend marriage to me only to have sex?"

She did not know how it was possible, but his dark eyes changed color, transforming into a deeper, gloomier glare. At length, however, a slow smile lit his face.

She said, "It is no joke, sir, and may I remind you that it is only fair of you to make your intentions known to me."

His smile didn't diminish as he slowly brought his

hand up to her cheek, the backs of his fingers gently stroking her skin. But she drew back from the tender graze as though stung.

Their eyes met, held, dueled. A moment danced before them as they stared, the look between them carnal and searing. She could not have looked away had she meant to, and she did not mean to. He held her captive while one moment followed upon another, until at last, without so much as a single word being uttered, he turned and trod away.

But Anna could not let it rest at that. She dared not. She hurried to catch up with him.

"Sir, I think I deserve an answer."

"This is my answer, white woman." He did not turn to look at her. In truth, the speed of his pace increased.

"But I didn't hear a word said about it."

"No words are needed," he responded, his gait becoming faster. "Had I meant to 'have my way with you,' it would already be done. I do not attack my prisoners sexually or otherwise."

"But you've never said and I . . . I . . ." she began, her voice breathless. "Perhaps I misunderstood. It is only that you touched me back there and—"

He stopped and turned on her so suddenly that she ran straight into him. But his arms did not come around her to hold her as they had before, and she found herself bouncing back from him, barely able to keep her balance.

He took a stand, albeit an annoyed one, one foot clamped solidly next to the other. He asked, "Who has told you that you are unattractive?"

"Several people," she answered, quietly.

"Who?"

"My mother for one," she said, looking away from him, pretending interest in her skirt. "Also several boys in the orphanage where I was growing up. That man on the train."

"What man on the train?"

"The one who abused your brother."

He sighed. "I am certain that his was an evil heart. You should pay no attention to that."

"There have been others."

He snorted, and when he at last answered her, he said simply, "They were wrong."

He did not wait to see the effect these words had upon her, she noted. He said them plainly, with no fanfare and no apology; in truth, he said them with what appeared to be great antagonism toward her. And with nothing else uttered, no other explanation given, he turned and trod away.

They were wrong?

Did that mean he found her attractive?

Anna felt like pinching herself. Had she, unbeknownst to herself, fallen asleep? Was this no more than a very real dream?

A hair-raising streak of lightning, followed by an instantaneous clap of thunder made her jump, rousing her from her speculation, making her realize that she was more than awake. It also brought her duty clearly back to mind.

Hastily, she glanced over to where the children still slept. How could she have forgotten the reason she had sought out this tall brave in the first place?

Annoyed with herself for what she considered her breach of responsibility, she picked up her skirts and hurried after the man.

She gasped. *What the . . . ?*

The man was in the act of unsaddling the ponies.

"Sir?" she called.

He did not hear her, and she watched in horror as he slapped the animals, the action sending the ponies running.

"Sir!" She screamed the word.

If he heard her, he did not acknowledge her.

"Sir." A spurt of energy had her catching up to him. But it was too late. The damage had been done; the horses were gone. She ran after the animals to no avail, stopped and spun around on him. "Sir." She said the word as though it were an accusation. "Why did you do that?"

He did not answer her, and with a rudeness that should have sent her scurrying away, he turned his back on her and strode off in the opposite direction. But she was not to be ignored so easily and she caught up to him.

"Sir," she said again, "why have you let the horses go? Surely you must know that the children and I cannot travel without them."

"You are all going to have to," he said over his shoulder, still sparing her not even a single glance. He kept his pace fast.

"But, sir—" She reached out to grab hold of his arm; she missed.

"The ponies are too easy to track," he commented, making no mention, if he had even noticed, that she had tried to take hold of him. "We will have to make our trail **without those animals.**"

She literally had to run to keep up with him. "But the children—"

"Will walk."

She stopped completely still, rebuffed and curiously angry. Oh, how she wanted to stomp her foot, to argue with him; indeed, she felt like grasping hold of him and forcing him to face her until he gave her more than a few syllables in answer to her questions. But another rumble sounded from the skies and she thought better of the action. Quickening her own strides, she ran forward to catch up with him.

"All right," she said, "I will give you quarter about the ponies. Perhaps you are right, but I must point out that the children and I have no shelter from the storm."

He nodded toward their camp. "The rocks will be your shield against the wind and the rain when it comes, plus these." He held up the trade blankets that he had pulled off the ponies.

"But—"

"There is nowhere else for us to go. We cannot outrun the storm, nor do we want to be caught as the tallest object on the prairie when the worst of it hits. No, we will stay here."

What could she say? "All right, but—"

"The children will not be able to sleep long, either," he added. "It will be your duty to awaken them and get them ready to move as soon as this storm passes. It is then that we must be on our way."

"On our way? But, what if it is still dark? Surely you would not have us leave a perfectly good shelter in the middle of the night?"

He gave her a patient, although a suspiciously exasperated look. *"Haahe,* we must leave, especially if it is in the middle of the night, and you will have to prepare the children."

"Sir, really, I feel that I must protest that—"

"Unless," he added, interrupting her, "you want to be caught on foot by any hostile war party roaming the countryside."

"I thought you said that—"

"Nahkohe-tseske, Little Bear, while it is still night, we will need to find a place to camp during the day that will not easily catch the eye of a war party. From here, until we reach the safety of the north country, we will be in constant danger from both the whites and the Indians. The Indians will want to kill you and the children, the whites will want to kill me and my brother. No matter which group would find us, we would not be safe."

"Then you mean to take us to safety?"

"Perhaps, if you please me well enough."

"Please you? But . . ." As her eyes met his, she felt a surge of awareness, the same sort of biological urge that had sprung up between them only a few moments ago. Her pulses leapt, sending a cascade of pleasure radiating throughout her body. He, however, appeared immune to it. She spoke up quickly, hoping that she sounded as though she, too, were unaffected. "Sir, if it is your plan to help us and take us to the nearest white settlement, I can assure you that the soldiers would listen to me, if they found us. If I were to tell them our story, and I most certainly would do so, I feel assured that these people would not fail to see that you have helped us, and they . . ."

Her words ended when his eyes narrowed and a sneer came to his lips, accompanied by a growl that made her want to jump back, away from him. But this man did not frighten her quite so easily, and she held her ground.

Straightway he observed, "Look around you, white woman; look at where you are. Do you see a great many of the same white settlements here that you might find on your eastern shores?"

"Of course not, but—"

"You are in Indian country, *Nahkohe-tseske,* where your people and mine are at war. There would be shooting first, talking last, and no amount of your pleading would make a difference, so do not talk to me of it again. *Hova'ahane,* we will *not* go to any white settlements and until we reach the destination I have set, we will sleep by day and travel at night. I have spoken."

" 'I have spoken'?" she muttered to herself.

Anna sputtered out the word, "Sir," but found herself speaking only to air. He had again turned his back on her. However, not to be put off, she called out to him, this time more audibly, "Sir, might we have a few more words about this?"

He did not answer, which was becoming quite annoying. Nor, she observed, did he seem to be in the mood to turn around and converse with her. In truth, he quickly trod away from her.

"Why, you pigheaded, obstinate mule," she swore, stomping her foot. "I have more to say on this and you shall listen to me, by goodness. I demand it! Do you hear?"

Perhaps it was the cursing; perhaps only the anger in her voice that caused the trouble. Whatever the reason, he stopped; he paused a moment. Then he turned, treading back toward her, his every step a menace. He had set his shoulders rigidly and had pressed his lips together until his chin more resembled an object made of stone than of flesh and blood. At length, he bit out, "Do not antagonize me."

"But—"

"Know, white woman, that my mother, my father and my little sister, as well as three other members of my family are dead because they believed they could talk with these warrior-whites and bring peace. They, too, thought they could reason with these people. All are dead because of it. The great peace chief, Black Kettle, is dead. Yellow Wolf is dead. You do not understand what is going on here. I have said all that I am going to say on this. No more argument. We leave as soon as the storm abates."

Anna drew back, while he spun away from her, leaving her once more with nothing more to do than stare at his backside.

But rather than be annoyed, this time she drew within herself. His mother, his father, his little sister? All dead? She had not meant to anger him, nor to bring up painful memories. She had simply been defending her own.

He was also right, she acknowledged to herself at last. She did not know this country, nor the attitudes of the people who lived in it. She did not have the knowledge of how to avoid Indian war parties, nor even how to find her way across this land.

Briefly, she recalled the words of the unknown man who had sat behind her in the train only earlier this day. An element of irrational glee had filled the man's words when he had been speaking about the killings at Sand Creek, even of the women and children.

Perhaps this tall brave was right. It was entirely possible that, if such unreasonable hatred existed within the hearts of the people here and, if the soldiers found her with this man, there *would* be killing first and questions later.

Abruptly the truth of her own situation struck her, and her head reeled under the weight of that cognizance. She and the children were completely dependent upon this man; utterly, fully dependent. Not only did they have this tall warrior alone, to look to for their food and their shelter, they were entirely reliant upon his goodwill for their safety and protection.

Stung to silence, Anna continued to stare at his retreating figure. She would have to trust him; she had no choice.

Thus, she followed him more meekly when he made his way back to their temporary camp. She watched as he set up his guard on the hill overlooking it. Still, without another word, she slunk up beside him, took the blankets he had proffered to her earlier, and turned to scoot down the hill toward the children.

"White woman." His words caught at her and she swung around to him. "Know that my offer is no longer open to you."

"But I thought that—"

"Perhaps if you had agreed immediately, it is possible I *might* have been persuaded to lead you to a white settlement. But you did not respond quickly enough to what I proposed."

Anna could only stare at the man, her lips mouthing the word, "Oh." But no sound came from her throat.

And having no ready response, she wound her way back down the hill.

With sightless eyes, she surveyed the spot where she would spend the rest of the evening, her gaze softening when it lit, at last, upon her most precious charges. Sitting down, she took one of the children into her arms, and swallowed noisily.

What, in heavens name, was she to do? How could she have come to this?

She inhaled deeply, beyond tears as she realized that she, who for most of her life, had been given good reason to feel vulnerable, had never felt so defenseless in all her life.

Perhaps when the Indian boy returned, the one who had championed her, things might be better . . . maybe.

Chapter 8

❝*H*ova'ahane! Hova'ahane!❞
   War Cloud muttered the words to himself as he watched the storm begin to whip up its fury. Although he did not fear the thunder or the lightning, War Cloud was not so foolish as to trod upon a flat prairie during a storm.

He lay on his stomach, on top of their rock shelter. In his right hand he clutched a sawed-off shotgun while his spear rested beside him in an ever-ready position. His bow was slung over his shoulder, with his sheath of arrows lashed across his back. Even though it unlikely that a war party would be traveling in this weather, War Cloud's eyes still scanned the prairie. One could never be certain with these warrior-whites. These men seemed to have no method to their attacks, nor did they appear much for a fair fight with men of their own make, character and advantage.

From the Indian point of view, these warrior-whites appeared as little more than cowards. These "soldiers" hid behind the walls of their forts like scared rabbits. And when they did venture out to do battle, they concentrated their attacks upon villages of women and children, not upon their equals, the warriors. It was something no Indian mind could comprehend.

That his own people, the Cheyennes, were retaliating in the same brutal manner as these whites, attacking outposts and settlements along the frontier, War Cloud refused to consider. An eye for an eye. This was how it was.

A shuffling noise sounded from below him, and War Cloud peered down to see one of the children turn over in sleep. The rustle of their clothing beneath the blankets reminded him of the events that had brought him to his present situation, and without pause, frustration surged through him once more, causing him to mutter a quiet, *"Eaaa,"* in response.

Although War Cloud was not the sort of man to long dwell on things that could not be changed, he could not help indulging himself in a moment of self-contempt. He, who had refused to engage in any more worthless peace talks with the whites; he, who had led several of the conflicts between the warrior-whites and the Cheyenne Dog Soldiers; he, certainly no friend to these whites, now found himself aiding and abetting not just one or two of these people, but thirteen.

He tightened his mouth, while a muscle twitched furiously in his cheek.

And yet, he thought, if he were honest, he would admit that a part of him was glad to have the company of the white woman . . . She certainly possessed a sharp tongue, he considered, a half grin pulling at the edge of his lips.

Nahkohe-tseske, Little Bear. It was an apt name for her.

Reluctantly, War Cloud recognized hers as an indomitable spirit; plus, he acknowledged, it was possible that without her interference, his brother might be lying dead, a sacrifice to the hostilities of war.

There was more, although he refused to consider the tangled emotions that had sprung up between himself and the white woman.

Lust. That had to be the explanation for his actions. Yet, if that were true, how did he account for his urge to comfort the woman, to take her in his arms and hold her until her cares melted away?

An image flitted across his mind, the likeness that of the white woman. And despite his own trepidations, he caught himself recalling the way the wind had whisked her hair against her face; the manner in which that unflattering dress had moved against her body. It caused a stirring within his blood and made his heart beat a little faster, and War Cloud again acknowledged this for what it must certainly be: lust, pure and carnal.

It was odd, too, because she was not what he considered pretty, yet . . .

He shook his head, quietly admonishing himself, and with silent determination, set his mind to other things. He brought his attention back to his surroundings, keeping a look out for any sign of an enemy. There would be little rest for him this night—for the next few weeks, in fact, since it would be some time before he could lead these people to the relative safety of the north country. Until then, neither he nor his brother would be able to relax their vigil. Both his own and his brother's safety, as well as that of the woman and children, rested upon his competence.

War Cloud heaved a deep sigh. And although he knew it did no good to ponder the mistakes of the past, he could not help but wonder what he could have done differently to avoid his current predicament. In truth, he could find no error on his part, except perhaps earlier when the whites had stolen his brother from him.

That he had left Lame Bird with a cousin in a Kiowa camp had been a mistake. The Kiowa and the whites had been at peace and it had seemed the best thing to do at the time. But the camp had been raided anyway, his brother taken captive and recognized.

The ultimate miscalculation, War Cloud had come to realize, was not being aware of how notorious his own person had become. That the white man considered War Cloud an outlaw seemed ridiculous to him. His was a spirit at war; his purpose that of a warrior, not an outlaw.

But no matter, War Cloud had made a mistake in not giving credit to the white people's intelligence, never dreaming they would make the connection between himself and his brother.

It would be the last time War Cloud ever repeated that error. He would keep the boy close to him in the future and he would remember, too, that so long as these wars raged over the plains, no one was safe from attack.

"E-na'estse-ve!" The wind rushing by him seemed to speak to him in Cheyenne.

War Cloud paid it little attention.

"E-na'estse-ve!" She is the one. The whispered words came again.

War Cloud frowned. Was he hallucinating, or was he having a vision?

He glanced around him, in every direction, but he could see nothing except storm clouds. He waited, frown-

ing. If it were a vision, something else would make itself
known to him.

War Cloud lingered, belly down on the ground, his
senses alert. But nothing else happened for quite some
time, no other words spoken, even the wind beginning to
still. Perhaps, he decided, he was merely dreaming wide-
awake.

"*E-na'estse-ve!*" The low voice came again when War
Cloud would have relaxed. This time the voice came
from the direction of the clouds.

War Cloud narrowed his brows. He knew that voice,
had heard it at some time in his past. Glancing back
briefly toward the sleeping figures of the whites, War
Cloud tried to determine if anyone else had heard it.

No one moved. No one stirred.

Again, "*E-na'estse-ve!*"

War Cloud came up to a sitting position and, glancing
toward the heavens, asked in a whisper, "*Nevaahe
ta'hohe?*" Who is that?

No response came to the question, and War Cloud tried
again, a little more loudly, "*Nevaahe ta'hohe?*"

Still nothing more was said, nothing to explain what
was happening.

And yet, the voice was familiar. Frowning, War Cloud
made the connection and asked, "Is this the voice of my
ancestor?"   •

Instead of an answer, the low voice repeated, as though
War Cloud hadn't asked his own question, "*E-na'estse-
ve!*" She is the one.

"*Nevaahe?*" Whom do you speak of?

"*Ve'ho'a'e. E-na'estse-ve.*" The white woman. She is
the one.

War Cloud again surveyed his surroundings. Nothing. There was nothing there, except . . . Again, his brows narrowed, and he let out his breath. "I have not heard from you for many years, my ancestor," answered War Cloud. "I thought you had given up on me when I failed to be successful in marriage many years ago."

No direct reply was forthcoming except that the wind whisked by War Cloud as though it were somehow angered. Then came the voice again, saying, "You are the one, and so is she. The time has come at last."

War Cloud moaned, and shaking his head, uttered, *"Hova'ahane*. I am not the one. I have tried to destroy the spell that binds you and that binds me and my kin." He addressed the spirit as though he were speaking to a live person. "But, Grandfather, I grow tired of the game. Five times I have been ready to marry. And in all these experiences, none of these women have stayed with me. All are gone; all left me for another. The curse holds strong."

"It will be different this time," came the softly spoken words.

"It will not be different!" Irritated, War Cloud found himself raising his voice. Calming himself and glancing back toward the sleeping figures below him to ensure that he had not roused them, he added, "Go away, Grandfather. The last time you spoke to me, I had more trouble than I could handle."

Now, it is true that these were odd things to say to a spirit, made even more strange by the fact that War Cloud should be so annoyed. Amongst all Cheyenne, as well as with most Indian tribes, the object of a vision, as well as the being who gave it, was revered, perhaps even feared. However . . .

"Yet," the voice said gently, "did not the white men come as I said they would? Did they not build their homes on your land? Are there not now more of them than the blades of grass upon the ground?"

"Haahe, all these things became true," War Cloud whispered, "but not for many years and not before I was laughed from the camp. My wife left me after only a few days to run away with another because no one would believe these strange things that you told me."

A strained silence followed this statement, the land mimicking the stillness, although a few drops of rain began to splatter on War Cloud's face. At length, the voice continued, "Your wife would have left you no matter what you did or said, for the curse over our family prevents your happiness, and hers. You know that either she had to leave you or she would die."

War Cloud sulked, knowing in his heart the truth of these words. Yet, still, he was unwilling to relent and he ordered, at some length, "Go away!"

"I cannot," came the voice. "I am as reliant upon you as you are on me."

"I do not rely on you!"

"Do you not?" came the voice, oddly inflected with laughter. "And yet you seek to cross the prairie with many white children and expect to do it without incident from the warrior-whites?"

War Cloud grunted. "I must do as I must do. I am now honor-bound to do this because of my brother. Now, go away and do not seek me out again. I am not the one to end your plight. I have already tried to help you, to help my clan; I have failed. Perhaps my brother is the one who can at last break this bad luck. Why do you not talk to him?"

A hush filled the void left by these words, and then the vision of an old man materialized before War Cloud, there upon the prairie. War Cloud came up onto his forearms as he announced, "Since I was a young man, you have come to me and have spoken to me, Grandfather. *Haahe,* yes, you have given me wisdom, you have shown me truths many times, but these truths are not always easy to accept. I would have you leave me alone."

Several hushed moments passed before the image asked, "Tell me why you speak as you do."

War Cloud forced himself to curb his irritation. He reminded himself that it was not his ancestor's fault that his own people had not believed the truth of the old man's prophecy all those years ago, just as it was not his fault that War Cloud found himself escorting a group of white people. At length, he said, "Grandfather, you may speak to me wisely as you have done in the past. It is only that sometimes these things that you tell me are not only hard to do, they are difficult to believe. Grandfather, I would live in peace with my people and with myself."

The image came to within ten feet of War Cloud and there it halted. It said, "There will be no peace for you or any of our family until you put this curse to rest, my son. I know these things are hard to understand and they are hard for you to do, but you must set your mind to it. The white woman's heart is good."

With a quick jerk of his head, War Cloud announced, "I am already helping her and it matters not if her heart is good or evil. I have pledged myself. It is enough. I will take her north."

"This is not what she wants."

"She has no choice."

"But you do."

"I have not the choice," argued War Cloud. "If I do as she asks me, I risk the murder of myself and my brother. If I take her north, she may survive."

"Or she and the children might be killed by those amongst our own kind whose hearts have become as hardened as the earth upon which you walk."

"It is a risk," War Cloud acknowledged, "but it is the only way."

"*Hova'ahane,* there is another way," said the spirit. "Do as she asks. I will be here with you. I will guide you."

"Enough!" The wind whipped around War Cloud and rain began to splatter in his face in earnest. But he would not be swayed by these things. "I will need no guide, for I know the way north. I will do as I think best, not as she suggests or as you will it. I would be rid of her as soon as I can, Grandfather, and be on my way."

"Yet, she could be many things to you. My son, it takes but one act of kindness for one such as she."

"But she . . . she is . . ."

"One act of kindness . . ." With these words, the image disappeared, amidst a hair-raising crack of thunder.

"*Saaa,*" War Cloud muttered to himself, scoffing, yet even as he did so, a hand touched his arm. Despite himself, Sun Cloud jerked and spun around, sitting up and staring into a pair of round, green eyes . . .

Chapter 9

Anna slept fitfully.

The wind felt as though it were nudging her, talking to her. Worse, she was having a gruesome nightmare.

From somewhere far away from her body, she watched as her captor talked to an apparition. Watched him as though she were somehow a part of the conversation.

But she wasn't.

Oh, how she wanted to come awake. She kept prodding herself, hoping to open her eyes, but they remained tightly shut.

And still the voices spoke, in words she could not understand.

A crack of thunder cut through the air and Anna awakened with a start.

Her breathing came in fits and spurts and Anna drew her hand to her heart, as though to shield herself. She was frightened . . . frightened and . . . She glanced around her, at the children.

At least they slept peacefully. Oh, how she loved every single one of them.

Watching them, Anna realized what she was going to have to do, and the sooner it was done, the better she would feel about it . . . she hoped.

So it was with a determination that might have rivaled even the most stouthearted of men, that Anna rose to seek out her captor.

"Sir." The white woman's gentle voice reached out to him. "I must speak to you."

War Cloud calmed himself and, still holding her gaze, found himself asking, "Did you see? Did you hear?"

"See what?"

Sun Cloud let out his breath and narrowed his brow, asking, "Did something awaken you?"

"My thoughts awoke me; they worry me, sir," she said, and War Cloud relaxed. "I have at last fully confronted the fact that I, and I alone, am responsible for these children, and my mind does not rest easy." Her look puzzled, she stopped for the beat of a moment, then, "I am sorry, sir, but I heard nothing."

"Hova'ahane." He shook his head. With a deep sigh, War Cloud settled his glance on the horizon, his face an unreadable mask.

"Sir, please, I must speak to you."

Still not looking at her, he said, "I am listening."

He heard her sigh before she began, "Sir, forgive me for coming upon you as I have, it is only that I feel I must repeat my concern about the children."

"Humph!" was his only answer.

"Please listen. There is a way for you to take us to a white man's town. You and your brother would not have to come with us into the camp, just lead us close to it."

"And what do you think the white people will do after you or the children tell them that Indians led you to them?"

"We would not say anything?"

He scoffed. "Think you not?" His chin shot up and he slanted her a glance. "And what will you say when they ask you how you came to find a camp of white people hundreds of miles from the raid upon the fire horse? With no weapons? With no food?" He growled. "You would fool no one."

"But by the time others became aware of it, you could be gone."

He bristled, releasing his breath in a dismissal before he said, "You think as a white person."

"I *am* a white person."

He gave her a quick glance. "*Haahe,* so you are. But if you are to survive here, I would urge you to direct your attention to the barely noticeable things that surround you. You must start, white woman, to think like an Indian. Do you understand?"

"I . . . I don't think so."

"Humph!" he said. "I want you to do something."

She nodded. "All right."

He waved his hand in the general direction of the prairie. "Observe what you see around you."

She looked.

"What do you see?"

She hesitated, then, "A storm, clouds, night."

He nodded. "What else?"

"The prairie which goes on into nothing, grass, rain . . . nothing more."

He nodded again. "Ah, now you see it."

"What?" Her voice cracked. "I see nothing."

He remained emotionless and said, "That is the point. There is nothing more there. Do you observe that I am afoot?"

She nodded.

"Tell me one of the most frequent possessions of the white man."

She looked puzzled, at last guessing, "Guns?"

"Horses, Little Bear. The whites have horses. I would be easily found, hunted. No matter the lead I might have on these people, once they found out about me, they would have advantage, even if I captured a horse or two. No, the whites would find me and kill me."

"But I am willing to negotiate."

He turned his head slowly toward her and repeated, "Negotiate?" He said the word slowly, his tongue slurring the syllables together as though he could barely believe what he heard.

She nodded. "Yes, sir," she said, "I am willing to give you something in exchange for this small favor you would do for the children."

He looked her up and down, watched as she gulped, watched as her glance fell to the ground.

He waited for her response and when it came he could barely hear it, she spoke so softly. He asked, "What was that again? I did not hear you."

Again he watched as she balked, at last uttering, "I would do as you ask."

That stopped him; stopped him so completely still he had to remember to breathe.

He muttered, "As I ask?"

She nodded. "I . . . I would be . . ." She gazed away, then down. "I would be . . . yours."

Despite himself, War Cloud found his body stirring to life with the image that her words aroused in him, and he found that his voice was hoarse with anticipation when he asked, "You would do this . . . for the children?"

Again, she nodded.

"But you know nothing of me, of the Cheyenne, the Indians, nor what might happen to you."

He watched as she threw back her head and gazed toward the heavens. "It does not matter. If it means a better life for the children, then I would do it."

He studied her closely. He said, very, very softly, "Little Bear, look within your heart and ensure that this is what you want, for there would be no going back and it could prove dangerous for you. If you make this bargain with me, I would see it through. Know that."

"I have already thought it through, sir." She gave him a shy look. "If you will have me, that is. I know that I am not much, sir, but I promise you that if you do this, I will do all that you ask.

He snorted, looking away from her. "Do not speak of yourself that way."

Her glance at him was puzzled. "What way?"

"The way in which you regard yourself, as though you have no worth. Know, *Nahkohe-tseske,* that I have looked into your heart and what I have seen there is good. I will not hear anyone say anything different about you, not even yourself."

This seemed to quiet her, at least for a moment. But

then, as though she could not resist it, she beseeched, "Sir, may I invite you to do the same with me as you had me do only a moment ago?"

He gave her a blank look.

"Look at me, sir," she explained. "Just look at me and please see the obvious."

He stared at her.

And she waited. After a pause, she asked, "Well, what do you see?"

"A white woman. A woman with eyes that show nothing but kindness. You are the first white woman I have ever known. Perhaps if more of your women were like you, your men would not grow up to be such cowards and liars."

"Sir! I do not like to hear my own kind spoken of in such a manner."

"I do not like to see my own kind dead," he countered.

She gulped, sighed, then said, "Do we have a deal, Mister Tall Brave?"

His glance swept over her once again, and despite himself, he found his nerve endings prickling with his acute awareness of her proximity. "I will have to think on it, Little Bear. I will have to think on it."

"How long will it take you to think?"

He shrugged. "It will take as long as it takes me to decide."

The expression on her face fell. She muttered, "Like you, I will not hold the offer open for long."

He shrugged. "My decision will not be rushed. If the offer is no longer open when I am ready, that is your loss, and perhaps mine, too."

She sighed. "Very well. However, please do not be long in deciding, Mister Tall Brave, for I fear I will not rest well until I know which way it will be."

He nodded, then added, "War Cloud. My name is War Cloud."

He caught her swift smile at him, watched as she offered her hand. "That is a very interesting name, Mister War Cloud. Although I told you once before, let me introduce myself again. I am Anna," she said. "Anna Wiley. How do you do?"

He took her hand, ignored the awareness which swept through his body at her touch, then glancing up into her eyes, he stared at her, trying to read her thoughts. At length, he uttered, whispered actually, "You are certain that you have thought this thing through and that this is something you are willing to do?"

She nodded. "I have."

He squeezed her hand before letting it go. Staring away from her, he said, "I think, Miss Wiley, that I have decided."

"But—"

"Miss Wiley." He grinned, and placing his right hand up at an angle to his head, he snapped his wrist, bringing his first finger down at the same time, the sign for, "It is done." He uttered quickly, "We have a deal."

Chapter 10

***

Anna caught her breath. He had accepted her offer. The odd part of it was that she did not feel as though she were a sacrificial lamb. Instead, she felt . . . elated.

Rain beat at her face, yet despite the discomfort, she found herself returning the man's grin. Cool water ran over her lips and into her mouth as the clean taste of the rain freshened her breath, and she found herself uttering, "Thank you, Mister War Cloud. Thank you very much."

He shot her an odd look, a corner of his mouth pulled up into a grin. As they stood there facing one another, knee to knee, chest to chest, she could not help but observe little things about him; how his long hair, now soaked, framed his face; how one eyebrow, cocked upward, accentuated the devilish leer on his lips. She could only wonder what the man was thinking that would make him smirk so, but she was not left to wait for long.

Before another moment had passed, he uttered, "I only hope you will get along with my wives."

The rain drowned out the last of his words and, uncertain she had heard him correctly, she murmured, "Pardon?"

"Haahe, I do not know how my wives will take to another woman."

Luckily for her, the rain hid her reaction to this choice statement and, although unnerved, she found she was able to keep her voice even as she said, "But sir, I thought you said that the Cheyennes have only one wife."

He nodded companionably. "Most do. Some have more than one—sisters."

She compressed her lips and held her tongue, afraid to utter a word. Well, what had she expected? She knew very little about his man, after all.

Clearing her throat in preparation to say something—anything—she cast him a swift look, not at all pleased by what she saw there. In her youth, she had read that Indians were taught to be stoic, that their countenance expressed no measure of their innermost thoughts. Well, she decided, that observation was certainly in error. For this man wore the most self-satisfied look that she had ever seen.

Why, she wondered, did he appear to be so pleased? What did he expect of her? That she would back out of their bargain so quickly?

That was when it struck her. Of course. This was exactly what he thought. This man must have enough experience with the white man to realize that if a man were already married, there could be no pact between him and a white woman. Plus, she had told him this, herself.

Well, this tall brave would just have to think again, for he had bargained without knowing the intensity of Anna's determination.

She gazed up into the midnight sky and said, pretending a nonchalance she did not feel, "The rain is starting to get heavier. Do you think we could find better shelter for the children?"

The wicked glint in his eye told her he was not at all fooled by her attempt to change the topic of discussion, and he responded, "Very much bother are white women, but perhaps"—he ran his gaze up and down her body—"they are worth it. I will have to see."

Insulted, as he had surely intended her to be, Anna straightened away from him. But when she spoke, she kept her voice calm as she commented, "I can assure you, sir, that I will be no bother to you, or to your wives." She sent him her own smug expression as she continued, "For there will be no reason at all for us to have much contact. Now, as I was saying, about the children—"

"There will be much reason for it," he interrupted her.

"Excuse me?"

"You will need to perform your feminine duties, will you?"

If he had meant to embarrass her, as she suspected was exactly his game, she refused to rise to the bait. Instead, she lifted her head at an angle and said, "Sir, Mister War Cloud, I feel that this conversation is inappropriate in view of the fact that the rain is getting heavier and the children are having to sit out the storm without protection and—"

"I disagree."

"You do? But—"

"I feel our words are very appropriate. You would desire to know all that you can about the man you are to give yourself to, would you not?"

She shut her eyes, took a deep breath, and counted to ten. The man was being very deliberate and very antagonizing. At length, she opened her eyes to stare directly at him. She said, "It does not matter what you have done in your life previous to this moment. No matter your present marital status, you are now the means to the children's salvation. I must think first of them and only secondarily of myself. Yes, it will be a sacrifice for me, for you are right. I do not know you, I do not know your ways. But then again, one cannot pick and choose one's own sacrifices. If a person could, then they would hardly be a concession, would they?"

She almost wished she hadn't made such a gallant speech, for as soon as the words were uttered, the humorous gleam in War Cloud's eye disappeared, to be replaced by a moroseness she could little explain. In essence, his features hardened into an unreadable mask. A moment passed quickly, followed by several more, before he observed unemotionally, "No, one cannot choose one's sacrifices."

He got to his feet, pulling the buffalo robe up from the ground with him. "*Ta-nasetse,* go on." He pushed the robe toward her. "Give this to the children," he ordered. He started to turn away, but before he did so, he glanced down quickly at her, at her dress, which was swiftly becoming plastered to her body under the constant pour of the rain.

The glint in his eyes softened and his touch became gentle as he brought the robe up around her shoulders, his fingers lingering over the exposed skin there as he said, "Or perhaps you should use it yourself, I think."

She glanced up quickly to catch the hint of affection in his eyes before he dropped his hands to his side. He said,

"I would not like you to become ill. I will need you to prepare the children to travel yet this night."

"But—"

A fleeting smile crossed his lips. "Do not argue," he said. "A good Indian woman does as she is told."

"Sir, I must remind you that I am not yet your—"

"And she does not talk so much either. Now, go. When the storm dies, we will travel."

She nodded. "All right. Mister War Cloud, do you know where there is a white settlement close to here?"

"*Haahe,* we will find one."

"Thank you," she uttered once more and then impulsively, she came up onto the tips of her toes and reached out toward him. Before she lost her nerve, she pressed a light kiss to his cheek.

That he turned his head before she knew what he was about, that he pressed his lips against her own in what was her very first kiss, were all actions she had not anticipated. Shocked at herself for the quick warmth that stole over her body, startled further to realize that this man might actually want to kiss her, and even a little afraid of his intentions for doing so, she would have drawn back at once, had not his arms come around her waist, preventing her escape.

However, he did not draw her in more closely toward him. In truth, such an action would have been far from necessary. Her body fell, of its own accord, against him without her consciously willing it.

Was this supposed to be his punishment for her? she wondered. If so, this man had reckoned without knowing the feminine mind. For the kiss did much more than simply stimulate her; alas, it inspired her. And she found herself wanting more . . . of him, of the kiss.

Cool water seeped into her mouth. This, all mixed up with the sweet taste of his lips, heightened her senses and sent a streak of longing racing along her nerve endings. Her breath intermingled with his, and when he opened his mouth over hers, she offered no resistance.

As it happened, it was he who broke off the embrace; he, who turned away from her, presenting her with his back. But it was not an action of repulsion and she knew it.

Briefly, she smiled, gazing in full at the fall of his wet, dark hair down his back, watching in wonder as his shoulders rose and fell with the depth of his breathing. Oddly, such shortness of breath comforted her. But when she spoke, all she uttered was a soft, "Thank you, again, Mister War Cloud. I give you my promise that you will be proud of me." And with these few words left between them, she turned from him and fled back to the comfort of the children.

But such a kiss could not be so easily erased from her memory. She replayed the feel of his lips against her own over and over within her mind. No matter the tiredness of her body, despite the late hour of the night, she sat up, wide-awake. Pressing her fingers to her lips, she recalled the refreshing taste of his mouth, the clean scent of his breath, the textured feel of his skin beneath her touch.

And with a curious sense of contentment, she at last fell to sleep, her dreams haunted by the dark, mysterious presence of the man known as War Cloud.

Lame Bird returned to them in the early hours of the morning, announcing that the whites were to the south and east. With this information well taken, War Cloud set his path to the west and north, toward the Arickaree Fork of the Republican River.

The storm had lasted but a short time and after Anna had prepared the children for a long trek, War Cloud led their party out over the prairie, the moon and the stars his only guide. War Cloud had hoped to make their next camp on an island in the fork of the Arickaree River. Here there would be shelter and a means of defense, if it became necessary to keep one.

The silvery sky of morning was upon the horizon when War Cloud led them to the island. Normally dry at this time of year, the river was high at present due to the recent storm, but neither he, the woman, nor the children had trouble in fording the stream, particularly since the deepest part of the water was no more than thigh level on the littlest orphan.

The sandy island lay several feet above the height of the water. With bushy willows, tall grasses and small, woody alders, the island would make a perfect camp. There would be plenty of firewood, good places to hide if the need arose and shade for sleeping. Plus there would be food, if only in the form of fish.

Any other kind of sustenance was going to be a problem, War Cloud considered.

Upon his return, Lame Bird had brought with him a few prairie chickens and rabbits. The nourishment, however, had been devoured at once and watching the children as they ate, War Cloud had realized how difficult it was going to be to lead these people to safety—if only because of the diminishing food supply.

No longer was game in sufficient quantity to enable

one to live easily off the land. True, War Cloud could augment the nourishment with fish, but even that would soon be gone when the water fell, as it was certain to do. The arid Kansas winds would see to that.

Perhaps tomorrow, while letting the children rest, he would try to find some other game—a buffalo or antelope—and dry the meat.

Presently, Anna prepared the children for bed. He listened to her soothing voice as she sang a calming song to them and found himself barely able to keep his own eyes open. Luckily Lame Bird had volunteered to sit watch, and exhausted, War Cloud had readily accepted his offer. After leaving the boy with directions, he had sauntered away from the others and had discovered a hidden spot, beneath the shade of a willow.

Perfect for a quick nap.

Content, War Cloud sighed and had only settled down, when he saw her.

While one side of the island sloped gently through the water to a line of hills about three miles away, on the other side, the land rose tall in the form of a wall, leaving nothing but prairie rolling off in the distance at its peak. It was toward this side where a person would find the most privacy, for this natural wall would provide protection.

Here is where she stood and he observed that she glanced all around her, obviously searching for the best and most remote spot.

It did occur to him that he should let her know he could see her. But on the other hand, he reasoned, perhaps there were some things which were better left unknown. After all, when would he have another opportunity to observe this woman unaware?

And observe her, he wished to do. Not only because he was male and she, female, but also because she was becoming . . . well, what was she becoming?

True, he could admit that he admired her; true, his respect for her grew ever more distinct; yet he feared there was more to what he felt than these things. She had put the lives of her children before her own, and on more than one occasion.

She had objected to moving her charges, too, in the middle of the night, yet she had done it, nonetheless, and had accomplished the task without complaint and without incident from the children.

He realized that her duties must be toiling, yet she handled the others always with courtesy and with kindness.

She would make a good wife. The thought came out of nowhere and silently he admonished himself. For no matter what happened, he knew he could never marry—her or anyone else.

Still, despite all this, he gave her his full attention.

The early morning sunlight cast a pinkish glow over her skin as she worked over the arduous task of undoing a long series of buttons at the front of her dress. Grimacing, War Cloud wondered how long it must take her to dress on a daily basis, if it took her this long simply to undo those buttons.

Once more, common courtesy caused him to debate with himself. She had not gone very far in undressing; there was still time to warn her of his presence. It was the polite thing to do. Certainly if she had been a Cheyenne woman and he were caught watching her . . .

But she was not Cheyenne and he was tired and . . .

She raised the dress over her head and War Cloud drew in his breath, making a barely audible hiss. For a moment, he forgot to think, until he realized that the anticipation was for nothing.

She was still fully clothed.

He could barely hold in his amazement. For beneath that outer gown she wore another dress, this one more delicately trimmed with lace and ribbons and much prettier than the horrible brown one that she wore over it, at least in his opinion.

Watching her, it came to him why it was that the white woman's backside was always so puffed out and fluffy. There were loops and stiff ruffles on the back of this skirt. No wonder. She was no different than her Indian counterpart, as he had begun to wonder; her clothes were merely differently arranged.

War Cloud came up onto his elbows that he might have a better look at her. So much prettier was this undergarment than the ugly brown thing, he began to wonder why she wore the outer dress. Was she trying to make herself unattractive?

But she moved at that moment and his thoughts ceased. He watched her graceful motions as she took hold of the ugly creation, washed it and hung it on a bush.

Maybe he would steal it away from her. The impish urge was almost uncontrollable.

He did, however, control the impulse. She stood up and in response, he sat up at attention. He saw that she scrutinized her environment, as though she suspected that someone watched her, but when she seemed to find noth-

ing, she untied the ribbons that held her skirts in place
and slipped them over her head.

If he had hoped to see her naked as a result, he was to
be extremely disappointed. She wore an even odder-look-
ing garment beneath this.

War Cloud shook his head. How could one woman
wear all these clothes out here on the hot prairie?

This garment, though not a skirt, nor even leggings,
was ruffled with lace and ribbons around the legs. The
thing more resembled the white man's pants than some
other article of clothing, although not quite . . .

And though this thing, too, was much more comely
than the ugly brown dress, he could not help but observe
that this woman would be most uncomfortable in it, particularly under the Kansas heat. This garment she slipped
off as well.

Yet, still, to his astonishment, she was not naked. Beneath this she wore another piece of clothing, this one
hugging her curves with ties all the way down the front of
the thing to her waist. It was only then that he realized
how tightly this woman was bound.

She struggled with those wrappings, and one moment
followed upon another as War Cloud watched in utter
amazement. Briefly he wondered if he should come to
her assistance.

However, once again, he decided against it. If he made
his presence known to her now, it would embarrass her,
and the disrobing would surely cease, and, though it
might be so very wrong of him, he did not think he was
quite ready for the display to end . . . at least not yet.

He watched as she labored with the knots on that

ridiculously tight-fitting vestlike thing, watched as the article came loose and she threw it aside, her hands and fingers coming up to rub at her waist and middle as though the circulation there had stopped. And in fact, maybe it had.

Yet there was still another garment beneath this one, this next piece of clothing being in the shape of a slip. Now, this was the kind of dress War Cloud was accustomed to seeing on women, although Anna's was more flimsy than the cloth dresses worn by the southern Cheyennes.

Gazing at Anna, he could not help but think how much better she looked in such a simple article of clothing, without all the trappings of her civilization.

He held his breath as he watched her fingers come to the fastening of this dress. Would she take this one off, too?

It appeared that she might. With a hasty study of her surroundings, she undid the bindings that held the dress in place. She slipped the garment off, and he watched as she stood before him the very way in which she had come into this world.

Unwillingly a very male part of him, which had already been awakening, made its presence more than well known.

Her breasts might be small, he thought, her hips tiny and her waist even more infinitesimal still, but she was all feminine curves and valleys, and when she reached up to release her hair, the brownish tresses of her locks fell straight to her waist. He shivered.

Beads of perspiration had been accumulating along his upper lip and he suddenly felt the need for a cold bath.

He should look away, do something else, make his presence known to her. Something, anything. He knew it.

He did nothing.

Lust. Lust was his reaction to this display, and he had best control that urge. A man should not spy on a woman who was not his wife in this way. And yet, she had as good as offered herself to him.

He reminded himself that he did not intend to take her offer to heart. He could not. While he might be willing to use her to break the curse—and in so doing, help her across the prairie—that was the extent of his concern for her.

Wasn't it?

If that were the case, however, and in light of his resolutions, then what was he doing watching her? How could he justify it?

He could not, he decided.

Still, he did not look away.

It did enter his head to wonder how this woman could have ever reached maturity without realizing that she was attractive. If not beautiful in the traditional sense, there was still much about her to lure a man to passion. He wondered how she might appear if she ever tried to make herself pretty.

Was it possible that she could be a beauty? Maybe.

But it little mattered. Given the goodness of her heart, she would make some man a good wife.

He was not, however, that man. He could never be.

As he watched her, the morning sun chose that moment to shine directly onto her hair, adding to it a shimmer of gold. It was a rare occasion, indeed, when War Cloud beheld that hair color on another human being and he found himself unable to look away from her.

If the truth be known, he never let his eyes stray from her until she had finished her bath. He watched as she reached up to wash her hair, observed as she scrubbed herself with the sand from the stream. And all the while he surveyed her, he thought he might go quietly out of his mind.

As soon as she finished, he was going to take a swim in that same cool water, he told himself.

So enchanted was he by her that it came as a surprise when he heard the sounds of horses.

He put his ear to the ground, listening. Trouble.

He sat up slowly, casting a look in all directions, that he might determine the direction of the riders. But he could see nothing.

He was going to have to warn the woman and the others. He would also have to prepare them, as quickly as possible, to face an enemy and, realizing he could delay no more, he stood up, away from his cover.

His eyes met hers as he did so and, as he stared at her all over again, he knew a moment of regret, for he had enjoyed her beauty . . .

Chapter 11

He caught her gaze, took note of her startled glance, which quickly turned to anger, yet by a series of signs, he told her to seek cover. She started to speak to him, mayhap to scream, but he cautioned her to silence.

Then he crept to where Lame Bird was supposed to be keeping watch.

"*Saaa.*" He let out his breath. The boy was asleep. No wonder his brother had not raised the alarm.

War Cloud once more put his ear to the ground, listening, trying to determine where the riders might first appear. At last he lifted his head, stared at his young brother—who had come suddenly awake—and by a series of signs, told Lame Bird that there were Indian ponies coming this way; four of them.

There was no need to mention as well that no matter whether the Indians were from an allied or an enemy tribe, if the two of them were found with these white people, there would be trouble.

"What is it?"

The white woman knelt down to his side. Her hair, wet from her bath, fell to her waist and a few locks of it caught against his arm, causing shivers to run over his skin.

She must have hurriedly dressed as well, he surmised, for the only clothing she had pulled on was that one slip he had glimpsed earlier upon her; that and one skirt. She held the ugly brown thing in her hand, as though ready to pull it over her head, but he cautioned her not to do it, to remain still. But whether he took this action for their safety or because he disliked that brown thing, he spared no time to consider.

Using only signs, she asked again, "What is it?"

He gestured back in the same manner, "Four Indian ponies are approaching. Let us hope they have not picked up our trail."

When she started to pull the dress on again, he reached out and restrained her.

"Go and prepare the children to run for shelter if the need arises," he signed. "Keep them quiet. No moving, no whispering. Complete silence."

Snapping her right hand in the air, the index finger coming down at the same time—the sign of agreement— she moved off to find the children.

The riders came in sight; four Indians. They appeared to be Cheyenne, though War Cloud reserved judgment. Although their clothing appeared to be Cheyenne, it was odd because he did not recognize them, and he should have, *if they were Cheyenne*. Perhaps they were from an allied tribe, the Arapaho?

Good manners would demand that War Cloud stand up and reveal his presence, yet instinct and perhaps some suspicion made him hold back. He would be sure.

That was when he heard the four of them speak, and he

congratulated himself on his good judgment. These were no Cheyennes or Arapahos.

These were Pawnee, most likely. Cavalry scouts masquerading as Cheyenne.

The Indians dismounted and led their horses toward the water, letting the animals drink to their fill. War Cloud watched them without looking at them too closely, knowing that an intense regard would cause them to "feel" the eyes of another upon them.

If these men were cavalry scouts, he reasoned, then they were out hunting his own people. Duty demanded that he should kill them while he could.

However, that action might be more suicidal than brave, for he did not know how many more of the warrior-whites were in their rear. Better he remain alive to warn his people than to die an honorable, yet useless death.

Again, placing his ear to the ground, War Cloud listened. But he could ascertain nothing. If there were soldiers behind these men, he could not hear them.

What were his options?

He and his brother could attack—always a good plan—but if they were killed, the woman and her children would die, if not at the hands of the Pawnee scouts, then from exposure or from some other wandering war party. If he held back, he would have to warn his people that Pawnee scouts had been spotted so close to their country. It meant he would have to take the woman and her children into the camp.

Impossible.

A child's scream split the air, interrupting his thoughts. *Damn!* His cover blown, War Cloud acted at once; his senses, his body, trained all his life for combat such as this.

Swish!

His arrow found its mark; one Pawnee fell. He sent another arrow hurling through the air almost at the same time, but it met with nothing. The other three of the enemy had been alerted and sought cover too swiftly.

As quickly as the first man fell to the ground, the horses shrieked and reared, stampeding back in the same direction they had come.

"Damn!" War Cloud cursed again. Those horses would alert any party that was attached to these scouts that there was trouble.

A movement in the bushes alerted War Cloud to danger and he sent another arrow whizzing toward that place.

Thud! He heard a groan, saw a man fall.

Lame Bird crouched down beside him, and War Cloud gestured the boy to move off to his left where the grass grew tall. So far the enemy did not know who it was they fought, nor exactly where they hid.

Then it happened. The two remaining enemy arose in a combined effort and simultaneously scrambled back up the cliff's grade, scratching their way upward toward the prairie. Abruptly, they were too far away for an arrow; too distant for him to use his shotgun.

There was nothing else for it. He could not allow those two to rejoin a greater force.

Taking care to keep his cover, War Cloud moved forward, following these men, but when the two did not turn to fight, he gave it up and, splashing into the water, swiftly forded the stream, following after the runaways.

He clawed his way up the incline and, once on the level

prairie, sprinted after the two, hoping he could outrun them. Still, they kept their distance, retreating fast.

Dashing across the prairie as fast as he could, War Cloud sped toward them, but he could not catch them. He did, however, manage to capture one of their horses. Grabbing hold of the animal, he jumped onto it and made a clean dash after the two, who were, luckily for him, still afoot.

The end came quickly for one, that one being no match for a mounted, Cheyenne warrior. The other, however, would not give up so easily, and when War Cloud delivered what should have been a fatal knife-thrust, the man leapt onto him and pulled him from the horse.

Though stunned, War Cloud recovered rapidly enough and, grasping hold of his knife, lunged at the brave. But the Pawnee now held the upper hand, being armed with saber as well as knife, and no sooner had the fight begun when the Pawnee took the offense.

War Cloud darted one stab at him, another, then remembering a move that had once won him a fight, he jumped up in the air, stretching out both legs at the same time. He kicked his opponent as hard as he could.

The fellow, dazed by such a move, went down, but was back on his feet before War Cloud could finish the fight. War Cloud managed to kick the saber out of the man's hands at least, sending it out of reach, which caused the odds to be fairer.

The two men, on their feet, circled one another. One jab followed another, joined by another, still to no effect.

Without warning the Pawnee executed a lunge, grabbing hold of War Cloud and throwing him down. War Cloud made a desperate attempt to stop the downward motion of the man's knife, held that arm imprisoned in the air, straining . . . He almost had it . . .

A gun fired, and the Pawnee, surprise mirrored on his face, went stiff in War Cloud's grasp.

Realizing what had happened, War Cloud threw the man off him, and none too gently, either. As he leapt to his feet, anger shot through him.

"Who did that?" he asked in English before he'd had a chance to glance behind him. When he did so, he noted the alert poise of his brother, the woman, Anna, beside him, the gun in her hand and the shock of what she had done on her face.

He did not need an answer. Instead he asked another question, "Why did you not let me finish the fight? You killed him."

"He was going to murder you," came the female response.

"I was winning."

"I didn't see it that way," she countered.

"*Saaaa.*" Outrage stirred within him as he let out a breath, perhaps in an attempt to release some of his anger. It did not work. He trod right up to her, each step toward her a threat. He said, "You are not to interfere again, do you understand? When a man fights, it is to be a fair fight to the death. Anything else is a dishonor. Now, come help me turn these men facedown."

Although Lame Bird made a move to help him, the woman stood rooted, questioning, "Why?"

He sighed, annoyed. "Because it is bad luck to keep these men facing the sun."

"No, I didn't mean that." She paused a mere beat. "You didn't turn the men over at the train fight."

"Those men were white," he answered. "I did not care how their bodies were left."

He fingered the scalp lock of one of the dead Pawnee and unexpectedly heard the woman shriek. He glanced up at her, observing that she held her hand to her breast as though she were having difficulty breathing. She said, "You . . . you're not going to . . . to scalp these men . . . are you?"

"Hova'ahane." He threw the dead Pawnee's head back down to the ground, scalp lock still intact. Rising, he commented, "What good is a trophy when there is not one of my people here to sing its glory? Besides, you have brought dishonor to me today. I would have finished the fight fairly."

He watched her bristle. "And I, sir, would have my children safe," she declared, while she placed her hands on her waist as if to emphasize her words. However, the action gave emphasis to her small bone structure. It also caused War Cloud to note that not only had she discarded that ugly contraption of brown, this new piece of clothing complemented her in a way the brown dress never could have. She continued, "I did what I had to do. I saved your life that you might save ours. Perhaps now we are even. I no longer owe you my life."

He said nothing, his lack of response his acknowledgment.

Bending, he turned one of the men facedown, and straightening back up, he said both to her and his brother, "We will need to leave camp immediately. The warrior-whites cannot be far behind these scouts."

His brother nodded, while the woman said, "I will go and prepare the children."

War Cloud tried to rein in his reaction to this calm, logical statement, but he did so in vain. She had dishonored him on the field of battle, and this, combined with the aftereffects of combat, caused him to round on her. He said, "Go prepare the children, as well you should. It is this that you should have been doing from the start of the trouble. What would you have done if the Pawnee had won this fight? And you out here instead of hiding yourself with the children? Do you not know that your duty, when there is a fight, is to take the children and flee to safety? What good is it for me to fight if you get yourself killed?"

She raised that chin of hers straight up in the air and she countered, "What good are you to me dead?"

"*You* would at least be alive, and that is the point."

"But I would not survive without you to guide me."

Inwardly he cautioned himself to remain calm, yet for all his good intentions, he found himself closing what little distance remained between them, where he drew his face close to her face, menace in his tone, although his voice was barely over a whisper. He hissed, "You would survive. Do not doubt it. Yours is not a faint heart, that you would bow to death so easily. No, if there is another fight, I would have you know from here, now, until the end of our journey, you are to take the children and flee to safety. *That* is your duty. Do you understand?"

Her eyes spit fire, but she nodded, if a quick jerk of her head could be called a nod. She started to argue, saying, "But—"

"I will not debate this with you further. Do not cross me again. Now, go see to the children."

She opened her mouth, closed it, opened it again.

"I . . . I . . ." All at once, she threw back her shoulders as she countered, "I will do exactly as I see fit and I might as well let you know, Mr. War Cloud, that I will not be taking your orders now or in the future, and if I see fit to save you in order to ensure your life so that you can help me and the children, then that is exactly what I will do. And you should know, too, that if I leave now to go and see to the children, it is because *I* think it the best thing to do, not because you tell me to do it. Do *you* understand?"

Shocked by this sudden outburst, War Cloud found himself able to do little more than gape at her. With her brown-gold hair falling around her shoulders, with the blush of anger on her cheeks and the light of battle in her eye, she was beautiful . . .

Stunned to silence, he stared at her, watched as she flung herself around on her heel and headed back in the direction of the island.

He was looking at her still when his brother turned to him, asking, "Why were you so harsh to her?"

War Cloud could not answer right away. In truth, he barely heard the question. At last, however, sanity returned and, dragging his regard away from the woman, he shrugged, saying, "What she did was unthinking, and brought me dishonor."

"But she did not know."

War Cloud sighed and turned away from the sight of her. *"Haahe,* you are right, my brother. Still, it is enough that I am leading her and the children to safety. Must I also be kind to them every moment of the day?" He trod away from his brother, toward the waiting horse. "We had best leave quickly. You round up the remaining ponies while I go and erase all traces of our camp."

His brother signed agreement, while War Cloud went on to observe, "It is strange that the warrior-whites are this close into Dog Soldier country. It is not a good sign. They must have some reason to feel confident in their force." He paused, then noted as though talking to himself, "The sooner we release these whites back to their own kind, the safer we will be, I think."

With a shrug, Lame Bird nodded and sprinted off to go capture the other ponies.

Chapter 12

If those Pawnee were attached to the warrior-whites—and War Cloud was certain that they were—it was important to catch the remaining three ponies quickly, lest the animals return to their owners. Luckily Lame Bird accomplished the task in little time, returning to their camp as War Cloud was preparing to leave.

Climbing up the incline to the prairie, War Cloud met his brother at a distance from the island. The two exchanged greetings, whereupon War Cloud took possession of one of the ponies, leading it by its reins.

After a time, Lame Bird said, "*Na'neha,* my brother, I have been thinking. Our people will need to be warned of the danger, if there is any." As he talked, both Lame Bird and War Cloud slowed their step. Ahead of them, still on the island, waited the white woman and her children. But both brothers held back from going there. Lame Bird continued, "Why do you think our enemy was so close to Dog Soldier country?"

War Cloud inhaled deeply, his brows pulled together in a frown. At length, he said, "I believe they are the advance guard for a troop of warrior-whites. I cannot be certain, but it is the only explanation that makes any sense." He fell silent, until after a brief pause he said, "I am troubled by the Pawnees' manner. Did you see that they were overly confident? They showed no concern about traveling through our country, though the sun is high. It was as though they had no fear of meeting up with a Cheyenne war party." War Cloud's frown deepened. "I do not like it."

"Their trail is still fresh," said Lame Bird. "I could double back on their tracks and see if they lead me to the warrior-whites."

War Cloud nodded. "*Haahe,* that is a good thing to do. Follow us first, however. If there is danger in our country, I will need you to follow behind us and erase our tracks. Then go back and see what you can discover. Do not be gone longer than the night, however."

"*Haahe,*" said Lame Bird. Then, "If we go to Tall Bull's Dog Soldier camp—as we must—what do you plan to do with the woman?"

War Cloud hesitated. "I have no choice but to take her and the children into the camp."

"But she will not be safe there."

"I realize that," said War Cloud. "But the tribe must be warned. Perhaps our people will honor the old ways and not harm these captives."

"Perhaps." One of the horses nudged Lame Bird and absentmindedly, the boy began to pet it. Lame Bird said, "Will you give some of the captives to families who have lost a loved one in these wars?"

War Cloud grimaced. "I cannot."

If this statement startled Lame Bird, the youngster hid the fact well, for all he said was, "Why can you not?"

"Because I made a pact with the woman, promising her that I would take her to one of the white outposts where she can find homes for the children."

"Na'neha!" Lame Bird appeared startled. "It would be very dangerous to take these people to a white camp. Do you forget what happened to our cousin?"

"I do not forget."

"But the children could find homes with our people."

War Cloud sighed. "I thought so, too, at first. There are problems, however."

Lame Bird remained silent, a way of encouraging his brother to continue, but when War Cloud said nothing, Lame Bird went on to say, "Perhaps I could stay with the woman and children while you go into Tall Bull's camp and tell the elders and the chiefs what you have seen."

"I thought of that as well, but the plan is not sound. Have you forgotten how difficult it is to provide food for all of these people? You know that I cannot predict how long I would have to be in camp.

"And what if you were to be found by more Pawnee scouts, or worse, by the warrior-whites?" continued War Cloud. "No, *nasemahe,* my younger brother, I made a mistake once in leaving you in the Kiowa camp where I thought you would be safe. Yet look at what happened. You were recognized by those men of the white race who have no spirit. And you were captured when the Kiowa camp fell. *Hova'ahane,* I swore that I would never repeat that mistake again."

Lame Bird nodded. "Then I think, *na'neha,* that you should tell her what you are doing and why."

"Why should I? She is a hostage."

"Because she is more than that, and I believe, too, *na'neha*, that you know it."

War Cloud remained silent. What could he say? To deny his brother's claim would be to lie.

Yet, for all his attempt at truthfulness, War Cloud could not quite admit to the eagerness with which he awaited more contact and more conversation—even to their sparring—with the white woman. In essence, such acute awareness of the woman puzzled him.

"I think," said Lame Bird, "that if my brother were to look into his heart, he might discover that part of his anger at the woman today was the shock of seeing her so close to danger."

War Cloud cringed, his brother's words being too close to the truth.

Lame Bird continued, "If I were my brother, I would find a time that is right and tell her. It is the only way, for I do not believe that she would willingly follow you into one of our camps unless you convince her that she must."

War Cloud grinned. "I fear you speak the truth, *nasemahe*."

Lame Bird smiled, while War Cloud laid a hand upon the lad's shoulder, an expression of affection.

War Cloud said, "I will think on this, *nasemahe*, my brother." And with no more to be said, the two siblings began their descent down to the island.

But War Cloud's concerns could not be put aside so easily, for he could not help feeling that there were sentiments at play between this woman and himself that he dared not examine too closely. Certainly his body behaved as though it would like nothing more than to roll her upon the ground.

Startled at the direction of his thoughts, War Cloud tightened his mouth. He could not afford to develop feelings for this woman—for any woman.

So it was with a feeling of relief that War Cloud sent up a prayer to the Above Ones, thanking them for making this woman the same as his enemies, a white woman. At least in this way War Cloud could ensure that he would never fall in love with her . . .

Because they were in country controlled by the southern Cheyenne, War Cloud had explained to Anna that he would not have to run off these particular ponies. Their party would be able to keep the mounts, thus allowing ten of the children to ride.

It left only three of their party to walk, since neither War Cloud nor his younger brother had demanded to ride. That this action on his part had done much to stir Anna's admiration, she refused to consider. She was still too angry at him.

Collin, because he was one of the older boys, had volunteered to walk. It was interesting because, as though by some mutual consent, a friendship had sprung up between Lame Bird and Collin. Even now, as she glanced behind her, Anna could see the two boys pulling up their troop's rear, with Lame Bird instructing Collin on how best to erase a trail.

Anna, herself, trudged along after the four ponies, carrying the youngster, Patty, on her hip. But the Kansas heat and humidity were almost tearing her apart.

That, along with the incredible pace that War Cloud kept, might account for Anna's constant lagging behind their group. Still, she was happy. The children were riding and not wearing themselves out unnecessarily, and Collin was happier than she had ever seen him.

She chanced to send a glance up, far ahead of her, there to catch sight of War Cloud's tall form. She frowned. He looked entirely too lively and spry, she feared, while she felt as though she were wilting.

She reminded herself that she was not too happy with him. In fact, so angry had she been that after the island fight, she had vowed she would never again speak to the man. How dare he order her about as though she were no more than his slave to command?

But she had to admit that when he and his brother had caught all four horses, putting the children upon them without even a hint from her to do so, Anna had felt herself weakening toward him. Kindness and humility fairly exuded from such an act, and Anna had realized, as she had watched, that these were not the actions of a lord and master.

Unfortunately—at least in her consideration it was unfortunate—any resentment she might have been harboring toward the man had died a quiet death right then.

Though these actions by no means wiped away War Cloud's harshness toward her, she had also realized that perhaps some of his anger had been misplaced because of the fight. It was not because of her.

It did not make his anger any better and it certainly did not excuse him. It was only that she understood.

She watched War Cloud now as he led their small party. He had given Collin a weapon to use, handing over some knives, as well, to the other older children. A necessity, he had said, out here on the plains.

"Are we ever going to stop and rest?" asked Patty.

"Yes, dear, we are. But not until we're out of danger."

"I'm hungry."

"I know, darling, so am I. But we must keep going until there is little likelihood that we will be attacked. As it is, we're taking a chance, moving about in the daylight. But War Cloud says that we have to be on the move quickly."

"I like his name."

"Yes, I do, too," Anna answered.

"He's handsome, isn't he, Miss Wiley?"

Surprised by the astute observation, whatever Anna might have said in response, stuck in her throat. What could she say? she wondered, when in truth, she considered the man more than merely handsome. His look was exciting, exotic and more thrilling than the rather simple image that the word, "handsome" evoked. But yes, she admitted to herself, he cut a very handsome figure, indeed.

Patty gave her a strange look. "Don't you think so, Miss Wiley?"

"Hmmm?"

"Don't you think he's handsome, Miss Wiley?" the child asked again.

Anna gulped. "Yes," she said at last. "I believe I do."

Patty grinned and drew her arms around Anna's neck. "I think he likes you, too."

Anna scoffed. "I think not."

As though Anna had not said a thing, however, Patty continued, "When he looks at you, his eyes go all soft."

"They do?" Anna cast the youngster a brief glance. Such adult observations from this child—her Patty, her artist.

"Yes, they do," confirmed Patty. "Maybe you should marry him. Do you think you might, Miss Wiley?"

Anna did not know how to respond to the youngster. She was certain the children knew nothing of the pact she had presented to War Cloud, a pact he had accepted, she reminded herself, yet . . .

"What do you think, Miss Wiley, do you think you might marry him? If you did and he liked me, too, maybe you could adopt me yourself."

Anna wanted to cry. "Oh, Patty," she murmured, catching her breath. "I would love to adopt you, but it is impossible."

"Why is it?" answered Patty. "I think you're pretty when you don't wear that ugly dress."

Anna could only smile, such was the honesty of children.

"And besides," continued Patty, "I think I'd like to stay with you forever."

Anna's heart constricted with pain since, if the truth were known, she would love to keep Patty with her. But it could never be, and Anna could barely keep her voice level as she said, "And I'd love to have you with me forever, Patty."

"Would you really?"

Anna could not speak this time; her voice wouldn't let her. She nodded toward Patty instead.

Patty gave her one of the biggest hugs Anna had ever received, before she settled back onto Anna's hip. Quite astutely, she asked, "Am I too heavy?"

"Not at all, dear," Anna lied. "Don't worry about it. You're just fine, darling, just fine."

Yet, with the combination of the sun beating down on

her and the ungodly humidity, Anna thought she might surely collapse at any moment. As it was, it was all she could do to place one foot in front of the other.

Also, amidst the scurry to leave, Anna had somehow lost the brown dress. And though secretly she rejoiced at its loss—since the garment had been too hot for comfortable travel—more guardedly she would admit that she felt more vulnerable without the outer layer of clothing; more feminine, prettier perhaps, but definitely more defenseless.

The situation also left her to travel in nothing more than her chemise and skirt, a circumstance that, had she lost the dress only a few days previous, would have startled her no end. Now, however, she felt little embarrassment about her predicament, only the joy of knowing that the lack of excess clothing was helping to keep her a little cooler.

She was glad to note that ahead of them, War Cloud appeared to have stopped and Anna, upon drawing closer, saw the reason for it. Their party had come to a stream. Frustration gave way to joy and she felt her step quicken in anticipation.

The horses were the first to wade into the water, and despite their precious loads, the animals lowered their heads to drink.

The children, who were none of them experienced riders, sent nervous glances back at Anna, and drawing at last level to the water, she set Patty down on the shoreline and ventured into the stream. The task of taking each child from the horse and carrying him to shore became quite lengthy, exhaustion settling within her too soon.

Shortly, however, Collin came up to give her a hand,

while Lame Bird and War Cloud sat beside the stream, watching.

She knew she crossed cultural barriers when she called out to War Cloud, "You could help."

He simply shook his head in response and smiled at her. He said, "Next you will want me to wear dresses."

She gave his figure a quick glance, deciding that even in a dress this man would look much too masculine and all too handsome. However, she would keep that observation to herself.

She said, "In the white man's world, men help the women with this chore."

Again he smiled back at her, observing, "When my skin changes to white, I will help you."

That sassy statement had her biting her tongue. Darn the man. He had almost made her laugh.

At last her chore was done, and she began to help each child to drink, finding the task unnecessary. Instinctively the children knew what to do.

War Cloud watched them with seeming patience, she noted, although now and again, she observed him scanning the area around them.

Presently, he stood up and paced toward her.

Drawing to her side, he said, "Wait here with the children and do not follow me. I am going to see if there are signs of an enemy nearby. If there is no evidence of an adversary, we might stop here for a while and rest. Also, I think there might be some shelter ahead for us, and if there is, we will go there for the afternoon to rest." He pushed a knife into her hands. "Do you still have your gun?"

She nodded.

"Do not be afraid to use it, or this knife. Your life may depend on it."

Again, she nodded.

And then it happened. He brought up his hand to run a finger through a lock of her hair, his gaze upon that single tress, intense.

What was he thinking? What was he doing? Did he find her attractive? He could not, and yet . . .

Anna could not speak. Alas, she could barely breathe.

In a whisper he said, "Leave your hair free."

Anna swallowed with difficulty and wondered, did his eyes really go soft whenever he looked at her?

She stared up at him; she could do little else. At the same time, she tried desperately to read his thoughts. But it was impossible.

Murmuring softly, "I will," she wondered, *Will what?* Will stay with the children? Will leave her hair down? Will become his wife?

She almost groaned at the direction of her thoughts and she worried briefly that he might be a mind reader. But he pushed away from her so quickly, she felt as though she had been left in midair.

She prompted herself to feel her feet beneath her and she wiggled her toes as if to make sure she still stood on solid ground. And letting her breath out slowly, she watched as he trod away from her.

He was giving her a moment of reprieve, a moment in which to collect herself. But she knew that opportunity was as fleeting as a drop of moisture under the Kansas heat. Something was happening between herself and this man and she did not know what it was. She wondered if he did.

And, though she could little understand it, he seemed to find something in her that was attractive. And, the good Lord forgive her, she liked that attention . . .

They camped beneath a grove of cottonwoods and willows, the majority of the trees growing next to a babbling stream. Anna noted that several of the willows had boughs which hung down, dipping into the water. Glancing toward those branches, she knew a moment of camaraderie with the plants.

She felt miserable in the heat. Even though War Cloud had led their party only a few miles away from where they had recently stopped for a drink, the journey here had seemed interminable.

Frankly, Anna felt as though she were shriveling up under the relentless sun, and the children did not appear to be faring much better. War Cloud, however, looked as fresh and undisturbed as when they had first started their trek; a circumstance that found her casting him envious glances from time to time.

How did he do it? She would have to remember to ask him about it at the first opportunity.

However, once they had stopped long enough to set up camp and she'd had the chance to contemplate him more thoroughly, she had observed that War Cloud appeared anxious. She had inquired about it, but had received no more than his typical monosyllabic replies in response.

Still, when she inspected his countenance fully, she knew with certainty that something bothered him. Was an enemy in their vicinity?

She wished she had the nerve to quiz him extensively

about it, but she knew it would do her no good. Perhaps it was no more than exhaustion, anyway.

But no matter, her energy resources were exhausted and she did not feel she had the strength at present to pull out of him whatever were his concerns. At least not right now. Perhaps later.

And so it was that with this thought uppermost in her mind, she curled up onto her side and fell into an exhausted sleep; a sleep filled with visions of a handsome Indian who somehow found something in her that was attractive.

Chapter 13

She awoke to the sounds of evening. Off in the distance trilled the melody of hundreds of crickets, while closer at hand came the quavering refrains of doves. An occasional burst of the night hawk's warble accompanied the evening's racket, and she would have to have been deaf to miss the incessant croon of the locust.

Listening, Anna extended her arms above her head while a wave of contentment washed over her. She sighed longingly, breathing in the humid and earthy, although somewhat cooler, air. She stretched, leisurely, as though she had all the time in the world.

As the evening continued to fall about her and she breathed deeply, Anna decided that the air here smelled fuller, cleaner and healthier than it had in any other part of the country. It was also less humid since evening had descended upon them, and as she opened her eyes, she stared straight up into the branches of a tree. That those limbs waved in the wind seemed somehow romantic, the natural clamor of the stirring leaves thrilling to her, as though the wind and the trees were giving notice of another imminent storm.

How long had she slept? she wondered. She remembered that War Cloud had set up camp late in the afternoon, right here beneath these few shade trees, but beyond that she recalled nothing. She had gone to sleep almost at once.

She became alert for sounds that would tell her that the children might also have awakened. She heard nothing, however, that would cause her to think they had, and moving sluggishly, she turned onto her side.

She caught her breath at once; held it, then let it out slowly, noiselessly. Directly in front of her sat War Cloud, his back to her, and she allowed herself a short while to study him.

What a fine figure he cut, she decided. He had let loose his long, black hair and the effect was astonishing to her. Why, she concluded, his hair might be as long as hers. Odd, she had become used to seeing him with two braids caught at both sides of his face, and for some reason that hairstyle, or perhaps her lack of observing him closely, had failed to give her a clue as to its true length. Nonetheless, at present those locks fell gently down his back, their descent unencumbered by the quiver of arrows he usually wore, although a strand or two of his hair waved now and again in the wind.

Wondering what he might have done with his quiver, she flashed a quick glance down to his side, observing that he had set it in a ready position next to him, along with his spear and shotgun.

Uninterested in the weapons, however, she returned her study to the man himself, noting that his shoulders were broad in the extreme, his back unusually straight even though he appeared to be leisurely reclining. Plus, if she allowed herself to look there, glimpses of his buttocks and bare legs peeked out at the sides of his breechcloth.

Previously, she had refused to stare at that portion of his anatomy, considering such curiosity indecent. Nevertheless, she began to rethink her attitude.

She had to admit that, while she had practically melted under the Kansas heat, this man had remained cool. God willing, she conceded, there might be some logic to his style of dress.

At present, he sat before her cross-legged and alert; he alone being watchful while the rest of their party slumbered.

She was impressed. Such vigilance would require discipline and a willpower of steel, she decided, for she realized how horribly tired she had been after their afternoon march. She had been unable to keep her eyes open.

Yet he had not only led them here, he had remained on guard. Admiration for his hardiness stirred to life within her, as well as an awareness of . . . what? It was more than mere thankfulness; it was a sense of respect she felt, as well as perhaps a feeling of . . .

What made her want to reach out and touch him? Her fingers itched to do so, as though they possessed a will that was independent of her own.

Regardless, she might have done it, but in that instant he looked quickly over his shoulder. Gasping, she cast her glance in another direction. A nervous sort of trepidation washed over her, reminding her of the sensation she'd had when, as a child, she had been caught in the act of stealing a sweet.

If he noticed anything peculiar, however, she did not

know it, for his response at seeing her awake was no more than a brief, "Humph!"

"And good evening to you, too," she countered, staring back at him, her voice perhaps more brisk than was necessary.

He did not respond to her, however, and after a short while, she asked, "Have you seen any sign of an enemy?"

"Humph!" came the response she was beginning to expect from him.

She sat up, straightening her petticoats around her. "I was only wondering," she justified, although why she needed a reason to ask him questions was beyond her.

Again came that terse, "Humph!" Although in a trice, he added, "Had there been sign of any enemy, I would have awakened you."

If she was supposed to be properly chastised for the simple act of asking a question, she refused to rise to the bait. She said instead, "Would you like me to sit watch while you rest?"

He did not respond. At least not in words. She did notice his entire body stiffening, however.

She tried again, "Would you?"

She heard a low, guttural sound come from his throat and then, "First you try to entice me into doing women's work," he reprimanded, "and now you try to take my duty from me. What is it you wish? Would you rather I wear dresses?"

"I . . . The thought hadn't entered my mind. I am only trying to be kind to you. I realize that you must be tired."

"Humph!"

"I was trying to be helpful."

"Then maybe you should do your women's work without complaint. That would be helpful."

"Why, I . . ." She bit her tongue. Differences in culture, she tried to tell herself. That was all this was. The two of them were merely experiencing a divergence in etiquette. There was no reason to feel anger. She simply did not know what he expected of her, and he did not know what she considered polite behavior. Although sometimes, she admitted to herself, she had the impression that this man deliberately antagonized her.

Still, what did he consider women's work? She said, "If you are talking about what happened earlier today, there by the stream, I think you misunderstood. I was merely commenting that a white man is more considerate of his woman when he sees that she is tired and is yet required to do physical work."

"Were you?"

"Yes, I was."

"And is it more considerate," he asked, "that the man be caught off guard by an enemy or by a wild animal when he is helping his woman?"

"What do you mean?"

"Is it not better that a man stand on guard, watching out for the weaker ones, ready to fight an enemy if the need to do so presents itself?"

"I . . ." She stopped. She did not know what to say. Unfortunately, for the sake of argument, what he said made perfect sense.

He did not wait for her to continue, however, and he went on to say, "In my camp you would have been chastised for asking me to help you. It is a man's duty to protect his family, not to do the women's work. Most Indian women take pride in what they do and do not wish their man's assistance. Were I to have tried to help a Cheyenne woman in this way, she would have been insulted."

"But—"

"She would have thought that I was telling her, with my 'help,' that she was not worthy of my protection. Is it this, that you wish from me? Do you not feel deserving of the safety I give you?"

"I . . ." She paused for the beat of a second. "No," she continued, "I . . . thank you, I guess. But you see, it is the way of things in my society that a man, because he is stronger than a woman, will help her with physical work."

"Humph! Look around you, *Nahkohe-tseske*. You are no longer in the country of your people."

"I know, but . . . there are so many things I do not know about your country, Mister War Cloud, as there are things in my society that would be strange to you, also. Could we not call a truce as regards our differences?"

He did not answer right away and she explained further, "Please try to understand, I am not attempting to be difficult. I simply do not know what you expect of me. And, if you are honest, you will admit that you know little about what is considered good behavior in my society."

"Humph!" came the response that was beginning to become irritating. He said, "I do not care to know it."

She cleared her throat. "That may be. However, we have been thrown into one another's company against our will. We could try to understand one another, couldn't we?"

He did not answer, and unexpectedly, she took courage from his silence.

She came up onto her knees and scooted toward him, settling herself beside him. She chanced a glance up at him, immediately catching her breath. There were lines of worry upon this man's face, and she found herself asking at once, "Is something wrong?"

"Humph!"

One of the children stirred in his sleep and she sent a hasty glance toward that spot, letting out her breath as she watched the child settle back down. Returning her attention to War Cloud, she asked once more, "Is something worrying you?"

Again, no response.

"Something is, isn't it?"

"I do not worry . . . so much," he added.

"I see," she acknowledged. "Then might you tell me what it is that isn't worrying you . . . so much?"

He shrugged. "I suppose I must tell you sooner or later. I have known that I must."

She drew in a quick breath and threw back her head, as though she were to meet a conflict rather than a simple statement of fact. Although she asked only, "What is it?" she watched as a muscle twitched in his cheek.

He snapped his head to the left, chin out, a gesture she was beginning to recognize as typical for him. After a short while he said, "Those Pawnee at the fight were very close to Dog Soldier country. They took a great chance in coming this close to my people's land; this they knew. It makes me believe, because of their lack of fear, that they must have been the advance guard for a column of warrior-whites. If this is true, then these whites are seeking out my people in order to kill them. I have sent my brother and his white friend, Collin, back along our trail to see if my suspicions are true."

"Oh," she uttered without pause, "this could, indeed, be a problem." After a moment she asked, "Forgive me, War Cloud, for I know you have more to say, but I must ask you, what are the Dog Soldiers?"

His brows drew together and that same muscle tapped angrily in his cheek, but he did not hesitate to answer, saying, "The Dog Soldiers are a Cheyenne military society. It is one that used to be an esteemed order of the Cheyenne people. However, many years ago the leader of this society disgraced himself by killing another Cheyenne. Even though the act was committed in self-defense, the laws of our tribe banished him.

"There were many of his relatives and friends who followed this leader into his exile, and together, they set up their own camp, becoming a militant society. They are now the most feared of any group of warriors, for they will fight to the death to protect what is theirs."

Anna moistened her dry lips and swallowed, hard, as a thought occurred to her. She asked, "And are you a part of this society?"

"I am one of its leaders."

"I see," she said, as one thought followed upon another and she asked, "And the fight at the train, those were your men who struck us?"

He nodded.

"And so it is really you who are responsible for the deaths of all those people," she pressed on.

He must have heard the censure in her voice, for he sent her a glance laced with contempt. "I am at war with the whites," he said.

"But not those particular people," she uttered, stating her viewpoint on the matter even though she knew he would disagree.

"The bounty hunters captured my brother," he responded. "They abused him and knew I would come after him. They were prepared for what would happen and it was a good fight. Those whites are not as innocent as you would make them seem, I think."

She raised her chin. "I agree that the bullies got what was coming to them, but there were innocent people killed, too, a friend of mine among them."

"That is true, yet the law of the prairie is, a life for a life, and I have many more lives to take before I can say that I have avenged the deaths of my family and my friends."

She paused. While it was a fact that she might understand this point of view, she could never agree that one innocent life should pay for the death of another. "Yet," she breathed, "the laws of my God say differently. Only those who kill should be punished, not those who had no hand in it."

"Then you should teach these values to your children when they are young so that they do not kill innocent Indian women and children. Or are you like the other whites who believe that only a white life is of any worth?"

"That was a harsh blow, Mister War Cloud," she countered. "You must know, from my actions, that I do not share others' prejudice."

"Humph!"

She became silent. He did know that, didn't he? She said, "There are many other white people like myself who are not prejudiced and who want only peace."

"Had the white man wanted peace," came the instantaneous reply, "he would have talked peace at Sand Creek, because the Indians were there under a truce; we were there to talk about reconciliation. For many days there had been peace talks and the soldier-whites visited our camp often. Yet you know what happened. Either you speak with a forked tongue or your words contain no experience with these warrior-whites. Had the white man stayed his hand at Sand Creek, there would have been peace, for the Cheyenne wanted harmony to return to the land. I know. I was there."

Her expression stilled. She was certain that he spoke wisely, for as he said, he had been there and surely knew what the Indians had planned and what the warrior-whites—as he called them—had done. And yet, was it wise to blame an entire race for the injustices of a few?

Anna said, "The white man was wrong at Sand Creek. And if you were to visit with the leaders in the East, you would see that you would get their agreement on that."

"And if I could do that, how would that help the Indian people? What would that give them that they do not already have?"

"Understanding?"

"Humph! Our leaders visited our father in the East many times in a place called, Washington. Lean Bear went to that place in the year the white man calls 1863. Black Kettle, the great peace leader, went there in the year 1864. Bull Bear and White Antelope were there, too.

They are gone. They listened to the great white father who spoke of peace. They believed him and trusted him, only to be killed by these frontier warrior-whites who do not recognize Indian rights. Would you have the Indian give up his life, his women, his children and all that he holds dear to become no more than slave to these warrior-whites? You tell me now, what good would come from the Indian going there in the East?"

Anna's brows pulled together in a frown and she hesitated. She had not known all those delegations of Indians had gone to Washington on a mission of armistice. Nor did she understand why the white man in this territory did not listen to the words of those in governmental power, for she was certain the United States government would not sanction many of the military's actions here.

She said, "I don't know what to tell you. I really don't know what good might come of going there. Maybe you are right and it would do no good whatsoever."

No expression crossed his face, although the muscles in his neck worked violently. He observed, "Sometimes a man must make a stand for what he believes is right. The Cheyennes are making such a stand now."

"But—"

"There comes a point when a person must be willing to fight for what is right. There are some things more important than one's life. One's home, one's way of life, the people one loves, are all such a cause."

Anna, completely at a loss, sat watching him. Honor, duty and a sense of justice emanated from this man. Yet, though his words were filled with wisdom, she also recognized their hopelessness. She became aware, perhaps for the first time, that the Indians were on the correct side of the law. They were not the interlopers they were being made out to be. They were fighting for their homes and their right to live as a people, and because of this, they would fight to the death.

Yet they were doomed. She knew it and perhaps he did, too. The white man was better armed and had more friends in Washington to plead the side of his cause. It was the white man's words, not the Indians', that would be heard.

The realization of this made her want to reach out to him. She could not help it. He looked so proud and yet his cause was so hopeless that she found it almost impossible to withhold herself.

In truth, she could not. She placed a delicate hand on his shoulder, surprised to feel his muscles quiver beneath her touch.

Dear God, this man is vulnerable.

The thought came as though from some deep recess within her. Despite his gruffness, his curt manner and stoic indifference, this man felt things deeply.

Oh, how she would love to wipe away his worry. If only she could, she would wave her hand and dispel all the troubles that existed between their two peoples. How she wished it could be that simple.

But she was not capable of such magic and she found she could only give him a lesser compensation, her words. She said, "I am so sorry for the trouble between our societies. Please, tell me more. Is it merely the threat of the cavalry in this country that worries you? Or do you think you will not be able to warn your people in time?"

"I will get to them in time," he commented, his features rigid. Nor did he spare her a glance.

"Then what is it?"

He shifted uncomfortably, though his profile remained majestic. After the beat of several moments, he answered, "I must take you and the children to the camp of my people."

She digested this in silence. At length, she commented, "They will want to kill us, won't they?"

"*Haahe,* they will." He sent her a quick glance, as though to measure her reaction.

What had he expected? That she might rant and rave? Did he think she would stoop so low as that? Or worse, that she would not understand?

He really did not know her, if he could think these things about her. She asked, calmly, "What are we to do about it?"

He shrugged. "We will have to hope that my people will abide by the old Cheyenne custom that it is the worst of crimes to abuse captives. I fear, though, that the hostilities run so deep, that there will be a few weakened hearts who will not stop until they have your scalp."

"Oh," was was her only comment, as she struggled to remain as calm as she could, given the circumstances. "Could you not leave us somewhere else?" she suggested. "Could you go into camp, warn your people and then return to us?"

"And who would save you if the Pawnee or some other tribe might come upon you?"

"I have a gun."

"And who would feed you? Have you not noticed how difficult a task this is? There are thirteen of you."

Undaunted, she offered, "I'm sure we could manage for a few days."

"You would not last a day, and I must be in camp longer than a mere few days."

"And if your people don't respect the old ways?"

"I will not raise my hand against my own countrymen. I understand their hatred, although in your case I might make an exception."

Anna fell silent. She could not permit this man to take them into his camp. That was all there was to it. She was going to have to convince him to leave them here—alone. Even if it meant potential disaster, it would be better than taking the more certain risk to the children's lives in the Cheyenne camp.

"Please, Mister War Cloud," she said, "leave us here. We will manage somehow."

"I cannot."

"Then let us wait for your brother to return and send him into your camp. You could then stay here with us yourself."

"Do you think I have not already considered this? But there are problems with that, for my people would ask him where I am and he would tell them."

"I see. But he wouldn't have to mention us."

"Do you think not?" He sent her a sulking glance. "A scout is a trusted being amongst all the Indians. His must be a tongue that never rests in deceit. He must tell the people all he knows; he must tell it straight and to the best of his ability. My brother would have no choice but to mention you and the children. Besides, do you forget that I sent my warriors on ahead, before me? They know that you accompany me. If I did not come into camp, it would appear that I am hiding you. We would be sought out by the others and I would end up having to fight my own kin.

"This is not something I can or will do," he continued. "No, the best thing to do is to take you into the village as though there is nothing wrong. This might be your only protection."

"I understand," she noted, gently touching one of his hands. "And yet, it is a chance I am unwilling to take. Could you not lead us to a white settlement before you go to your people?"

"And delay reporting the danger?" He clenched his jaw. "Know that we are in Dog Soldier country where there are no white settlements. I would have to go very far out of my way to take you to one. By the time I returned, the warrior-whites might have attacked, perhaps killing hundreds of my people. No, I cannot do it."

"I see," she said, and she did. Nonetheless, she tried another tack. "I will not go with you to your village willingly."

"I know this."

"Then how do you propose to get me into your camp?"

"I will have to tie you up, I suppose."

She sat up stiffly.

Grinning, he glanced to his side and shook his head. "Though the idea has much merit," he said, "still, it has its own problems."

She sat up straighter, folding her knees under her as though she might jump up at any moment. She said, "I should hope so."

"There is one way to keep you safe, but I do not like to put it to you."

"Oh?" she asked. "Please, what is it?"

"You will not like it."

She cut a brief glance at him before turning aside.

"Still," she said, "you could tell me about it and let me decide for myself."

He grimaced. "Do not say that I did not warn you."

"I won't."

He sighed and waved a hand in the direction of the children, saying, "I think that all your children will have to be my own."

She arched a brow at him, as though she expected him to elaborate. When he did not, a look of noncomprehension crossed her face.

He caught her glance, appeared to understand her confusion and went on to explain, "And in order to make them mine, I would have to take you now as a man takes a woman . . ."

Chapter 14

She wondered if her eyes mirrored her shock. Yes, she knew she had pledged herself to marry this man, but now . . . ?

As a man takes a woman? Perhaps she was mistaken, but that did not sound to her as if War Cloud meant marriage. Or did he?

"A-are you saying you wish to marry me in all due haste?" she stammered.

"*Haahe,* we must commit the act that is shared between a man and his wife."

She froze. "The act . . . ?"

He sent her a knowing glance. He said, "*Haahe,* the physical deed that binds a man to a woman."

She could not look him in the eye and, as she felt a blush spread across her cheeks, she feared he would have little trouble reading her thoughts.

She commented, "I, ah, think that is a little drastic, don't you?"

"What means this word, 'drastic'?"

She hesitated. "It means extreme, rather harsh."

"*Saaa,* not drastic," he said, "but . . . necessary. If I am to keep you and the children safe in my camp, then you and all of them must pretend to be mine. It would have to be a good act, too, for we will have to convince the others."

"Pretend?"

"*Haahe*, pretend."

"But—"

"I have been pondering other ways to ensure you are safe. And though I have thought a great deal about it, I have found no other resolution that might work. Still, I have been looking within myself to try to understand if perhaps I am the problem. But I fear that even if I am, there is no other way, I think."

"I see," she said, although did she? She tried to swallow, realized her throat was too dry, and fell into silence. Nevertheless, a sudden kindling of inspiration had her asking, "What do you mean, that you could be the problem?"

He did not answer, his look at her irritated, before he shot his glance away. But in that brief glimpse, quick though it was, she realized that he invited her to read his thoughts.

She did not have such mental powers, however, and after a time, she proffered, "We wouldn't have to do the deed, so to speak . . . in order to make the pretense good, would we? As long as we're married, no one would know the difference but you and me."

He sent her a frown. "I have considered this. It would be easier on you at first."

"Good."

"It would also mean your death, most likely."

"What?" She drew her breath in so quickly, the air almost hissed. She asked, "Why?"

He twisted his chin to the left, obviously piqued. He said nothing.

One moment followed upon another until, almost beside herself, she touched his arm. Exasperated or not, the man needed to communicate his concerns to her, not let her guess. She asked again, "Why could we not just pretend the whole thing without needing to . . . to . . . ?"

He held up a hand, as though he might interject something, but he remained silent. When he did, at last, mouth some words, it was only to ask his own question. "Are you so innocent that you do not know my problem?"

She felt as though her head were spinning. She asked, "Know what?"

More silence.

Her curiosity was turning into a tangible quality by the time she spoke up, "Please, I don't know what it is that you're implying."

He grunted, and she had the strange suspicion that this big ferocious warrior was exhibiting signs of . . . reticence.

She prompted, "Know what?"

He said it so quickly, she could barely believe he had spoken. Worse, she had not heard him, his words being lost to the wind. She said, "I did not hear that. Could you say it again?"

He let out his breath in a rush before uttering, under his breath, "I desire you, and that is the problem."

Though said quickly, that comment made her go completely still. Had the earth suddenly opened up and swallowed her whole?

She cleared her throat, tried to speak, but all that came out of her mouth was a croak. Licking her lips, she glanced away from him, out into the night.

He desired her? This extraordinarily handsome man wanted *her*? In a sexual way? And this was a problem?

Strangely enough, her body was behaving to his declaration in a highly feminine way. Tiny flickerings of pleasure pulsed over her nervous system, the whole of it settling like butterflies somewhere in her midsection. It made her want to respond to him in kind, made her want to touch him, to hold him, to be touched and to be held in return.

But she could do none of that. Still, she knew she had to say something, anything, but what?

She gulped and tried to voice a response, at length coming up with the highly intelligent words, "I . . . I . . . ah . . ."

She gave it up.

He saved her the trouble and asserted, "Surely you have known this."

She? Known it? Again, she tried to speak; opened her mouth, closed it. It was impossible.

He continued, "I do not know how this has come to be a difficulty, especially since you are white. But recently . . ." He shook his head, staring away from her as he left the rest unsaid.

"Recently . . . ?" she prodded.

He took a deep breath and resumed, "The others in my camp would see through me at once, I fear. I could, of course, seek out a willing widow in the camp and take care of my carnal feelings in this way. But word of this would fly through the camp like a devil wind, and our secret would soon be out. I would be caught out in the lie, and because our people are at war, you would be imperiled."

Surely, she thought, the lump in her throat would diminish with time, wouldn't it? For she found she could do no more than moan.

But even the sound of her voice appeared to have an unsettling effect upon him, for when he glanced at her, such fervor filled his eyes, she thought his look might set her afire. She could feel a flush rising and a tingling sensation spread over her body all the way down to her toes. Indeed, so intense was her reaction to this man, her heart pounded as though to alert every perceptive point within her body that pleasure awaited. In fact, she feared her heart's beating was so loud, he could hear it.

He said, "You have already offered yourself to me. So this is not something you have not, yourself, considered. Would it be so bad to give yourself to me now instead of later?"

She tried again to speak; she wet her lips with that distinct purpose in mind. She opened her mouth. Nothing happened.

Meanwhile, he reached out and covered her hand with his own. He said, "I promise that I will try to make your first experience good."

She gulped. The good Lord be praised, the moment the man touched her, she was lost. A yearning for something she could not explain, something deep and consuming, swamped her so utterly, she found herself wanting to . . . caress him. It was practically a physical need.

Yet, on another level of awareness, his words about her, about the children, suddenly hit her. And she wept with realization. In truth, so caught up was she in the newness of these sensations, she had forgotten about the children and their welfare.

She blinked. How could she? How irresponsible of her, she inwardly scolded, perhaps criticizing herself too harshly. Nonetheless, she felt the lesser for her brief lapse in duty.

Possibly it was this sense of guilt, however, that at last gave her the ability to speak, and she found herself able to murmur, "And did you want to . . . to consummate this pact between us tonight?"

She heard his low groan, the sound of his voice sending shivers of erotica erupting along her already strained nerves. Ultimately, however, he commented, "I would have you consider it first. There are a few days before we will arrive in the camp of my people."

"And . . . and you think this will save our lives?"

"It is the only thing I can think of that will. For, as I have said before, many of my countrymen will want to take some of the children into their own homes—to replace those of their own lost in the war. And as for you, unless you pretend to be married to me, giving me full rights over you, there are some within my camp who may desire to abuse you, as many of our women have been used. *Hova'ahane,* I fear that I can envision no other way for us."

"I see." She drew in a deep, strained breath before muttering, "But I don't see where the pretense of a marriage comes into this. If we marry, we marry, and I suppose a woman must at some time realize that with marriage comes the act for which man and woman . . . that is to say . . ."

She glanced at War Cloud, who was giving her the strangest look—as though he were seeing her for the first time.

He opened his mouth to say something, closed it and glanced away from her. Momentarily, however, he said, "Know, white woman, that I am not offering you marriage. I never have."

Not offer her marriage? What sort of lie was this? She said, "You most certainly did. I even remember you proposing."

He scowled at her. "That is not possible . . . Try to remember back, *Nahkohe-tseske,* to a few nights ago, when you came to me on the hill and suggested that we lie with one another."

"I made *no* such suggestion."

"It appeared that way to me."

She began to fume. The man had to be insane. She had not made an indecent overture to him, she had been forming a pact, a treaty. Yes, it might have been a rather personal settlement, but that was all it was.

She reiterated, "I made a pact to stay with you *if* you performed your duty to take the children to a white settlement. It was a treaty between the two of us. Nothing more."

He leered at her. "I think it was a womanly advance, for I never agreed to marry you. You told me you would be mine. You did not mention marriage and . . . what was I to think?"

"But I meant—"

He held up a hand. "That is not what you said."

Fury rose up within her. But whether it was directed at herself or at him, she would have been hard-pressed to tell. Especially because it was true. That was exactly what she had told him.

But she had thought that he would understand her; that she could never contemplate such an act with him without marriage.

She sat back. Well, what was she do to now?

At length, she observed, "And so now you want to seal this arrangement with the . . . the intimate act of marriage without actually *being* married? Let us be specific. Is this what you are asking of me?"

"It is either that or get yourself killed."

She made a harsh noise with her tongue, scoffing him. "There must be some other way. I refuse to believe that this, and this alone, will ensure the lives of my children . . . You realize that you are asking me to become a woman of ill repute?"

He made no comment.

"I would run away from you first, that's what I'd do."

"Fine," he said. "Do it then, but I think you would get yourself and the children killed."

"Why?"

He shrugged, as though that were answer enough, and made a move to get to his feet, but she reached out to detain him.

She asked, "If I did leave, why do you say we might be killed?"

"Because," he said, sitting back, "you are in Cheyenne country. After Sand Creek and the Washita, the Cheyennes will exact revenge should they come upon you and the children. And you would not have me or my brother there to defend you."

"Your brother would be going on with you, then?"

"He must. It is his duty, as well as mine, to bring news to Tall Bull's Dog Soldier camp."

"I see. But, if I left, isn't there a possibility that I might come upon some of the warrior-whites, since it's their presence in your country that's the reason you are considering taking us to your camp?"

"True," he said. "You might. Go ahead and take that chance. I free you. You and the chilren are no longer my captives. Now, take them and go, for I must trek onward toward the Dog Soldier camp."

"But—"

"Do not keep arguing with me. You must make the choice. A few nights ago we made a pact. I agreed to help you in exchange for something you could give me that was of some worth to me. Now, while you might not honor your side of our treaty, I am still bound by it, thus I am offering you the only thing that I can to get you through this alive."

She heard him, and took note of the subtle insult in his speech, the part about breaking her word; still, another thought crossed her mind and she frowned at him. "Are you telling me the truth?"

War Cloud pulled his shoulders into a straight line; his head erect, his countenance infuriated. Obviously her question was just as offensive to him as his words had been to her, but she would not take it back. She needed to know.

He said, "To lie is something that the white man would do. Not an Indian. Besides, why would I deceive you?"

Anna was certain, because of the topic of their discussion, that her face was becoming even more scarlet than the red paint she had once witnessed upon this man's face. She said, however, "It would not be above some men to make up this threat of danger—to pretend there were unsettled problems when there weren't—in order to . . . to . . ."

She stopped. She couldn't finish the sentence. Somehow she knew that what she'd been about to say wasn't true anyway. Unless this man were an actor as great as any Shakespearean player, he was being as truthful with her as he could. There had been nothing fake in the worry she had witnessed upon his face.

In the meantime, however, War Cloud had pulled back, away from her, his features unreadable as he said, "Go! You are free. Go collect your children. I will help you on your journey by pointing you in the right direction." Again, he made to leave; but again, she held him back.

"Please, sir, I'm sorry. I should not have insulted you. But I am new to your country and I don't understand why, if there are white soldiers in this area, and if I left with the children, you think our chances of being killed are great."

He sighed; he glanced skyward as though looking for mercy, but he answered her question nonetheless. "Because," he said, "the soldiers are not looking for you. Because the warrior-whites do not track well. Because my people are looking for the soldiers and so there are many war parties out upon the plains. Because my people know this land better than the soldiers. Because my people would find your trail and track you. Because you do not know how to provide food for yourself and these children. Because if you are not found by the warrior-whites in time, you would starve—there are too many of you to feed."

He paused to take a breath, "Because—"

She held up her hand. "That is enough."

Whew, she thought. Make no mistake; had she only herself to think about, she would leave. But she was not alone. She was responsible for twelve other lives, twelve young children who depended on her to do the right thing. Would she *have* to agree to this man's plan?

Humiliated, she said, "Please, sir, is there no other way?"

He gazed away from her.

And she pressed on, "Couldn't we pretend a carnal knowledge of one another, just as we are faking a marriage? Could we not do this—at least until there comes a time when we might be properly married?"

He sighed. "I can never marry you."

"But if you take that which is only a husband's right to take, sooner or later you must come to terms with what you have done. Sooner or later you must make it good."

"Do not speak more to me of marriage, for I cannot marry you—ever . . . you or anyone else."

Her lips formed the word "Oh."

He squatted back down beside her, his gaze far away from her. He said, "I did not know you meant marriage when we made that treaty; otherwise . . ."

She nodded.

He sat silent for several more beats in time. At last he said, "Perhaps we could try to 'pretend' the physical act, as well. If so, I only hope that I can hide my passions from those who know me well."

"And do you think you could do it? Hide your, ah . . ." She paused as a wave of inspiration struck her, and she said, "What about your wives? Could you not seek to assuage your, ah . . . needs with them?"

She glanced at him only to catch a look from him so full of amazement, she did not know what to think. But he seemed to recover well enough and swiftly enough to say, "We have talked enough."

"But—"

He arose so abruptly, stooping over her so quickly, that for a second, while he picked up his weapons, she felt as though her breath had been taken away. And without so much as a single glance in her direction, he trod off as quickly as his legs would take him.

What had she said?

She watched his figure retreating into the distance, wondering at his strange behavior, yet marveling at his masculine perfection at the same time. In truth, she scrutininzed him and, Lord help her, she was not so innocent that she could not observe a pained gait when she saw one; nor the telltale evidence, when she at last allowed herself to look toward the man's midsection, of the truth that he spoke.

Anna knew she should be shocked at the direction of her thoughts, at the path of her gaze. But she was not. No, though she would be hard-pressed ever to admit such a thing, down deep within herself, she rejoiced.

The man had been telling the truth.

He desired her. Somehow the knowledge gave her strength.

Chapter 15

War Cloud was not happy with himself.

Not only had he admitted too much to her, conversely, he should have told her more. True, he had needed to confess his physical awareness of her in order that she understand the danger. But he had left out the most important threat: that inevitable peril from himself.

He should tell her. He should detail all of it to her, and he knew that he could not let the evening pass without speaking to her again.

That he had been careless with his facts, that he should be caught so completely off guard by his own fabrication regarding his marital state, made him realize that he had been dealing too readily in the realm of untruths.

But why not? She was white, which essentially made her an adversary. Why should he trust her with his secrets?

He sat completely still, lingering upon a slight rise in the land, while he contemplated his situation. Having tramped to this spot, which lay some distance away from her, he stared out into the starlit night and, centering his attention upon his deficiencies, debated what he should do.

While he had not wished to plague Anna with his personal troubles, he feared he already had entrapped her in them—and she, without knowing it . . .

This seemed to be a journey of firsts for him, he thought. The first time he helped the whites; the first time a woman had made a suggestive overture to him; the first time he would have to take what that woman offered without giving anything in return.

If only there were another way. Was there one? Had he overlooked something?

He reviewed his facts: If he took the gift Anna offered and married her, the curse would ensure Anna's ultimate demise.

Not good. What else could he do?

He could refuse her offer and do as she suggested: *pretend* that she was his wife. If he were strong enough, if he were good enough, he could do this.

Unfortunately, this was not quite a workable alternative. It was one he had considered briefly but had discarded. He had not lied when he had warned her of his passionate nature, or of the consequences to her and the children if he were found out in the lie.

And it could too easily happen. Sparked by Sand Creek, many of the Dog Soldiers were committing terrible depredations along the frontier, and no white woman or child was immune. That those same warriors would be in the Dog Soldier camp, that those same warriors would consider it their duty to assault and kill Anna, went without question.

And the children? It was hard to say what would happen to the children. Some would be adopted into the tribe. Others would not.

No, the danger was real. If War Cloud wanted to keep the woman and the children safe, he would need a shield behind which they could stand that no one in his camp could shatter.

A marriage bed with no marriage. It was the only real solution, but it was also one she would not sanction.

Of course, he could give in to her wishes and marry her—particularly since she was demanding it. It would solve his immediate problems. But it would give her so many more.

For, if she only knew it, the curse carried with it a complication, one that no one from their clan had at first contemplated.

Will be unlucky in love.

No one had known the extent of loss that would eventually accompany those words. The realization of it had not come easily; had been discovered by experience only.

He could not let her discover the truth of it in the same way, not and be true to himself and to his brother.

No, he had little choice: he must seek her out. He must confess it all, with no regard for his own welfare in doing so.

But how was he to do it?

Glancing in her direction, he realized that it mattered not how he said it, the only important thing being that it be said.

And if she ended up hating him, then he would have to live with that.

He bowed his head and set himself to do it. It might not a perfect solution, but it was all that he had.

* * *

She had not budged from the spot where he had left her, he noted, and he expelled a harsh breath before treading up to her. Without preamble, he uttered, "We must talk . . . more."

Her glance up at him was worried, puzzled and aroused all at the same time. Upon seeing it, his body answered hers involuntarily, making its needs so well known to him that he thought he might quietly go out of his mind.

She murmured, "Of course. Won't you sit down?"

He came down in his customary cross-legged position, settling quietly beside her. The mild wind caught at his hair for a moment, pushing it to the side, and he listened to the crickets absentmindedly, their noise soothing his nerves. Gathering his thoughts, he centered his attention on one thing only: how to start.

At length he confessed, "I am not married. There are no wives that I can seek out to satisfy my needs."

He heard the slight catch in her voice. It was the only reaction that he witnessed before she said, "I beg your pardon?"

He repeated, a little louder, "I have no wives. There is no one—"

"Thank you, Mister War Cloud. I heard you." She drew in a deep breath before continuing, "I had wondered." She frowned. "But I don't understand. Why would you say this to me?"

"I was trying to discourage you."

These last few words brought a scowl to her face. Nonetheless, all she said was, "Oh."

"Hova'ahane." Her thoughts were as easy to read as a buffalo bull's prints in mud, and realizing the direction of her thoughts, he sought to comfort her. "You misunderstand. I did not wish to discourage you because there is anything lacking in you."

"You didn't?"

"Hova'ahane." He inhaled deeply and took the plunge, stating, "I did it because of me."

She blinked. "I don't understand."

"I know," he said, nodding. "Bear with me, for I will seek to enlighten you. It is why I have sought you out again this night," he said. "There are some things about me that you must understand. And so, although I am reluctant to bear the matters of my family to you, I fear that I must." He sat as perfectly still as he could as he began, "Five times I have been ready to marry. Four times my brides left me before the deed could be done, and the last time, my wife ran away with another man only a few days after our marriage. After that, I swore I would never marry again."

Her expression was full of puzzlement. She asked, "Is there something wrong with you?"

He closed his eyes and sighed. *"Haahe,* there is a great deal wrong with me, I fear. I had hoped to keep from telling you this, for it is not something that brings me happiness, but I find that, if I am to protect you, you must know everything."

He could see that she was puzzled, but to her credit, she did not utter a word; she simply watched him. He started, "All of my family and all my kin are cursed. It is a bad spell, a very bad spell, for it will doom my entire clan if it is not broken soon. And yet, no one has been able to set my family free of it in these hundreds of years past."

He watched her closely, observing that Anna's expression changed not at all as she said, "And what is this spell?"

He hesitated, lingering over his thoughts for a little while before he stated, "The curse has to do with marriage, but that is all I can tell you. Know that the curse would affect you if you were to marry me."

"But I don't understand. How would it affect me? I am not part of your clan."

He turned to her with one eyebrow raised. "You would be part of my family if you married me." He kept his eyes on her as his words registered with her. He watched as her countenance became skeptical, watched as something resembling a gray cloud washed over her features.

"Nonsense!" she said, a glint of anger gathering in her eyes. "I must tell you, Mister War Cloud, that if this is your way of frightening me so that I will no longer plague you with demands for marriage, it is a wasted effort."

She pushed a lock of hair back from her face before continuing, "First of all, we have resolved the difficulty between us by agreeing to *pretend* to be married. Secondly, I do not believe in curses."

Her manner was so brisk that instinct clamored within him to get to his feet and leave; honor kept him seated. He said, "We have not 'resolved' our disagreement over the marriage bed. I tell you what I do so that you can understand why I must ask you to reconsider, if you wish your stay in my village to be without incident."

"But you said—"

"That I would try to *pretend,* yes, but it is not that simple."

As she sat up a little straighter, glaring into his eyes, he was reminded of a mountain lioness he had once seen fighting for her cubs. She said, "Now, let me repeat this so that I can be sure we are both talking about the same thing. I will only bed you if we are married; you will not marry me."

He nodded.

And she continued, "You are demanding husbandly rights without marriage, based on the fact that it will provide the children and me with safety once we reach your village."

"That is right."

"Am I right in assuming the only reason you will not marry me is because of the curse?"

Another nod.

"Well, then, there is no problem, Mister War Cloud. For as I said, I do not believe in curses. It will have no effect on me. You can then keep your part of our treaty and marry me."

"And if I do this, if I do as you ask, it will mean your ultimate demise."

"Why?"

He groaned. "Because, since that day when the curse first started, no one has ever married into our clan and survived it."

Her eyes were round when she asked, "What do you mean?"

"Those who marry us," he said, "either leave within the first few days after the marriage, or, if they stay, they die . . ."

* * *

"Are you telling me, too, that if I marry him, I will die?" Anna could barely believe she had heard War Cloud correctly the previous evening. But after he had delivered this coup de théâtre, he had fled from her so quickly that she had been left staring at the empty place where he had been. She had not been able to question him.

And she had fretted all night.

She now sat with Lame Bird, having cornered the boy upon his return to their camp this morning. She watched as the lad set up his watch on a slight incline.

Lame Bird nodded to her and signed, "Yes, if you marry him, you will die."

"Well," she stated, "I don't believe it." She followed these words with the gestures of sign language.

"And yet," countered Lame Bird in the same language, "what he told you is true. No one has survived a marriage to any member of our family."

Anna sat up on her knees, her attention drawn inward for a moment. She asked, "Then how does your clan . . ." She stalled. What was the hand motion for "procreate"? After a slight pause, she began again, asking in sign, "How does your clan have babies?"

Lame Bird looked up at her with concern. He signed, "Do not worry yourself with that. You should remember only that you must not marry him, if this is the reason you have sought me out. To marry him would kill you."

"Well, I don't believe it," she signed. "If that were true, then how did you and he even get born?"

"*Eaaa*," said Lame Bird, his glance falling to the ground. Nevertheless, he signed, "Sometimes the other person does not die for several years, and this allows children to be born. But it is said that fear of our curse has traveled so far afield, even into our enemies' camps, that there are few who willingly marry us—and stay with us. It has been many years since a child was born to our clan. I am the last. And now with many of us being killed at Sand Creek and the Washita, our family begins to despair that we might, indeed, be the last of our kind."

He finished, and Anna sat in silence until another thought came to mind. She asked with gestures, "And yet your brother tried to marry five times even though he knew this?"

"It is said that he did not believe in the curse when he was young," responded the youngster in sign. "He thought, as I once did, that the story was told only to discredit our family, for some of the stories were bad, very bad. It was not until he tried several times to marry that we both, at last, came to understand that the curse is real. Of course, our ancestor helped him to discover this, too."

"Your ancestor?"

Lame Bird nodded. "We have an ancestor who comes to my brother often. He speaks to him as he does to no other. Our ancestor believes that it is my brother who will, at last, be able to break the curse."

Anna drew back from Lame Bird, remembering a dream that she'd had only a few nights previous. She had seen, there in the fantasy, an apparition talking to War Cloud. Had it been real?

No, impossible.

Still, doubt colored her tone of voice as she said, "I do not believe in curses or in ghosts." She followed the speech with signs.

Lame Bird merely shrugged. "I understand," he signed. "There were many years of my life when I doubted it, too."

"Many years?" she queried. "You are still so young."

"I am not young!" came the instant gestures.

Anna grinned, though she signed, "No, you are not so young."

"Humph!"

"Lame Bird." She said his name aloud. "You must understand. I do not believe in curses. I do not believe in ancestors speaking to the living, nor do I believe in spirits wandering over the prairie. My beliefs are strong and they will protect me. So you see, there is no danger in your brother marrying me."

"Humph!" the lad said, then signed, "I forbid you to do it."

Forbid? This, from a mere boy?

Lame Bird continued with signs, "Why do you want to marry my brother so much?"

"Because if I do," she returned, "the children and I will be protected when we reach your camp."

Lame Bird nodded. "That is a good plan, for you will not be safe otherwise."

Anna nodded. "Yes. But there is another reason. Your brother and I also made a pact. We agreed that I would marry him and he would take me to a white settlement."

This simple statement seemed to startle Lame Bird and he rushed the gestures. "My brother wishes to marry you?"

Anna glanced away. "Not exactly," she said, following the words with the proper hand motions.

"What did he suggest?"

"He . . . well . . ." What could she say? "He thought I meant one thing while I meant another."

"Saaaa," said Lame Bird, knowledgeably. "My brother must want you in the way a man wants a woman he *wishes* to marry."

As Anna recognized Lame Bird's signs, she felt her cheeks grow so hot, she thought she might burn up with embarrassment. It was one thing to have such a conversation with an adult, but with a child?

Yet, Lame Bird went on, as though these sorts of things were discussed daily, "It is good." The youngster looked away from her, although now and again she caught him snatching quick glimpses at her.

She said and signed at the same time, "It is not good. I could never be a part of something like that without marriage."

"I disagree," signed Lame Bird. "Your life may depend on it."

Anna felt her insides churn as she translated the gestures. Was the boy, too, a part of this madness? She signed, "I find the story of the curse interesting, but not frightening. Therefore, it is my belief that there is nothing to be lost from marriage."

"My brother will never marry you."

Goodness, but she was getting tired of hearing that.

The boy sent her a sympathetic look. "Know that he would be proud to have you as his woman. But he cannot. Perhaps it might help if I tell you that no woman has ever been harmed by . . . keeping him company . . . to my knowledge. Know, too, that if you do this thing, it is not the same as being a woman of fleeting reputation. Do not confuse the two. You would do it to save the children, much as you saved me—only in a different way."

She heaved in a deep breath, deciding there was no reasoning with these brothers. Besides, she was more than a little uncomfortable discussing such a subject with a child of twelve.

Signing the hand motions for "Thank you," she came up onto her feet.

But before she could leave, Lame Bird caught her by the hand, pulling her attention back to him. He signed, "You should understand that in an Indian village, there is little that is unknown from one person to the next. If my brother claims you for his wife when he has not committed the husbandly act, and if he desires you, it will soon be found out. It is not so easy to hide things from very wise men."

Anna groaned. She signed, "But I could never do it."

"I understand," motioned the boy. "Still, it is good that he desires you. It has been many moons since my brother has shown any interest in a female."

"That may be good for him, but bad for me," she said, signing the general meaning of the words.

"Think you so?" Lame Bird queried and smiled a very adult smile at her.

And Anna thought she might like to melt into the ground, so great was her embarrassment. Without further sign language or conversation with the boy, she trod away. She would seek out War Cloud and have this issue settled.

She found War Cloud at his bath. However, thinking he was merely swimming, and not sparing a thought as to how he might dress when he went about such a thing, Anna padded right up to the shore.

She said, without waiting to see if he acknowledged her, "Mister War Cloud, we should get this thing settled between us before we go any further toward your Dog Soldier camp."

If she had thought to catch him off-guard, she was to be quite mistaken, for he merely glanced at her and, treading water, said, "Come join me in my bath, white woman, and we can get it settled easily right now."

"Oh!"

He laughed, and Anna was caught off guard for a moment at the pleasant sound of it. She said, "I have not come here for that reason, and well you know it. So turn your mind to other things."

He swam a little closer to her. "It is hard for me to 'turn my mind to other things' when there you stand and . . . here am I. I am told," he said suggestively, "that I scrub backs well." He raised a wet arm and, gesturing toward her, invited, "Come here, Little Bear, and I will show you."

"Mister War Cloud!" she uttered. "I have come here to do no more than discuss our pact with you. Nothing more. Now, perhaps I should turn my back while you get out of the water so that we might discuss this," she suggested, though she did not turn away.

"Why?" he asked, swimming a little nearer. "Were I to stand up, perhaps you could see if you like what you would be getting if you kept your part of our bargain."

"Really!"

"*Haahe,* really."

"Mister War Cloud!" she said again, beginning to get angry. "We still have much to discuss. We have not agreed on what we will be doing and . . . we need to talk."

"Do we?" he asked, swimming closer. "I have told you how it should be for me if you and the children are to remain safe. I regret that this puts you at a disadvantage. But seeing that it has and that you object, I have also agreed to try to pretend a sexual knowledge of you that I do not have. It is my opinion that this will not work, but I am willing to do it. The choice is yours. Now, what else have we to discuss?"

She ignored the question. "I . . . My concern is for the children, not myself."

"Then I will tell you what I think you should do, Little Bear. Throw off your clothes and join me, and you will no longer have anything to decide."

He swam still nearer to her and, without pausing to ask permission, stood up and came forward, dripping water all over her.

But it wasn't the fact that he was getting her wet that took her attention, it was more that Anna had never seen an adult man in such a state of undress. For the only thing hidden from her was enclosed beneath a tiny bit of cloth that covered his most masculine asset.

Tanned skin, taut muscles and broad shoulders, which tapered into a narrow waist and hips, met her regard.

She gaped. And he grinned.

Shaking off the excess water from his body, which fell onto her in cold pinpricks, he teased, "Perhaps you have reconsidered my offer?"

"And if I have?"

That question seemed to gain his attention as nothing else had, and he stared at her for so long she began to grow embarrassed.

But she rushed on. "When I make an agreement, sir, I try to weigh the facts before I hasten into anything. Now, although it is true that I did not know of this curse, or of your unwillingness to enter into the marital state when I made the pact, it makes the fact of the bargain no less valid. Mister War Cloud, I would see these children safely settled. I knew I took a chance when I put the suggestion to you, and I understood at the time that I did not have knowledge of your customs or traditions. The curse changes nothing. If you think that I am so weak-minded as to back out of it simply because others have done so in the past, then you are mistaken. I said I would be yours if you would help me, and I meant marriage and by goodness, sir, I will marry you, curse or no curse."

She peeped a glance up at him to see what the result of her declaration was, and she gasped. The man's features had hardened into a mask of concentration, and as he clenched his chin, his eyes danced with a fiery light.

All he said, however, was, "I will not marry you or anyone else."

"Fine!"

"Know that no matter what we do, I will not take you as a wife."

"Very well!" She made a movement so that she faced him fully, propping her hands on her hips. She said, "Make me a jaded woman, then, for I will keep my end of the pact no matter what you say, so long as you remain true to your own pledge and take me and the children to safety."

With her words, War Cloud's features mellowed and he swept a curious glance over her, every nuance of his look sending erotic stirrings bursting over her already stimulated nerves. But she ignored the feeling; she ignored him and she went on to say, "If I must, I will do this thing with you—but on my terms. It is a sacrifice that I must make and that is all it is," she said. And then once again, as though she had to remind herself, "That is all it is."

With this said, she crossed her arms over her chest, her pose most definitely defensive.

He, on the other hand, rather than being excited by her offering, appeared immune to her. And he watched her with narrowed eyes. At length, he said offhandedly, "You have a few days to think about it. Do not rush into any decision yet."

Darn it! The man made her want to scream. She hated to think what it had cost her, in terms of her pride, to bow to his demands. Why did he not simply take her, now that she had agreed to it, and get the matter over with?

She said to him, "I do not rush into anything. I think I know my own mind."

Regardless, his answer was none other than a grin. He said, "If I did not know you better, *Nahkohe-tseske,* your quickness to take this action might make me think that you are looking at this with more of a happy heart than I had, at first, anticipated."

"Never!"

However, he did not seem to hear her, and with one eyebrow deliberately raised, he appeared to take great delight in contemplating her with the most devilish grin she had ever seen.

Darn the man!

She turned her back on him and put a foot forward, but she had only taken a few steps away when he caught her about the waist and spun her around to him.

His fingers, cold from his bath, pushed back her hair before they smoothed over her face. And with his every touch, her body turned to a quivering mass. She felt branded.

He said, "You are the bravest woman I have ever known."

"Humph!" she uttered, immitating the sound she had so often heard from him.

And then he kissed her. He kissed her lingeringly, yet thoroughly, his lips encompassing hers as though they were a part of his own.

Anna surrendered, her body molding to his every nude contour, delighting in the sensation of his manly form against her. In truth, she felt as though she might dissolve into a puddle.

Raw yearning swept through her, causing her to feel as though her feet might not hold her. But she remained whole and upright, much to her surprise.

Then his tongue swept into her mouth and she lost whatever control she might have had over herself, collapsing against him completely.

She became lost in a world of seduction and rapture, certain that nothing existed outside of this man's lips and his body pressed up tightly against her.

He broke off the kiss all at once, and she should have regained control over herself, but he immediately began showering kisses over her face, her eyes, her cheeks; lower still to her neck, finding the sensative spot there.

"Little Bear," he whispered, "it will be good between us."

She could barely think. In truth, it was all she could do at the moment to nod. This was, indeed, good.

She could feel his lips against her face as he grinned, his cheek nuzzling hers. And he said, "I think our liaison will make you happy, while it lasts."

While it lasts.

Those last few words had the same effect as dousing her in cold water. Drat! He would have been able to take what he wanted had he kept his mouth shut.

And he knew it.

His teasing her could only mean one thing: he was forcing her to acknowledge that if she did this thing with him, she would be as much a willing participant as he.

Oh, how much easier it would be if he just took her.

But he was not the sort of man to do that.

Anna drew herself out of his arms and turned her back on him, feeling the very real evidence of his ardor against her. It made her want to turn and confess that she wanted this lovemaking as much as he.

But she mustn't do that, and so she did the only thing she could do. She took one slow step after another away from him, until gaining some little distance, she was able to run away from him altogether, back to the children. Back to some semblance of sanity.

Or was it?

Whatever the case, it was going to be a long, hot day.

Chapter 16

Was she supposed to pretend that nothing had changed between them? she wondered. Could she ever be her usual self with War Cloud again? When even the tiniest of glances from him had her remembering the way he had looked, the way he had touched her, the things he had said?

Even now when she thought of him, when she recalled the tone of his voice, the feel of his body against hers, and the fire in his eyes, it sent tiny pinpoints of pleasure sweeping along her nerve endings.

She put the question to herself once more. Would she ever be the same again? She somehow doubted it.

Shortly after their talk, War Cloud had directed her to attend to the children and keep them quiet. They would wait until evening for travel, he had told them, even though their party should have been safe, so close were they to Dog Soldier country.

But with war parties on the loose and warrior-whites sending scouts into the territory, there was no way to predict the safety of daylight travel.

True to his word, War Cloud led them from camp, out

onto the open prairie. With the stars as their only tool to navigate, Anna located the Big Dipper, found the North Star from that and observed that they traveled north and west.

Ahead of her, she watched the dim shapes of the ponies laden with their precious burdens. Luckily the moon had risen half-full and bright, though it cast eerie shadows over the landscape. Those ghostly silhouettes could have been frightening, too, she realized, if War Cloud were not here with her. But under his protection, with him leading them and caring for them, Anna felt little to no fear. In truth, if she were honest, she would admit that War Cloud set her mind at ease.

In more ways than one.

While she no longer harbored fear of her surroundings, she also had laid to rest a great deal of her anxieties over the children. No longer did she feel that she, and she alone, was responsible for the welfare of the children. She shared it now, with him.

Her own society could learn much about honor and trust from these people, Anna determined, remembering how fragile mere contracts could be. Until this moment, she had never stopped to consider that those in business appeared to expect a person to break his word if given the least provocation.

Not so these red men. Such uncompromising trust she had never before experienced.

Not even with the Orphan Society. Even there, she had been directed to put her signature to contract in order to "prove" her good faith. What was more, she was required to have any prospective parents put pen to paper that they, too, show their good intentions.

How much simpler it would be if, like these men of the wilderness, a man's word and his own personal pride in himself were more binding than anything another could think up or write.

With this little bit of philosophical rambling, Anna stared in front of her, and spotted the object of her thoughts, War Cloud, far ahead. Since morning, she had become more than a little aware of him, of small things that he did, and she had started to look at him as more than her captor, her protector or as a mere handsome Indian male.

Yes, he was attractive, no doubt, but he had become more than that to her.

He was a lover.

Odd, thought Anna, she was only mildly shocked by the thought. In truth, she might have been perhaps too comfortable with that image.

But, she continued with this line of reasoning, War Cloud was more even than that, although the man did evoke the most amorous urges within her. But what was it about him?

As she watched him move, she became aware of tiny things about him. The way he walked; the long length of his muscular legs; the way his breechcloth flapped in the wind; the way his legs and the rounded curve of buttocks peeked out beneath that breechcloth.

Funny, she had been led to believe—from pictures she had seen—that Indians wore shorter breechcloths. This man's cloth was long in front and back, almost to his ankles. He wore a belt of cartridges round his waist and on the right side of that belt hung a stunningly beaded, blue and white and silver buckskin sheath; his knife, she assumed, encased in it.

His back, what little she could see of it, was broad, muscular and bare. Around one arm he wore a beaded armband, and around the other, one of silver.

Also, he wore weapons of necessity: the quiver full of arrows lashed across his back, his bow in a ready position over his shoulder. And in his left hand he carried his sawed-off shotgun.

His feet, she had noted on numerous occasions, were encased in a sturdy pair of undecorated moccasins, obviously handmade—perhaps by his own hand.

It occurred to her that up until now, she had not bothered to study the man and she wondered how she could have missed this spectacle.

It would be so easy to undress him, she mused, at once shaming herself with the direction of her thoughts.

But truly, it would be so simple. A tug on that piece of buckskin between his legs would do much toward assuaging her curiosity.

And she knew how he would look.

She moaned. Enough was enough! She had to stop this constant speculation.

She forced herself to look away from him, not realizing until too late that in that small amount of time, he had doubled back toward her.

She literally bumped into him.

But he grabbed hold of her and settled her, one of his hands smoothing back a lock of her hair at the same time. He said, placing that wayward strand behind her ears, "You are lagging too far behind the others, and I fear I cannot protect you properly if the need arises." He let the rest of her hair fall over her breast and sent a quick glance to Patty, who had fallen asleep in Anna's arms. "I think," he continued, "that one of the ponies can carry another small load. Would you like to try it?" He motioned toward Patty. "With the child?"

His touch on her, no matter how light, was causing Anna's body to come alive, and she was having some difficulty coping with the sensations while carrying on a conversation with him at the same time. Especially when her body was practically screaming at her with the need to be held. But she could not very well tell War Cloud that.

She commented, "It is kind of you to think of it. Do you really believe the ponies could handle the load?"

"I think we should try it," he responded. "Otherwise I will have to slow our pace and we will not reach a good camping spot before morning." He brought his hand down to draw his fingers through Patty's hair before saying, "She is a very small girl. I think the pony will be able to take on her load. Come, let us see. Follow me."

And with that, he turned away, not looking back, clearly expecting her to follow him.

Of course, she did.

As they approached the pony, he swung around toward her and drew Patty from Anna's arms, and as he did so, his hand accidentally brushed her breast. At once, Anna's senses responded to him, sending a rush of longing through her that was all out of proportion to such a simple gesture.

Oddly, the sensations seemed to center in the middle of

her body and, after a while, she felt a very personal, very feminine part of her grow moist.

She tried her best to ignore the newness of these sensations, as well as the yearning for something she did not fully understand. She stepped back, letting him take Patty into his arms.

Anna paced around toward the pony's head and petted its nose, speaking to it in muted tones, all the while watching War Cloud as he lifted Patty onto its back. With the youngster settled, War Cloud took a step toward her, giving the reins of the animal to her. As he did so, his fingers lingered over Anna's.

At the contact, her pulse leapt and she cast a hasty glance at him, only to find him looking at her expectantly.

But, if he noticed anything unusual, he made no comment and he said, "You lead the animal and stay close to me and the others."

She nodded, gazing back at him and watching with fascination as moonlight bathed his features in the depths and shadows of misty light. Had he ever looked this handsome?

She murmured, "I will."

"I know," he said, while he reached out a hand to run his fingers over her cheek. And then dimly, as though he did not want anyone else to hear, he whispered, "I do not want to lose you."

With those words, raw yearning swept through her, making her senses surge until Anna felt weak with it. They were words, mere expressions, but for Anna, War Cloud might as well have declared his undying love for her, so intense was her response.

She could not speak for a moment and she looked away from him before saying, "I will stay close. I give you my oath."

And when he answered, "I will hold you to that," she chanced a look up at him, catching an answering glint of hunger in his eye. Did his words hold a deeper meaning? Was he awaiting the evening with as much anticipation as she?

Anything could happen, she realized, for it was her intention to marry this man despite his own sentiments on the subject.

No matter, she would keep her part of the bargain; she would do what she must to save her children.

She watched him as he spun around and walked away from her, realizing as she did so that she had never been more aware of another human being in her life.

Alas, she could not wait until they pitched camp.

She awoke to find him beside her, his back to her.

As was becoming customary, she had fallen asleep from exhaustion as soon as they had pitched camp. Every muscle in her legs, as well as her back ached. She wanted—no, she needed—to stretch. Still, she hated to move lest she disturb War Cloud. She suppressed the urge.

The scent of evening came to her on the wind, all mixed up with the odor of the grasses, wildflowers and dirt, and she closed her eyes to commit the smell to mind. She would remember it always, for it would remind her of War Cloud, even if the time came that he was no longer a part of her life.

But he was here with her now, and how she did long to

reach out and touch him; how she wished she had the courage to do it. He was so close, yet a world away.

She watched his shoulders move up and down as he breathed silently in and out. It was the barest of movements, and yet, to be this close to him, to be able to touch him and feel his breath if she wanted to, was an intimacy she had never before experienced. And she so desperately wanted to experience even more.

There it was, clearly expressed, she thought, at least to herself. She wanted this man. If she were to be completely truthful, she would admit that his declaration to make her his had stimulated her beyond thought.

Secretly she admitted, she wanted this tryst, marriage or no. It was a hard thing to learn about herself. No matter how strict her upbringing, no matter how moral her character in the past, she was afraid she might be willing to risk it all.

After all, he might not marry her; he surely gave her to understand that he would not.

And would it make a difference to her? Morally, yes, it would, at least it should. But on the other hand, she was uncertain it would be such a bad thing if, after they committed the deed, they went their separate ways.

Goodness! She brought her thoughts up short. How could she have ever entertained such an idea? Oh, the scandal.

She must think of something else—quickly. She could not afford to nurture the thought of anything else except marriage to this man.

As distraction, she glanced once more at the broad back of her protector.

What would it be like, she wondered, to be loved?

Would it be as exciting as it had been this morning? Would she lose herself so thoroughly to it that he became the center of her universe?

This morning had not been a bad feeling—not at all.

The odd thing was that, without the deed even being accomplished, she already felt more alive. As she drew in a breath, she realized that never before had she been so refreshed by the simple act of breathing in the clean fragrance of the grasses and wildflowers. Never could she remember the common squawk of the nighthawks and blackbirds invigorating her. Never had the wind and the rain so touched her soul. Even the sight of the tall sunflower stalks as they stretched up toward a midnight sky thrilled her as it never had previously. Would these things be even more intense after she had shared a night with War Cloud?

She pressed her lips together and despaired. She feared she could hardly wait to discover it.

And, the dear Lord help her, the fact that War Cloud did not want a permanent relationship did not seem to daunt her. Though she would be hard-pressed ever to admit it, she was aware that, while she might insist on marriage, deep within her, she had known that she might never be able to commit herself fully to this man. Not body and soul. They lived in worlds too far apart.

Though she had been truthful when she said that she would be willing to marry him, even then she had known that she would always hold a part of herself separate.

She only feared what this might mean about herself.

She grimaced as a muscle twitched in her back, but at least it brought her to the present. She really needed to move and stretch the kinks out of her body, and despite her reluctance to disturb War Cloud, she was going to have to act. Silently she drew her arms over her head and strained.

Although she thought she had twisted soundlessly, War Cloud looked over his shoulder, his dark eyes seeking out her own.

He said, "I am glad you are awake. I fear we need to talk." Thus, having spoken, he turned his head away from her and said no more.

She scooted onto her side. His back was to her, and she wished she had the nerve to reach out and touch him, perhaps to force him to acknowledge her.

But she still did not possess the courage.

She watched him instead. She knew he had to be as exhausted as she was and she wished to comfort him, at least a little. But she feared even bringing up the subject of marriage. Would she again receive the same lecture?

After a while, however, when he did not speak, she said, "Tell me what is on your mind."

She was close enough to him that she could feel the heat of his body, and it made her want to curl up to him.

But she did not. She watched him instead, observing that he twisted his head to the left before he spoke to her. It was the only sign he made that gave her an indication that he was not as comfortable with her as he might like her to suppose.

He began, "I have been thinking."

"Yes?"

"I have decided that we will not commit the marriage act after all."

"We won't?" She wondered if she sounded as disappointed as she felt. Perhaps she did, for he turned his head and eyed her, scanning her swiftly.

However, presenting his back to her once again, he uttered, "Had I not thought that you had already offered yourself to me, I would not have told you the things I did about myself and you would not have this problem."

"But," she said, "if I had not come to you with the bargain, you would not have agreed to take the children and me to a white camp, isn't that right?"

A growl sounded in his throat.

"And that is the important thing that we must not lose sight of—the children."

He said, "I will take you to a white camp, as I have promised, without your having to give yourself to me. The problem is mine. I will handle it in my own way."

"I beg to differ."

He shot a glance at her over his shoulder.

"Are you now telling me that there is no danger for me and the children within the Dog Soldier camp?"

"*Saaaa*, there is great danger."

"Then I don't see how this does *not* affect me. Know that I will do this thing with you in order that the children are safe. I will also keep my end of the bargain. Do you think I am so dishonest that I would go back on my word?"

"But you did not know." He moved his shoulders up and down. "You thought marriage would be your sacrifice, not a moment of passion that would leave you with no man to protect you and any children that might come about from our union."

Children? She hadn't thought of that. An unexpected

warmth rushed in upon her, causing her a moment's hesitation.

But she could ill afford to spend more than an instant in contemplation of it, and so she said, "It's doubtful that I would become laden in that way if we only did it . . . that is to say, if we only committed the act once . . ."

War Cloud turned his head toward her, a frown pulling at his features as he said, "It is not so unlikely."

But she took no notice of him and went on to say, "I don't think you should worry about that. After all, the thought of having a child is not an unhappy one. Know that I would never put a child of mine out on the streets. Somehow I would manage."

That this statement took him by surprise was evident. He swung his body around to face her, his countenance clearly puzzled. He said, "You would do this?"

"Yes," she answered at once.

"But you would have no husband, for I could not be that to you."

She shrugged as if it were nothing. "I would make do. I always have."

"If this be true," he countered, turning almost all the way around toward her, "then why do you not take all of these children as your own?"

"Because," she said without hesitation, "I could not afford to keep them."

He shrugged. "You could take one or two."

"No, I could not." She sighed. "I have given my word to the society that I will see these children safely placed in Christian homes—with a mother *and* a father. They need both. I could not provide that for them."

He nodded, as though in perfect understanding. At

length, however, his look grew more serious as he said, "I would not want a child of mine growing up without knowing me."

"Nor would I."

"If there were a child from our union, it would stay with me."

"I could not allow that."

"Humph!" he grunted. "We bicker for nothing, I think. We have not done the deed, nor are you with child."

She smiled slightly and said, "That's true," grimacing as her dry lips cracked with the movement. Involuntarily she licked them.

His eyes homed in on the movement. After a brief pause, he asked, "You would willingly do this with me?"

She hesitated. Dare she tell him the truth? Perhaps not all of it. She could relate some of her thoughts, those that would not mark her as an easy woman. She said, "Yes, I believe that I would. You see, I would do most anything to ensure the safety of the children, and if this . . . this physical thing is a problem for you, I would ease your . . . mind—and mine."

He groaned. What had she said? She sent him a quick glance.

And her stomach suddenly jumped into her gullet. Dear Lord, passion fairly emanated from this man's eyes.

She cleared her throat self-consciously and said, "But you would have to show me how to do it, for I do not know what to do."

He nodded. "I could do this, if you wish it." He stretched out a finger to tilt her face up toward his. His dark eyes stared into hers. "Tell me the truth that is in your heart," he murmured, "for if you do this out of fear, I will satisfy my needs elsewhere."

Once more she swept her tongue over her lips, the action again gaining his attention. And as he stared at her lips, she felt herself tingling under the intensity of his gaze. She shut her eyes and breathed in deeply before she said, at last, "But if you sought out someone else, would that not throw doubt onto our union?"

He shrugged. "I would make excuses."

She blinked her eyes open and asked, "Would your reasons be believed?"

Again, he lifted his shoulders.

"It would be a chance, wouldn't it?" she asked. "Whereas, if we did this, it would be easier?"

He made no response.

And she reiterated, after a while, "I will do this thing with you, War Cloud."

He gave her a quick nod and said, "Then I think we should seek somewhere more private, that we do not disturb the children."

Suddenly Anna could not speak. She nodded.

He made an outward gesture. "Do you see that tree by the stream?"

"Yes," she said, realizing he pointed to a willow that skirted the water.

He continued, "You prepare yourself and I will meet you there when the evening turns to complete darkness." And with no more than these few words said between them, he came up onto his feet.

"Where do you go?" she asked, wanting to reach out and detain him, to ask him what she should prepare for.

But she did not know how to ask. All she could do at the moment was stare up at him.

Her gaze came to his waist, moved lower as she looked for a sign that he still wanted her. She could only hope that he did.

But he turned his back on her, blocking her view, and said, "I must scout out the land and ensure that we are safe. I would not be surprised by an enemy."

"Oh." Her lips rounded on the word.

And he left the camp posthaste. As he walked away, she watched him until she could no longer see his image. Was it her imagination, she wondered, or did his step seem a little lighter?

Had she perhaps set his mind at ease? At least a little?

She hoped so. She would not have this act of love be for nothing.

Chapter 17

S he bathed. It was the only thing she could think of to do to "prepare herself." Because she had washed most of her garments as well as herself, when she stood next to the willow tree, awaiting War Cloud's arrival, she was clothed in her chemise alone.

She shivered. The undergarment was too thin to give her much protection against the elements, and now and again the breeze touched her in all the wrong places. As a result, goose bumps spread over her arms and legs and she trembled.

Yet, she did not leave. She stood waiting . . . and waiting, no matter that she felt more than a little foolish for doing so.

What kept him? Dusk had slowly turned to the pitch-black of night, and Anna hugged her arms around herself to keep off the chill.

Not that it was cold. In truth, the night was balmy and warm. It was only that, with low clouds filling the heavens, there were no stars or moon above to bring about a feeling of contentment or warmth. Plus, the heavy humidity in the air easily forecast the possibility of rain.

Would she and War Cloud be able to complete the marital act if it rained? Oh, why did he not hurry?

Anna began to wish that she had paid more attention when she had been younger and the other girls in the orphanage had spoken of the marriage bed and what was expected of a woman at this time in her life. As it was, Anna really had no idea of what was to come. Perhaps, she thought, if she had more of an inkling of it, she would not be so inclined to fret.

She heaved a deep sigh, had done no more than let out her breath when the wind blew up, seeming to whisper in her ear, soothing her . . . making her lids drop. Something startled her and she flung open her eyes, only to realize how tired she was . . . and she was still standing.

She sat down, leaning back against the trunk of the willow as the gentle breeze touched her face. Surely War Cloud would find her when the time was ready.

She heard the drums in the distance, watched the eerie light of their fire, saw the leaps of their dancers.

She edged closer. Was this where she would find War Cloud? Was it an enemy camp? A friendly one?

With amazement, Anna realized that there would be no friendly Indian camp for her.

Ah, there he was. Her hero, her protector. But what was he doing? Why wasn't he participating with the others?

Although he did not see her, Anna followed him through the camp. She would go where he went, see what he saw. She would understand what drove this man.

And then what would she do?

She would love him, she decided. She would simply love him.

* * *

It is as the wise men have said, War Cloud concluded, as he stood watching the shadows of those who have departed this world. These, his ancestors, were depending on him. The time was near. The curse could be broken.

Never before had War Cloud seen so many of the shadows of the dead gathered in one place. Never before had he seen so many of them drumming, singing and carrying on as though they were alive; some were even dancing, their figures no more than mere outlines.

Still, theirs was a feast for him; a time for encouragement. All his kin were here, his own father included amongst them. War Cloud watched their ghostly merriment with fascination, but he held himself back from them.

He had never enjoyed close contact with the dead, not even when a spirit spoke to him in a vision quest. Some of his people, even a few great warriors, trembled in fear of the spirits. While War Cloud was not afraid of them, his emotion toward them was far from joyous. If anything, he usually found himself to be more than a little annoyed after communication with them.

He expected it to be no different this time.

Troubled, War Cloud turned away and left their haunted circle to pace slowly toward the stream which lay not far away.

Coming upon it, he drowned out the clatter of the unearthly drumming and listened to the very real surge of water as it gurgled happily against its many rocks. The familiarity of this natural melody, along with the crickets playing their nightly serenade and the mournful cries of the wolves in the distance, calmed his soul, allowing him a moment of respite from his thoughts.

"*E-peva'e tsexe-ho'ehneto,* it is good that you came here, away from the others."

War Cloud was not surprised to hear the words of his ancestor Sky Falcon. He glanced up to see the ghostly image hovering before him, there over the water.

"*Henova'e he'tohe?* What is it? Why are you not with the others?" War Cloud spoke harshly, though he knew he should temper his words.

"I must talk to you," said the shadow of the ancient one, still speaking in the Cheyenne tongue.

"I need no talk," said War Cloud. "Always when you seek to counsel me, you try to encourage me to do something that is not in my heart to do. Know that I am committed to breaking this curse and to helping you find peace, but I must live my own life as I would have it, not as you would see it."

The ancient one, though in shadow form only, approached. It said, "I would not ask you to do something that is not in your nature to do."

"Humph!"

"*Henova'e he'tohe,* what is it? Why is your heart heavy when the rest of us rejoice?"

War Cloud paused, and then said slowly, "I fear the consequences of coupling with the white woman, Grandfather."

"Ah," said the old one. "Speak to me of it, my son."

War Cloud barely shrugged. "I fear that I am coming to like her too much, Grandfather."

"Humph!" said the shadow.

"I find that I worry about her," War Cloud continued as though the ancient one had remained silent. "And I no longer think of her as a white woman or as an enemy."

"What is wrong with this?" asked the shadow.

"I fear, Grandfather, that I could be her destruction, and it is this that troubles me."

"You will not harm her," declared the shadow all-knowingly.

"Perhaps not this night," answered War Cloud, "but what of the future? She is determined to marry. Yet, she knows that I cannot. What if I cannot prevent it?"

"Do not fight it so hard, my son."

"And what of love? I cannot deny that I already admire her. I have never known a woman like her. She is brave when others would cower. She gives of herself when others would hold back. Grandfather, what if I begin to love her? Would not my love for her take her away?"

"It is a hard thing to predict, my son," said the shadow. "But I think that it is only marriage that could harm her—if she is not strong enough to break the spell."

War Cloud nodded. "I do not want her to try to break the spell, Grandfather. I fear this."

"And yet," the ancient one said, "I believe that she is the one. It is as she says, my son. Her beliefs are strong. They will protect her."

"And what if they do not protect her? What if they fail her?"

The shadow of the old man appeared to pause as though in reflective thought, giving War Cloud the opportunity to continue speaking.

War Cloud said, "It is the man's duty to set the course of his life with a woman. It is my duty to guide *Nahkohetseske*, for there is much about the curse and about our family that she still does not understand."

"Think you so? She may grasp more than you recognize, I think. Remember that a warrior leads with his courage, my son, but a woman leads with her heart. Only this can I tell you. Follow her. You will not regret it."

No sooner had this message been uttered than the shadow vanished, the abruptness of its disappearance leaving War Cloud feeling annoyed and strangely empty. Pulling his mouth into a grimace, he turned aside and, spinning around, bumped into something standing directly behind him.

Out of habit, his body tensed and he bent, ready for action, grabbing hold of his knife at the same time. Instinct had him wielding the object in his hand ready for use. Looking up, he took stock of who stood before him.

Nahkohe-tseske's green eyes stared straight back at him.

"*Saaa,*" he said, relaxing his stance and sheathing his weapon. She had surprised him, for he had not been listening for the sounds of another soul sneaking up on him.

And it appeared, he noticed, that he had startled her as well, if her expression were a mirror to her thoughts. She stared back at him with eyes that appeared unusually wide and unblinking. He sighed and said, "You heard? You saw?"

She did not speak, merely glared at him.

He threw back his head and groaned. "So now you know."

One moment followed upon another until at last she muttered, "What have you done to me?"

War Cloud slanted her a frown and, when she remained silent, again asked, "Did you see? Did you hear?"

"I'm not sure what I saw."

He let out his breath. "Did you hear?"

"Hear what?"

Ah, he had forgotten that he had been speaking to the shadow of his ancestor in the Cheyenne tongue. She would not have understood, if she had heard anything at all. It was good.

She repeated, "What have you done to me? Not in all my life have I seen anything like . . . this that I saw tonight."

The sinew in War Cloud's arms went rigid as she spoke. He knew of no way to make this easy for her.

It was not a simple thing to do, to see the spirits, to speak to them. Few people were ever given the opportunity. He wondered if she knew the compliment his ancestor paid her.

Anna straightened away and glanced around her. "Was the image I saw here tonight the one you called Sky Falcon?" she asked.

He narrowed his eyes at her. "It was."

"I do not believe in ghosts, Mister War Cloud."

He shrugged. "I cannot help that."

"Did you hypnotize me?"

"I do not know this word, hyp-no-tize."

She stiffened her spine. "It is a new word in the English language," she explained, "and it means to put someone into a waking sleep, so that they are not seeing the things around them, but rather observing objects that another suggests to them."

"Ah . . ."

"Did you do this to me?"

He paused to collect his thoughts. When he did at last speak, he began slowly, as though only in this way could he bring her to understand. He said, "I do not cause all things that happen on this earth. If I can, I try to understand them, that is all. If you saw something this evening, know that it was you who experienced it—for I made no suggestion." His voice caught on the last word.

"Very well." She appeared to accept this without further difficulty. "And the drumming and singing?" she asked. "Have we camped next to a band of Indians?"

He stuck out his chin and jerked his head to the left. He said, "You heard them?"

She snorted. "A body would have to be deaf not to."

War Cloud let his gaze roam up and down Anna's figure, noticing for the first time the distinct upward tilt of her head. He commented, "You are privileged, then."

"What do you mean?"

She shivered, and War Cloud noticed for the first time the meagerness of her dress. He asked, "Are you warm enough?"

She nodded.

"Then follow me and we will go into this camp that you might see it for yourself. There is little I can do to explain it to you. You must see it for yourself."

"But—"

"*Ne-naestse,* come. If you have become aware of the noises of the evening, if you saw that which spoke to me, then I would have you see the rest, that you might better understand what is happening here."

And giving her no choice but to follow him, he tramped in the direction of the ghostly camp. Perhaps it was a good thing; she might think twice before trying to convince him again to marry her.

Chapter 18

Drums beat out a slow cadence while phantomlike figures danced to a centuries-old rhythm. With only an illusionary fire to serve as their lighting, it was difficult for Anna to make out more than mere outlines of those dim shapes.

She clung to War Cloud's arm in silent alarm and scooted close to him. "War Cloud," she whispered, "what is this?"

"It is a dance of my ancestors," he answered. "They are celebrating."

"Why?" she asked.

He paused for a long time. Moving closer to him, she nudged him and asked again, "Why are they celebrating?"

He stared straight ahead of him, and in the dim light, the only thing she could see of his features was an outline. She could not read his thoughts, nor observe his reactions. At length, he answered, his voice no more than a whisper, "They believe that the curse that binds my kin is almost at an end."

"They do?"

"*Haahe,* they do."

"Why?" she asked.

She felt him take in a long breath before he answered, "Because of you."

"Me? What has any of this to do with me?"

She felt him shift his weight from one foot to the other. And though it was obvious that the man was uncomfortable, she would not withdraw the question. She had to know. Impatiently, she waited for his response, still clutching his arm.

Finally he said, "They believe that you are the one to set them free. They have long awaited a time when the curse could at last be broken."

"They have? But why me?"

He straightened himself up to his full height before glancing quickly down at her. He said, "You are the first woman in all these years who is unafraid of the curse. Because of this, my ancestors believe that you are strong enough to overcome its power."

She had no reply to that. While on the one hand she might be flattered, on the other, these things he spoke of frightened her.

"Do you think I am the one, too?"

He sighed before he said, "I do not know what to conclude. I would like to think that you can help lift the curse, if only because I have been trying to overcome it most of my life."

"You are uncertain?"

He shook his head. "I fear the curse's power. If you are not the one, or if your power is weak, there would be great harm done to you."

She shivered, but asked, "How?"

"I have already told you the consequences of a union with me."

She nodded. "If I marry you . . . but I don't believe in curses."

He gestured toward the figures. "And do you believe in these?"

She stopped perfectly still. She did not, yet she could not deny what she was seeing.

"Ah," he said, "now you know my problem. I would like to think that you are the one. I fear the consequences if you are not. Know that your belief in yourself must be strong—for there might come a time to test you. Know this."

"I don't understand."

He shrugged. "Nor do any of us. Had we the knowledge of how to cast off the spell, it would be gone. Know only that there will come a time when you will need to be strong—if you are to help us."

"Help you? I am trying to, but I still don't understand. Tell me, what is it that you wish from me?"

He stared down at her, but it was too dark to see his features. He said, "I do not know. But if you are the one and we commit the marital act, you must be warned that there is great risk."

"Even if we have the liaison, but don't marry?"

He nodded. "I fear there is danger either way."

She frowned. "But if we don't marry, the curse would not affect me. Is there another kind of danger?"

She thought she heard him curse in English. But the words were said so quietly, under his breath, that she was uncertain. She asked again, "What kind of danger are you talking about?"

He looked away from her, his posture tense as he explained, "There is danger that I may fall in love with you."

In love with her?

She had to be dreaming. She pinched herself—only to find that she was still standing beside War Cloud.

Dazed, she found herself asking, "And you think there might be a risk of this happening?"

He shrugged. "I already admire you, and I desire you. There is a next step, and perhaps taking you to my sleeping robes might be that step."

Then by all means, do it, she said to herself alone. Aloud she voiced, "And if I fall in love with you?"

He sent her a swift glance. "Do you think that you might?"

She caught her breath and, unable to say the words, sidestepped the question altogether. At length, she nodded.

He said, "Then there is more trouble than I feared, for you must not stay with me. Promise me now, no matter what happens, that you will leave me when the time comes for us to part."

She remained silent.

"Promise me."

She groaned. "I cannot do that. Know that I do not put any faith in this curse. What if there is a problem and I am required to remain with you . . . for the children? I cannot see into the future easily enough to give you that promise. I am sorry."

He grimaced. "Then we must be careful, very careful with each other, and we must not nurture a feeling of affection between us. Promise me that you will at least try to do this."

What could she say? "I will try," she murmured at last. But she knew that even this promise had come too late.

She already felt more than a little affectionate toward War Cloud. If he only knew . . .

The shadows lingered, dancing under an overcast midnight sky, their outline highlighted only by the ghostly fire in the middle of their circle. Most of the figures were clean silhouettes, except for the special features a few wore on their heads—a buffalo headdress or a horned hat. All wore breechcloth and moccasins. All were clothed in mist and mystery.

She wanted to leave this place, but she dared not do so. Something kept her here, though she would have been hard-pressed to put a name to exactly what it was.

Presently, one of the figures distinguished itself from the others, and she recognized the image of the same old man she had observed speaking with War Cloud earlier, by the stream. The ancient one looked different now, however, with no more than a buffalo robe drawn over one shoulder.

A cloud sailed across the sky overhead, allowing a beam of moonlight to shine down on them. It bathed the image in an unearthly light, and for a moment, she saw the shadow distinctly.

Dear Lord, this was a likeness of no man she had ever before witnessed. Tattoos marred the ancient one's perfect complexion. They were everywhere on his body: on his cheeks, on his chin, on his arms. His long, gray hair hung down to his hips, while a single feather, attached to his hair, fell from his head.

The image came forward.

All at once another image joined his, that of an old woman, and in her arms the female shadow bore a dress—a white buckskin dress, heavily decorated with colorful quills and shells.

No sooner had Anna registered what was happening than the phantomlike woman touched her, sending a sudden chill over Anna's body.

Immediately, the ghostly dress encompassed Anna and she stood looking down at herself, enwrapped in the misty regalia. It fit her perfectly.

"Hova'ahane!" came War Cloud's voice. And he roared, "You will not do this to us!"

But neither the image of the old woman nor that of the ancient man or the dress faded. Alas, all three shone with spectral light.

Anna clutched War Cloud. "What is happening?"

War Cloud did not answer.

Instead another voice spoke to them in a language foreign to Anna, using words she did not understand, yet words she comprehended all the same.

The ancient one uttered, "From this moment, until forever, neither of you need ever be alone again. For you are united now in body and in spirit. I say to you, my son, that wherever you go, so shall she go. Your tears, your fears, you happiness will be hers. And all her experiences, her woes, her sorrows and even her joys you will share. Know that you belong together. So be it."

"Hova'ahane!" came War Cloud's plea.

But it was useless. The images disappeared.

Gone, too, were the drums, the singers, the fire and the dancers.

In the aftermath of swirling mist and uncanny images,

Anna turned curious eyes to War Cloud. She whispered, "Dare I ask what just happened?"

War Cloud turned to her with a heaviness in his stance that she recognized at once. He said, "Do you not know?"

"I am uncertain."

"They married us, and in a traditional manner."

Anna stared at him for the pulse of several moments, her expression changing from disbelief to indulgence. At last she uttered, "Good."

"Good?" He spun away from her as though he dared not stay in her presence a moment longer. He trod back in the direction of their camp, his long legs carrying him quickly away from her. Over his shoulder he called, "You might as well have sanctioned your own death."

She ran after him; she had no choice. "You will never make me believe in this curse, War Cloud, so do not try," she said. "I am happy that at least your ancestors have thought to do the right thing."

He swung around. "It is *not* the right thing! And I wish the spirits would let me live my own life." He spun back in the direction of their camp without awaiting her reply.

She caught up with him easily, however, and reached out toward him, forcing him to stop and turn to look at her. She said, "Fine, live your own life. You did not say a word. They cannot *make* you marry me. We spoke no vows."

His breathing was heavy as he watched her. All at once he pivoted away from her and held his arms up to the heavens as though, by his own actions, he could reverse the past few moments. He cried, "I do not recognize it! Do you hear me, my ancestors? We are not married!"

A fierce wind whipped at him, thrashing his hair behind his face. Her hair, too, blew in the wind, strands of it flogging her face so rapidly that she felt as though she stood in the midst of a whirlwind.

"I will defy you!" came War Cloud's utterance.

Outstretching a hand toward him, she touched War Cloud and said, "It is over. It is all right. We do not have to recognize the pact. It is up to us, after all."

Lowering his arms, he turned to her, and then it happened so quickly and so naturally, she could barely credit it.

He touched her, she grazed him with her fingertips, and they fell into one another, their bodies suddenly imprinted one against the other. The wind whipped up its worst against them. But they did not notice.

His arms had pulled her in so close, they shielded her, and she could feel every one of his taut muscles. She was aware, too, of the emotional quivering in his chest and she stood against him, utterly entranced with this man.

Though she might not agree with his reasoning, War Cloud protected her as no one else ever had. And she could not explain the closeness she felt to him at this moment, nor the forces that urged her to comfort him.

All she knew was that she needed to take away some of his pain, and her arms went around his neck.

"Shhh," she said, as though she soothed one of the children, and she pulled his face down to hers, her lips raining kisses over his shoulders, up to his neck, his cheeks, while her hands stroked through the long mane of his hair.

"It's over," she said. "I promise that I will not hold you to it. Between us will be the bargain that we are unattached."

She felt him nod; became aware of the strong grip of his arms around her.

Suddenly his hands ran up and down her spine and, as though he could stand it not one moment longer, he drew her to her knees, while he knelt in front of her. And even as he stole one kiss after another, his hands pushed the chemise from her shoulders.

A surge of fire swept through her. Oh, how she wanted this; how she wanted him.

"Love me, War Cloud, please." she begged.

His lips found hers in one kiss after another. Soon, his tongue swept into her mouth, pressing, urging, taking her sweet response as though, with his tongue, he would give her all the loving she needed.

"Please," she uttered. "Don't leave me."

"I will not," he whispered huskily.

His hands stumbled over the ties of her dress, and reaching down, she helped him, her own fingers unsteady.

Soon she was bare to the waist. She began to rub her breasts up and down his chest as though she would dance with him in this way as well.

He muttered something deep in this throat while she formed little cries on her lips.

Suddenly she found the courage to place her hands over the smooth fabric of his breechcloth. She tugged, shocked to find the maleness of him falling into her hands.

Another groan from him sent her reeling out of her mind.

He said, "You are innocent and I should be careful."

"No, do not be careful."

He muttered, "I would have you enjoy this, too."

She nodded as though she understood, although, in truth, she remained completely unaware of the significance of his words.

He said, "I cannot stop."

"I do not want you to."

Another moan sounded on the midnight air, but whether from him, from her or perhaps from the wind, she could not be certain.

He urged her legs apart and pulled her up onto him, his fingers touching her most private, most feminine spot.

A rush, not unlike a bolt of lightning, streamed through her and that same moisture that she had felt there at the juncture of her legs once before, seeped from her, welcoming him.

He said, "You are ready for me."

She nodded, not understanding what he meant, but certain he spoke the truth. She felt as though she might explode. She said, "Please."

Meanwhile his fingers were creating magic within her, sending flows of sensation up and down her body, and then he was positioning himself down there between her legs.

"Are you ready?"

"Yes," she said.

He surged upwards with no more preparation and she cried out.

At her whimper, he stopped, while she kept herself still, fighting the urge to pull back, away from him.

He said, "The hurt cannot be helped the first time. If you move against me, it will make it better for you."

"Move?" she asked.

"Twist and fidget against me. Do this until it starts to feel better."

"But it will hurt worse, won't it?"

"I promise that it will not."

"You are sure?"

"I am certain."

She wiggled a very tiny bit at first, experimenting. The pain was not so bad this time. She twisted then, moving upwards and then down.

A growl sounded from him.

She asked, "Do you like that?"

"Very much," he returned, and she repeated the motion, eliciting the same response.

But if she thought she could control the pace of their lovemaking, she was sadly mistaken.

A few more twists and pulls and he suddenly drove himself higher, taking her with him.

He positioned her on the ground below him, though he continued to kneel before her. Grabbing her legs, he pulled them onto his shoulders, while he thrust urgently within her.

Sweet heaven, it felt good.

She stared up at him solemnly, and he gazed back at her in the same manner.

"I think I have waited for this all my life," he ground out. "I do not remember wanting anything more."

She could barely stand it. She felt as though she were burning up with fever and she strained against him as he drove into her over and over.

And then it took her by surprise. She hadn't expected either pleasure or such intensity. Her whole body convulsed as pure bliss swept to every part of her.

But that wasn't all. In the midst of this most powerful experience, he thrust himself into her deeper and deeper, and she watched in awe as he spilled his seed into her, his expression of pleasure more thrilling than any Kansas summer storm.

They danced in the rhythm of love over and over, moving against one another as spasms of belated rapture overtook them. At last, spent, he collapsed over her.

It was a time of warmth, a time of giving, and she wrapped her arms around him to pull him closer. And as she felt him slip into a curiously peaceful slumber, she realized that she was in deep trouble. Very big trouble.

For she had lied when she said she would try to keep from feeling affection for him. She loved this man. Heart and soul. Dear Lord, help her. *She loved him.*

Chapter 19

❦

*H*ad it been a dream?

Dawn fell all about them, the first morning rays of light enveloping them in a soft world of pinks and silvers, misty dews and cloudy grays. Blackbirds and doves, meadowlarks and bobwhites welcomed in the day with their own special brand of cooing and songs while the dark-haired man and lighter-haired woman reclined on a hillside.

War Cloud had placed his buffalo robe between the ground and the two of them, a necessary protection from the moisture that clung to every blade of grass. Anna lay between his legs, his arms about her, the back of her head on his chest. Both stared toward the east and the beginnings of a spectacular sunrise.

Anna leisurely stretched out one of her hands to run her fingers down his arm. She felt his answering shiver and gloried in the lingering kiss he place atop her head.

She had awakened in the middle of the night to find herself in War Cloud's arms, both of them lying beneath the willow tree. Wondering if it had been real or merely a dream, she had related her strange experience to him.

247

War Cloud had simply smiled at her and made love to her over and over. It had been the most wonderful, the most natural, experience of her life.

With her ear pressed firmly on his chest, she listened to the beat of his heart, and she sighed, content in the moment.

She said, "What will we tell the children?"

"The truth," he said. "One should never lie to a child or seek to hide the facts."

"And what are the facts?" she asked.

He groaned and nuzzled his lips against her hair. "We will tell them that we will be going into the Dog Soldier camp," he said, "and that there is great danger for them there. We'll tell them that you and I are pretending to be married in order that we can protect them and that they are to pretend to be our children."

"And you don't think any of them might let it slip that these things are mere pretenses?"

"*Hova'ahane,* I do not. For knowing so little of the ways of the prairie, these children have been little trouble. Besides, they may be young, but they are not stupid."

"Hmmm," she said in agreement. "Is there anything else I should tell them?"

He nodded. "To stay close to me; to say nothing unless I tell them to and, once we reach camp and are settled, to stay within my lodge rather than run about the camp. In this way, they will not constantly remind the people that the great Cheyenne Dog Soldiers are sheltering a horde of white children."

"And will we reach your camp today?"

He nodded again. "Already scouts have spotted us."

She sat up in alarm, but he pulled her back to him, nestling her head once more against his chest. "I have seen the scouts on yonder hills since before sunrise. Had they wished us harm, it would have been done by now. Besides, seeing us as we are will heighten the illusion of the story we must tell."

She inclined her head.

"I sent them a message that I am coming into camp."

"You did? How?"

"With my robe," he said. "There is a signal used to tell them not to approach, that I will be coming in."

"There is?" she asked. "What is it?"

He drew his hands up, away from her, and with arms outstretched, demonstrated, saying, "Imagine that I hold the ends of the robe in each hand. I make this motion." He brought his left hand to his right shoulder and then his right hand to his left shoulder, both arms ending in the same position. He repeated the motion and said, "This means do not approach."

"And did they tell you anything in return?"

"Only an acknowledgment."

"I see," she said. "Do they know you will be bringing in twelve children, as well as me?"

"They know. News of your presence with me traveled with the war party, here to my people."

"Oh, dear." She squinted her eyes against the silvery rays of morning. "And did you also tell the scouts that we are married so that there will be no trouble?"

"No," he responded. "The scouts were too far away to communicate more than a simple message. As I said before, seeing us together in this way is enough. Once we reach camp, I will tell the others that we are married. There is no need to do more. But know that it is a marriage of pretense. You understand?"

"I do." She sucked in her breath and, after a moment, said, "I am scared."

His arms tightened around her. "It is to be expected. Know that I am here with you."

She hesitated before saying, "And do you think we will remain unharmed?"

"It is to be hoped."

She debated asking her next question, finally voicing the inquiry after a slight hesitation. "Must we be in camp a long time?"

"Long enough to tell Tall Bull of the danger and to be polite to the others."

"Tall Bull? Who is Tall Bull?"

"He is the leader of the Dog Soldier camp," said War Cloud. "He is a wise and brave man, as well as a fair man."

Anna fell silent until, after a while, she asked, "Before we go into camp, is there anything else you should tell me?"

"*Hova'ahane*, stay close to me."

"I will." She reflected for a moment on their evening together. It had been an incredible experience, and not even the otherworldliness of her dream could make it less. Leisurely, not realizing the backlash her next question was to have, she asked, "Is there anything else that you should tell me about the curse?"

He did not answer right away, and Anna, chancing a quick glance up at him, watched as early morning shadows splashed ethereal silhouettes across War Cloud's fea-

tures. It made it difficult to gauge his reaction, but she was
certain she could feel his instantaneous frustration. Why?

He looked away from her, off toward the sunrise, and
said, "There is much I should tell you."

Suddenly he seemed so serious. Why? she wondered,
but she only acknowledged, saying, "All right. If our
lying together will make me a part of this, perhaps I
should know as much about it as I can."

He let his breath out in a deep sigh. "What would you
like to know?" he asked.

Settling back against him, she gave it some thought
and said, "Perhaps you could tell me if there is any way
to break the spell."

He inhaled slowly and paused for a second, at length
answering, "It is said that an act of kindness will end it."

"An act of kindness? That is all?"

He frowned. "It is not so easy. All of the men of my
clan have tried to commit many acts of kindness upon
womankind. It has not worked. The curse holds strong."

"I see," she said, falling temporarily silent. "Why upon
womankind?"

"No one knows," he replied. "When the curse first
came about, it was uncertain it could be broken at all.
Later a medicine man fixed it so that the power of the
curse could be released at some unnamed time in the future, but none know how. All that is known is that it must
be a completely unselfish act given for the good of womankind."

"Hmmmm." Despite the topic of their discussion,
Anna felt like purring, so good did it feel to be held in
this man's arms. And she luxuriated in the touch of War
Cloud's naked chest against the thin fabric of her

chemise. "Tell me," she said, winding a lock of his hair around her fingertip. "When you agreed to help me with the children, is that why you yielded so readily?"

He nodded. "Perhaps."

She frowned. "Were you only trying to break the spell, then?"

He drew his brows together and clenched his jaw, remaining silent. At some length, however, he said, "Do not fret. I promise that there was more to it. That first night on the prairie, Sky Falcon came to me and said that you were the one, that the time was near. I did not believe him, nor would I take his advice. I was going to bring you to the Sioux in the North, but when you seemed willing to give yourself to me, I decided that I would help you. It did not matter if you were the one to break the spell or not."

"It didn't? Why? Why did you decide to help me?"

He moaned. "Because you amused me."

Amused him? Was that all he had felt for her? "Oh," she said, unable to keep the note of distress from her voice. Had he not intimated at that time that he had desired her? Had that not been true?

But he must have sensed her anguish, for he kissed the tender part in her hair and brought up a hand to knead the muscles in her shoulders while he said, "Do not feel bad. You were white and I hated all whites. Even Sky Falcon could not persuade me to change my mind. *You* did. That I should agree to your plan was a great honor to you."

Still she was not reassured and she said, "But if that's true and you were only amused by me, then you must not have meant it when you said you desired me."

His voice held a note of humor when he commented, "Did my actions this evening look to you as though I lied about this?"

A sigh fell into the silence between them and she realized it was her own. *No, his actions spoke well for him.* Still, she was unsatisfied with his answer and she remained silent.

"Know, *Nahkohe-tseske,*" War Cloud said, stroking her shoulders as he spoke, "that since that first night we met, I have been truthful with you. My concern about your welfare and the children's is genuine."

Anna heard him and, while on one level, she might believe him, on another she could not be mollified so easily. She said, "But you did not tell me about the curse at first, even though you agreed to help me. Did you not care then that you might involve me in this and that the curse carried the penalty of death?"

He shrugged as though it were nothing and said, "You were white."

"So? I am white now."

"It is as the wise ones say," he commented, as though he spoke to no one but the wind. "The whites ask many questions."

"Stop that." She sat up.

"What?"

"Every time I get too close to you, you pick on my race."

"There is a great deal about your race to 'pick on.' "

"Do not *do* that." She gently slapped one of his legs before settling back against him.

He took her scolding good-naturedly enough and inhaled deeply before he said, "It is hard for me to think well of your race, but I am sorry. You are right. You have not proven yourself to be anything like the other white people that I have known. To call you white is a great insult to you and I will try to remember that."

"Hmmm," she said, setting her lips into a frown. "I think, War Cloud, that your answer to me is even still an insult. Tell me, are all Indians your friends?"

"You know they are not."

"Then," she countered, logically, "you must admit that there are different types of people even amongst races."

His massage upon her back lightened. Gently, he turned her around until he could see her eyes. And staring down at her, he said, "I know where your tongue is leading you, *Nahkohe-tseske,* and I do not wish to go there with you. Know that the white man has proven himself to be lower than even the Crow or the Shoshone. Those tribes, at least, do not kill women and children unless forced to do so, nor do they slaughter us while pretending to talk peace."

Anna stilled beneath his earnest expression. "I am so sorry about that incident at Sand Creek," she said as though she had personally done the damage.

"I do not want your sympathy."

"Then what is it that you want from me?"

Rather than answer, he kissed her hair, the sensitive skin at her neck, her ear.

And she moaned.

He whispered, "Does that tell you?"

She turned her face away, and though she smiled, she could not help commenting, "I am uncertain. Although I am flattered by your attention, I little understand it. I

know my limits, War Cloud, and long ago I came to terms
with the fact that I am not a pretty woman."

"Do not say these things about yourself."

She presented him with her back and sat forward. She
said, "Let us not discuss that subject, either, at least not
right now."

"*E-peva'e*. All right." He brought his arms around her
waist, pulling her back into his embrace, all the while
whispering against her ear, "Know that I find you beautiful."

"Stop!"

"You do not believe me?"

"No." She shook her head.

"Here." He set her a little away from him and, turning
her around, took her hand and guided it to his chest. "Do
you feel the beating of my heart?"

She tilted her head to the side, her eyes staring into his.

"Know that when you are near to me, my heart beats
fast, as though I am running while remaining perfectly
still. Now, while I admit that upon first seeing you, without any knowledge of your spirit, I might have passed
you by; it is also true that from the start, no matter how
unattractive you tried to make yourself, there was something about you that drew me to you. Yes, I witnessed
your valor and your love for your children, but there was
more. No, long have I been of the opinion that you are,
indeed, as beautiful in body as you are in spirit."

Anna did not know what to say. She could not dispute
him, for he spoke with too much sincerity.

"But even knowing this," she countered, as though she
had to challenge him, "you were ready to have me die?"

"Remember that I have never offered you marriage."

He folded her back into his arms and said, "*Nahkohe-tseske,* you appear ready to find fault with me perhaps a bit too easily. Let me ask you a similar question."

"Fine," she granted.

"Have you told me the complete truth about your intentions toward me?"

She cut a glance up at him. "I think so."

But he insisted. "About everything?"

She turned her head away from him. Of course she had not told him *everything.* Yes, she had been truthful; it was only that she had left out certain parts.

But there were some things a girl had to hold secret within herself, after all. She could never tell him, not ever, that she had envisioned walking away from him. It was not a thought that filled her with pride. In view of the fact that she had pleaded with him to make love to her, it would make her seem callous, as well as perhaps a little wanton, too. Plus, it would not do a great deal to satisfy his dignity. No, she could never tell him that.

He said, however, as though he had read her thoughts, "I think neither of us is saying the exact truth that is in our hearts. Perhaps it would be good if we were completely honest with each other."

She bobbed her head once, as though she agreed perfectly with him, although silently she continued to hold her own doubts.

He said, "I will tell you about the curse, all that I know, but you must also be honest with me regarding why you are falling in with my plans so easily. Do not be mistaken and think that I have not noticed this about you."

She quickly sucked in her breath.

And he prodded, "Is it a pact?"

She remained silent for a moment or two. And he urged, "Do we have a treaty?"

What could she say? At last, she complied and said, "Very well."

"I will go first," he said, "for there are some things about the curse that I have not told you, and you are right, you should be aware of it all, for despite our efforts, there might come a time when it could still influence you."

"Good," she agreed.

"The story of the curse goes back long, long ago to my ancestor, Sky Falcon. Although he is being punished for cheating on his wife, the truth is that he was not completely deceptive to her. And that is the sad part of the story. His love for his wife was deep and true. But Sky Falcon had been a merchant in his younger days and had known many a young girl in an intimate way. Because of this, his father-in-law would not accept him as a husband."

"Then how did he come to be married?"

"Spirit Woman, she who was the love of his life, eloped with him. And they were happy for many years amongst his own people. But always did Spirit Woman's father sit in anger. Hatred festered within him. And at last he devised a plan to kill Sky Falcon and get his daughter back. But the plan had terrible consequences, for in the end, his deception took his daughter from him forever."

"How did it happen?" she whispered.

"I do not know all of it, but here is what my father told me and what his father before him told him. Old Lost In Timber plotted with a witch, Dark Star. Because both Lost In Timber and Dark Star had great powers, they were able to make Lost In Timber take on the form of a mountain lion. Together Dark Star and her 'pet' came into the camp of my ancestor, Sky Falcon. There Dark Star set out to seduce my ancestor, but she could not do it by fair means, for Sky Falcon's heart was true.

"It is said that this witch managed at last to take over Sky Falcon's mind by having him touch a magical pelt, and she would have taken him into her intimately had it not been for Spirit Woman finding them.

"Still," continued War Cloud, "all might have been salvaged, had not Lost In Timber, whose spirit had been living within the mountain lion, attacked Sky Falcon. In order to save her husband, Spirit Woman offered her life to the witch in exchange for her husband's life.

"This was quickly done and Spirit Woman was taken into another world. Meanwhile old Lost In Timber became again his own self, but it was too late. His daughter was gone.

"It was his own fault," said War Cloud, "but old Lost In Timber could not see it. And so angry did he become, that he cast a powerful spell over Sky Falcon, as well as over all Sky Falcon's kin for generations to come. Always would this clan from that day forward be unlucky in love, and so unfortunate would they become that their seed would at last die out from this world."

Anna sat within War Cloud's arms, listening to his gentle voice, so close to him, yet so far away. She dared not move. The story he told her was beautiful in a way, but alas, it was too strange for her to accept. Yet she understood that this man fully believed it. Unfortunately, it brought too clearly to mind the differences between her and War Cloud, and a peculiar sensation filled her soul. It was as though she felt herself grow distant from him.

Odd that only a few moments ago she had felt practically one with him.

But never had it been more evident to her that she had stepped into the midst of a culture she did not understand. Curses? Witches? People turning into animals and back again?

She said, unable to help herself, "It is unbelievable."

"And yet," he countered, "you saw the proof of it last night."

"Did I? I had a strange dream. That is all." She suddenly grew tired and closed her eyes. And of course, the truth was, she had reason to be tired; she'd had little sleep. Still, only a few moments ago, she had been the picture of health and energy.

He asked, "Was it a dream?"

"Of course it was," she said. "Although I do admit to envisioning your ancestor in my dream. Tell me, War Cloud, why does your ancestor appear to haunt you?"

War Cloud swept his arm out in front of him, indicating the world at large. "Because," he answered, "Sky Falcon can find no peace until the curse is broken. Old Lost In Timber ensured that even in death Sky Falcon would not be united with his wife. And so Sky Falcon searches. He seeks her and someone who can at last break the spell."

"And you all believe that I am the one to do this?"

War Cloud shrugged. "The wise men know that only a strong heart can afford to be kind. You are both."

This was a piece of knowledge that she had never heard before and she took a moment to assimilate it. *It took strength to be kind?* Was it the mark of a society of bullies where the opposite was held true, even revered?

Miserably, she had no answer to her question and found herself asking War Cloud, "And what if I decide to help you and I fail?"

"Then we all fail," he said. "It will not be the first time."

Her fingers had been sifting through the sweet-smelling grass that grew beside them. She picked up a long piece of it and, putting it in her mouth, asked, "What must I do to help?"

"No one knows," came his answer.

She paused. "But if no one knows, why tell me any of this?"

"Because," he said, "if you decide to continue on with me, there is danger. You must know that the spirits want us married. It is why they came to you last night in your dream. If you marry me and do not die, the curse will end. My ancestors think your beliefs are strong enough to withstand the danger. That is all."

"I see." She threw the blade of grass away and twisted around to look at him. "And you? What do you think? Do you agree?"

"I think it is too great a risk to take. I believe that we should continue on as we have decided we will do. We will take the children to safety and you will go back east where you belong. You will remain alive; the children will remain alive; all will be well."

"Except that the curse still exists."

"It is not your worry."

But strangely enough, she thought, it was becoming more and more her problem, although she decided to keep this bit of information to herself.

"And now," he said, "you must tell me what it is that you wish to keep secret."

She sighed, the change in topic coming a little too quickly for her. Must she tell him those things she would rather not say?

"You promised," he urged.

She pouted before she remarked, "You must give me your word, then, that you will not think unkindly of me if I tell you this."

"It is done," he answered.

She glanced away from him, wishing she did not have to say the words, but at last she uttered, "I . . . I was . . . had a thought once—when we were going head to head—that it might not be so bad to be able to have a night with you and then walk away."

He nodded.

"I was ashamed I had the thought. But even knowing this, I could not wait to commit the act that would bind us together."

"I know this."

She held her breath for a moment and then said, "In my society, such a woman is not well thought of."

He did not speak for several minutes, and while Anna waited, the world seemed to stop spinning. At last, however, he began to speak, saying, "When two people are thrown together, as we have been, it would seem strange if neither person found something about the other to admire. Both of us are unmarried. Both of us are young and the threat of passion would be difficult to suppress. You are not to be blamed for what has happened. The fault, if there is one, is mine. Had I not told you of my plight, you would not have thought of it."

"I am not so certain." With this admission, she felt his surprise, though he uttered no words to express his reaction. She explained, "I found you attractive from the first moment I saw you."

He seemed to accept this well enough, since all he muttered was a "Humph." Nonetheless, after a brief hesitation, he went on to say, "It matters little who is to blame. The past means nothing. What is important is what we do from here. The spirits are trying to marry us. I do not like it."

With these words he fell into silence, and she followed his lead, both quiet, both seemingly engrossed in their own thoughts. At last, he commented, "I think the best thing to do is to pretend that the act of mating did not happen between us. My needs are satisfied for the moment. There is no cause to do it again."

Almost at once, Anna's composure slipped, although she did her best to pretend that his words had no effect on her.

Unblinking, however, he continued, "I think that, as hard as it is, we have no choice but to continue on as we were. I will lead you to the white settlements as soon as I warn my people of the danger to them; you will place your children and I will help you. After it is done, I will go north to visit my relatives as I have intended doing all along, and you will return to the East. It is the best thing to do."

Was it? Anna found herself compelled to disagree with him, the desire almost overwhelming, but because she could find no logical explanation for the emotion, aside from her own passion, she remained silent.

The odd thing was that he was telling her these things even while he held her within his arms. And she was reluctant to remove herself from the warmth of his embrace.

Was there no other solution? Truly?

At length, he observed, "It is a good thing that you do not want to be my wife and that you have told me this. For therein lies your safety."

"But that's not true. It was only a thought."

If he heard her, he did not mention it. He sat up and positioned her a little distance away from him, and though she missed the safety of his arms, she made no comment.

"Soon," he told her, "you will need to awaken the children. For this day, we go to the Dog Soldier camp."

She murmured, "Then we will be traveling in the daylight hours?"

"*Haahe,* we are in Dog Soldier country and there is no longer a need to travel at night. Scouts have spotted us and will protect us until we reach camp. You should go and prepare the children now."

She sat forward, but before she left him altogether, she turned back to him. "War Cloud?"

He arched a brow in her direction.

"It was a thought I had, that is all. Do not think that I will not still endeavor to have us married. Plus, I am not convinced that going our separate ways is the right thing to do."

"*Haahe,* I know." He smoothed the backs of his fingers over her cheek. "But I am. Now, go."

She could think of nothing else to say and so, with little more to be debated, at least for the present, she went.

Chapter 20

By midmorning Lame Bird and Collin returned, reporting that they had spotted troops to the east, following the trail of Tall Bull's camp. These were the troops under Major Eugene A. Carr, a man well known to the Dog Soldiers. He had been hunting Indians all winter, it seemed, finding few to battle.

But now it was summer and the Indians were more willing to fight. Thus there had been skirmishes between the two forces almost daily.

Something had happened to Collin, however. He limped.

"We were surprised by two Pawnee scouts," said Lame Bird in Cheyenne, gesturing the meaning of his words in sign language so that Anna could understand. "The Pawnee," continued Lame Bird, "had dressed themselves to appear that they were Sioux—who you know are friendly to us. These Pawnee had waved their robes to the two of us." He pointed to himself and the other boy before continuing, "We did not know that these Indians were anything but friends, and when they asked us to approach, we did so. They attacked. In the skirmish, my white friend, Collin, was hurt."

"I told him to leave me," said Collin, "but Lame Bird would not do it. After running off the enemy's horses, Lame Bird then rescued me by pulling me onto his pony and, since the enemy had no mounts, we were able to escape."

Anna stood staring at the two of them with something which must have been akin to shock fixed upon her face. For the moment, speaking seemed beyond her.

"It was a knife wound," said Collin into the silence. And then, as though he were proud of it, he pulled up his pant leg to indicate a raw, red scar.

Anna sucked in her breath.

"I tried to heal it as well as I could," said Lame Bird in sign language. "I could not find the best herbs to attend to it because we had to keep moving. We did not know if the Pawnee might catch their horses and give us chase."

Anna smiled at Lame Bird and said, "You did well," giving meaning to the English words by signing. She added, "That was a very brave thing that you did."

Lame Bird stuck his chin up in the air and straightened his spine. But there was a sparkle in his eye when he signed, "And would you have done less?"

Anna shook her head and, casting a glance at Lame Bird, gestured, "I would have done the best I could." She touched Lame Bird's shoulder while, under her breath, she remarked, "It reminds me that I have not uttered a proper thank-you to you, young man." And as though to rectify the error at once, Anna signed, "I would give you honor, too, for coming to our aid—mine and the children's—back there at the train fight. I . . . That was another brave thing that you did for us and I thank you."

Lame Bird grinned at her slightly before he signed, "As was yours in rescuing me. Perhaps," he added, "we are kindred spirits."

Anna smiled. "I think that you may be right," she said and, reaching out, put her arms around the youngster, hugging him close.

Lame Bird returned the embrace effusively until, as though embarrassed, he turned away to leave Collin in Anna's charge. But Anna soon discovered that she had the same problem as Lame Bird. She did not have the proper herbs or medicine to treat the wound.

Hopefully, thought Anna, when they reached Tall Bull's camp, they could all rest for a few days and allow Collin to recover. Silently, she said a prayer.

They found the Dog Soldier camp at a place the whites called Summit Springs, on the South Platte. Here the Indians had set up camp because the river was too flooded to cross.

It was the first time Anna had ever witnessed an Indian encampment, and had she not been so nervous, she might have admired the sight of it perhaps a bit more than she did. Stretched out for miles over a high plateau, the tepees complemented the land as though they were attached to it and a part of it.

Buffalo skins, bleached white on the bottom and darker toward the top, fell over tall lodgepoles neatly arranged in circles. There were literally hundreds of these lodges, beautifully painted and strewn over the land, the only curious thing she noticed about the dwellings being that their entrances were all set toward the east.

Closer and closer they came to the camp, near enough

that Anna could hear the shouts and laughter of children. She huddled her own charges in toward her and put her arms protectively around them. No one spoke.

At first, upon entering the camp, the buzz of happy voices and the rhythm of drums swept through the village. But as soon as the people caught sight of War Cloud leading herself and the children, the camp became quiet. And if ever it could be said that silence was deafening, this was the time.

Soon, however, as War Cloud had predicted, incomprehensible words came at her. Anna needed no translation to recognize the jeers. Some picked up stones. A few threw them; others threatened.

"E-tsevestoemo," War Cloud sang out, grabbing stones from as many people as he could and forcing those close to him to set down their weapons. *"E-tsevestoemo*, (She is the one who is my spouse)" he shouted at the crowd.

Quickly he ushered Anna and the children through the camp and into a tepee, out of sight.

No one followed them, although Anna became more than a little aware that several Indians stood outside the lodge. She could literary "feel" their hostility. Still, no one made a move to harm them.

Anna did not understand and she asked War Cloud, "Why do they not follow us in here or try to pull up the lodge's covering, if they want to hurt us?"

"Because," War Cloud said, as he watched her settle the children, "you are in one of the lodges of the chief, Tall Bull. No one will harm you so long as you remain here. Even the worst of our enemies would be safe here so long as they do not step foot outside the lodge. Now, stay here. I will be gone but a moment."

And then he left without another word.

But he was back quickly enough, bringing an old woman with him.

Anna glanced up at the Indian matron, noticing that the woman stood watching her with a look that could only be called disbelief.

War Cloud, however, appeared to be anxious to be on his way and he instructed, "Do not leave this lodge. Remember that so long as you remain in this tepee, you are safe. This woman is Blue Star. She is white, although she has been with us so long, no one remembers that about her anymore. She will help you."

White? Anna stared hard at the woman, receiving a similar scrutiny in return.

White? This person certainly looked like no white woman Anna had ever seen. The old one's face was literally covered with paint and her graying hair, caught into two braids, had turned almost completely white, hiding whatever color it might once have been. She wore a southern Cheyenne cloth dress and moccasins.

Anna said, "Hello?"

The woman gazed at her in wonder, as if she knew the word but could not put a significance to it.

War Cloud said, "My brother and I, as well as Collin, must go to the tepee of the council chiefs. There we must tell them what we have seen. None of you are to leave here. Do you understand?"

Anna nodded but protested, "Must Collin accompany you?"

"*Haahe,* but he will not be harmed. I promise this. That he sustained an injury in battle with the Pawnee will make him a hero in the eyes of our people."

Anna gazed at the face of her young charge, recognizing the light of excitement in those youthful eyes. "All right," she agreed, "but please send him back here soon so that I can attend to his wound. And Collin, do exactly as War Cloud tells you."

Collin nodded and War Cloud said, "It will be done." Turning, he bent over to exit the tepee, Lame Bird and Collin following quickly after him.

After they left, Anna glanced at the old woman once more and smiling, tried again, "Hello?"

But when the old woman returned, *"Pave-eseeva,"* and when she seemed to have no more to say, Anna gave up trying to communicate.

Under the cover of darkness, they left the Dog Soldier camp as quickly as they had come.

"A war party of Sioux have arrived and have reported that the soldiers are close to the camp," said War Cloud, returning to Anna and the children in the early evening. "The Sioux advise that we move camp and cross the river at once, but Tall Bull will not do it. He says it is too dangerous."

Anna fixed her eyes on War Cloud and muttered, "And so the Indians will not cross the river because it is too dangerous? But we will? We, who have much less experience with these kinds of things? And in the middle of the night no less?"

Though he appeared to listen to her, he seemed unaffected by her questions. "We must and we will do it. Try to understand, while you might be safe in this lodge, there is too much danger for you here in the camp, even though I have said that you are my woman and that these children are my own. Plus, with the warrior-whites so close to us, we cannot stay here. If fighting were to start, no one would know you from the enemy. Possibly no one would care. *Hova'ahane,* we cannot stay."

"But, War Cloud, how can we possibly get across the river safely?"

He shrugged lightly. "We will manage," he said. "We leave tonight. Prepare yourself and the children."

Anna sighed. She had hoped to rest here for a little while longer. She could have used more sleep, and she had wanted Collin to have more time to recuperate.

But perhaps it was for the best. If the soldiers were close and there was to be fighting, she did not wish to be in the middle of it. Besides, if she were honest, she would admit that she was becoming used to traveling through the night.

She awoke the children well before midnight. At least one good thing had come from arriving in the Dog Soldier camp, and that was that they had been given ready access of War Cloud's pony herd. All of the children rode, most traveling double, and with one mount for each adult, plus one for Collin and one for Lame Bird, they left camp with twelve horses total.

Now they only had to ford a flooded river.

Raging water filled Anna's vision while the thundering mass of swirling liquid rippled under the beams of a crescent moon. Mixtures of dark brown and white foam swept over its bed like a streaming herd of stampeding buffalo; loud thumps of rocks, as they were picked up and set down, adding to the general cacophony.

Mists filled the air, partly from the water, partly from

the fires the Indians had set to erase their trail. Smoky. The air smelled smoky and wet all at the same time. And while beads of moisture fell over her face, she watched the natural disaster in utter fascination.

Whatever were they going to do? It looked impossible.

She was not given long to ponder their plight, however. Approaching her with one of the ponies, War Cloud said, "You must stay with the children. The water is too swift to allow us to cross it in the usual way."

Anna tilted her head. "What is the usual way?"

"With a float made of buckskin," he answered easily enough. "You stay here. Lame Bird and I will have to take the children across two at a time."

The gaze she gave him must have communicated her confusion and she asked, "How?"

"Each child will ride a pony, my brother and I will swim alongside the animal to the other edge of the river."

"But how will you get back for the rest of us?"

"Lame Bird and I will swim back here with one pony. Then we will take the next two children, until we are all safely across."

"But that could take all night," she protested.

There was a hint of humor in his eye when he admitted, "It is a good thing we have most of the evening ahead of us, is it not?"

She barely acknowledged him before she offered, "I could help. It would go faster."

"And have you ever crossed a river as swift as this?"

The answer was more than obvious, and she remained silent.

"*Hova'ahane*. You will stay with the children. Someone must remain with them. *Ne-nastse,* come on."

War Cloud led a pony to the edge of the river, the water's shoreline dotted with bushes and grasses. Anna followed him, trying to think of some other way of getting across.

She said, "Could we not go upriver a bit and see if there is an easier crossing?"

War Cloud shook his head. "Scouts have been sent out and have found no ready passage across. Besides," he said, bending to pick up one of the children and swinging him easily into his arms. He smiled good-naturedly at the youngster, as if to say that Indians forded surging rivers every day. "Besides," he continued speaking to Anna, "there is not the time to go upriver. Warrior-whites are in Dog Soldier country, and we are not in a position to do battle with them without suffering severe losses." He positioned the boy on the back of the animal, saying to the child, "We are going to cross this river, do you understand?"

The boy nodded.

Handing a set of buckskin reins to the boy, he said, "Your job is to hold on to the horse no matter what happens. Do not let go. Do you think you can do that?"

"I will try," said the boy.

"*E-peva'e,* it is good," said War Cloud, returning to lead a second pony to the edge of the water. Taking hold of another child, War Cloud settled the youngster on the horse in much the same manner as he had the first child.

Lastly he motioned to Lame Bird.

"You will come back," Anna said before War Cloud stepped into the water.

"Do not doubt it."

"No," she said, "you misunderstand. I am telling you that you *are* to come back. I would have you be careful."

He turned to her, reaching out a hand to run the backs of two fingers gently over her cheek. He said, "I will."

"You'd better."

He grinned and, pivoting around, urged the horses into the water.

Anna watched them with a mixture of hope and despair, refusing to take her eyes off of them until their figures were mere specks in the distance. Time passed slowly as she awaited War Cloud's return. She could not see a thing.

It must have been close to an hour later when War Cloud and Lame Bird approached Anna and the children once more, but they came from much farther downstream.

Upon seeing them, Anna let out a deep sigh. The two of them might be soaking wet, but they were alive.

She rubbed her hands up and down her sides in nervous anticipation. "That took a long time."

"It cannot be helped," War Cloud responded, coming straight at her and not stopping until he had taken her in his arms. Without pause, without stopping to think, he rained one kiss after another on her lips, her cheeks, her eyes.

And she returned his passion, pulling his head down to her and covering him with kiss after kiss on his neck, his shoulders, any area of skin available to her.

His arms around her felt as though they bestowed life, and she sobbed against his shoulder, not caring that he was drenched from head to foot. She admitted, "I am scared, for you, for the children."

"I know," War Cloud said, "but this must be done. You must not show the children your fear. It will go better if you keep them calm." He raised his head to send a penetrating look into her eyes.

At last he set her away from him and quickly, as though he dared not think too long about it, turned away to pick up another one of the children.

Ten pairs of wide eyes, however, stared back at both her and War Cloud. But Anna, having no ready explanation to justify what the children had witnessed, simply remained quiet.

War Cloud immediately set back to work and, after settling one child atop a fresh horse, he led another youngster to a different animal.

He said to Anna, "Perhaps you could rub down the pony that I brought back, that he might be ready to cross the stream again later."

Anna nodded and, grabbing the buckskin reins, led the animal to a pasture of grass.

Meanwhile, War Cloud set the other child on top of the horse. He gave this youngster a grin as well and asked, "Are you ready to show me how brave you are?"

The lad responded to the encouragement and said, "I will be courageous, I promise."

War Cloud acknowledged the boy with a simple, *"Haahe,"* and a smile. "The river current is strong and you must hold on tight to this horse, for he will get you to the other side. Can you do that?"

"I can," came the young voice.

"I could help you," volunteered Anna again, having come up beside them.

"You will stay here," War Cloud said, unrelenting.

"You will be the last to cross." He sent Anna a cautionary glance. "Do not disobey me in this. The water is a dangerous place even for those who are experienced in the ways of this land."

Anna pouted, but he grinned at her and changed the subject. Pointing toward the sky, he said, "Do you see those stars?" He directed her attention to the Big Dipper.

She nodded. It was practically the only constellation visible this night.

"Watch it carefully for me. When the last brother is aiming down toward the prairie, tell it to me. For that will mean that morning is coming soon."

"All right," she said. "Which star is the last brother?"

He showed her. "It is the end star there, the one in the handle. Do you see it?"

She did and she inclined her head.

His look at her was hungry and proud all at the same time. The feeling of affinity lasted but a few seconds before he was turning away to run back to the ponies and the children. Once more, War Cloud and Lame Bird set out across the river.

Time passed even more slowly this time, and yet, as he had before, War Cloud returned for two more children.

It took five trips and what must have been six hours before Anna noticed that the last brother was pointing directly toward the prairie. There were two children yet to swim over to the other side.

She told War Cloud as soon as he returned, "Morning will be here soon."

Tipping his head up at an angle, he looked in the direction she showed him and commented, "We must hurry, then, for I would have us gone from here before the light of day."

Anna, catching his gaze, looked up to him and volunteered, "I could follow you with a few of the horses that remain here. It would make it easier on you."

"*Hova'ahane*. Lame Bird and I will have to return for the ponies that would still be here anyway. No, you are to stay here and guard these horses until we return."

Anna frowned. She felt urged to get across that water as quickly as possible. What would happen when morning came? Would there be more trouble in the camp?

Unfortunately, she could not predict the future with any sort of accuracy, and the waiting seemed interminable.

Morning was dawning on the eastern horizon when War Cloud and Lame Bird at length returned for their last load.

Neither of the Indians appeared distressed, despite their intense physical effort. And though Anna espied exhaustion in War Cloud's face, he made no mention of it. Neither did she.

Lame Bird led two riderless ponies to the water and was already crossing it on one of them when War Cloud turned to Anna.

"*Ne-naestse*," he said, "come here." He held the reins of a pony out for her, and she settled on its back with little assistance. Then War Cloud was leading her pony into the water.

He said over his shoulder, "You have done well and I am happy that you did not disobey me, for I fear," he admitted, "that I am too tired to scold you."

Her heart went out to him. "Thank you for what you are doing."

The pony was in the water up to Anna's thighs when War Cloud answered, "No thanks are needed." He grinned at her. "I am required always to be kind to women, after all."

She smiled back at him when suddenly the pony shifted from a walk into a full swim. Anna gasped as the pony plunged forward, leaving only its neck and head above the raging waves. Cold water encompassed her up to and above her waist. The current pushed them downstream, but War Cloud held them firmly, making sounds to the animal and shouting, *"Ta-naestse!"* over the roar of the water.

Anna almost lost her seat, crying when a current threatened to pull her into the stream.

"Hold tight," came War Cloud's command, and Anna leaned over the animal to clutch fast on to it. No sooner had she complied when War Cloud swam close to her. He pushed an arm around her waist and brought her fully back into her seat.

Anna bulked as she realized how demanding this night had been for him. Still, oddly, despite his exhaustion, she felt safe and protected.

They passed through the rest of the water without further incident, and soon the pony found its footing on the rocky bottom of the river.

"E-peva'e," he said to the animal, petting it as he led it onto the shore.

There Anna beheld all the children. War Cloud had set Collin to watch over them.

War Cloud dropped the reins of Anna's horse and said to her, "Lame Bird and I will go back across the water to get the remaining horses, and then," he paused, though he did not look up at her, "we will find that white settlement."

The joy of seeing the children all safe and settled paled against another, more pressing concern and, as Anna hopped down from the horse, she said, "Do not go back. We traveled here to your village on no more than three horses, and now we have eight. It is enough." She had come up behind War Cloud and no matter that the children watched, she placed her hand on his shoulder. "Please stay here."

He turned his head toward her touch. "We will make better time and it will be easier on us all if we have all the horses. Lame Bird and I have gone across the water too many times for it to be dangerous. I would have my remaining ponies."

"Please, don't," she pleaded again, but it was no use. He would have his way about this and taking one of the more rested mounts, he and Lame Bird set out for the other side.

She had a bad feeling about it, but short of taking the man hostage and refusing to let him leave, what could she do?

Anna turned away and pivoted back toward the children, scrutinizing each one. Most of the darlings were dry, she found; a few of the more recent ones to cross the river, however, were still damp, and Anna set about drying them.

Already the sky was growing light in the east, causing Anna worry. But she tried to calm herself; what danger could there be? War Cloud and Lame Bird were Cheyenne; they would come to no harm in the crossing.

The series of shots came as a surprise.

At the sound, panic swept through her and looking

quickly back across the water, Anna surmised the reason why. Soldiers and Pawnee scouts swarmed over the Cheyenne encampment.

Dear God, had War Cloud and Lame Bird reached the other side? Please, dear Lord, please don't let it be so.

"Miss Wiley," one of the children asked, "are War Cloud and Lame Bird going to be all right?"

Anna's throat felt so tight, she could hardly speak. As it was, she could barely make out the shapes of the horses at the water's edge, confirming that neither War Cloud nor Lame Bird had reached those animals yet.

Could it be that upon hearing the shots, they'd scrambled back across the water? Or would they do that?

If their people were under attack, would they not be inclined to . . .

Dear Lord, War Cloud and Lame Bird would try to help their own people!

Explosions, gunshots, the neighing of horses, as well as the screaming of women and children, split through the morning air. Even from here, Anna could smell the gunpowder and could sense the utter fright in the air.

She froze. She cared about these people. She did not know why. But she did.

Though she and the children were white, no one in that camp had hurt them, at least not once she and the children had reached that tepee. Given the same circumstances, would they have been treated as well if they had been Indians coming into a white man's town?

She had to rescue these people. She had to help her men.

She glanced at Collin and felt a moment of camaraderie, for he seemed to understand.

Collin said, "Go to them. I will watch everyone here. We will hide until you return." He placed the reins of one of the animals in her hands. "I have been watching War Cloud and Lame Bird come and go across the water. The current carries them downstream, that way." He pointed. "You should find them somewhere down there. Be careful."

She squinted her eyes against the morning sun and said, "I will."

The battle raged off in the distance, but closer to the shore, she could see several women and children venture into the stream. Soldiers chased them, shooting at them, but amazingly enough, the women and children kept going, kept running.

Holding tight to the mane of her pony, Anna swam toward the other side of the river as fast as she could. Perhaps she could carry some of those women and children with her back over the river. She had to try.

As she approached the shoreline, she became aware of two figures fighting off the advance of the soldiers while the harried women and children fell into the river.

War Cloud and Lame Bird!

Anna had never witnessed, much less been in the midst of, a battle until this moment, and she would never forget it; the sounds of the shooting, the explosions, the screaming, the utter fear. Nor would she ever forget—or even come to terms with—the terror that twisted its way into her gut. A shot rang out close to her; she saw a woman with a child drop.

Dear Lord, the soldiers were shooting women and children!

War Cloud advanced upon the man who had done it, War Cloud having no weapon but his knife, for his gun would still be wet.

Anna cried out, but her wail could not be heard over the noise of battle. She screamed over and over, watching as War Cloud battled the soldiers.

In truth, Anna had never been so relieved for the incompetence of the military as she was at that moment; for the soldier missed War Cloud completely, though her hero approached the man as though he were unafraid of the bullets. And then the two became locked in hand-to-hand combat.

But she could not simply stand and watch. Forcing her pony to follow her, she gained her way to the shore, there to be met with a terrified woman and her children. She wanted to go to War Cloud's aid; she desperately needed to ensure he remained alive, yet she knew that she could not do that.

Gazing one last time at War Cloud, she knew what she must do, and pushing the pony into the midst of the fleeing Indians, she said, "Come on, using gestures to communicate."

Setting the horse back into the water, she swam beside the woman and her children, much as War Cloud had done with her, guiding the animal through the tempestuous water and toward the other shore.

Once they reached the shoreline on the other side, she tried to communicate with hand motions to the woman that there were other horses not far away.

"Take them," she said. "Take them and run far away from here."

Despite the language problems, the woman seemed to

understand, for she headed off in that direction, and Anna, hugging her poor pony's head, encouraged the animal back into the water.

Most of the women and children were already braving the river, despite its current, but Anna was able to help another party across the water.

War Cloud still fought, defending the flight of the women and children. Presently he was joined by a few other warriors who had escaped the village and were now keeping the soldiers back, thus allowing their families to flee.

But their plight appeared grave, for soldiers poured out of the village. Even as the last few women made their way to the shore, the men followed, scrambling after them and taking a stand, fighting a hasty retreat.

Soldiers pressed down on War Cloud and Lame Bird. Their situation looked desperate, unless . . . Anna had an idea.

"War Cloud! Lame Bird!" she called out. "This way!"

Did he hear her? And if he did hear, would he know to come to her? Would he trust her, a white woman, at a time like this?

"Nahkohe-tseske, ase-sta'xestse!"

She had no idea what he had said, but she knew one thing. "I am not leaving without you."

"Ne-ve'neheseve! Ase-sta'xestse!"

"I have a horse. Hurry, we can get away."

Both older and younger brother glanced around them, as though to take stock of how the fight went. What did they see? Anna could only hope that, with no more women and children streaming from the village, the two brothers would decide to leave.

She watched in nervous wonder as both War Cloud and Lame Bird began a retreat toward the water.

"Come!" she said, holding the reins of the pony and forcing it to be still as she stood beside it. "Come! Run hard! You can make it!"

War Cloud caught up to her. "*Ta-naestse!* Go on!" he said in English as though only now realizing that he had been speaking in Cheyenne. "We will follow."

She did not wait for another command. Setting the horse into the water and bringing her men with her, she set out across the river, swimming by the pony's side. A stray bullet whizzed past them, followed by two more shots, and then nothing.

Was it over?

Anna glanced back as War Cloud and Lame Bird guided the pony across the water. The Indian camp was completely destroyed. Even from her far vantage point, she could see the raging fires destroying the once grace-ful Indian village.

Over the thunder of the water, she asked War Cloud, "What happened?"

War Cloud, swimming behind her, peered back toward the shore before returning his glance to her. And in his eyes she glimpsed such a look of despair, she knew she would never forget this moment.

"I fear," he shouted to be heard over the water, "that my people should have crossed the river in the night, as we did. Had they done this, they would not have been taken by surprise. I do not want to think what this will mean. This was the last of the Dog Soldier camps."

Anna did not know what to say, either, silence seeming to be the only option.

At some length, she said, "There were several women and children who escaped. I saw what you and Lame Bird were doing, holding off the soldiers so they could get away. That was very brave of you."

He shrugged.

And she urged, "Let us go to the children and be away from here as quickly as we can. I do not see any of the soldiers following us across the river. Perhaps we will make it over there safely after all."

"Perhaps."

It was all he said.

Chapter 21

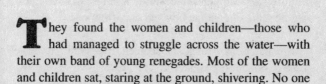

They found the women and children—those who had managed to struggle across the water—with their own band of young renegades. Most of the women and children sat, staring at the ground, shivering. No one spoke. Now and again, one of the women let out a wail.

War Cloud took command at once. *"Ne-ve'-ea'xaame,"* he said to the women. Then in English to Anna, "We will take these few Cheyenne women and children with us."

"Yes," she said.

"Maybe," he commented, as he rubbed down one of the ponies, "we will have to go all the way to the land of the Sioux before we will be able to find a white settlement."

Anna nodded as she began to throw blankets onto the ponies' backs, but she did not voice a word. It was not so much what he said as what he left unsaid that bothered her.

Was he, too, trying to invent reasons why the two of them should remain together? If they did not marry—and from War Cloud's viewpoint, they must not—sooner or later they were going to have to part.

She did not want to think about it. Curse or no curse,

duty or no duty, Anna was not certain she wanted to leave War Cloud.

But, she reminded herself, she had time to consider these things; lots of time. For now, she had best put these thoughts behind her, because these women and children were going to need help, if their party were to leave this place and remain ahead of the soldiers.

Soon, they had set off once more across the prairie, the children and women protected by no more than one desperate man, one Indian boy and one white one.

She had been wrong, she decided. She would not have time to ponder her situation.

Two days later, their bedraggled party rested at the crest of a hill, overlooking the rolling line of a wagon train. Stretching out to the horizon, the oxen-pulled prairie schooners crawled across the land, their inhabitants completely unaware that a party of women and children, plus two Indian males watched them.

At the sight, Anna's spirits plummeted.

But she should feel joyous, shouldn't she? Well, shouldn't she?

After all, this wagon train could be the answer to her prayers. Here, before them, was a white camp. It could mean that she might at last be able to fulfill her duty to the society and to these children, for it was almost a certainty that there would be some good people down there who would be only too happy to take the children.

But at what price? She stole a glance at War Cloud. Was she really prepared to leave him? Never to see him again?

Anna squared her shoulders even as the thought crossed her mind. Did it matter? Hers was a specific duty to these children and to War Cloud. She had given both of them her word of honor; she had no time for her own selfish desires as to what she wished and did not wish.

And yet . . .

As she wistfully gazed down at those wagons, winds blew up from the west, blowing her hair back from her face and outlining her clothing against her body. War Cloud had come to stand next to her. And though he did not touch her, his hair, whipping in the wind, lightly grazed her shoulders, the silky strands mimicking his own potent caress.

Though faint, the brush of those locks set off tiny explosions all along her nerves, and Anna shivered in response, remembering another time when she had dared to run her fingers through this man's dark mane. It seemed so long ago.

Without looking at her, he commented, "My people tell me that they will not go down to those wagons."

Anna turned her head to acknowledge him. Holding a hand over her forehead and squinting up at him, she said, "I do not blame them." Staring at him one moment more, she reminded herself of what she must say to this man. Her heart beat heavily in her chest and she determinedly looked away. She blinked once before she said, "The children and I will be fine from here. War Cloud, I . . . I . . ."

"Think you that I would have you and the children go down there alone? We do not know what awaits you there. Until I am certain that you and the children will be safe, I will accompany you. My brother will stay here with my people and protect them until you and the children are taken in by those people and I am convinced that you will be treated well. After, I will return here."

She would not have to leave him now? Anna's throat constricted and she shifted her face away from him so that he would not see the rush of emotion across it. Staring back down at the long line of billowing white wagons, she found it almost impossible to speak.

After all, what did a person say to a man like War Cloud; a man who had not only saved her life, but was the only man she had ever known intimately? A man whom, in less than a few hours, she would never see again? What words could possibly express her sense of gratitude, her loss?

Alas, she found herself unable to utter a thing, and so she contented herself with doing no more than staring away from him.

"We will wait until darkness," he said, his voice deep, though tightly controlled. And somehow Anna found herself nodding agreement.

Truly, she could do no more than that.

By the time the sun threw its reddish-gold rays over the land, Anna had bathed each child. The Indian women had helped her, though they did not withhold their puzzlement over why these children could not bathe themselves.

Anna tried to explain with signs that if she did not do this task for them, the children would miss cleansing important areas of the body—like behind the ears and under their arms. Nor would they necessarily wash their hair.

And she would have each child looking his best. Their very futures depended on it.

Too soon, it was time to begin the trip down to the wagons. Anna had bathed herself, of course, but she had given up trying to tie her hair up into its customary severe knot.

Darn it all, she did not know why she was making such a fuss over herself. She would have to go as she was. It would hardly matter, she decided.

What would those people think, she wondered, upon seeing her come into their camp with so many children? What would they think of the handsome Indian man who accompanied her? And with she, herself, dressed only in her chemise and petticoats?

Would the white people applaud or crucify her?

Startled, Anna realized her mistake and backed up to that thought. White people? Not her *own* people? Had Anna begun to think and act like an Indian, too?

Perhaps that was not such a bad thing, but when had she changed?

Standing high on a hill, Anna reflected on that, watching as the wagons stopped and drew together into a circle, which, of course, would be their nightly ritual to protect against attacks.

War Cloud had been suspiciously absent throughout the day, Anna had noticed. But he approached her now and with a curt nod, asked simply, "Ready?"

Anna straightened her spine. It occurred to her that she might never be ready to leave this man. But she could hardly tell him this. Not when he remained so adamant about returning her to her people. And so she said, "We are."

He acknowledged her with a slight jerk of his head, and setting out on foot, he guided them toward the wagons, leading ten of the children sitting atop four ponies. Collin and Anna pulled up the rear.

Even from this distance, with fiddles and harmonicas filling the air with music, Anna experienced a fleeting desire to sway to their rhythm. It had been so long since she had heard anything like it.

She carried Patty on her hip, the youngster looking more drawn and skinny than Anna had ever seen her. In truth, Anna was concerned for the young girl, but she kept a smile on her face as Patty stated, "I don't want to go down there."

Anna brushed her fingers through the girl's long, straggly hair and kissed the top of her head. "Everything's going to be fine now."

Patty moaned, the sound of despair in her tone disconcerting to Anna. Patty said, "What if no one wants me this time, too?"

Anna's breath caught and her heartbeat must have increased tenfold, for she could hear it in her ears. It never failed to happen. As they'd journeyed across this country, there had been many times when certain children were not "chosen." And each time a child was left behind, Anna felt his or her hurt as though it were her own.

Perhaps it was that hurt that made it difficult for Anna to answer Patty with an instant rebuttal, for Anna's stomach felt as though it had lodged in her throat. At length, she said, "Shhh, calm yourself. There will be so many people who will want you, they will have to fight over you. Do not fear."

Patty, however, would not be stilled and she cried, "But none of the others wanted me."

Anna felt as though she might cry, too. Her voice trembled as she said, "That's not completely true. I have always wanted you."

"You do?"

Anna could feel Patty's tears, there against her shoulder and, placing the child's head in the crook of her neck, Anna said, "Remember when you wanted to stay with me and War Cloud forever?"

The youngster nodded and hiccuped at the same time.

Anna gulped in a breath of air and plunged in where perhaps she should have been more cautious. However, she affirmed, "*We* want you, Patty."

Big brown eyes set in a too thin face stared back at Anna. "You do?" came the high-pitched question once again.

Anna tried once more to hold back her tears and, pressing her lips together to fight off the urge, she said, "Yes, we do. But first let's see if we can find a good home for you here, shall we? After all, you would not want to grow up as an Indian, would you?"

Patty placed her arms around Anna's neck and hugged. "I would not mind being Indian. And you know what? I hope no one down there wants me. Then I can stay with you and War Cloud forever. I love you, Miss Wiley."

Anna bit her lip. Truly, she tried to keep her composure. But it was no use. This time Anna cried. And sniffling, she said to the youngster, "I love you, too, Patty. I love you, too."

Hugging the child tightly and being hugged back in return, Anna realized the truth of her declaration. Silently, she said a prayer for the child, for herself, for War Cloud, even as tears fell over her cheeks.

While the people on the wagon train cast suspicious glances at War Cloud, they welcomed Anna and the children into their camp openly, with shouts and outbursts of joy.

Food and water appeared before them as though conjured up by a magician's wand. No one asked a question, not even when it became evident that most were curious as to what Anna was doing in the middle of the prairie with all these children and one Indian. And while she and the children accepted their hospitality heartily, Anna kept looking around her, scrutinizing the faces in the crowd for a dark one with very long, black hair.

She found him some distance away from her, staring back at her, arms crossed over his chest.

He wouldn't leave her without saying good-bye, would he?

Anna related her story in brief to these people, accepted their congratulations and their compliments regarding her bravery. But her mind was occupied elsewhere. Once again, she cast a look in War Cloud's direction.

Thunder sounded in the distance, but it barely made an impression on Anna. Laughing, pretending interest in a witticism directed at her, Anna arose and said, "Excuse me, won't you please?"

"Certainly." "Of course," came the round of voices.

Anna trod off in the direction of the lone Indian. She

picked up the hem of her skirt, glancing down at it at the same time. These were new clothes, at least new to her. Someone had lent her a shawl; another woman had given her an outer coat and dress, and Anna had accepted them graciously, but at this moment all she longed for was War Cloud's arms about her.

She approached him slowly and as she did so, she kept her eyes fastened on his, each step she took carefully calculated so as not to draw too much attention to herself. He watched her closely as well, and she could not help but wonder what he was thinking.

Did he, too, regret their parting? Did his heart ache for her as much as hers was aching for him? She hoped so. Somehow, she did not want to experience this hurt all alone.

Presently, she drew level with him. "Has anyone given you trouble?" she wanted to know.

He shook his head, but made no further response.

Once again, she asked, "Has anyone inquired how you came to be mixed up with us?"

He looked away from her before replying, "I pretend I do not understand English. It makes my being here simpler."

"I see," she said. "Well, I for one have told them how you and your brother saved me and the children, and I must say that you are regarded as something of a hero."

He raised his shoulders briefly, as if to say it was nothing.

She stared at him but fell silent, as did he. In the background Anna was aware of laughter, of happiness and of the warmth of fellowship. As another round of thunder rolled across the sky, she disregarded the noise; it was

simply an accompaniment to this moment with War
Cloud. At length, Anna observed, "All of the children except two have new parents and new homes."

He gave her a curt nod. "This is good."

"Yes, it is," she replied. "This wagon train is going to
Oregon. There the children will have a new start on life. It
is a very good thing."

As he listened, War Cloud lifted his head and reposi-
tioned his arms over his chest. Hesitating briefly, he
asked, "And you?"

"I . . . I don't know. As I said, there are still two children left who have not been chosen by any of the families. If I cannot find homes for them here, I must go
somewhere else." She glanced away from him, out into
the night. "I know it is selfish of me to ask, but if, by any
chance, I cannot find homes for these last two, could
you . . . ah . . ."

Why could she not outright ask him? Was it because
his answer was too dear to her? Or was it simply because
she feared his response?

He did not wait for her to finish and he said, "I found
some Lakota scouts with this party. They have agreed to
take my people north as soon as these wagons move on."

Anna did not comment and he did not look at her as
he said, "I told these scouts that I would accompany
them."

"Oh," she said, "I see."

He glanced down at her, but she would not return his
gaze. She did not wish him to look into her eyes; he
might see too much.

But perhaps he did not need to observe her directly to
know her thoughts, for he sucked in his breath and said,

"But I would not have you travel across the prairie alone. If you cannot place these two children into homes, I will take you to another white town."

Anna sent him a hurried glance. "You would?"

He nodded. "I would."

Odd that her mood should depend on the whims and decisions of this one man. Still, there was no use denying it. Anna felt her spirits lift, and for the first time this evening, she experienced a real desire to smile.

He said, "The Cheyenne women and children told me what you did for them at the soldier fight. They told me how you swam with them across the river, helping them to escape."

Anna did not know what, if anything, to say, but she was saved the effort, for War Cloud continued, "That was a brave thing that you did."

Anna turned her face aside. "I would not see them die. The soldiers were little more than bullies, shooting at women and children who had no means to protect themselves. It was hardly fair."

War Cloud inhaled deeply before commenting, "You are a good woman."

"Thank you."

But he was not finished and he carried on, saying, "I regret that my actions have made you less pure in body than you are in spirit."

Anna froze. Regret? Impure?

How could he say such a thing? It was simply not true. Especially when the memory of their time together brought Anna such happiness. Nothing, she decided, not anything that filled her soul with so many good emotions could ever be wrong. Did he not feel it, too?

Regret? No, never would she regret what had happened between them. She would treasure her memories of that time always.

As she thought of what she might say to him, she drew her brows together and said, "I disagree."

He frowned.

"I feel more pure now than I did before we met. Mister War Cloud, I feel I can safely say from experience that a person is not quite whole until he has experienced love from another. No, you may regret what took place between us, but I never will. I . . . I will cherish it."

Having said what was on her mind, she pivoted away from him, presenting him with her back. She had to; she could not bear to see his response.

But he reached out to touch her, the light brush of his fingers keeping her from leaving. He said, "Know that if there were no curse, if there were not so many risks, if things were different between us . . ."

She let out a small cry.

"Little Bear!" He pulled her into his arms, the outline of his body firm against the backside of her own. His head came down against her hair and she heard him drag in his breath, as though he gloried in the joy of inhaling her fragrance. His lips nuzzled her neck. "Little Bear, know that I—"

"I seen that Injun somewhere around here." Behind them came the voice of one of the settlers.

"Damn!" Stepping back, War Could dropped his arms from around her, and Anna glanced down at the ground.

War Cloud's curse word echoed her own thoughts, she decided as she brought up her hands to chafe her upper arms. She would give almost anything at this moment to simply declare herself tied to this man . . . forever.

Two men came up behind them, but Anna chose to ignore them, as did War Cloud.

Turning around, Anna took a deep breath to steady her voice and asked as casually as she might, "Tell me, have you had anything to eat?"

She watched as he shrugged. "The white man is not so ready to share his food with an Indian, and I am not quite willing to eat from his hand, either. I will hunt in the morning and I will eat then."

Anna frowned. "But you must be hungry."

"It is nothing," he said, and then, still neglecting the white men who watched him from the side, added, "Little Bear, know that I would have things different if only I—"

She coughed, sweeping her glance in the direction of the men who were eavesdropping. She asked War Cloud in a voice perhaps too loud, "Would you have something to eat if I brought it to you?"

"I might."

"Then," she said, "wait here while I go and get you some food." And without so much as one more word, she spun around and trod off in the direction of the cook.

"Damn!" she muttered to herself as a tear fell over her cheek. But she would not brush it away. Too many eyes might see it.

What had she gained by her admission to War Cloud? A few more days with him, maybe a week or two.

There was going to come a day, however, when she would no longer be able to think of excuses to keep him with her. And then what would she do?

She would think of something, she decided. She would have to think of something . . .

The music of the fiddles, played against a background of thunder, etched its way into her soul as Anna stood on the sidelines and watched the dance. Men and women from the wagon train twirled around the ground, which had been set up as though for a ball. She recognized the steps of lively jigs, of waltzes and of quadrilles. She watched, too, as the people gossiped and laughed with one another. She stood among them as though a part of them, and yet not.

No one had asked her to dance.

Earlier in the evening, Anna had ensured that the children had been safely tucked into bed, most having new homes and new parents to fuss over them. It had been a happy time, yet sad. Happy that they had found homes; sad that she was going to have to leave them. Truthfully, Anna had felt pulled in two directions.

Plus, she had a worse problem: Patty and Collin.

Poor youngsters. No one had wanted to take Patty or Collin into their lives.

It was not as if something were wrong with the two of them—not really. It was only that given their physical difficulties, those two had been looked upon as more liability than asset. Collin with his limp might or might not be able to produce a hard day's labor on a farm; Patty, because she looked more skin and bones than child, appeared too close to death's door. Patty would need a great amount of nursing before she could be of any use around the house, if she survived.

Anna had not informed either of them of this fact,

however. She had merely tucked them into bed same as she did every night. She had assured herself that in the next town, things would be different.

Still, Anna had cried. Would it really be different?

She had left the two children to sleep, had been intent upon doing that herself, when she had discovered the excitement: there was to be a dance.

A dance. My goodness, she had thought, how she would love to dance.

As a sign of goodwill, a few of the women in the wagon train had lent Anna some fancier clothing, so that she might be able to go to it properly dressed. But Anna had to admit, once she had donned the finery, the effect was not a particularly pleasing one. She was simply too tall, and the dresses they had lent her fell too short.

But she dared not take the dress off, for she had only her chemise and petticoats. She could not go to a party that way.

And her hair? Well, the women had helped her to put it up again into its familiar knot at the back of her neck. But was that attractive on her? She did not think so.

And why should she care? Never had she agonized so much about her appearance.

Maybe, she thought, it might be because out on the prairie, with War Cloud beside her, Anna had felt pretty. He had even told her she was beautiful. And there had been a time when she had believed him.

But perhaps she had believed him too soon. Certainly she was no Cinderella.

No one had asked her to dance.

She could not really blame them; her height put men off.

But the music haunted her. Oh, how she wanted to dance.

No one would know it, though, she determined. Pride would prevent her from making her feelings known. And so, pasting a smile on her face, she stood apart from the others, watching, waiting, hoping.

Soon, she would leave, but it was still too early to do so. After all, the dance had barely begun and was being given in her honor. Besides, maybe the threatening storm would come and she would be saved the effort of making an excuse to leave.

In the meantime, she would simply have to watch the others . . . and dream.

Because no one had asked her to dance.

Chapter 22

War Cloud stood at the edge of the promenade and watched as the white people demonstrated their own brand of dancing. He remembered seeing this kind of entertainment when he had briefly scouted for the army. He had even learned how to do it once.

But that had been a long time ago.

Where was she?

She should be out there in the center of the dancing, being honored by her people. For she was the true hero.

His eyes scanned the many dancers, but there was one that he could not find: she who haunted his dreams.

She simply was not there.

Perhaps he should go and find her. He glanced away, out toward the outer edges of the dancing. Where could she have gone?

His eyes grazed over a tall figure, there on the sidelines, skimmed over her and went on, only to return. Anna? Was this his own Anna?

He barely recognized her. He had become so used to seeing her with her hair falling about her shoulders and in her pretty, though fairly revealing garb, that he had forgotten how badly the white man's own kind of clothing fit her.

Her face was still tanned from her many hours in the sun, and he knew, if he approached her, that her green eyes would sparkle in that special way that she had when she looked at him. But someone had dressed her and had put her hair up in a fashion that did not compliment her.

Still, what did it matter? Hers was a spirit that was indomitable. Hers was a nature that was pure and was kind. What difference her style of clothing?

That was when it struck him. These people were ignoring her. Why?

She was the heroine, not them. She should be the first one and perhaps the only one dancing, being honored.

His eyes narrowed as he watched her face. He recognized her smile as one that was strained and he knew her well enough to realize that beneath her outward composure, this woman hurt. Was she grieving because she was not out there stepping to the music along with the others?

Unlike Indian dancing, War Cloud was aware that the white man's way required a partner. Was no one willing to accompany this wonderful woman?

Anger stirred within him.

What was wrong with a people who could not see how magnificent his Anna was? Could they not look past the ill-fitting clothes and unbecoming hair to the woman herself? Could they not see the beauty that was his own *Nahkohe-tseske*?

Like an arrow hitting its mark, War Cloud collided with a truth that should have been apparent to him for a long time. But it hadn't been.

She was beautiful. No matter Anna's apparel, no matter her hair, no matter the color of her skin. *This was the most beautiful woman War Cloud had ever known.*

How could he have been so stupid that he had not seen this before now? Her skin color, her race, nothing of that nature meant anything.

Certainly he desired her; certainly he had experienced lust with her. But all along, his interest in her had been more than these things. He had simply been unaware of it.

He loved her. He loved *Nahkohe-tseske.*

He groaned. When had it happened? When had this woman become so valuable to him that he would risk anything to see her happy? And when had he stopped thinking of her as a white person and fallen in love with her?

Had it been from the start? That first time she had dared to shield her young charges? Challenging him and his warriors to do their worst?

War Cloud thought back to the raw, eager feelings he had experienced with her, when they had been out there on the trail. Had it really been lust he had felt all those weeks ago? Or had he simply wanted, as nature had intended him to want, the woman he loved and admired with all his heart?

He loved her. Love, simple and strong.

He felt joy with the realization. He felt elation. And yet he despaired. It was going to be the hardest thing he would ever have to do to walk away from her. *And he must walk away.*

He groaned. How would he ever do it?

By not letting her know. That was how he would do it. He would admire her; he would love her and he would let her go, when the time was right.

But he would not think of these things at the present

moment. That time was distant. Now, as he stared across the camp's makeshift dance floor, he knew what he was going to do.

And the white people could be damned if they did not like it.

This was *his* woman and right now she hurt.

The fiddle had begun a waltz, and Anna swayed to the three-quarter beat, closing her eyes. Lost in her own dreamworld, she barely registered the fact that the laughing voices had gradually silenced.

Opening her eyes, she still did not perceive the cause for it until the reason was almost upon her. And then she stared out across the dance floor, straight into the deepest set of dark eyes that she had ever seen.

War Cloud approached her.

He was not going to ask her to dance, was he? He could not. Did he not realize the infamy that such an action would cause?

But as he took one deliberate step after another toward her, she began to realize that she simply did not care about scandals or about what these people might think of her. She had not braved a train attack, a Pawnee fight and a raging river to worry about the petty prejudices of a people who should know better. Who were these people to judge her?

And the music so filled her soul.

He did not say a thing as he stepped up to her. He simply held out his hand. And she took it, smiling at him.

No words were spoken between them. None were necessary.

She fell into his arms. As she expected, silence prevailed as they paced onto the dance floor. But these two were beyond censure, for the music had not stopped playing.

One step followed upon another, and together War Cloud and Anna were soon swaying to the bewitching rhythm of three-quarter time. She stared up into his eyes, he down at her; her gaze was grateful, his insistent.

He grinned, and it occurred to her how infrequently she had witnessed this man's gorgeous smile. The expression lit up his features and softened his eyes, making him look more boy than rugged man.

She returned his smile.

He leaned forward to whisper, "You are beautiful."

How could it be? Only a moment ago she had felt as if she were the most pitiful creature alive, and now she knew with certainty that she must surely be pretty, if only because he said so. Still, she could not help protesting. "But I—"

"I will not hear you say another word about it." His arms tightened around her. "These people have eyes but do not see with them. Know that you are the most beautiful woman I have ever known."

Her smile turned radiant. There could be no mistaking his words, nor the adoration shining clearly from his eyes, and lost in the wonder of him, she twirled around and around, there on the dance floor, lost in the magic of his arms. She grinned . . . and she grinned. Soon she was laughing, and War Cloud joined in with her.

They might be in the middle of hostile country, perhaps even in the midst of a quarrelsome group of people, but it did not matter.

They had fallen in love and both of them knew it without speaking a word.

Whatever were they to do?

The melody ended. Another song took its place. The people pressed in around them; some looked shocked at the couple's behavior, others indulgent.

Anna stopped, as did War Cloud. Gradually he let his arms drop from around her, but he did not take his eyes from her.

He stared at her; she back at him.

Others' bodies began to dance around them, some even bumping into them. Still, neither she nor War Cloud moved.

At last he broke eye contact to look around him. He appeared to take stock of where he was, what the others around him were doing and, gazing back at her, he spoke more eloquently through expression than mere words could have.

He would be alone with her. Now.

Anticipation washed through her, her stomach twisting with the knowledge of what the night might yet hold for them.

He took her by the hand and turning, led her away, out of the throng of dancers. And he did not stop until he had taken her far from the center of the celebration.

Others watched them; others whispered, and Anna heard them, but it never occurred to her to pull away from him. Why should it? She trusted War Cloud with every fiber of her being.

Besides, none of these people knew what she knew. She had been lucky enough—or perhaps unlucky enough—to have experienced the worst and the best from these Indians, and she knew them for what they were: a people, same as any other people, with perhaps different ideals and goals, but certainly an honorable people who did not deserve to be called "savage."

She followed his lead as he took her past the fires of the wagon train, out and away from their circle, out onto the prairie. And looking back, Anna was happy to discover that, while these travelers might be willing to damage her reputation with gossip, no one had actually come after them. Perhaps no one wished to tangle with War Cloud.

He stopped at the edge of a hill, beneath an overhanging rocky edge and as he did so, he drew her into his arms.

As though she were lost in a dream, she stared up at him, dazed, if only by the strength of her devotion to him. In the distance she could hear the music, accompanied by the rush of the winds over the grasses. But as romantic and alluring as these sounds might be, Anna barely registered them.

Hazy moonlight shone down from over her shoulder, silhouetting War Cloud's face, and she noticed little things about him all at once: the way the dim lighting cast flickering shadows over his features, the way his high cheekbones threw his eyes into shadow. And though she could little see his eyes, she had no trouble reading his thoughts.

This man wanted her; and the good Lord help her, she desired him as well. She loved him.

One of his hands came up to sweep his fingers over her cheek, while with his other hand, he held her fingers entrapped in his. She closed her eyes, drew in her breath and pressed herself forward, wanting no more than to experience the feel of his body against hers.

But he had other things in mind, apparently, for he kept her a hairsbreadth away from him. Presently, he reached around behind her head, there to seek out the pins that held her coiffure in place. And all the while his fingers groped with their task, his stare never left her face and his gaze touched her like a potent caress.

He said, gently, "I have always liked your hair down."

"I know," she whispered. Tenderly, as though he were one of her children, she brought her fingers up to the hard contours of his face, there to run her fingertips down his cheek, watching with pleasure as a shudder, barely perceptible, shook his body.

Oh, how she needed this; how she needed him. Worse, she *had* to touch him, to feel him, to tell this man that she loved him and that she would follow him anywhere. But most of all she ached to show him that she would be his for the rest of her life.

A cloud passed over the moon, making it difficult to see more than a mere outline of his shape. But it did not matter. He brought his face close to hers, and she inhaled swiftly as the balmy scent of his skin imprinted itself into her memory forever.

Delicately, he nibbled on her neck, fondling first one of her earlobes and then the other. Her body stilled as she tried to hold on to her sanity, for delirious sensations had spread throughout her body, making her feel dizzy.

One of his hands massaged her through her dress, up and down her back, that hand coming dangerously close to her buttocks, until with one low pass after another, he felt her there also.

Ah, how she longed to open up to him, to give him everything in her that there was to give. She stretched her arms around his neck.

Had she been less hungry for him, had she been less inclined to open up to him, it might have occurred to her that someone from the wagon train could spot them here. And whether it was as it should be or not, she might also have realized that if she were seen in this way with War Cloud, there would be trouble for him . . . for her.

But how could she think of these things when she was beyond rational thought?

Especially when War Cloud's fingers were beginning a silent descent down her spinal column, creating outbursts of havoc with his every touch. She groaned and fell in toward him. How could she not do so? It felt that good.

He said, "I must lift your skirt. Do not be alarmed."

She nodded, and the dear Lord help her, she assisted him. He lifted her up and positioned her with her back toward the smooth wall of the stone cliff. With the bulk of her weight pressed against that wall, he guided her legs around his waist.

He whispered into her ear, "Do you know what you do to me?" even while he directed her hips to join with his.

She did not answer, not trusting her voice.

He continued, "I should find us a spot where we would be free from the eyes of the whites. I should take you slowly, also, to show you my admiration, but forgive me, *Nahkohe-tseske*, I cannot wait."

She murmured, "I do not want you to."

"Someday," he said, "there will come a time when we will spend the whole day wrapped in each other's arms. Someday we will have this."

Did he know what he was saying? she wondered. Did he realize that he was giving her a future with him?

Did that mean he was ready to marry her? And to the devil with the curse? Did he love her?

She forgot to think any further as his fingers found her most vulnerable, most feminine spot, and before she could utter a sound, he joined his body with hers.

"Nahkohe-tseske," he breathed into her ear. "Know that I would keep you with me if I could."

She whispered, "I know."

"Do not be angry with me," he muttered.

"I am not angry with you."

"And yet you should be. I do you a dishonor. You are the sort of woman that a man marries. The kind of woman that he devotes himself to for the rest of his life."

"This is no dishonor, sir."

He groaned and brought his hand up to her breasts, his fingers beginning a massage upon her delicate skin, the sensations he created sending her head spinning. Yet he was still deeply sheathed within her, his hips thrusting and gyrating against hers.

She heard a whimper and it took her a few moments to realize the sound had come from her. She whispered, "I love you."

"Hova'ahane," he uttered, and while she registered this Cheyenne word as a negative response, his caress on her told her the very opposite: that she very likely held this man's devotion as no other woman had ever done. But what good did that do her? He would never marry her.

Unless she broke the curse.

Damn the curse! She loved this man as she had never loved another soul, and she would be condemned to hell before she would let a centuries-old curse come between her and the man she adored.

But he disentangled himself from her all at once, mumbling in hushed tones, "Though I might not be able to give you the one thing you deserve, *Nahkohe-tseske,* I can at least give you this."

And with no more said, he grabbed her under her arms and gently pushed her upward. With the majority of her weight still held up against the wall of the cliff, he positioned her high above him, and said, "Put your legs around my neck."

What? She uttered a slight protest. "But I don't understand—"

He did not offer a word in response, however. He simply pushed up her skirt and ducked his head underneath it. And where the male part of him had once caressed her, he began to kiss her there, too, over and over.

He could not have knocked the breath from her chest any better if he had been trying. *Dear heaven above!* She had not known such sensation existed.

What he was doing to her was scandalous in the extreme, naughty and perhaps indiscreet, and she was shocked beyond herself. Yet, for all that, it was the height of ecstasy.

"War Cloud." She made a halfhearted attempt at protest, but when he answered her with a "Shhh," she did exactly as he bade.

His tongue found her moist cleft and the sensitive spot above it, and with a sigh, she spread her legs even farther, opening to him, trusting him with this her most precious gift.

He made love to her in a way she had never dreamed

possible, and as surges of euphoria ebbed and flowed within her, she moved against him until she thought she might explode.

Her breathing became rushed while her body labored toward a fulfillment that it understood instinctively.

His kisses became firmer, his tongue more insistent and tiny cries escaped her lips until all at once she burst with excitement, fiery rushes of intoxication sweeping over her. Over and over the pleasure rushed within her, until she felt herself at last relax.

She thought that he might have let her slip down to him, then. But he did not. He kissed her in the same spot again and again, and only gradually did he lower her to him, and then only far enough to give him access to her breasts.

She still wore her chemise, but this did not hinder him. He kissed her through it.

When he at last settled her down farther, so that he could join his body to hers once more, he kissed her neck, her hair, her cheeks, and finally her lips. The scent of him, and of her, as well, was caught on his breath, but it was not repulsive.

Alas, it was exhilarating.

Holding her under her buttocks, he locked his gaze with hers as best he could within their darkened paradise. It was as though he elicited her agreement before he thrust himself into her.

She groaned as she took him fully into her. For a moment, her body went limp. It felt so good.

He moved with her and within her, up and down, driving and bearing against her as though he practiced a private dance with her. Gradually he set up a rhythm, one that she met easily.

Without stopping a thing she was doing, she reached out to run her fingers through the long, coarse locks of his hair, and as she did so, she murmured, "Thank you for that, War Cloud. That was wonderful."

"*Ne-a'ese,*" he said. "It is I who should thank you. You are all I have ever wanted, and more."

He strained against her, one thrust of his hips giving way to another, over and over.

And strangely, she began to feel the beginnings of a more arousing sensation rising up within her again, and she gave in to the feeling, meeting his every motion, move for move.

After a short while, his breathing became more strained and she could perceive the rush of heat within him. She knew he was nearing the climax of his own pleasure.

She gazed at him, watching him in wonder as his muscles contracted against her. It was powerful; he was powerful and he was magnificent, and she felt herself responding in kind to him.

All at once he exploded, as though her loving had set him off like a blast. And she met him beat for beat, glorying in the ultimate satisfaction as liquid fire, raw and frenzying, swept over her.

Dear God, she thought, she had never felt closer to another human being in her life. How was she ever supposed to walk away from this man?

Truly, she thought, she could not do it. It would be like denying a piece of herself. It would be like dying.

It was not a pleasant thought, and shoving such dispiriting ideas to the back of her mind, she set herself to thinking about something else.

She pressed lingering kisses to his chest, amazed at the soft, yet firm texture of his skin.

Ah, she thought, *this is so much better . . .*

Chapter 23

The remote sound of thunder awoke them.

He was the first one to move, pushing himself up and away from her. And though his fingers caressed her hair, moving down to her face and her cheeks, his first words were not romantic as he said, "We must awaken the children who are to travel with us and we must leave here at once."

Oddly, despite her unusual position, she had been drifting in and out of consciousness for some minutes, but upon hearing him talk, she came fully awake. He gave her bottom a few gentle taps, and as he allowed her legs to slip down to the ground, she wondered how long they had slept.

Thirty minutes? An hour? The distant sounds of the fiddles and a harmonica told her that not much time had elapsed since they had first come here, but that was not enough detail to settle her mind. Perhaps the pioneers danced the whole night through.

War Cloud stepped back, away from her, and she tried to stand up on her own, but it was nearly impossible. As the stinging sensation of free-flowing blood came back to her limbs, she collapsed.

But he caught her, holding her next to him for several moments. She felt his chest rise as he inhaled, felt him hold that breath for a moment and then exhale, his sigh warm against her skin.

He said, "Would that we could stay here the night through, but we must leave." He dropped his arms, setting her away from him, and the night was so pitch-black that she could barely see him unless he stood directly in front of her. However, he was not so far away that she could not identify certain elements of his features and the outline of his body. Clearly, she could see that he was straightening his clothes—what little of them he wore. She gasped back a sigh.

Whereupon she began to stamp her feet, hoping to restore some feeling to them and to her toes. Briefly she fell in toward him and chanced a glance up at him, only to come away, startled. Concern had etched itself upon his features and, not bothering to be bashful, she asked straight out, "What is troubling you?"

A muscle ticked in his cheek and his mouth tightened before he admitted, "There are many things."

"Such as . . ." she prompted.

He paused, and in his eyes, there for a moment, she could have sworn she descried a look of apology. For what? she wondered.

But when he spoke, all he said was, "There is danger for us here, I believe."

"Is there? Why?"

"I do not think I was reasoning too well this night," he explained. "If I were to consider the reaction of those people to our dance, then I would conclude that these white people do not think well of the Indian. In truth, there are probably some here among these settlers who would like to see me dead. By being here with you and by accompanying you, I have obtained some protection from them, but I think it could be fleeting, especially since they now know we are lovers."

"How would they know that about us?" she asked. "And even if they did, what does that matter? I don't think anyone would dare to harm you."

"Do you not? Tell me, what punishment would befall anyone who killed me? Would the white man's law discipline him, or would it be more inclined to honor him?"

"War Cloud, I don't think—"

"Hear me out." He held up one finger as though to ask her for silence, and continued, "Only a fool would have failed to miss what was happening between us when we danced. And I fear that if we do not leave this campsite tonight, at first light, there could be great trouble for me, possibly for you, too, for you have taken me into you."

"But," she sputtered, "I have told these people how you saved myself and the children. You are a hero. Surely these few people would grasp that because of this, we might have feelings for one another. After all, we have been on the trail together for several weeks. No, I think you are wrong. I think I could make them understand if I were able to talk to them."

"Think you so?" he asked, and even in the darkness, Anna glimpsed one of his eyebrows rising with doubt. "Remember," he persisted, "that you are not supposed to love me, and I am certainly not supposed to *make* love to you. Our two cultures are too greatly opposed for this to be done without problems, I think. And what if one of the children should tell his new parents about how you really came to be traveling with me? No, if I am right about this, I think that even if you tried to talk to these people, before you finished, I would more than likely be hung up from the nearest tree."

"No, you must know that I would not let that happen."

He shrugged. "I think that you might not be able to stop it. Do you remember when I told you that my cousin, a chief, once brought a white woman, whom he had ransomed, into a fort? He was hanged with very few questions asked, so I am told. Yet, he had never done damage to the woman.

"No, I have made love to you. I think that this is enough to incite these people to take up arms against me once they start to reason it through."

"Hmmmm," she said. "I suppose you could be right." She glanced away from him and began to put her own clothes back to order, and she asked, "What would you like me to do? Do you think the children whom I have placed into families will be all right?"

"*Haahe,* I think no harm will come to them. They are white. They are innocent, and the people will look upon themselves as their defenders. But you said there were some who were not taken into families?"

"Yes," she said. "Patty and Collin. Patty, because she is too thin. I do not think she is well, War Cloud. And Collin because he limps. I think that he was also looked upon as a possible burden to these families." She added, "Do you have a plan?"

He drew his brows together and frowned. A minute, or perhaps two, ticked by as he lapsed into silence. At length, however, he said, "I think that this is what we should do. Together we will walk back into the camp of the white settlers as though nothing has happened between us. It is then that you should go and awaken Patty and Collin. Once done, we should leave in haste, before anyone has a chance to think twice."

"Then you don't believe we should sneak away?"

"I do not. That would only cause the settlers to assume that we have done something wrong. No, we should walk in as though we have every right to be there. And in truth," he said, as he reached out a hand to smooth back her hair, "we do."

She made a grab at his fingers when he would have pulled away, and turning her head toward him, encouraged him to comb his fingers through her hair. She said, "That feels good."

"Hmmm," he said. "Then I will have to remember to brush your hair every night that we are together. Perhaps, if I do this for you, you will always remember me."

She turned her face toward him and said, "I will need no such reminder." She had uttered the words lightly, though only a simpleton would have failed to notice the seriousness underscoring each syllable.

And War Cloud was no ninny. However, he held his own counsel on the matter, though his fingers stilled for the pulse of a second as they trailed through her hair.

After a time, Anna said, "I have one question."

He nodded.

"If we are to be so open about what we are doing, and there is someone from the camp who might wish us harm, don't you think they might follow us?"

"It is possible," he responded with a shrug. "But I do not believe they will try. These white settlers will need their scouts to show them the way through Indian country, and I do not think they will want their few scouts to be gone, following four people who have done them no harm. Besides, a storm is almost upon us and, even if some of these white men do decide to follow us, our trail will most likely be washed away by morning."

"I see," she said, taking a deep breath. "But," she said, persisting, "I still think that these people would more than likely understand if I were to speak to them. I think you might be perfectly safe here."

He looked sullen as well as thoughtful. He did answer, but only after a slight pause. "You could be right, but I am unwilling to take the chance and stay here until morning."

And, truth to tell, Anna had to admit, she was inclined to agree with him.

Tilting her head to the side that she might see him better, she said, "Nor am I willing to take that chance either, War Cloud. Not at all."

She felt a drop of rain on her arm. A flash of lightning, followed by an ominous peal of thunder, more than mirrored her apprehensive mood. They were traveling south and west, she noticed. The only reason she even knew this was because she had gained their direction the previous evening—from the Big Dipper constellation.

They traveled with no more than the one pony—this being for the children. But the weather, the midnight hours, meant nothing to her. Anna had become used to tramping over the prairie with only the light of the moon to guide their way.

But there was not even a moon this night. Clouds filled the darkened sky.

Collin and Patty rode the pony while Anna guided the

animal by its reins. Both of the children were so tired, they slept sitting up in the saddle. Luckily War Cloud kept their pace a little slower than usual, perhaps because of the children.

Scooting up close behind him, Anna asked, "Why do we go south?"

"Because," he responded, "the wagon train goes north. I do not wish any trouble with them. Besides, not too far from here is Fort St. Vrain, the nearest white settlement. You will probably be able to find someone there to take in the children."

To take in the children. She froze and then stumbled as the pony pushed her forward. So this was it. Fort St. Vrain was the name of the place that would mean the eventual parting of ways for her and War Cloud.

"Fort St. Vrain?" she asked, catching up to him. "Isn't that awfully close to Sand Creek, where so much of your trouble started? Perhaps we should find another place. Aren't the people there fairly prejudiced toward the Indians?"

"It is and they are. But there is no need to find another place. I will not go into the fort with you," he said. "I will give you the horse, and you and the children will go the rest of the distance without me."

"I see," she responded. But she did not understand; not really. Perhaps she never would.

"Fort St. Vrain was not always a place that was prejudiced toward the Cheyenne," War Cloud clarified.

"Was it not?"

"*Hova'ahane,* in the early days when Bent's fort was built for trade with the Cheyenne, Bent's partner, Ceran St. Vrain, built this fort on the South Platte to trade with the Lakota and the Arapaho as well as the Cheyenne. It was only in later years that it became a fort for the warrior-whites. My father knew St. Vrain well and said he was an honest man."

"Hmmm," she said. "Did St. Vrain sell the fort to the military, then?"

War Cloud shrugged. "I do not know," he said. "I only know that trade no longer happens there and that the warrior-whites now rule it."

"Oh," she uttered, and fell silent. They spoke no more for some time, each perhaps reflecting on his own private thoughts. Another clap of thunder, however, had her commenting, "It looks as though we are walking straight into a storm, and I fear for the children."

Though she spoke in muted tones, she was certain he had heard her, even though all he said in reply was, "Humph!"

At one time, such a brusque response might have bothered Anna, but it no longer did. Over the past few days with War Cloud, she had come to understand him better, and she knew that the terse rejoinders were simply his way of letting her know he had heard. War Cloud did not consider his manner abrupt.

Anna said, "The children are not well, War Cloud, either of them, and though I know we want to put some distance between us and the settlers' wagons, if we can, we should seek shelter before the storm hits."

"Humph!" was once again War Cloud's answer, but Anna said nothing more. He had heard her; she trusted him to do the right thing.

At last he called over his shoulder, "Up ahead, maybe a

mile or two, there are caves. I found them yesterday when I was scouting this area, for I knew that I might need a place to sleep that was far enough away from the settlers' wagons to be safe. These caves should stay dry and we can sit out the storm there."

"Good," she said. Then, as something else occurred to her, she asked, "Your brother, will we go back there for him?"

"He will meet us in a day or two. I sent word to him with the Lakota scouts from the wagon train. He will follow us."

"That's good," she said and lapsed into silence, to collect her thoughts and recall again all that had taken place this evening.

It had been easy to gather up the two children, and it seemed there had been little cause for concern.

True to his plan, Anna and War Cloud had trod back into the midst of the settlers' camp, War Cloud halting at the edge of the festivities. But Anna had gone on forward, heading directly to where she had left Patty and Collin.

Awakening the children had caused a minor stir, since a few of the women had wanted to know what she was doing and why. But Anna had gone on to explain that because she and War Cloud were to travel at night—due to the danger of wandering war parties—they were leaving camp at once.

Several of those women had offered Anna sympathy for her plight, as well as giving her blankets and food, all of which she had graciously accepted. A few—very few of the women—had stood apart, whispering from behind upraised hands.

But other than that minor difficulty, there had been no trouble.

Anna sighed, deciding that this was one less worry, and she focused her attention upward, to try to gain better bearings from the night sky. But clouds still hid the moon as well as most of the constellations.

She had no idea where they were, could only put her trust in War Cloud, that he would know this terrain. And, of course, he did, at least he knew it better than she.

Anna heard a movement behind her and she glanced back to find Patty awake.

"Miss Wiley," the youngster called, her voice weak, "are we there yet?"

Anna dropped back to take Patty's hand in her own. Although she had no idea where "there" was, she said, "Not yet, dear, but soon. Why not go back to sleep? When it is time I will awaken you."

"All right," said Patty, and with a gentle pat on her hand, Anna trod forward once more, increasing her pace to reach War Cloud.

She called his name as soon as she came within hearing distance of him. "How long is it before you think we can rest?"

He did not speak at once, and Anna had to stumble quickly forward in order to keep up with him. Following, she awaited his reply, and at length, he said, "Just a little farther. The caves are up ahead of us, and I am trying to get to them as quickly as I can. This storm," he pointed overhead, "is going to be a violent one, I think."

"Do you?" she asked. "I have heard the skies grumbling all evening, but it has not amounted to much yet.

Do you think this one will be worse than the other storms we have encountered?"

"I do."

"Why?" she asked. "What makes you think so?"

He pointed toward the midnight sky. "I saw 'earrings' on the sun this afternoon. My northern kin say that when this happens in the winter, it is a sign that there will be savage winds and cold weather. But we are in warm weather and maybe it will not be so bad. Still, we should use caution and get to these caves with all possible speed."

Anna heard what he said, but he had puzzled her and she asked, "Earrings on the sun?"

"Haahe," He affirmed. "The Blackfeet call them sun dogs; the Shoshone, earrings. They look like fires on each side of the sun. The Lakota say that the sun's cheeks are afire."

Anna gazed skyward, as if she forgot for the moment that it was pitch-black outside. Realizing what she was doing, she sent Patty and Collin a concerned look, but both children appeared to be sleeping once more, one leaning on the other as they sat upon the pony.

Anna shivered. It was a strange sensation. One moment she had been warm enough, the next cold. It appeared that the temperature, even as they were walking, had suddenly and unexpectedly dropped. She had read of this sort of thing happening in this part of the country, but never had she thought to experience it.

A drop of ice hit her in the face, suddenly followed by the stinging sensation of several others. Sleet? In the middle of July?

War Cloud rounded on her and said, "The storm is already starting. Do you see those rocks?" He pointed to a cliff ahead of them. "This is the place where we are going. We are almost there. I will run ahead of you to ensure that there are no snakes or bears inside the caves. If it is safe, I will give you a call like this." He stepped back and, bringing his hands up to his mouth, made a howl that sounded so close to the cry of a wolf, Anna would not have been able to tell the difference. Lowering his hands and stepping back toward her, he said, "When you hear that call, you come."

"I will," she said, staring at him earnestly. She added, "You will be careful."

He sent her an easy grin. "I always am," he replied. "But I must warn you that it is not a simple climb to that shelter. It is hard enough in the daylight in good conditions. I fear that you and the children might not be able to make the climb easily. Perhaps I can carry one of the children or maybe we should find another spot."

Anna gave Patty and Collin a quick perusal. She said, "We need shelter now. Do not worry about us. I think that if we can brave flooded rivers, warring Pawnee and murderous soldiers, we can surely dare to climb icy rocks."

He nodded. "I think that you can do it, too."

Anna acknowledged him with a brief dip of her head, though she held him back when he would have gone. "War Cloud," she said and, as he spun around toward her, she brought his hand to her lips, kissing his fingers. She said, "Stay alert."

"I will," he affirmed, and he returned her gesture, only he went on to kiss every single one of her fingertips.

Anna caught her breath. No matter the rain, no matter the sleet, no matter the two children who sat a horse behind them, this man set her senses afire.

Raindrops fell onto his face as he glanced at her, but in his eyes she espied a blaze that she knew was matched by an answering light in her own.

However, she simply said, "Do not do battle with bears. And remember that I love you."

He groaned, a sound so seductive she felt the effects of it all the way to the tips of her toes. But when he spoke, all he said was, "I know," and then he turned and was gone.

Anna was convinced that she was not the type of person who could easily be left waiting. Especially under these conditions. The sleet was pelting them harder, and even Collin and Patty were starting to complain.

Where was War Cloud? It seemed he had been gone forever.

"What are we waiting for, Miss Wiley?"

Anna had been staring off into the night, at the spot where War Cloud had disappeared. She turned back toward the children and said, "We are waiting for a signal from War Cloud. There is a cave on that hill and he has gone there before us to ensure that there are no snakes or bears hiding there."

"You should have awakened me, Miss Wiley," said Collin. "I would have gone with him."

Anna smiled at the boy, realizing, perhaps for the first time, how their adventure had changed him. Whereas before Collin had seemed withdrawn and solitary, at present he appeared more self-confident and sure of himself.

Anna stepped back toward the two children and said, "Next time I will, Collin. I promise."

Even as she spoke, the wind whipped up behind her and Anna glanced skyward. This could not be doing the children much good.

Could something have gone wrong? Should she continue to wait or should she take matters into her own hands and go and find War Cloud?

She should go to War Cloud, she decided. Anything had to be better than standing in the sleet, waiting.

Anna trod forward and had taken no more than a few steps when she heard the doleful lament of a wolf. That was her signal.

She turned to the children and said, "Did you hear that?"

"No, Miss Wiley, what?"

"The cry of the wolf. That's War Cloud's signal."

Anna paced as quickly as she could toward the cliff and found War Cloud waiting for her at the bottom of it.

He said, "Come, hurry. The rocks are already slippery. We will leave the pony here, under the trees, but bring the blankets from its back."

Anna nodded agreement.

Without letting another moment go by, War Cloud took Patty into his arms and pulled both Collin and Anna along after him. "Careful," he warned. "Though the climb is not steep, one must walk along a ledge for a short while to get to the cave."

"Ah," Anna said, but became silent when a sheet of ice suddenly hit her. Dear Lord, the sleet had turned to hail. She placed her arms over her head in an involuntary action.

"Hurry," War Cloud encouraged, though Anna needed no urging.

He took them high up onto a ledge and, scooting along it, dropped suddenly down, out of sight.

"War Cloud," Anna screamed, but he popped his head back up just enough so that she could barely see him, his forehead on a level with the ledge.

She asked, "Where is Patty?"

"She is inside the cave. Come, and hold tightly to the wall of the cliff. Here." He grabbed hold of Collin, and dropping down, both man and boy disappeared.

Anna waited, barely daring to move.

War Cloud's head appeared once more, again at the height of the ledge. He said, "Come closer and I will be able to grab hold of you."

Anna held her breath and followed in the footsteps of the others, though at a much slower pace than the children. Her feet slipped over the rocks once and she screamed. She had never been particularly fond of heights.

"Steady, *Nahkohe-tseske,* you can do this," he coaxed. "Come. Only a little farther and I can grab hold of your hand."

Moving sideways one slow footfall after another, she inched along the cliff, her back stiff against it. He held an arm up to her and urged, "Come. It is not much farther."

That depended on your viewpoint, Anna thought. From where she stood, he could have been miles away.

Sleet blurred her vision and was making the rocks icy, perhaps even perilous, yet she scooted forward one careful inch at a time.

"*E-peva'e.* It is good, you are doing well, keep coming," he encouraged.

Rain, mixed with hail, beat at her face until she felt as though she were being blinded by it. She looked down and froze, paralyzed with fright. She could simply go no farther.

Off to her left she could see the dim outline of War Cloud's hand, stretching up toward her. Still, she could not force herself to move. Perhaps, she thought, if she could jump toward his hand, she might reach it. Dare she try?

Never. She could barely force her feet to scoot forward at all, let alone take a daring plunge.

"*Nahkohe-tseske,* you have almost made it. Move toward my voice."

"I cannot!"

"*Haahe,* you can. A few more steps. Come."

But Anna stood paralyzed, unable to budge, unable to say a word.

War Cloud scooted up onto the ledge beside her. "Take my hand," he bade as he reached out to her.

She made a wild grab for him and as she did so, she bent forward too suddenly and slipped completely off the ledge.

Screaming, she scrambled for something solid; found a slippery rock and clutched to it.

"*Eaaa,* hold on." War Cloud's voice seemed to mirror his fear. She heard him scoot back along the ridge. "Hold on," he encouraged.

Something inched toward her. What was it? His hands, thank the Lord. She felt War Cloud's hands take a firm grip on her wrists; felt her own fingers slipping, though she tried in vain to cling to the rocks. But the muscles in her hands and fingers ached with their load and they convulsed until she feared a mere few seconds stood between her and death.

Like a flash, she remembered War Cloud's warning about the curse. Was she to be its next victim?

Slowly, one by one, her fingers could not hold on and she slid off the rocks. She screamed, but heaven help her, she did not fall; War Cloud held her fast.

He called to her, his voice strained, "Get ready, for I am going to bring you up here. Are you set?"

She cried. It was the only sound she could push past her throat.

With one gigantic pull, he hoisted her up, onto the ledge, both of them falling back into the safety of the cave.

Anna shivered, partly with cold, mostly with fear, as War Cloud folded her into his arms.

Murmuring softly to her, he whispered, "It is all right. You are safe."

Anna, however, could not utter a word.

"My beautiful, brave woman," he whispered. "You must be afraid of high places."

Anna nodded and managed to say, "I am."

"Why did you not tell me?"

She raised her shoulders and shook her head as she whimpered, "It did not seem important."

War Cloud grunted, but made no further comment. In due time, however, he said, "Come farther into the cave. I will build a fire."

"Yes," she said. "Please."

"Do you feel calm enough to look after the children?

They will need your help to make them better. Do you think you can do this?"

Anna gave War Cloud a nod, smiling and sniffling at the same time. It might not be her finest smile, but it was the best she could produce at the moment.

Chapter 24

"**A**re you all right, Miss Wiley?" Collin asked.

Anna grimaced and glanced toward the children. She said, "I am fine," though she continued to have her doubts.

"I was scared for you," said Patty.

Oh, dear, thought Anna, she must have given them a fright. She scooted toward the children until she could take them both into her arms. Holding them tightly, she said, "I am fine now, although I do not know what I would have done had War Cloud been a little less brave." She gave each child a quick kiss.

Collin wiped at his cheek immediately and squirmed out of her grasp. However, he continued to look upon her fondly.

And Anna continued, "But at least we have a safe place to sleep for the night." As she glanced up, she caught a glimpse of her hero in the act of building a fire.

As though he sensed her attention, he turned his head, and she caught his eye before he bent once more to his task. Admiration had shone clearly from his eyes. That and what else? Had it been fear?

After a time, he said, "I think we will camp here a few days before we move on. There is plenty of game, so we will have a good food supply. This will help us to remain here and give the children the rest that they need in order to regain their strength."

Anna sent him a grateful smile but made no reply.

At length, War Cloud commented, "Lame Bird is to meet us in a place barely a day's ride from here. When I am out hunting, I will find him and bring him back here."

"And then what will we do?" asked Collin. "Is there a reason why Patty and I are the only two who remain with you, Miss Wiley?"

Anna had no ready answer to give the youngster. Her heart ached for these two. How could she tell him that he and Patty were the only children still unchosen?

Gently she touched Collin's arm while she prepared to respond. She swallowed, opened her mouth to speak and closed it. What could she possibly say?

In the meantime, War Cloud had gained his feet and had stepped toward the children. As though it were his obligation to handle the matter, he said to Collin, "A man has many duties in life, my friend. You have already proven yourself to be a brave man. You must be even braver now, for we go to Fort St. Vrain."

"Fort St. Vrain?" asked Collin. "What for?"

Realizing that she could not let War Cloud bear the entire brunt of the task before them, Anna came alive and said as soothingly as possible, "We still seek families, Collin. For you and for Patty."

Collin looked dumbfounded at first, and then as comprehension dawned, his expression sank, his look one of despair.

But it was Patty who spoke up first. "But I thought we were going to be *your* children, Miss Wiley."

Anna caught her breath. She had almost forgotten. This was exactly what she had told Patty. Had it been only this morning when they had arrived in the settlers' camp? Had so little time elapsed? It seemed like forever since she had told the lie to the girl. But then, Anna had been so certain that she would not find herself in this situation.

Realizing she had no choice but to tell the truth, Anna sent an apologetic glance toward War Cloud as she explained, "I told Patty that you and I were going to take her as our own child, War Cloud . . . after we married."

War Cloud's countenance hardly changed, not even when the significance of what this surely meant became clear. However, his mouth tightened and he frowned. But his glance at Anna was not a look of censure. No, it was more an expression of worry. Nevertheless, he leaned down toward Patty and said, "If Miss Wiley told you this and she believed it, then the fault is mine. For without her willing it, she must break this promise to you."

Patty's eyes became wide as she stared at War Cloud. Still, he went on to explain, "It is I who led Anna to believe that she and I were going to marry. But the truth is that I cannot marry anyone. Know that our *Nahkohetseske* is doing the next best thing for you by taking you to Fort St. Vrain. Know also, neither she nor I will rest until you and Collin are safely settled."

Having said this, he began to rise, but Patty pulled him back down to her and insisted, "But I want you, War Cloud. I want *you* to be my father."

Anna tried to remember a time she had ever felt more

miserable, but she could not. Nor could she think of any words to say that might ease the situation.

War Cloud, however, did not seem so afflicted. Gently he reached out a hand to stroke Patty's hair as he commented, "If ever I were to have a daughter, know that she would be you. But it can never be."

"Why?"

"Because there is danger for the women in my life," he answered. "And so, because of this, I have decided that I will never marry."

Patty's eyes appeared to grow big in her face and as she gazed up at War Cloud, she solemnly placed her small hand on his and said, "But we like danger, don't we, Miss Wiley?"

Anna could hardly stand it. She came down to kneel next to all three of them and catching War Cloud's eye, stated, "That we do, Patty. We like danger very much."

"Even if that danger means death?" War Cloud interjected.

"Yes," both females answered.

War Cloud scowled, giving them both a low growl. He said, "Our adventure this evening makes me think that your Miss Wiley and I already test the patience of the spirits." He paused and then said to Patty, "But come now, we speak of things we cannot change. For now, your duty is to eat well for these next few days and regain your strength. Do you think you can do that?"

Patty nodded. "I will do my best if you will try to keep us with you."

War Cloud raised an eyebrow toward the girl, but to his credit, he said nothing.

* * *

Collin had wanted to go with War Cloud to meet Lame Bird. But Anna would not hear of it.

"Tomorrow," she said, "tomorrow, you can go hunting with them both. For today, you are going to rest here, while I tend to your leg."

Mumbling something about females and something else about squaws, Collin submitted to her doctoring.

It was later in the day when War Cloud came to her and told her that they were going to have to be on the move yet again.

"Why?" she asked.

"Because I found the tracks of three bears outside the cave this morning. And though it is not yet time for them to begin their winter sleep, I think perhaps that we have been resting in their home."

In their home? Anna thought as she swept her hair, which had turned sun-burnished golden, behind her ears. She said, "Yes, well then, perhaps we should be going."

They left that afternoon.

The adobe walls of Fort St. Vrain stared at her from far off in the distance. Set against a backdrop of snow-covered Rocky Mountains, the place did not appear to be her idea of any sort of haven.

Instead, that haven stood beside her. If only he knew.

Anna had positioned herself on a cliff that overlooked the fort. Built of adobe and cottonwood, it sat next to the South Platte River, a strategic position; one that had for so many years seen great trade conducted with the Indians; one that had also been part of a mutual truce and peace. Currently, however, the fort was overrun with the United States military and at best, it had now come to symbolize the declaration by the government that the Americans had come to stay.

It seemed sad. Sad that an era so full of promise had passed. Sad that the intention—which had been to place two completely different cultures together and prove that they could coexist peacefully—had been betrayed.

The prairie wind blew in her face as she stared off at the structure, that breeze reminding her of how much she had come to love this land and this wilderness . . . this person standing beside her, too.

But it did her no good to think this way. This was the end of their journey together, the end of their association. War Cloud had made that plain to her: once she left him, there would be no going back.

Oh, that she could stay here instead of taking the journey into Fort St. Vrain. But short of pleading with War Cloud, what could she do? Especially when he seemed determined to do the "right" thing by her.

If only he knew what was in her heart. If only he knew that leaving him would be a certain death for her. Better, she thought, to die of the ungodly curse than of the raw loneliness that would surely follow upon her departure.

But she could not tell War Cloud this. Or could she? If she did not say what was in her heart at this moment, might she never have the chance to do so again? Might she always regret that she had never tried?

That thought was enough to decide her.

She could not leave this way, not without at least daring to speak what was in her heart.

Swallowing what felt like a little fear, as well as an overabundance of pride, Anna reached out to him. Touching his arm, she said, "War Cloud?"

He did not speak. Instead, he nodded.

She tried to say the words, found that she could not. Her eyes watered and her voice caught in her throat. *Darn the wind,* she thought, bringing up a hand to brush back strands of her hair, which had flown into her face. It was the prairie breeze, after all, that was stinging her eyes, making them water, wasn't it?

She took in a gulp of air and said, "War Cloud, I do not wish to go down there."

He did not answer; he remained immobile, his gaze apparently fixed on something in the distance.

She continued, "I know what you have said about the curse, but if that is the only reason we cannot marry, I think it is not enough. Why don't we try it? You know that I do not believe in this curse and I think my faith is strong enough to withstand whatever might come."

She watched him; stared at him as he shut his eyes, as though he were forcing himself to remain calm.

She glanced away, and as she did so, in her peripheral vision she could have sworn she witnessed her hero, this big, fearless warrior, bring up a hand to take a swipe at his eyes. But when she turned back around toward him, she found his features composed, despite the telltale hint of redness in his eyes.

He said, "You know that I cannot do that. I fear we are already testing the curse's strength. I would not willingly be the cause of your demise."

She lifted her head to catch a swift gust of wind. She said, "You might be that cause anyway."

He looked at her, she back at him and she was surprised to discover puzzlement on his face. Feeling as though she were taking another chunk out of the armor she used to face the world, she went on to explain, "If I go there, to St. Vrain, I think I might die of a broken heart. Perhaps it would be better if I stay here with you and die a more natural death."

Her words seemed to raise a storm within him, for no sooner had she spoken her mind than he turned to her and took her into his arms. He said, "I would not have you die at all."

"But you know that—"

He silenced her with a kiss, his lips searing hers with the knowledge that, had their circumstances been different, he might readily change the course of her life.

But things were not different, the curse still existed, and when he lifted his head, all he said was, "Know that I cannot alter what must happen between us. And you cannot, either."

Cheek to cheek, she whispered in his ear, "I would change it in an instant if I could."

"Would you?" he asked.

She frowned. "What do you mean?" she asked.

"Would you dodge your duty so easily?"

She turned her head toward him until her lips met the hard contours of his face. She asked, "My duty?"

"*Haahe*," he said. "Was it not you who once told me that you had to find Christian homes for these children?"

"Yes, but . . ."

"If you stay with me, then they will remain with me, too, and you know that I am not of that faith."

"But they *want* to stay with you."

"Does it matter? Did you not give your word to your people in the East? Did you not promise to find the children only the best homes?"

She heard her own words in what he said. Out there on the prairie, before she had really come to know War Cloud, she had told him these things. How dare he use her own arguments against her. Did he not realize that things were different now? That she was different now?

She said, maintaining her position, "Yours and mine would be a fine home for them."

"I do not doubt it," he said easily enough. A little too easily, for he went on to say, "But that is not the point and you know it. You gave those people your word of honor. Can you so easily reconsider?"

"I do not reconsider it without a great deal of thought."

He brushed a lock of her hair back from her face, his look at her pure adoration. "No," he said, "you do not. I believe you. Still, I must force you to keep your vow. And I have my own duty to perform. I told you I would help you to place these orphans and I have." He sent a weak grin down at her. "Come, it is not so bad. We will always have fond memories of each other, will we not?"

Tears gathered at the corners of her eyes. She could not help it. And she said, as the last of her pride died an ungallant death, "I do not want memories. I want *you*."

He sighed. "And I want you, but you know in your heart that it can never be. We come from different worlds. We have had a brief romance and it was good. But it is now time to resume our lives. Our experience will not be for nothing, however, for our lives will forever be shaped by what we have shared with each other." He grimaced and then admitted, "I do not hate the whites so much anymore."

A tear slipped down her cheek.

He wiped it away with the tip of his finger, bringing

that same finger to his own eyes, there to commingle their teardrops. He said, "As easily as this tear becomes a part of me, so will you always be with me. When you think of me, I will be there with you. Come, do not cry. Yours is a brave heart. You must do this thing. You know that you must."

What was she supposed to do? What was she supposed to say? Try as she might, she could think of no other argument against his own. Whimpering, she said, "Kiss me, War Cloud. Kiss me once more, only this time, please kiss me as though you love me, if only for a moment."

He blinked, surprise etched into his features. He did not utter a word and yet his arms tightened around her, pulling her so closely in toward him, she could barely breathe.

He lowered his head toward hers and she gazed up at him, trying to commit every tiny nuance of his features to memory. For the rest of her life, she would think of him as he was now.

And as his lips met hers, she wondered if the wetness on his cheek was from the heat of the day or from another source. Whatever it was, as his lips met hers, she tasted the salty flavor of tears, but whether they were from her own eyes or his, she would never be certain.

Yet, tears or no tears, his tongue swept into her mouth as though he might like to make love to her right here in this place and at this time, and she answered his ardor with every ounce of her being.

She felt the gentle rocking of his chest, and tearing his mouth from hers, he hugged her so fiercely, she could perceive every loving contour of his body against her.

She felt his shoulders tremble as though even his muscles protested the strength of his resolve.

And then he set her away from him, turning his back on her and spinning away. Quickly, he strode out onto the prairie.

Anna wiped the tears from her face and watched him for a scant moment before she spun around to confront the children. She said, "We must go."

Neither of the youngsters uttered a word. With no more than a brief nod to her, they both followed War Cloud. Meanwhile, Anna turned to Lame Bird.

She wanted to reach out to him, to take him into her arms, but she knew he would protest. And so she remained beside him, mute, with tears running down her cheeks.

What could she say to the lad? she wondered. If not for him, she would never have had this adventure; in truth, she and the children might be, at this moment, dead.

Anna inhaled deeply and, assembling a ghost of a smile, said, "I will miss you." She followed her words with the gestures of sign.

Lame Bird said nothing, however, and gazed away from her. She added with both words and sign, "You will take care of him for me, won't you?"

Lame Bird nodded and said, *"Haahe."*

Too soon, both Patty and Collin were seated on the pony. As Anna approached them, she heard War Cloud talking to them, his words reminding her of her own to Lame Bird. He said, "You will be fine. You will take care of yourselves and watch her for me, won't you?"

It was Patty who spoke up; Patty who said, "I will. I love you, War Cloud, and I love Miss Wiley."

Anna heard War Cloud speak, but what was said, she could not hear.

At last War Cloud spotted her and this time, as he turned to her, he said, "You must go. It is late morning, which is the best time to approach a fort. The soldiers will be relaxed and will not be so heavily on guard, for they will be taking turns having their midday meal." He nodded toward her. "Go now."

Anna spun toward him one more time and mouthing the words "I love you," she turned to leave.

She glanced back only once, to see both War Cloud and Lame Bird watching them. She observed War Cloud as he signed the words, "You are in my heart," his wrists coming up to his heart in a perfect hug.

It made her want to turn around, run toward him and simply refuse to leave. But she could not do it. He wanted her to go, and sweeping the last tear from her cheek, as though she could just as easily sweep this man from her life, Anna turned away.

Chapter 25

As Anna strode into the courtyard of Fort St. Vrain, it was evident that the fort was alive with activity. But Anna, lost in her own thoughts, barely perceived it.

Upon entering the fort, she had asked the soldier at the gate to escort her to the officer in charge. The man had led her to a Colonel Robinson. She waited in his office now.

She glanced at the downtrodden faces of her charges. Like her, they clearly did not wish to be here.

It had become evident to her that War Cloud had feelings for her—she had no doubt of that. But, whatever feelings he held within him, they were not enough to enable him put his trust in her.

Besides, he did not love her. He had never told her that he did, and she had reason to believe that he never would, no matter how long she remained with him. Under such circumstances, what good would it do her to stay?

The colonel, a man in his late forties, chose that moment to stride into the room. He said, advancing toward her, "Miss Wiley, is that correct?"

Anna nodded, offering the man her hand. "I am with the Society of Orphans, sir. I am in this country to try to place children with the settlers. These are the last two children to find families. It is why I have come here."

"I see," said the colonel. "But might I ask you how you came to be here?"

Anna sighed. "It is a long story, Colonel. Perhaps after we have had an opportunity to refresh ourselves, I can relate the details of our journey. At the moment, I am interested to learn if there is a reverend or priest here who might help me to find parents."

"Yes," said the colonel. "Yes, of course. You do have papers stating your cause, do you not?"

"I am afraid I lost those long ago."

"I see," he said, and then again, "I see. Well, be that as it may, won't you come with me?"

"Certainly." Anna arose and, taking the hands of both Patty and Collin, followed the colonel from the room.

On the way out the door, the colonel commented, "The guard tells me that you and the children have come to us riding an Indian pony."

"That is right."

"Might I ask you how you came to be in the possession of an Indian pony in this country?"

"We were given it."

"I see," said the colonel. "By whom?"

Anna heaved a deep breath. She said, "Excuse me, Colonel. Though I am sure you are needing and wanting a great deal of information from me, I must tell you that we have had a harrowing journey. I am not prepared at the moment to go into the necessary details. Perhaps later, if you would be so kind."

"Yes, yes, of course. Of course. Excuse my manners,

Miss Wiley. It is only that we've had a rash of visitors to our fort in the last few days. Seems a bounty hunter's come here all the way from a little south of the North Platte. He's looking for a renegade."

"Well," said Anna, "I wish him luck."

The colonel turned to her with a light in his eye that Anna could little understand. However, when all he said was, "Right this way, please," she obediently followed him.

"Miss Wiley." It was Patty speaking to her.

"Yes?"

"Why did that big man ask you so many questions? Doesn't he know that you are tired?"

"I don't know, Patty. Perhaps he seeks information that he thinks we might have about the Indians." Anna lowered her voice. "And we mustn't tell anyone about the Indians, do you agree?"

Both children nodded.

"But, Miss Wiley." It was Patty again speaking to her. "Why can't we go back to War Cloud?"

"Shhh," said Anna, glancing at the colonel, walking ahead of them. "Not quite so loud."

"I'm sorry." Patty pouted until all at once she said, "But I don't understand. Do you love War Cloud?"

Anna sighed, not wanting to answer the question, but this was little Patty, after all. The girl deserved an explanation. Truth be told, Anna was literally breaking her word to the youngster. She said, "I love him very much, Patty. But there are problems."

"What problems?" asked Patty.

Anna sighed. "Problems of a personal nature, I'm afraid. Problems that go back a long way in his family, long before we ever met him."

"Hmmmm," said Patty. "I still don't understand. If you love him and he loves you, why can't you marry him?"

"Because," said Anna, "there is a curse in his . . ." She stopped. "What was that you said, Patty?"

"What?" Patty wanted to know.

"The part," Anna explained, "about War Cloud loving me."

"Oh, that. I just don't understand, if two people love each other, why they can't marry. Is it because he's Indian? Is that why you won't marry him?"

Anna leaned in toward Patty. "He loves me?"

Patty nodded, then asked, "Didn't you know?"

"He never told me."

Patty beamed. "Well, he told me so."

"When?"

"This morning, when I told him I loved him and I loved you, he said that he loved you, too."

"He did?"

Patty nodded.

"Did he tell you anything else?"

The little girl moved her shoulders up and down. "Only that there were some things love required a person to do and that sometimes, if a man loved a woman well enough, he had to let her go." Patty frowned. "What does that mean, Miss Wiley?"

Anna glanced up and away from Patty. She asked, "You are certain about this?"

The youngster nodded.

Anna spun away from the colonel. She began to hurry

in the opposite direction. Not that the man noticed. Since he had taken the lead, with Anna and the children in tow, he had not glanced back at them once.

"Miss Wiley?" It was Collin speaking. "Why was the colonel taking us toward the sheriff's office?"

Anna did not think. She barely had enough time to work out a plan of escape. She said, "I don't know. Maybe the people we sought were in that office." She began to run. "Children, did you see what they did with our pony?"

Both youngsters shook their heads. Collin asked, "What are you going to do, Miss Wiley?"

"I think that I am going to take a horse in exchange for the one that we brought here with us."

Astonishment colored Collin's face. He asked, "Why are you going to do that?"

"Because," said Anna, "I am going back to War Cloud."

Patty jumped up and down. "Goody! Can we come with you?"

"No, you will find homes here—good homes. You are both to stay here."

"But we want to come with you. You promised, Miss Wiley. You said that if you married War Cloud, we could be part of your family."

"But I want you to have good, respectable homes, children." Anna tried to reason with Patty. "Don't you see, I want you to be happy."

Patty glanced up at Anna, and so adult was her expression, Anna was taken slightly aback. The youngster said, "What good is a 'spectable home if you are not with me, Miss Wiley?"

Anna began to answer, stopped and swallowed whatever protest she had been about to make. What was wrong with her today? Anna wondered. She was much too inclined to break into tears.

Dropping to her knees, Anna took Patty into her arms and said, "You know, I think you could be right. After all, what's the point of having white picket fences and apple pie on Sunday if you're not with the people you love?"

Patty laughed and gave Anna a big grin.

Anna returned it and stood up, glancing around her. "Now, the hard part. How to get out of here without creating a stir."

Whereupon she took both children by the hand and strode swiftly across the yard, glancing back only once at the retreating back of the colonel. Luckily for them, the man still had no idea that Anna and the children had been taken with another notion.

The gate to the fort was still open, Anna noted.

Perhaps, if she and the children were quick enough, they could find a mount and leave here without causing much anxiety . . . or perhaps they might find a wagon. A wagon?

There stood one in the center of the fort.

Anna rushed the children toward it, and raising them both into the back of it, said, "We'll leave here and find War Cloud again . . . somehow. Are you sure you want to come with me?"

Both Collin and Patty grinned at her. "We're sure. Let's hurry," said Patty, and Collin nodded.

Anna ruffled Collin's hair, much to his chagrin, and hurrying around to the front of the buggy, she hopped onto the driver's seat. Without pausing to think of the repercussions of "borrowing" an entire carryall, she took hold of the reins and set the horses moving in the direction of the gate.

She heard a shout behind her, a man's voice.

"That's the one I'm looking for, Sheriff. She fits the description given to me by the scout at the wagon train. She's the one who's been traveling with the renegade Indian, War Cloud!"

Oh, dear, thought Anna. So much for her theory that she and War Cloud had caused little stir.

Dear Lord, why hadn't Anna put her facts together before now? Especially since War Cloud had once told her that he was a wanted man amongst the whites.

There was no time to reconsider her actions, however, though she would not have done so even had she been given the chance. Urging the horses forward, Anna set the wagon straight for the fort's entrance, willing herself not to stop.

Goodness knew what these people would do to her and the children, she thought, now that they knew she had been accompanying War Cloud. Perhaps it was a good thing that Patty and Collin wanted to go with her. There would be no "good" homes for them here.

Seeing the drama being played out in the courtyard, the guards began the task of closing the gates, but Anna held on to her nerve, driving the horses forward.

She didn't have time to think; she could only act, and as she cleared the gates, she realized she had done so with no more than an inch to spare.

Hopefully, it would take the soldiers some time to mount and come after her, and by then she would be gone and would be hidden. But what chance did she have against trained professionals?

"Yaaaa!" She drove the horses faster, using the quirt to urge them into a race across the prairie.

War Cloud watched Anna until her figure was no more than a mere speck on the prairie.

Lame Bird commented, "I will miss her."

War Cloud, however, barely acknowledged his brother, and even then it was simply by a slight tip of his head.

"I had grown accustomed to seeing her with us," said Lame Bird. "I had hoped that she would stay."

War Cloud made no comment. Instead he said, "*Tanaestse,* let us leave this place and go north to the Black Hills. There we should be able to find our northern kin."

But neither male made a move to leave.

"*Nohaso,*" said Lame Bird, "maybe we should go to the fort to ensure she is well received. Sometimes the whites are difficult to understand, and because she was with us, they might think to do her harm."

"I have been having much the same thought," War Cloud admitted. "*Nohaso,* perhaps we should go there. To make sure."

Lame Bird began walking in that direction.

"Wait!"

Lame Bird stared back at his brother.

"We must have a plan. What if the whites recognize me? I would be taken prisoner and killed and you might be murdered, too. We should have a strategy, for we do not even have any horses with which to outrun the soldiers should we need to."

"*E-peva'e,*" said Lame Bird. "It is good. You are right.

We should have a plan. But first let me ask you a question." He sent his brother a patient look and asked, "*Nameho-sane-me?* Are you in love?"

"*Haahe*," confessed War Cloud. "I am."

"Then let us hurry," said Lame Bird. "I have a bad feeling about that place."

War Cloud had not thrown away the dress that had been given to Anna at the settlers' camp. Thinking to present it as a gift to one of his friends' wives, he had tucked it away in his blanket.

He put that garment to use immediately, for he feared it was the only scheme he could envision. He would have to pretend to be female.

"You are not such a bad-looking woman, even if the dress is too small," commented Lame Bird, cocking his eye in War Cloud's direction.

"*He'kotoo'estse!* Be quiet," said War Cloud, refusing to look directly at his brother. "And remember what I told you. If shooting starts, you are to run from the fort as fast as you can."

Lame Bird lifted his shoulders. "I will remember."

As War Cloud and Lame Bird approached the fort from the east and as the wind was loud in their ears, they could not see or hear that the gates to the fort had slammed closed. In truth, they noticed nothing amiss until one lone wagon sped out from the fort. And upon that wagon sat a woman—his Anna.

Something was very wrong.

Literally tearing the dress from his back, War Cloud reached toward Lame Bird for his weapons, the youngster handing them over promptly.

The carryall tore straight for him and Lame Bird. War Cloud alerted his brother, "We must catch that wagon and urge the horses to run even faster. Something is wrong if Anna is having to leave in a hurry."

"*Haahe,*" answered Lame Bird.

"I will grab hold of the horse in front while you jump onto the wagon. *Ta-naestse!* Go!"

Both men sprinted toward the speeding vehicle, and only when the wagon was almost upon him did War Cloud become aware of the soldiers riding out of the fort. *Eaaa,* what had happened? He and his brother were going to have little chance against the faster mounts of the soldiers.

Still, if this was all he had, he would force these animals into a pace that would at least give the warrior-whites a good chase.

After all, *it was a good day to die.*

War Cloud sprinted toward the lead nag, vaulting onto it in a single leap.

A gun fired.

Were the warrior-whites trying to kill Anna? Why?

War Cloud goaded the horses to an even faster gait. As he did so, he wondered what had happened. It made no sense. Why would the warrior-whites be shooting at one of their own?

Unless . . .

Had they made the connection between himself and Anna? And even if they had, why would they shoot at her?

He had to use his wits, he realized, for they were outnumbered as well as virtually unarmed.

Up ahead of them loomed a hill. If he drove the horses

toward it, he might gain enough time to turn and face the soldiers, letting Anna and the children escape.

It was a desperate attempt; one that he would have to make count.

He ran the horses straight to the hill, bringing them to a halt so swiftly, the wagon tumbled onto its side. But Lame Bird had anticipated his brother's move and had prodded the woman and the children to lunge from the wagon before it rolled.

Anna did not hesitate to act. He watched as she spurred the children on toward cover, and War Cloud, seeing it, strode out to meet the soldiers. He only wished he had more than six arrows in his quiver. Those and his sawed-off shotgun were the only weapons he had in his defense. Well, perhaps he also had his wits, which had always seemed as good a defense against the warrior-whites as any other.

No sooner had he set up a stance than Collin joined him. Seeing the lad, War Cloud said, "Go back there with Anna and Patty."

But Collin would not be put off and he asserted, "I'm as much a man as Lame Bird. If Lame Bird can stand off the soldiers, then I can, too."

War Cloud did not give any further argument. No, much as he did not like it, he would not insult the boy by making him into a child. Especially after Collin had already proved his worth.

War Cloud said simply, "When the warrior-whites come, stand behind me. And if I fall, take Anna and Patty to a good shelter. Promise me you will do this."

A shot fired toward them.

"Promise me," War Cloud demanded.

"I will."

"Good. Now, keep moving around and stay behind me. A target in motion is harder to hit. Stay alive. The longer you live, the more of a chance the women have to escape."

War Cloud drew an arrow out of his quiver and, taking quick aim, let it fire.

Another shot discharged at them, missed. War Cloud and the boys kept on the move. More shots followed.

"No! Stop this at once!" It was a woman's voice.

"Damn!" War Cloud cursed, recognizing that voice, comprehending the danger. Would his *Nahkohe-tseske* never learn? It was her duty to leave, to hide, to find cover. But most of all, it was her responsibility to stay alive.

"Stop shooting this instant!" Anna yelled at the soldiers.

"Go back," War Cloud shouted at her. "Take cover!"

More guns fired, followed by a scream and then nothing.

"No!" It was War Cloud's cry. "No!"

Spinning around, he turned his back on the soldiers and ran to Anna. *Hova'ahane,* a bullet had found her in the chest. Was it fatal? *It could not be fatal.*

War Cloud reached down to feel her pulse.

"No-o-o-o-o!"

The warrior-whites steadily approached, guns drawn, but War Cloud paid them no heed.

"Anna, please don't leave me!" he cried.

But it was useless. Her body contained no life.

Anna floated above her body. She could hear War Cloud and yet she listened to him in an unusual way. Not with her body's ears.

What had happened? Was she still alive?

Anna looked at her body as though from above it. Was she dead?

She heard a chuckle from somewhere behind her. Behind her where? She had no physical form with which to orient herself.

The evil laugh sounded again, and a voice said, "So, you thought you could marry one such as he."

What was this? Spirits talking to her? It could not be. She did not believe in these things.

A face appeared before her. A horrible face; an Indian countenance, yet not. Tattoos marred every inch of this one's features. It was hideous, like no human being she had ever seen . . . except that once—Sky Falcon's had looked similar.

She formed a thought. "Are you Sky Falcon?"

A roar of anguish followed the question. Anna winced, more than a little disconcerted to realize her thoughts had communicated. "So," came the voice, "you think to insult me, too. Perhaps you would like me to kill your lover, as well as you, that you might spend eternity with each other."

How could this be? How could she be speaking in thought to a being no longer alive? Again, unable to help herself, Anna thought, "*You* killed me?"

"From the time you left the fort until your death, you as good as married that one. My curse over his family holds firm. None such as you can break it."

Anna had no idea what was taking place. Yet she seemed to have no ability to stop it and, unable to prevent it, she thought, "Then you are . . . the father of . . ."

"I am he who is known as Lost In Timber, proud medicine man of the Cocopa tribe."

"And am I dead?"

"Perhaps."

It could not be, she considered. If she were dead, she would be in the company of her Maker. Of this she was certain. She could *not* be dead. She thought, "The Cocopa tribe? But that tribe boasts no more than a few souls." Anna's thoughts took form. "It hasn't for hundreds of years."

"Be quiet!"

"Be gone, old man. I do not know what happens here. But I do recognize that if I were dead, I would be in company with He who is my God. You may as well realize that you have no power over me."

A rush of angry wind swept by her. Oddly, she felt no effect from it.

"Ah," came the voice of Lost In Timber, "you are wrong. I have great power over you. I can cause you, like Sky Falcon, never to be reunited with your love, not even in death."

Anna laughed, or at least she thought she laughed, if that were possible. She thought, "You are outdated, old man. You have no influence over me at all. I love War Cloud and I *will* live my life with him, and I have faith that I will be joined with him once again. You have no power over my beliefs. Now, be gone!"

"Think you not?" The old man raised an image of a hand toward her, fingers outstretched, and the instant he did so, a devil wind blew at her, encompassing her, taking her with it and disorienting her until she felt depleted of her own sense of space and time. At the same instant lightning bolts crashed around her.

In truth, all these things might have frightened her at

one time, but they did not do so at present. Anna had not lied when she said she simply did not believe. Only He who had given her the breath of life had the right to take it from her.

And so it was with this thought uppermost in her mind, she said, again, "I grow tired of this, old man. You have no power over me. If I were dead, then I would have gone to meet my Maker. You have nothing to offer me but fear and superstition, and I will have none of it."

Anna barely dared to think. But it occurred to her that if she could bring this old being to acknowledge that he had failed with her, might he not conclude that his powers had deteriorated? Could that possibly be the impetus to break the curse?

She had to try. Toward this end Anna reiterated, "Admit it, old man, your power is gone."

Old Lost In Timber roared, "Nonsense, I am as powerful today as I was when I was alive."

"Are you?" Anna questioned slyly. "You have no body with which to experience the world; you have no family who loves you. You don't even have a rewarding afterlife. And no one upon the earth believes in you anymore. No, old man, you are about as mighty as . . . as . . ." She pointed back to earth. "As that rock."

"You lie! It is I who took you away from your husband. It is I who will keep you from your husband. So long as you both remain separate, I can make you suffer."

So long as they remain separate? Again, she dared not think.

She protested, "*You* have no rights, nor any influence over me. No one, least of all I, gave you license to play

God. Go away, old man, I grow tired of your game. Soon I will awaken and will be in the arms of my husband and you will see. Your power is gone."

Anna paused in the silence that followed. She waited, and she waited. Had her ruse worked?

And then all at once the old spirit roared, "Think you that I have no power? You will die, I tell you. You will die."

"You are wrong, old man," she retorted. "I will not die at all. I will not die at all . . ."

"Take me in her place if someone must perish," War Cloud pleaded as he knelt over her body. Speaking once more to the Above Ones, he beseeched, "Take me."

Anna suddenly coughed, and gulping in a rush of air, she opened her eyes.

War Cloud leaned over her. "You live!"

"War Cloud." She coughed again, reaching out to touch him. He grabbed her hand.

"Come close," she whispered.

War Cloud leaned over her, bringing his ear to her lips as she breathed, "There is a chance that we can break the spell. His power exists only as long as we remain separate. We must confront him together."

"Who?"

"Lost In Timber," she muttered. "You must come back with me into the spirit world. Do you think you can? You have spoken to Sky Falcon all these years. Can you do it?"

"I can."

"Take my hand," she said.

He did so, but he also said, "We must wait a moment before I leave this body. The warrior-whites are almost upon us, and I must stay a little longer in order to protect you and the children."

Lame Bird knelt down on one knee next to him. The lad said, "You can go, my brother. The warrior-whites are leaving. Look."

It was true. Gigantic dust devils had descended upon the earth, landing directly in front of the soldiers. And at the top of those winds stood the image of a figure, that of Sky Falcon.

Said that image, "Go with her, my son. These warrior-whites will not bother you. I will see to them. Be brave."

War Cloud squeezed Anna's hand and said, "Tell me what you want me to do."

"Close your eyes, and no matter what is said, or what is done, we must never lose sight of one another; we must never become separate. His power works only if we do not remain together. Do you understand?"

"I do."

Anna breathed in another rush of air and, taking hold of his hand, slipped back with him into the land of the spirits.

Anna was immediately shrouded in fog.

"War Cloud?" she called out in thought. But there was no answer. How had they become separated? "War Cloud?"

She did not understand these things of a spiritual nature. She had held his hand. She should be holding it still.

Yet, he was gone and she could see nothing. Worse, there were no markings to guide her: no voice, no old spirit, nothing with which to orient herself.

"War Cloud?" she called again.

"I am here," came a very faint reply.

"Where?" Anna heard a clash of stone weapon upon stone weapon.

Does War Cloud do battle with Lost In Timber?

"War Cloud?"

No answer. "I love you," she called.

Swish! She heard the whisper of a flying arrow. Where was he?

"War Cloud," she called out, "please answer me. I must find you."

Nothing.

"I love you."

All at once, the smell of battle, the horrible stench of fear engulfed her.

She thought again, "I love you."

"I am here."

What had made him hear her this time? Why had she heard him?

She tried again, "I love you, War Cloud."

She caught a brief glimpse of him.

Love? Talking about love seemed to pull him closer to her.

Hurriedly she said, "Do you remember when we first saw each other? I thought you were the most handsome of men."

She caught a vivid flash of man against man, enmeshed in a fight to the death. She rushed through the mist toward them. She reached out—the image disappeared.

She caught the flash of a facsimile: an image of her wrapped in War Cloud's arms. It was War Cloud, calling to her with his thoughts.

"My darling," Anna tried to yell, realized that she could not and thought instead, "I saw your image of us. Keep doing it, my love. I will find you."

Another likeness flashed, as though it were right there before her, but too soon it was gone.

"Remember, my love," Anna said, "the Pawnee fight, how angry you were at me? Remember how you told me you had to have me or you would perish?"

"I am here," he called.

Anna caught sight of War Cloud struggling beneath the knife of old Lost In Timber.

She ran toward the sight, but again, when she reached out for it, it vanished.

She caught the flash of one of his thoughts; they were there, making love.

She felt herself move closer to him, and said, "Do you remember our first kiss, do you remember the night we spent in each other's arms?"

Suddenly he was beside her, though he was locked in battle with Lost In Timber. Had he always been there?

Cautiously she crept toward them and reached out to him. "I am here, War Cloud," she said. "Reach out and I will touch your hand."

Struggling to comply, War Cloud extended an arm toward her. Immediately she groped in his direction, even though howling winds raced at her and around her, threatening to disorient her. But she held her position and tried to take hold of his hand.

She could not get it, not quite, and her hero struggled beneath the weight of old Lost In Timber.

Grasping at straws, for Anna knew not what to do, she yelled out, "Do you see us, old man? Do you see that we are here before you? Do you observe us together, not apart? Admit it. You cannot destroy us, or our love. Your magic has failed."

Anna outstretched her hand, her fingertips inching slowly towards War Cloud. She almost had it and she said, "I love you, War Cloud."

"*Ne-mehotatse,* and I love you," came his response.

They touched.

"*No!*" old Lost In Timber screamed, staring in disbelief at both War Cloud and Anna, standing together, their fingers firmly interlocked. And as their thoughts became more and more as one, their strength built until it appeared as though their love, their only defense, was more weapon than mere magic. "*No!*" screamed the old man again, but it was no use.

Without so much as another word, old Lost In Timber disappeared, leaving nothing behind except perhaps a bit of dust and a cloud of mist.

Anna awoke with a choked breath, finding herself physically wrapped in War Cloud's arms.

Slowly he raised his head, and gradually he smiled at her. Anna returned the gesture.

He was the first one to speak. "You live."

Her smile grew until, at length, she laughed. Finally, she responded, "Yes, I think I do, as do you, too."

"*Ne-mehotatse,*" he said. "I love you, my sweet, courageous *Nahkohe-tseske*. I love you, I love you, I love you."

As happiness consumed her, Anna sat up, discovering to her amazement that her wound was nothing more than a scratch. What was more, the soldiers were gone; she could see them retreating to the fort, the whirlwind chasing them.

And what an odd sight it was. Sky Falcon's image stood as a central figure within the wind storm. But there was more. As though she had always been there, another figure appeared beside Sky Falcon. As Anna watched, Sky Falcon took the young woman in his arms and the two of them embraced. Together the figures ascended into the sky.

"Did you see it?" War Cloud asked her. "Did you see my ancestors?"

"I did. I saw them," said Anna. "Funny, because it looked as though Sky Falcon's wife had been by his side all the while. It was only that neither one of them could behold the other." Anna glanced up at War Cloud. "Like us."

He nodded. "Like us, save one difference. You would not let me go, not even in death. And I would have braved the gods themselves to keep you with me."

He kissed her then, and as a surge of pure contentment swept over Anna, Patty came to sit beside them. Along with her, she brought Lame Bird and Collin. Patty slipped her arms around Anna, her small voice crying, "Are you all right?"

"I am fine."

The little girl gave her a hug. "I am so glad. I was afraid I had lost you, Miss Wiley."

Anna took Patty in her arms, placing her between herself and War Cloud and, motioning to the two boys to come and join them as well, Anna declared, "Mother. Please, Patty and Collin, from this day forward, please call me Mother."

Patty laughed, a beautiful sound, whereupon she threw herself into Anna and War Cloud's embrace. Anna laughed until she cried and truth to tell, had she taken a moment to watch War Cloud, she might have been surprised by a tear of joy clouding her big warrior's eyes, too.

Taking them all into his arms, War Cloud vowed, "My family. My life."

Epilogue

Oklahoma, 1973

"**I**t is said that they lived until a great age," the old man concluded. "And always were they a model of happiness for all of the people."

The little girl sighed and fell against her elder, giving him a hug. She said, "That is a wonderful story, Grandfather. But tell me, what happened to Patty? Did she become well?"

"That she did, my girl, that she did," said the old man. "Patty became an artist for her people, catching their image on canvas. She lived to an old age, in this country here where we sit. In truth, she died not more than a score of years ago, and many is the night when she would tell this story over and over."

"And Collin and Lame Bird, Grandfather," asked the young girl again, "what happened to them?"

"Collin and Lame Bird, as is tradition, became blood brothers. Both of them took up arms and fought in the Custer battles. But to the Cheyenne, Collin is better known by the name Little Coyote."

"Little Coyote? Did you know that he was my grandfather?" asked the young girl.

"That he was. And you, my son." The old man turned to the young boy. "Do you know who your ancestors are?"

The youngster nodded and said, "*Haahe,* I do."

"And how do you know this?"

"Because," said the boy, "my sister has the green eyes of *Nahkohe-tseske.*"

The old man nodded. "They were heroic people, your ancestors, but you must understand that there is much greatness yet to come. The future is before you, and their spirits live in you, my son and my daughter. Do them honor, and remember that the purity of love has always been and will always be stronger than any evil the world has to offer up against it"—the old man grinned at the two youngsters—"so long as you remain united. You are living proof of that. *Naa-hetsetseha hena'haanehe.* And now, that's the end."

With these final words, the old man arose from his seat and, taking one last look at the children and at the countryside around him, limped toward the west, toward the place where the sun sets.

Two pairs of dark eyes watched the old one until he was nearly out of sight, and then, as quickly as he had come to them, the old one disappeared, never to be seen again.

Some say that the old man was Sky Falcon, come back to ensure that the story would never leave the minds of these his people, the Cheyenne.

But the young boy knew the old man for exactly who he was, he who was his kin.

Hova'ahane, the youngster thought, he would be true to his promise. He would never let the story die.

Note to the Reader

From all the accounts that I have been able to gather, the attack upon Tall Bull's camp of Dog Soldiers is as accurate as I could make it and still be fiction. The only thing that I have changed about the battle is the time it took place. The actual attack occurred around noon.

If you are at all like me, you might have had some other questions from reading that account. I've tried to answer a few:

1. Was the river really flooded?

It was and it was also the reason that Tall Bull stayed in camp.

2. Did the Sioux really warn the Dog Soldiers about the impending danger?

They did, and history has it that the Sioux fled the Dog Soldier camp in the night—same as my hero and heroine.

3. Did the Dog Soldiers really defend the flight of their women and children by standing off the soldiers?

Yes. One of the customs of the Dog Soldier was that when the battle was turning against them, they were to give their horses to the women, turn to the enemy and fight on foot. The Dog Soldiers were also the warriors who were known to wear the "dog rope." This was a sash of buffalo hide that was worn over the right shoulder. At the end of this sash was a wooden pin. Only the bravest warriors were allowed to wear the dog rope.

These warriors, when the tide of battle was going against them, would dismount and drive their pin into the ground. If this was done, the wearer could not leave. He was to stay at that place and defeat the enemy or die trying—unless some other Dog Soldier was able to pull out the pin and let him flee. The driving of the pin was such a brave act that doing it alone often provided the turning point of many of their battles. The last instance of the dog rope being used was in 1869, in Tall Bull's fight. Wolf with Plenty of Hair died in this way.

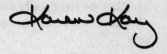

Glossary

Included are some definitions for terms used in this book that the reader might find unfamiliar. I hope this helps.

Black Kettle—Great Peace Chief of the Cheyenne Nation. He was killed at Sand Creek.

Cocopa tribe—a tribe in the southwestern United States, originally living near the Colorado River. Having a population at one time estimated at around three thousand, now boasts about six hundred souls, mostly living in Mexico.

Dog Soldiers—a military society within the Cheyenne Nation. It was, at the time of our story, one of the most feared societies on the plains.

Haahe—Cheyenne word for "yes." Historically used by men.

Hova'ahane—Cheyenne word for "no."

371

Lakota—this is the tribe that is currently often referred to as the Sioux. The Brule Lakota are a band within the tribe. As a note: Dakota, Lakota and Nakota are really the same sort of word referring more to dialects than to different tribes, although the Dakota generally lived east of the Missouri River, the Lakota were generally the western band of the same tribe, and the Nakota were usually thought of as the northern relatives.

Na'neha—Cheyenne word for "my older brother."

Nasemahe—Cheyenne word for "younger sibling."

Orphan trains—in the mid-1800s, New York City and a few other eastern cities had an overpopulation of homeless children. The orphan trains, originally envisioned by the Reverend Charles Loring Brace, were to be the solution to this problem, a solution that he hoped would save the children. He formed the Children's Aid Society and began the practice of sending the children west where he hoped they would find families who would take them in as their own. In the West, he supposed that the farmers had food in abundance and would welcome a helping hand. The trains ran for about seventy-five years, and the children generally ranged in age from seven to fifteen. Soon the practice caught on and other orphan societies sprang up to help send children west. There were sometimes as many as one hundred or more children in these "trains," many of the children having been taken from prison. To their credit, railroads offered reduced rates to these charities. The orphan trains came to an end around 1906 under Theodore Roosevelt when social workers began to emphasize the importance of families keeping their children, and new laws were passed to help mothers and children stay together.

Pawnee—a tribe of Indians on the Platte River in Nebraska. They had permanent villages and engaged in farming. One of their ceremonies included the rite of the Morning Star, which demanded a human sacrifice. For this reason and perhaps others, they made enemies of some of the other plains tribes, specifically the Lakota, the Cheyennes, and the Arapahoe.

Tall Bull—the leader of the Dog Soldiers at the time of this story.

Spotted Tail—the leader of the Brule Lakota at the time of this story.

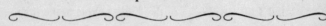